THE
LAST
LIGHT
OVER
OSLO

Also by Alix Rickloff

The Girls in Navy Blue
The Way to London
Secrets of Nanreath Hall

THE LAST LIGHT OVER OSLO

A Novel

ALIX RICKLOFF

wm
WILLIAM MORROW
An Imprint of HarperCollins*Publishers*

THE LAST LIGHT OVER OSLO. Copyright © 2024 by Alix Rickloff. All rights reserved. Printed in the United States of America. No part of this book may be used or reproduced in any manner whatsoever without written permission except in the case of brief quotations embodied in critical articles and reviews. For information, address HarperCollins Publishers, 195 Broadway, New York, NY 10007.

HarperCollins books may be purchased for educational, business, or sales promotional use. For information, please email the Special Markets Department at SPsales@harpercollins.com.

FIRST EDITION

Interior text design by Diahann Sturge-Campbell

Airplane image © Ivan Cholakov/Shutterstock

Map designed by Nick Springer, Springer Cartographics, LLC

Library of Congress Cataloging-in-Publication Data has been applied for.

ISBN 978-0-06-328620-7

24 25 26 27 28 LBC 5 4 3 2 1

This book is dedicated with love and admiration to Daisy Harriman

"I hope I make it sound electric, for it was."

*"Democracy at home and abroad offers us
a vista of endless possibilities."*

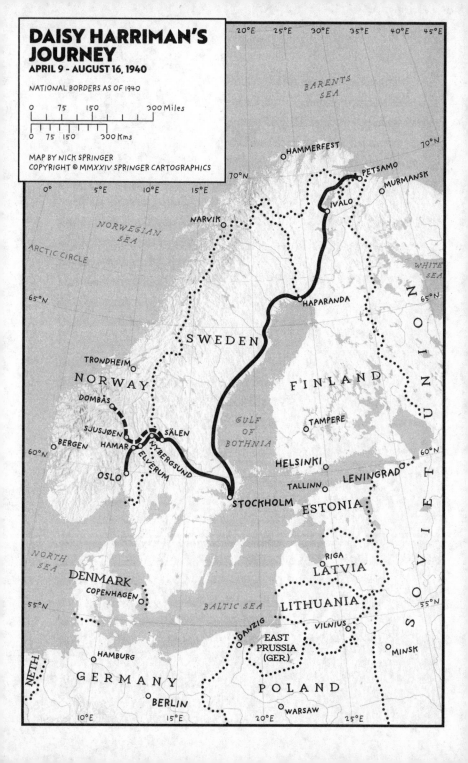

DAISY HARRIMAN'S JOURNEY
APRIL 9 – AUGUST 16, 1940

NATIONAL BORDERS AS OF 1940

0   75   150   300 Miles

0   75 150   300 Kms

MAP BY NICK SPRINGER
COPYRIGHT © MMXXIV SPRINGER CARTOGRAPHICS

CHAPTER 1

March 1940
Oslo, Norway

My dearest Anne,

It's 1914 all over again.

    This disturbing thought has been rolling around in my head ever since the news broke last September that Great Britain would come to the aid of Poland and join the fight against Germany. But never has it seemed so near as it has after this long deadly winter. My mind keeps returning to our years in France during the last great cataclysm, and I want to weep all over again for the failures that have led us back, barely twenty years later.

Caught up in a web of memories, Daisy paused, her pen resting on the paper. The afternoon light faded to silver, fog shrouding the Oslo city streets surrounding the US minister's residence. Kim dozed at her feet, the old German shepherd whuffling as his back legs twitched in dream. A few cars grumbled their way up the narrow street of Nobels Gate and turned into the legation's drive. It would be the wives. Five of them were meeting downstairs. Daisy had begun these weekly knitting parties as a way to support the Norwegians and show US solidarity, two neutral countries standing shoulder to shoulder. But the afternoons had become a welcome respite, a way to keep hands and minds distracted when every broadcast and newspaper article brought unsettling news.

The new heating system rattled and groaned as it fought a losing battle to warm the residency. Not for the first time, Daisy wished her office had a fireplace like the one in the drawing room. She shifted in her chair, feeling every one of her sixty-nine years in the groan of her hips and the ache along her back, but immediately dismissed her discomfort as nothing an aspirin and a small sherry wouldn't cure. Besides, it was only four in the afternoon. After her knitting circle, she had meetings at the foreign office followed by a cocktail party at the French embassy then a small reception at the palace. She would be lucky to find her bed before the wee hours of the morning.

It was times like this when she questioned the wisdom of accepting President Roosevelt's appointment. She could be tucked up comfortably at home in Washington, DC, with nothing more daunting than a cozy dinner with friends or a leisurely hack in Rock Creek Park ahead of her. She blamed it on Ethel. Her daughter had practically dared her to take the ambassadorship. An adventure, she'd called it. As if Daisy hadn't already lived a life greedy with excitement. A box seat on America, her friend T had once called this strange luck of hers that allowed her to be witness to the country's shaping. Was it luck, or was it her unquenchable curiosity and enthusiasm that led her to places few women dared venture?

A dot of spreading ink drew her back to the present, the period at the end of her sentence now outlandishly large and spidery. She thought about starting her letter over and decided against it. Mail delivery had grown spotty since war had broken out, and she wanted to make sure the letter went out this afternoon. Her sister-in-law's declining health kept her trapped at home these days, making Daisy's regular correspondence more important than ever. A fact made clear to her when Anne's latest note hinted that Daisy's silence must mean she was off on another of her little jaunts, traipsing about the Arctic with craggy fishermen or playing starry-eyed tourist in Saint Petersburg.

A rather unfair assessment of the situation, Daisy thought. Those trips had been part of her work. The best part, of course, but work nonetheless. If she didn't know better, she'd think Anne had been talking to Jefferson Patterson. While an enormous help in so many ways, her former deputy chief of mission had never quite approved of those trips either. He saw them as time not spent at her desk. Time not engaged in the serious work of the legation. He'd never quite blamed it on the fact that she was a woman, but it was there beneath the polite words and the accommodating smiles all the same. Still, she preferred his veiled condescension to Vice Consul Whitney's more obvious disdain.

A tap at the door brought Kim instantly awake and alert, but it was only Miss Kristiansen with the tea tray. Accompanying the pot of Earl Grey and plate of jammy biscuits was a less savory stack of folders and a bundle of envelopes with very red, very official-looking stamps.

Daisy's secretary offered Kim a treat from her skirt pocket then poured out a cup, adding sugar and lemon. "Just as you like it, Mrs. Harriman," she said with a smile.

"Thank you. I'm sure it will help me choke down the news from Washington."

The US legation had been fortunate to gain the services of this daughter of an American nurse and a Norwegian merchant seaman. Petra Kristiansen spoke both languages fluently along with Danish, French, and a smattering of German and was also a skilled clerk and typist. But it was that certain Scandinavian something that made her invaluable to Daisy. She had a confidence and easy grace that allowed her to move in any circle and adapt to any situation, all while looking positively flawless.

If Daisy had been forty years younger, she'd be jealous as hell.

Thank heavens Petra and that young assistant military attaché had formed an attachment. It didn't pay to have a girl that pretty stirring up drama among the unmarried staff.

"There is an important cable from the president, ma'am, and"—Petra slid an envelope to the top of the pile—"a letter from Mrs. Vanderbilt."

"Oh dear. I haven't even finished replying to her last letter. I hope it's not bad news."

Feeling only slightly guilty, Daisy set aside FDR and tore into Anne's letter, but only a few words in and she was setting down her cup with a rattle that nearly broke the saucer before she rubbed at her temple, where a headache threatened.

"Is anything wrong, ma'am?" Petra asked.

"Wrong doesn't begin to cover it."

Anne was fine, thank heavens. But Daisy's goddaughter Clementine was missing.

Not missing as she had been since she'd run away from home on the eve of her wedding, precipitating the scandal of the season. But truly missing as in not a soul had seen or heard from her in months. The last anyone knew, she was living in sin with a jazz musician, trailing after him like a camp follower. But that had been before the war. There was no telling where she might be by now.

"Sorry, Franklin. Family comes first," she muttered. Crumpling her earlier letter, Daisy tossed it in the trash, uncapped her pen, and started over.

Dear Anne . . .

* * *

"*VELKOMMEN TIL OSLO, Frøken Jaffray!*"

Cleo winced at the young woman's perky salutation as she handed back Cleo's papers. It was far too early in the day. Cleo had had far too little sleep. And the dangerous steamer crossing from Hamburg dodging British mines had left her pea green with seasickness and jumpy with nerves. She put her passport and travel documents away carefully, taking time to guarantee they would be safe. Papers were more valuable than gold these days. "*Takk*," she mumbled. "Thanks."

The woman smiled wider. "You are American?" She switched to English, her accent thick but understandable. Thank heavens. Cleo knew exactly three phrases in Norwegian, gleaned from looking over the shoulder of a fellow traveler with a guidebook—*thank you, please,* and *I do not understand.*

"That's right." Cleo wobbled as the ground under her feet continued to sway ominously, her stomach rising into her throat. She and boats had never been friends. Not as a girl in Newport retching over the side of the very eligible Jimmy van Speakman's sporty little ketch. Not now with tons of steel and three decks between her and the Baltic. If there had been any other way to get to Oslo, she'd have taken it in a shot. Train, taxi, horse-drawn sledge. But she was broke, her purse containing only a tiny jumble of various coins and none of them adding up to enough for anything but the price of a third-class steamer ticket. If only the necklace she wore was real, she might have arrived in style trailing her luggage with a handsome young porter to help her. But the pink costume diamond, while gaudily pretty, wouldn't even buy her a sandwich and a cup of coffee from the steamer's canteen. Still, it meant more to her than any treasure from Tiffany's. "Can you tell me how to get to the US legation?"

Immediately, the woman sobered as if suddenly noticing Cleo's scuffed and mismatched luggage, her worn coat with the matted fur collar, and her general air of nervous tension that had only grown worse since she'd left the Hungarian city of Kassa alone and nearly broke. No doubt, she wasn't the first American caught out by this ridiculous war that the customs clerk had come across. But at least here she was safe. Norway was neutral, like the US. There would be no checkpoints. No daily humiliations. No smirking soldiers whispering sordid invitations one always risked turning down.

"There is a taxi stand outside," the woman said, already starting to turn away to the next passenger.

Being rushed through the weather in a warm dry taxi sounded the height of luxury, but even stretched, Cleo's coins wouldn't be near enough. "And if I decided to enjoy a nice walk to clear my head? How far would it be?"

The woman snuck a glance out the windows of the terminal to where a cold sleet slanted like needles from a slate gray sky. She chewed her lip for a moment before digging in her pocket. "Here." She handed Cleo a few banknotes. "Take this."

Once pride would have prevented Cleo from stooping so low as to accept a handout. Not anymore. It was amazing what poverty and fear did to one's vanity. She'd learned to live with the poverty, but she'd never grown used to the fear. Even now, the copper tang of it seemed to settle at the back of her throat, sit like a stone in her stomach. She rubbed her arms as if she could wipe herself free of it.

"*Takk*," she repeated. "*Takk* very much," and hurried out onto the sidewalk in case the generous official changed her mind.

Outside, the sleet numbed her cheeks while the March damp gnawed into her bones. She thought New York winters were harsh. Scandinavian springs were ten times worse. She shrugged deeper into her hand-me-down coat. Not much farther, and she could finally rest. At least that was the hope she'd carried with her the last few weeks.

Aunt Daisy would help her.

Aunt Daisy would find Micky.

She repeated this mantra to herself as she bumped and joggled her way through the press of fellow passengers queueing for taxis and buses. Businessmen, sleek as cats. Workers with faces chapped by wind and sun. Soldiers in uniform. And then were the refugees like her, flotsam being blown this way and that by the war. Things might be quiet now—the Finns ceding territory to the Russians, the Germans and the British sizing each other up like boxers before the bell—but it was only a matter of time until they all came out of their corners swinging.

One taxi stood waiting at the end of the row. Cleo picked up her pace despite the blister on her heel and the suitcase bumping against her hip. She reached the taxi just as a businessman in an expensive wool coat and a fedora pulled low against the chill handed off his bags to the driver.

"Twelve Ole Fladagers Gate, my good man." A Brit. That was a relief. They were always the easiest to sway. Must be those centuries of noblesse oblige imprinted on their brain cells. Cleo hunched deeper into her coat and shivered. Not a hard act to pull off. She was freezing cold, her head and stomach swimming, and she'd not eaten in twenty-four hours.

"Please, sir," she said in her best little matchgirl voice. "I'm desperate to get to the American legation. The war, you see and my"—no doubt his middle-class paunch equaled middle-class morals—"my husband. He went missing in Poland after the Germans invaded. I'm hoping the US minister . . ." At mention of Germany, the man bristled, eyes going hard. She sensed his outrage on her behalf and doubled her efforts at looking pathetic. Easy after these last uncertain months when subservience was the difference between life and death. "But I see you're in a hurry. I'm sure there's a bus or something . . ."

A sympathetic smile lit his round face. "Nonsense. We can share a taxi. I'm in no hurry. I can drop you off and still make my meeting. Those Krauts have bloody nerve. We thrashed them once. We'll do it again."

Cleo gave a watery smile as she slid into the cab, leaning her head against the window to watch as Oslo slid by in a blur of handsome buildings and broad avenues swept by snow. They swung past the university, a theater, around the royal palace, with the Brit acting as tour guide in between his diatribes on the sorry state of the world, the duplicity of the Nazis, the courageous Allied soldiers, the havoc in the markets caused by such global instability.

Her eyelids grew heavy. There was nothing she could add that he would understand. Once she found Micky, she would do what she should have done in September—go home. This war wasn't her war. This fight wasn't her fight.

She wasn't her father.

She was just sliding into sleep when the man's hand on her shoulder jolted her awake. "The US legation, Mrs. Jaffray."

When had she told him her last name? She was obviously more exhausted than she thought. But he gave no sign of recognition or made any type of connection between her and the minister. If he had, he'd have probably lobbied for an introduction or an audience or some kind of special favor. "The residence is that one there. The chancery offices are housed in that smaller building across the way." He pointed at an unassuming structure that looked like it had once been a carriage house or garage.

The familiar fear clenched her belly, though whether it was fear for Micky or fear of her upcoming reunion with her intimidating godmother, she couldn't decide.

The driver set her bag on the curb before diving back into the taxi and disappearing up the street and around the corner with a rattle and a puff of black smoke.

She pushed through a high gate into a walled courtyard. Grounds stretched away to one side and what appeared to be a tennis court, the net put away for the winter. The residence was large and rambling, steps swept clear of snow and ice. The chancery itself was less than impressive and gave off a stark, utilitarian air.

She imagined people staring down at her from the windows, wondering who she was, why she was here. She expected guards to pounce any moment to whisk her away, but there was only one young man in an officer's cap and a heavy wool army overcoat, sleet dripping from his dark hair and damping his ruddy cheeks.

"Can I help you?" he asked politely. His features beneath the cap were blunt and plain. Not handsome, but friendly. His nose was slightly crooked. His brows were sharp arrows sloping over clever brown eyes.

Instinctively, she rounded her shoulders, sucked in her cheeks to make her face appear hollower, glanced up at him through lowered lashes. "Please," she said in a soft, wobbly voice perfected over months of living under occupation. "I'd like to speak with Mrs. Harriman. It's very important. A matter of life or death."

He gave a sorrowful shake of his head. "You could be in the pictures with acting like that," he replied, unmoved at her attempt at waifishness. "Not *good* pictures, but still . . . there's a certain Betty Boop feel about you. Maybe it's the big eyes or the bobbed hair."

His words shocked her out of character for a moment, her hand unconsciously touching the unflattering cap of dark curls at her ears, necessary after a week in that horrible hostel outside Budapest. Heat rose in her chest to burn her cheeks. "One learned very quickly in German-occupied Poland to use whatever advantage came to hand. I'd pretend to be Minnie Mouse if it kept me safe for one more day."

Shame replaced his earlier amusement. "Sorry. You are?"

"Cleo Jaffray." She narrowed her Betty Boop eyes as she paused to prepare the dagger stroke that would cut this tinpot soldier down to size once and for all. "Minister Harriman's goddaughter."

"Mrs. Harriman is in meetings all afternoon. She is not to be disturbed." Cleo had been greeted by Aunt Daisy's personal secretary, Miss Kristiansen, Sonja Henie in a brown pencil skirt and beige cardigan, her only adornment a blue-and-gold enameled brooch in the form of a butterfly pinned at her throat.

Cleo tugged at her own soiled blouse and tried not to shrink under the stare of this statuesque blond Valkyrie. "I'm sure she'd make an exception for family. You can tell her it's the prodigal goddaughter. She'll understand."

Perhaps it was naive, but of all the scenarios that had played out in Cleo's mind as she made her chaotic, frightening escape from Poland to Norway, her godmother not being available when she arrived hadn't ever crossed her mind. She'd imagined standing before Aunt Daisy properly penitent. Suffering whatever brutal dressing-down she cared to mete out. Letting the abuse spill over her, her mind as numb as her frozen fingers. Just so long as when the shouting was over, Aunt Daisy would agree to help. Now she felt unaccountably let down. An actress awaiting a cue that never came.

Miss Kristiansen looked over Cleo's head to the soldier who had introduced himself as Lieutenant Bayard. "I checked, Petra," he said. "She is who she says she is."

"Very well. I'll let Madam Minister know you've arrived." Her English was nearly as perfect as her ivory complexion, cornsilk hair, and glacier-blue eyes. Too perfect. Cleo didn't trust perfection. She'd had a lifetime of it stuffed down her throat until she choked.

"I'll show Miss Jaffray somewhere she can freshen up while she waits." Cleo hadn't realized how raw she'd become until she flinched when Bayard stepped forward, taking her elbow in the same way a guard might escort a prisoner. "Come on. You look dead on your feet."

The last few weeks on the road seemed to have caught up with her all at once and now her swaying had nothing to do with a long night spent on the ferry. The room he led her to was on the top floor off a small hallway. Not exactly the servants' quarters, but neither was it a VIP suite reserved for embassy dignitaries. Somewhere in between.

Like her.

Despite its lack of square footage, it was cozy and inviting, though at this point a broom cupboard would have seemed the height of luxury.

"So Mrs. Harriman is family?" he asked.

She'd offered enough information to get her inside. More was . . . complicated. But if it would get him to go away and leave her to wrap herself in the enormous duvet on the bed and sleep, she'd answer whatever questions he asked.

"She's my godmother really, but I've always called her Aunt Daisy. She was my father's second cousin on her mother's side."

"Was?" He either followed this convoluted family tree or didn't care enough to question it further.

"He died in France during the last war, but she and my mother are still close."

Aunt Daisy had been invited to the wedding. Cleo had seen the invitation on the top of the gilt-edged pile waiting for the post. The afternoon before the big day, she'd heard the bustle of her godmother's visit to the house on East Fifty-Seventh from her upstairs bedroom, her bag open and stuffed with what she thought at the time she couldn't live without. For a moment, guilt pressed weighty fingers on her heart, but ten months and far greater regrets had dulled the sharpest edges, and the feeling quickly passed.

"What brings you to Oslo, Miss Jaffray?"

"I'd have thought it was obvious." From her old coat to her scuffed shoes and battered valise, she could hardly be confused for a tourist in town for a spot of shopping and a look at the local sights.

"Humor me," he said simply. She studied him for any sign his interest could be used against her, but his gaze remained unreadable, his features thoughtful rather than prying. Habit had her starting to dissemble and deflect, but she was far too tired and her half-truths felt as heavy as boulders. Maybe it was better to confess everything to this stolid, square-jawed officer than to her godmother, who would be scowling as ferociously as any of society's infamous Four Hundred. Aunt Daisy had always been an open-minded and progressive soul, ahead of her time in so many ways, but even *she* had her limits. It would make sense to have an ally, someone in Cleo's corner who could go to bat for her if her godmother chose to be difficult.

"Right. It's a long story, but I've come to ask for her help."

Cleo couldn't say what woke her. Her skin wasn't damp with sweat. Her heart didn't race. Her body didn't feel frozen in shock and terror. The room was dark, but beyond the window, she could see the golden halo of streetlights, lamps burning in windows, the wash of car headlights sweeping over the ceiling. The haze of the city reflecting off the clouds made the air glow pink and peachy.

No steady drumbeat of marching boots in the street outside. No screams or sudden gunshots that left your stomach soft as a poached egg. No breath-stealing anticipation of the shouted request to prove her American citizenship as if she hadn't proven it the day before and the day before that. The authorities had finally suggested she and Micky pin an American flag to their clothes and tack another to the door of their apartment—just in case. They didn't have to ask in case of what. They did as they were advised in a vulgar counterpoint to their neighbors' Star of David armbands.

Still, Micky had chosen to stay, and she, unwilling to go without him, stayed too.

Cleo refused to look back to those moments when they could have made different choices. Regret was too painful.

A hiss of ice tapped at the window like fingers. She rolled deeper into the duvet, closing her eyes, but the tapping increased until she realized it was someone at her door. The darkness and her own blurry exhaustion had made her think it was midnight when more likely it was early evening—dinnertime. Her stomach growled, reminding her it had been at least a day since she'd had anything more to eat than a bar of waxy chocolate and a tepid cup of coffee.

"Coming." Dragging the duvet around her shoulders, she answered the door to find neither the lieutenant nor a helpful maid bringing her food, but Aunt Daisy herself. She was dressed in a grandmotherly wool twinset and pearls, her silver hair coiffed in soft becoming waves, but her stature and the burning light of curiosity gleaming in her eyes made Cleo take a cautious step back.

"Clementine Verquin," her godmother demanded, staring down her long regal nose, "where have you been? We've been worried sick." Even as Cleo's confidence shriveled at the tone, Aunt Daisy surprised her by pulling her into a perfume-scented hug. "Thank God you're safe."

Cleo fought the urge to sink into that embrace and weep like a baby. Instead, she stepped back and lifted her chin in a bid to meet her godmother face-to-face. "It's Cleo these days. I go by

Cleo. Not Clementine and certainly not Verquin." Just saying it left a bad taste in her mouth.

There was only the veriest pause before a shift took place behind Aunt Daisy's eyes, a filing away of information. "Very well. I never did approve of your mother naming you after the village where your father died. Maudlin, to say the very least. But I was up to my eyes with the Red Cross. By the time I found out, it was too late. The deed was done."

"I'll try not to hold it against you, ma'am," Cleo quipped then immediately regretted it. She was going for contrition, not wit. "Have you heard from my mother?"

"If you mean, has she forgiven you, the answer is yes. I'm not sure I have."

Cleo had been expecting that, but it still hurt. She'd always looked up to Aunt Daisy, the maverick in the family. Not content to remain simply a wife and mother, she'd stepped onto a bigger stage. Become a force in New York, then in Washington. Reveling in the political back-and-forth, the drama and the deals, Aunt Daisy had championed women's rights and workers' rights, causes she believed in even when those fights put her at odds with family and friends.

Cleo had always harbored the tiny flicker of a hope that of everyone, her aunt Daisy would understand why she'd run and, more importantly, why she'd returned.

"I'm truly sorry for all the trouble I've caused."

"Sorry? That's all you have to say? As if it's the least bit adequate. Your poor mother had to face an entire church full of people and tell them her daughter had run off and there's poor George Cliveden looking like a confused codfish through the whole thing. She barely left her house for three months until the worst of the talk died down, and George . . . I suppose your loss was Miss

Sweeney's gain, but still . . ." She gave Cleo a very familiar, very heavy what-am-I-going-to-do-with-you sigh. "I should give you the proper drubbing you deserve, but you look as if you've been punished enough, so we'll say no more on the subject."

Funny, but now that she started, Cleo felt an urge to come clean. She couldn't excuse her actions, but she wanted to at least try to defend them. "I thought I could marry him, Aunt Daisy. I really did. But the closer it came, the more it felt like the walls were closing in, and Mother wouldn't listen. I panicked. I thought once everything settled down, I could come back and explain."

"You always did prefer asking forgiveness over permission. Your father was the same way."

Was he? Cleo wouldn't know. All she knew of Paul Jaffray was the stories she'd been raised with, the somber portrait over the drawing room fireplace, the clothes still hanging in the wardrobe, the silver-backed brushes on the shelf, and the box of medals Mother kept as shiny as the day they'd been pinned on his chest. Paul Jaffray had been handsome, charming, honorable, selfless. He'd been a hero. Perfect in every way.

Cleo hated him for it.

"Yes, well. She forgave him for running off, didn't she? Me? I was disowned and cut off without a dime."

She waited for Aunt Daisy to launch into the same old sorry reasoning that had dominated Cleo's childhood. When taxed, her mother had always flung words like *liberty* and *democracy* and *principles* around as if that made his abandonment all right. Her godmother merely clenched her long hands together in front of her—strong hands, ropy with blue veins, but long-fingered, long-boned. "She was angry, and I suppose there are only so many times one can watch a loved one leave before it becomes too much to bear."

The guilt Cleo had tried so hard to avoid crashed over her as if the last year had never happened. The midnight escape down the back stairs, the taxi to the wharf, the open sea with freedom at the other side. She had run as fast and as far as she could. Another comparison to her father that left her bleeding. Would it never end? She'd fled halfway around the world and yet he still haunted her.

"I'm sorry," Cleo repeated, feeling put in her place. Daisy Harriman might look the part of someone's doting grandmother, but there was steel in that spine and razor-sharp intelligence in that bright gaze.

"It's your mother you should be apologizing to. Write to her, Cleo. Tell her what you told me."

"She won't understand."

"Give her a chance. You might be surprised."

They dined alone in Aunt Daisy's upstairs sitting room. The butler brought trays up from the kitchen, and Cleo tore into her food as if afraid he might grab it from under her nose. She felt Aunt Daisy's stare like a blade at her neck, but she was too busy eating to care. It was only after she'd mopped up the last bit of gravy with her dinner roll that she sat back in her chair. The silence had given her time to form her words, prepare her arguments. And if need be, build a defense.

"When was the last time you had a proper meal?" Daisy asked.

Surprised but relieved at the turn of the conversation, Cleo shrugged, trying not to remember last summer and the noisy, happy dinners with Micky and his friends. The laughter and shouted conversations over bowls of stew or plates of sausages and potatoes. And the music. So much music. Those dinners crackled with energy and life. So different from the meals they shared after the Nazis arrived in Zakopane, where every word was parsed for potential trouble and there was little room for food in a belly tight with anxiety.

"You aren't the first American citizen turning up on my doorstep looking for help getting home." Aunt Daisy slid one finger down the seam of her napkin. "I've had them lining up five deep on some days. Passage out of Bergen, Trondheim, and the other coastal cities is practically impossible to find, and even the overland route through Russia is risky right now."

"I don't want to go home. That's not why I came to see you."

For the first time, her godmother registered surprise. The napkin slid from the table to the floor, but she made no move to claim it. Like the woman checking Cleo's passport at the steamer terminal, Aunt Daisy seemed to focus for the first time, not on the frayed collar of Cleo's cheap flowered dress or the chopped, uneven cut of her short hair, but on her face, as if she'd suddenly seen her for the first time. "No?"

Cleo had told the British businessman she'd lost her husband, but Aunt Daisy would see through that lie in a wink. She was no man's fool and no woman's patsy. "I've been in Poland. I was living there with a musician—an American musician—named Micky Kominski, who I met on the ship to Le Havre last summer."

To her credit, Aunt Daisy remained still as stone, giving nothing away. Cleo was reminded of that lieutenant from earlier in the way her godmother could make herself go perfectly silent, her face open, waiting. It invited further conversation. Shared confidences. Spilled secrets.

FDR knew what he was about when he sent Daisy Harriman here as his emissary.

"He's gone missing," Cleo continued, swallowing back the lump choking off her breath. "I came to ask your help to find him. Please."

Aunt Daisy maintained a careful watchfulness over her plate of roast chicken and potatoes. Still keeping quiet. If it was supposed to ease Cleo's nerves, it was doing just the opposite. Daisy bent and retrieved her napkin, settling it back on her lap. She sipped at her glass of wine. There was an intensity in her eyes, as if she was running through a mental list. At last, she cleared her throat. "Impossible."

CHAPTER 2

Dear Anne,

It's Tuesday, which means in an hour I shall leave my office behind for the pleasant company of the legation wives. I wrote you about the group I've organized for the Red Cross. We meet in the residence's drawing room twice a week to knit sweaters, mittens, gloves, anything a skein of yarn and our needles can create. I can hear you chuckling now, imagining me at the head of a battalion of knitters when I should be doing something important like sorting out international crises or imploring Roosevelt to step in and bring this madness to a halt (as if he were Santa Claus with a bag of gifts). There are plenty of doubters here too, but not all diplomacy is done in high-powered meetings. My knitting engenders more warmth and fellow feeling among the locals than any amount of cocktail receptions would.

There was a platter of sandwiches and another of cake. An urn of coffee had been set up on a sideboard. Someone had snapped on the radio. The deputy chief of mission's wife, Margaret Cox, stood in a corner conferring with a group of ladies over a box of completed clothing ready to be sent on to the Norwegian Red Cross for distribution while others clustered on chairs near the windows to catch the light. Their needles flashed in their capable hands, their voices a high chatter that Daisy leaned into like a plant reaching for the sun.

"Mrs. Harriman, I really must insist." Vice Consul Whitney chased after her with a sheaf of papers. "We need those letters as soon as possible, and Herr Brauer has been most anxious to meet with you. I would think the German minister is more important than these women and their needlecraft."

"I'm sure you think so. And I shall phone the Germans the moment I'm done here."

Mr. Whitney gave the impression of softness with a loose, jowly face and thinning brown hair combed over to hide a bald spot. But there was nothing soft about his expression, furry brows drawn low over ice chips for eyes, or his voice, which was a bear-like growl. "Mrs. Harriman, please . . ."

"Even prisoners are allowed an hour of exercise once a day."

Creases bit into his stern features, and she stifled a smile. She really shouldn't bait the poor man, but he made it so easy with his constant chiding. "I'll take Miss Kristiansen along. I can dictate and knit at the same time. Will that suffice?"

He huffed his concession.

Battle won, but their war at a standoff.

Strauss gave way to a radio announcer, and the conversation died back as everyone strained to listen, whether they were fluent in Norwegian or not. Daisy could stumble her way through a conversation, but she didn't need to know her *vær så god* from her *vær så snill*, sitting, as she was, so close to Miss Kristiansen. The girl's face gave all away. It smoothed like glass, the smile tipping the corners of her eyes fading, her pen dangling thoughtlessly from her fingers. Across the room, Mrs. Mejlaender, the American wife of a Norwegian, translated for those who needed it.

Finland's lopsided peace treaty with Russia. The loss of three more merchant ships to German subs. The British mining the waters off Norway's coast. Conversation faltered, then grew louder as the news ended and the soothing strains of Chopin took over.

"This phony war is all well and good for those taking their ease behind the Maginot Line, but what about us?" someone commented. "That's our good men dying out there."

"You think the Russians will stop with Finland?" said another. "What they want is an ice-free port. Norway should take care. They'll be attacking in the north before long."

"Who says they'll stop in the north?" came the tart reply.

The response to this remark was a loud and firm repudiation, though Daisy felt a thread of unease ripple through the women. A few glanced in her direction as if seeking reassurance, a clue to the true state of affairs in the tilt of her head or a vague facial expression. She gave them her best poker face. "Petra dear, will you . . ."

The girl was white as the snow lying thick on the lawn. No doubt she was thinking of her family living in the northern port city of Narvik. Daisy recalled there was a brother working as a fisherman, a sister employed as a doctor. She touched Petra's arm, and the girl startled with a visible shudder. "Are you all right, child?"

"Fine, ma'am," she replied, giving nothing away.

The door opened, bringing a gust of cool air from the hall along with Clementine. No, she must start thinking of her as Cleo, a name as direct and unadorned as the woman who now bore it. She was bundled in a borrowed coat and a pair of overlarge winter boots that slopped when she walked, but her sapphire-blue beret was tilted at a rakish angle and there was color in her cheeks, filled out after a week of solid feeding. Cleo had yet to speak of her time spent in Poland and Daisy hadn't pushed. It was obvious by the shadows in her agate-green gaze and the way she startled like a deer that the girl had been through an ordeal. But there were limits to Daisy's patience and her resources. Cleo stretched them both on a daily basis.

"Aunt Daisy, I was hoping to—"

"Shush." She waved her to sit down, one of the wives making room beside her on the couch.

Cleo smiled her thanks but otherwise ignored the invitation. "I really have to speak with you. I was chatting with a gentleman I met at a bar off Arbins Gate near the palace. He's just arrived from Copenhagen on business and swears he—"

"Spotted young Mr. Kominski getting into a taxi," Aunt Daisy finished the sentence for her.

Cleo frowned. "No."

"Across a hotel lobby," Aunt Daisy continued. "Eating supper at a restaurant. I'm sorry to be harsh, my dear, but sooner or later you'll have to face up to the fact that Mr. Kominski died in that café bombing."

"But that doesn't explain his letter."

That infernal letter. The start of Cleo's quest that had sent her to Oslo in hopes Daisy could solve the mystery. She appreciated her goddaughter's faith in her abilities but finding one missing man in the middle of a war was like finding a needle in a haystack—one that was burning as you searched.

"The letter asking me to meet him under the clock at the train station in Kassa arrived three days *after* the bombing."

Daisy needed to tread carefully lest Cleo take it into her head to leave on the next train to carry on the hunt alone. Now that she'd laid her hands on her erstwhile goddaughter, she wasn't about to let Cleo out of her sight again.

"Please, Aunt Daisy. Just one phone call. You promised to help."

Had she? As far as she could recall, she'd warned Cleo of the impossibility of learning anything at all, but that hadn't stopped her from pestering, badgering, and otherwise irritating everyone around her until they gave in just to shut her up. A dubious but effective strategy.

"Miss Kristiansen, escort Miss Jaffray to the chancery offices. Tell Lieutenant Bayard I'd like him to make inquiries about a Mr. Michal Kominski formerly of New York City and lately of Zakopane, Poland. Last possible sighting in Copenhagen."

"Of course, ma'am."

"Do you mean it?" Cleo's face brightened with hope. After months of seeing that desperate eager light in the gaunt faces of those arriving at the chancery, exhausted and frightened, Daisy recognized it immediately, and her heart went out to the girl.

"This is the last time. Whatever we find out, you leave for New York afterward. No more arguments. No more delays. Your mother needs you at home. You're all she has left."

Cleo's gaze dropped submissively to the floor, but Daisy sensed no surrender in the set of her shoulders. "It needn't have been that way, you know," she muttered. "There were gentlemen buzzing round, even as recently as five years ago. She always sent them packing."

This was news to Daisy, though unsurprising. Letitia Jaffray had been a beautiful bride. Widowhood had only honed her elegant features to a fragile brilliance men couldn't resist. "I didn't know that."

"She kept it quiet. Afraid she'd be cornered into a marriage she'd regret." Cleo looked up, her gaze meeting Daisy's in an obvious challenge, which she chose to ignore.

Daisy could have warned Cleo from the outset that George Cliveden wasn't her type, but the girl had been a stove-toucher since the beginning. Had to find things out for herself, no matter the consequences.

"Your parents loved each other very much, Cleo. Maybe more than they should have."

"My mother loved. I doubt my father did, or else he wouldn't have run away the first chance he got."

Daisy wouldn't argue the point; there was just enough truth in the accusations to make her uncomfortable. "So we have an agreement? You'll go as soon as I can book passage?"

"I'll tuck my tail between my legs and endure a feast of crow from Mother and all of New York if I must. Just find out what happened to Micky."

Miss Kristiansen led Cleo away to the chancery to make the call. As they walked together, it was hard not to make comparisons between the two young women. Cleo's short dark curls beside Petra's shimmering blond crown. Petra tall and willowy with a dancer's gait and a quiet dreaminess. Cleo bearing the Jaffray shoulders and enough brash confidence to power a city.

They passed Mr. Whitney coming back for a second round, the vice consul's face bearing its usual sour, disgruntled frown. "I apologize for interrupting your little tea party, ma'am, but Ambassador Sterling's on the phone for you from the embassy in Stockholm. There's a reporter from *Life* magazine asking for your comment on the 'City of Flint' article in last week's issue, and the German foreign minister has sent around an invitation for an evening next week."

She and Mrs. Cox exchanged a look, the other woman deftly taking over the room.

Daisy's hour of freedom was over.

No ONE IN the city of Copenhagen had ever heard of Michal Kominski.

Cleo was back to square one.

She turned up the collar of her coat and angled herself out of the wind as she set a match to her very last cigarette. She'd rationed them the past week, doling them out to herself sparingly, one a day, no matter how much her body cried out for nicotine. She'd hoped Aunt Daisy would take pity and loan her a few dollars, kroner . . . whatever they used for money in Norway. But Daisy, while generous in allowing Cleo to replenish her wardrobe on her godmother's shop accounts, hadn't seen fit to extend that generosity to cold, hard cash. Probably afraid Cleo would take it and run.

Maybe she would, though running implied there was somewhere to go. A destination. Answers to the questions that kept her up at night, clutching her costume diamond like a nun might clutch her cross or rubbing the pad of her thumb back and forth over the constellation of smaller glass stones that decorated the setting, like a child might derive comfort from the edge of a favorite blanket.

Cleo flinched at the sudden roar of a bus heading up Nobels Gate and instinctively tucked herself farther back against the corner of the residence. She told herself it was to keep out of the wind, but her hands shook, and her heart beat rapid as a jazz snare.

She took a deep breath and exhaled slowly. She was safe.

The panic slowly subsided, leaving her slightly ill and guilty as hell.

She was safe, but what about her friends and neighbors still in Zakopane who hadn't had the benefit of the Stars and Stripes sewn onto their collars?

"Isn't that your job? To help Americans in trouble?" Cleo had pleaded with her godmother, but Daisy remained immovable. Information coming out of Poland was sparse and often unreliable. If Micky had not died outright in the bombing as the Germans claimed, there was no telling where he might be. It would be best if Cleo returned to New York as soon as possible. The situation in Europe was too unstable to linger.

"*You're* staying."

"I have a job to do."

"So do I" was Cleo's blunt response. That ended the conversation, but she was under no illusions that Aunt Daisy would leave things as they were.

Cleo stamped her feet against the cold. Smoke and breath mingled when she exhaled. Across the way, those at the chancery worked late. Lamplight gleamed over a crust of snow while above, the moon slid in and out of thin streamers of cloud.

A taxi drew up to the gate. Cleo moved to the far side of the building, out of the spear of headlights, only to find herself intruding on an intimate moment. At least that's what it looked like at first glance. Two figures locked together in the darkness. Then the wind died, and the voices, soft and insistent, carried.

"I don't know what to do. Every ship is booked." Cleo immediately recognized the precise English of Petra Kristiansen. "There are endless lines at the ticket offices. Some people are paying twice, three times the going price. The trains are no better. And the journey east through Russia is long with so many complications and dangers. It's impossible."

"Trust me," Bayard responded. "We'll find a way."

A scuff of her shoes or perhaps the glow of her cigarette betrayed Cleo. The two of them sprang apart, Petra hurrying to the waiting taxi while Lieutenant Bayard stood watching until the car backed out and disappeared up the street.

"I'm surprised to see you out here, Miss Jaffray." Unruffled by her intrusion, Bayard lit his own cigarette.

"Aunt Daisy's entertaining and Mrs. Nilsen chased me out of her kitchen, telling me I was underfoot," she answered, throwing him a sideways glance. "Speaking of which, I didn't interrupt an elopement, did I?"

The tip of his cigarette glowed red, the rest of his face in shadow except for the pinprick gleam of his eyes. "Petra's American grand-mother has been staying with the family. They're trying to get her back home, but the Finnish war has made booking passage nearly impossible. I told her I'd see what I could do to help."

"Why doesn't she ask my aunt for assistance?"

"Petra doesn't want to bother Mrs. Harriman when she's al-ready so busy with others seeking the same escape. We've had families turning up all fall and winter, some with nothing but the clothes on their backs. Madam Minister has worked hard to help as many as she can."

"Is this your way of telling me to stop pestering her?"

"It's my way of telling you the truth. If anyone in the White House or the State Department back in thirty-seven had thought war was on the horizon, they'd never have appointed Mrs. Har-riman to a ministerial post to start with. Now that it's come, the only reason she hasn't been recalled is that Norway's a small country, out of the path of the fighting. But that doesn't mean she has an easy job. Or that there aren't those here and in Washington who would love to see her fail."

"You care about her."

"Of course I do. She's the US minister and my superior."

"No, I mean you *care* care about her."

"She reminds me of my—"

"Dear old granny?" Cleo interrupted, unaccountably irritated on her godmother's behalf.

"I was going to say my father. He served as a noncom in the last war. Tough as old boots. Never demanded anything of his men he wasn't willing to do himself. They'd have walked into the cannon's mouth for him."

"And did they?"

"Yes. Far too many of them. He wasn't the same man when he came home."

"But he came home." She couldn't help the twinge of envy. What had allowed one soldier to survive and another to die? It was a question she still asked. The answer still eluded her.

"Most of him did," Bayard replied. "I sometimes think he left the best parts of himself on the battlefield. And here we are right back again for a second go-round."

"Surely it won't come to that. Not here in Norway."

"Maybe. Maybe not. You were in Poland. You saw how quickly it all went south."

"I was there," she replied with a long shaky draw on her cigarette. "The invasion happened so fast they passed us by in the first few days with barely a scratch to show for it. The worst of the fighting was miles away, so you could almost forget there was a war on."

A bang of trash bins around the back of the chancery made her jump. Fear knifed through her, every nerve firing until she wanted to be sick. Her cigarette fell from trembling fingers to hiss in an icy puddle.

"Almost," she added quietly.

CLEO TOLD HERSELF no news was good news, but the days dragged and Aunt Daisy's updates came less frequently as she spent more time in staff meetings or away at the Norwegian Foreign Office. To combat her growing frustration and ease the pressure that closed like a vise around her chest, Cleo took long walks, meandering through neighborhoods around the legation before venturing down into the city's center, where she explored every narrow street and winding, dogleg alley.

This afternoon, she'd taken advantage of a spring thaw to wander her way up and down the main avenue of Karl Johans Gate, glancing into the cathedral's close, poking her way around the university's buildings, circling the royal palace that stood solid and uncompromising at the top of its hill before finding herself at the entrance to Frogner Park.

Oslo's largest park didn't have the same scrappy hustle as Central Park back home. As a girl, she would escape the stifling museum atmosphere of the big house on East Fifty-Seventh to lose herself among the park's paths and grottos. She'd buy a hot dog from a vendor's cart or toss a coin into the upturned caps of the hopeful buskers. Sun herself on the lounges by the boathouse in the summer or skate on the pond in the winter. It became a refuge from her mother's more strident melodramatics.

Paul Jaffray had been dead for nearly a quarter century, but his wife mourned him as if she'd received the telegram yesterday. The memories of him choked off any hope of life for his daughter, or so it seemed. A bud nipped at birth.

Cleo had met George Cliveden in Central Park.

She was feeding the pigeons on a bench overlooking the tennis courts. He'd asked her for the time as he waited impatiently for his doubles partner.

It turned out his mother knew her mother. The two women played bridge together and attended the same charitable committees. He was a good dancer. Athletic. He played golf when he wasn't working in his father's law offices. He knew the right people, was of the right class, attended the right schools. Was, by any measure, a "good catch."

He'd taken her out to nightclubs. To dinner. To the theater.

And that would have been the extent of their relationship, if not for a fight with her mother.

Letitia Jaffray gave the impression of softness from her round cheeks to her curvy body to her high, girlish voice. Cleo knew better. If anything her mother's pillowy quality cushioned every attempted blow. Arguing with her mother was like punching a feather bolster. Exhausting. Pointless. Impossible.

The fight had started out in the usual fashion. Her mother had scolded Cleo for some minor infraction, calling upon her late husband to back up her argument.

Your father would never have . . .

Your father always . . .

If your father was here . . .

Cleo had heard the incessant complaints over her shortcomings all her life. But this time, she'd had enough of never measuring up. When she slammed out of the house, she'd no idea where she was headed until she stood outside George's apartment building.

The next thing she knew she was engaged.

An extreme attempt to finally impress her mother that backfired in spectacular fashion.

"Se opp!" The bicycle nearly clipped Cleo as it whizzed past, handlebar bell jangling, the man pumping the pedals as if he was late to a fire.

It seemed like half of Oslo was wandering the gravel paths patchy with melting snow, taking in the spring sunshine after one of the coldest winters ever. Along with the occasional mad-dash bicyclist, the park was awash in dog walkers and pram-pushing mothers, men in somber suits, and smartly turned-out secretaries enjoying chilly alfresco lunches before returning to their offices for the afternoon.

Cleo headed north past a small lake where a few ducks paddled. The trees, still bare after months of snow and ice, arched overhead. Fumbling in her handbag, she found a lonesome bronze øre coin amid her lipstick, compact mirror, and cigarette lighter. Squeezing the coin tight in one hand, she closed her eyes and made her wish before tossing it into the water. The same wish she'd made since that horrible morning outside the shattered, burned-out café in Zakopane. It hadn't worked yet, but Aunt Daisy aside, she wasn't giving up.

"Kim, *kom tilbake. Dumme hund!* Stop! Bad dog!"

The dog, rather than heeding the commands, snuffled Cleo's legs, its head nearly at the height of her waist. Cleo smiled and dug her fingers into the grizzled fur, scratching its head, which was nearly buried in her coat pocket. "Hello, Kim old boy. Are you misbehaving for Miss Kristiansen?"

The first few days after her arrival, Cleo had thought about befriending Aunt Daisy's secretary in hopes she might be another useful ally, but it hadn't taken long for whispers about Cleo to begin to circulate among the chancery staff.

Spoiled. Easy. Brat. Tramp.

She was used to being snubbed by the rule followers and the straight arrows of the world so she wasn't surprised by Petra Kristiansen's frosty attitude, only a little disappointed.

"I am sorry for bothering you. He is usually very well-behaved," Petra said as she snapped the leash back on the dog's collar.

"It's all right. Kim and I go way back. Aunt Daisy's had him since he was a puppy; the two are practically inseparable."

The woman's features flattened as if she was still unable to compute how Cleo and the American minister could possibly be related. Cleo oftentimes wondered the same thing. "He's usually docile as a lamb on a walk. What happened?"

"There was a work van. He pulled loose to chase it."

"Of course. Old Kim's never met anything with wheels he didn't want to catch. The herder in him, I guess. He'd never pull a stunt like that with Aunt Daisy. With her, he's good as gold."

"Madam Minister is in a conference on mineral imports. I'm glad he recognized you or I might still be chasing him."

"Not me exactly." Cleo shoved her hand in a pocket, pulling out a dried bit of beef and tossing it to the dog, who gulped it down with greedy smile. "He must have smelled Aunt Daisy. The coat was on a rack by the door."

The two fell in step together as Kim seemed to want to go wherever Cleo led and Petra was forced to follow the strong pull of the shepherd. "I hear your mother's family is from Chicago," Cleo ventured as an icebreaker.

"That's right," Petra replied.

It was like pulling teeth, but Cleo had been raised in a world where small talk was considered more necessary to a woman's education than math or reading. Right up there with flower arranging and how to hire staff. The more Petra resisted, the more Cleo was determined to get her to talk. She loved a good challenge. "Chicago's fantastic. Not as fantastic as New York, of course, but it has its charms."

Petra paused for a traffic light, and now those assessing blue eyes that had stared through Cleo since she'd arrived regarded her closely. "If you love America so much, why did you leave? And why do you not go back when you have the chance?"

Ouch. She should have seen that one coming. "It's a long story."

"They say you ran away from your wedding."

Cleo wished she could find those elusive "they." She'd teach them to mind their own business. "It sounds worse than it was."

"You didn't love your fiancé?"

Did Petra not know how small talk worked? What happened to discussing the weather or the shocking price of a pair of stockings? She'd bypassed that and gone straight for the jugular.

Cleo decided to parry with the unvarnished truth. "I thought I did. Turns out not enough to marry him." Petra didn't seem to know what to say to that, thank heavens. Cleo took the opportunity to follow up with some nosy questions of her own. "What about you and Lieutenant Bayard? Are you two setting a date yet?"

"It's not like that. He is a friend. Nothing more." If Petra was disappointed, she kept it well hidden. "He is merely helping me find passage for my grandmother."

"Is she here in Oslo?"

"She is in Bergen with my mother while they try to make travel arrangements."

"I'm sure she'll be fine," Cleo said, trying her best to sound confidently reassuring. "She's a US citizen, right?"

Petra's smile was polite, but she clearly did not share Cleo's optimism. She tightened her hand around Kim's leash, yanking him from a particularly interesting tree. "So was your Mr. Kominski, was he not?" Some of Cleo's shock must have shown on her face. Petra flushed with embarrassment. "I am very sorry. I should not have said that. It was cruel and unkind."

"It was. But you're not wrong."

CHAPTER 3

Dear Anne,

I don't know how much has been reported in the American papers about the Altmark, *a German ship attacked in Norwegian waters by the British in a brazen violation of Norwegian neutrality. It's become the stuff of fairy tales here—heroic boarding parties swinging cutlasses, maltreated prisoners of war held deep in the ship's hold. Add Errol Flynn and you'd have a Hollywood blockbuster. But it's left the Germans furious, the British defensive, and the Norwegians caught smack in the middle. I've done what I can to smooth a path for both parties, but tensions remain high. It's moments like these when I wish you were here. I could use a good healthy dose of your common sense and some of that Harriman charm.*

He's here now?" Daisy stood from her desk, where she'd been reading over the notes from her morning meeting with Vice Consul Whitney. A diplomatic pouch had arrived from Washington in the early hours, necessitating a frenzy of activity as reports were studied and responses drafted. Of course, it had also brought a pile of newspapers and magazines from back home, treats that had grown rare since the start of hostilities. Daisy had set them aside to be savored later with tea and sandwiches in her sitting room. A treat that would have to be deferred if this unexpected visit lasted too long. "For heaven's sake, send him in."

Miss Kristiansen disappeared only to return in the company of a somber gentleman in a dark suit, his hair cut close against his skull, his broad features and prominent ears giving him the look of a pugilist rather than a diplomat. Crow's-feet gathered at the corners of eyes colored with the weight of his position. "Herr Brauer, I'm sorry to have kept you waiting. Is there a problem?"

Silly question. Of course there was. The last few months had been nothing *but* problems, and there seemed no end in sight. Daisy tried not to forecast too far ahead, but it was clear it would be a case of delicate needle-threading for both Norway and the United States when it came to remaining on the sidelines in this conflict. A good thing she enjoyed embroidery.

She hid her concerns behind a bland smile of welcome as she motioned the German minister to a chair. His answering smile was equally opaque. "Not at all, Mrs. Harriman. I am here merely to extend an invitation to a small reception I'm hosting on the evening of April the fifth. I would be very much honored if you would come."

"You came all the way here for that?"

His features remained unreadable, but there was resignation in his gaze, a decision in the set of his shoulders that concerned her. "An honored guest deserves a personal invitation. Besides, my wife wanted to make sure nothing was lost in the post."

"How is Frau Brauer? Settling in with the new baby?" A pretty woman with delicate features and a chic sense of style, the German minister's wife had recently given birth to their first child, a daughter who was, by all accounts, already the apple of her father's eye.

"She is well. And the baby is thriving. Frau Brauer would

welcome your attendance. It would give you both a chance to chat about feedings and nappies and such."

The dig wasn't subtle nor was it a surprise, but she'd found early on that pretending a complete lack of understanding was usually her best defense. If they continued to press, she would ask them to explain the joke, which usually had them sheepishly swallowing their tongues. She'd no need this afternoon. Brauer seemed to realize his error. A wash of pink colored his cheeks, though his eyes remained hard, and he made no attempt to backtrack.

"I have a previous engagement with the Norwegian foreign minister and his wife that evening, but tell Frau Brauer I shall do my best to get there if only to ease her mind—mother to mother."

It was Brauer's turn to ignore the dig. Or perhaps it had passed him by, distracted as he seemed to be at her mention of Norway's Dr. Halvdan Koht. His somber face paled, and there was a bone-tired weariness about him that she didn't believe could be completely blamed on a new baby in the house. "If you have Dr. Koht's ear, I would ask that you press him to speak to his parliament about Britain's continued mining of Norwegian waters. My country can't let such blatant provocation stand. Norway must be made to see this."

Hitler was furious over what he saw as Norway's bending toward British interests. Tensions had only increased with Russia's invasion of Finland and King Haakon's renewed calls for neutrality alongside his push for defensive preparations. Britain's mining of the waters around Norway pushed Hitler into a corner where he must respond or back down, and it was clear he wasn't one for backing down.

"I'll speak to the foreign minister." Daisy tried one last time to offer an olive branch as she escorted him out. "The Norwegian parliament is doing all it can to remain correct in the letter of the law in all ways. It wants only peace for its country and an end to this war, as do we all."

"The king's late wife was a daughter of England, was she not?" Herr Brauer countered. "Sooner or later, the British will twist him round to their way of thinking."

"The United States doesn't want Norway drawn into the war any more than you do."

They paused at the door. He crushed the brim of his hat in his hand, exhaustion replaced by a grim glitter that sent a shiver up her spine. "Your country has interfered before, Mrs. Harriman. Forgive me if I find your guarantees somewhat lacking."

She watched him cross the courtyard to his car, his driver holding the door for him. Just as he ducked his head to enter, he was intercepted by a woman rushing over the wet macadam, hands tucked into the sleeves of her overlarge coat, a riot of dark curls escaping her headscarf.

Dear God, what was Cleo doing now?

Daisy couldn't hear what was said, but she knew that look. Before her goddaughter could cause an international incident, Daisy hurried out to mitigate any looming disaster. She arrived just as Herr Brauer bowed over Cleo's hand with a show of continental gallantry. "I will do what I can, Miss Jaffray." He glanced back at Daisy, once again the diplomat, a smile touching his thin lips. "I see where she gets her persuasiveness, Mrs. Harriman."

"Believe me, Herr Brauer, if I was half so glib, we'd not find ourselves in this predicament."

"Until the fifth, then."

Cleo waved him out of the drive before immediately turning to Daisy. "I know I shouldn't have, but it seemed too perfect an opportunity to pass up, and it worked. He said he'd make inquiries."

"He's an honorable man. If there's anything to be learned, he'll let you know."

Daisy was less sure that evening after she hung up the phone. If her information was correct, it began to make sense why the Germans might not be forthcoming. Zakopane wasn't just a resort town catering to the influx of German officers looking for a week or two of relaxation. It was the location of a new SS-Junker School, a secret police training center for SS and Gestapo officers.

Had that been why Kominski was so reluctant to leave? Because he saw a chance to land a blow for the Polish resistance? Or was it sheer coincidence that he'd disappeared after a bombing had taken out twenty German officers? Daisy didn't believe in coincidences. And then there was that damned letter. Was the man dead? In hiding? Could Daisy risk finding out with so much riding on the diplomatic knife edge she walked? She picked up the phone once more.

"Get me the Bergen ticket office of NAL. I need to book a single passage on their next ship to New York."

SNOW FELL OVER the narrow streets of Zakopane, feathering Cleo's hair and dusting her lashes. She had to find Micky, but every street she took led her back to the ruins of the Czarny Kot. The Black Cat was gone; nothing left of the café but blackened beams, melted glass, burnt bodies. She could hear voices in the wind, of those who'd been killed and those who'd simply disappeared as if they'd never existed. She clamped her hands over her ears, but Micky's voice seeped between her fingers. He called for her. He needed her. He begged her to help him.

"Cleo!" His voice was insistent.

"I'm coming," she cried. "I can't find you. Where are you?"

"Cleo, dear! Wake up!"

Her eyes flew open to find Aunt Daisy standing over her, the table lamp her godmother had switched on shining in Cleo's eyes. She must have fallen asleep, the magazine she'd been leafing through on the floor at her feet. Her heart raced, her hands clenched shaking in her lap, but she fought the panic back. Her hands uncurled. Her breathing slowed.

Aunt Daisy regarded Cleo thoughtfully as she held something out. "I've booked passage for you on the SS *Bergensfjord*, scheduled to sail for New York. Lieutenant Bayard will escort you as far as the Bergen quayside. I've cabled your mother to expect you."

"You're sending me away?"

"No. I'm sending you home." Aunt Daisy's stare pinned Cleo to her chair. "Where you should have gone to begin with."

"What about Micky? I can't leave."

"I'll do what I can to find out what happened to him." As Aunt Daisy said this, her gaze slid away, unable to meet Cleo's eyes. It was just for a moment, but Cleo knew that look. It was the look of someone who would say what needed to be said to make her go away.

"What about Herr Brauer? He said he'd help."

Aunt Daisy wouldn't be drawn into an argument. "Be packed and ready to go in one week."

Over the next few days, Cleo continued to try to change her mind, but whenever she sought her out to plead her case, Petra Kristiansen put her off. Madam Minister was in a meeting. She was leaving on a trip to the airfield at Kjeller or just arriving back from a fact-finding visit to Trondheim. She was preparing to host a dinner or on her way to attend a dinner elsewhere. The night before she was due to leave for Bergen, Cleo watched the taillights of the car heading out the drive, Aunt Daisy's feathered hat bobbing from the back seat.

"Damn!" Cleo said, shocking two chancery typists getting off work. They tutted their way past her on their way to catching the bus.

She turned to go back inside where it was warm and dry, but

the idea of one more evening spent leafing through magazines, listening to the radio, or staring out at the lights of the city was too dismal to contemplate. She was tired of the waiting, the wondering, the constant stress of feeling helpless. A walk, even without a destination, felt like forward momentum.

A few streets south of the residence, the glare of neon lights and the soulful strains of "In a Sentimental Mood" drew her into a crowded nightclub. Tables surrounded a small stage where a five-piece jazz band played over the clink of silverware and the hum of conversation. Cleo's eyes instinctively sought out the trumpeter. Too tall. Too blond. Not Micky.

"Har du en reservasjon?" A man in a starched penguin suit blocked her way. The way he waggled the menu in his hand, it was obvious what he asked.

She waved him away, satisfied to stand at the back and listen. It had been months since she'd heard Ellington. Upon their arrival in Zakopane, the Germans had immediately and officially outlawed jazz and forbidden anyone from either performing it or listening to it. That hadn't stopped them from breaking their own laws and hiring Micky to play at their private parties, his talent making him a favorite among the officers. He would come home early in the morning, still humming Goodman and Miller, his mood valiantly lifting her own.

"Miss Jaffray? I thought that was you." It was Lieutenant Bayard, with Miss Kristiansen, very obviously on a date, if his freshly pressed uniform and her silk charmeuse was any indication. "Care to join us?"

Petra's face blanched even whiter than her normal milky perfection. Yes. Definitely a date. So much for "just friends."

"I really shouldn't." The last thing Cleo wanted was to be a third wheel with Petra shooting daggers at her across the table.

She should go. Back out in the snow. Back to her quiet room with its noisy ghosts. And tomorrow, back to New York to face her mother and the judgment of New York society.

As if reading her mind, Bayard pulled out a chair. "You can't celebrate your last night in Oslo sitting alone in your room." He looked to Petra. "You tell her. She has to stay for a drink."

Cleo had to hand it to her. Petra didn't even bat an eye at being cornered. "Of course. Please stay."

"Just one drink then I really have to go." She accepted the wineglass the lieutenant filled from the bottle of red on the table between them.

Petra toyed with the brooch decorating her collar, the same gold-and-cobalt-blue butterfly Cleo had often seen her wearing. Was it a recent gift? A family heirloom? "Are you happy to be leaving Norway, Miss Jaffray?" she asked politely, if pointedly.

"No, but it doesn't seem like I have a choice." Cleo tossed back her wine as if she'd bellied up to the bar and returned Petra's cool stare with one equally dismissive. "And so long as Aunt Daisy avoids me, there's not much I can do to change her mind."

Bayard, clearly sensing a standoff, stepped in. "Mrs. Harriman went to a lot of trouble to secure that ticket," the lieutenant explained. "Passage out of Norway is tough these days and getting tougher."

"I get it. I do." Maybe it was the glass of wine hitting her empty stomach or maybe the band on the stage reminded Cleo of similar dinners where friendship and conversations had come easy, unlike here where she could feel Petra's suspicion in every chilly glance. "But I can't leave. Not yet. I know it's crazy, but I can't move on until I know for certain what happened to Micky."

"And if you never find out?" the lieutenant replied bluntly. "What then?"

Cleo thought about her mother, frozen at the very moment she'd received word of her husband's death. Unable to move on from that tragedy. Existing but no longer living. Would that be Cleo's fate? She shook off the idea along with her doubts. She touched the necklace at her throat as if reassuring herself it was still there. As Micky wasn't. "I'll find him. I know it."

"An admirable sentiment and one that does you credit, but what makes you think you can do what Mrs. Harriman can't?" Petra challenged. "If I were you, I'd take the gift that's been given and be grateful. Others would kill for the privilege you're tossing away like trash."

"Others like you, I take it?" Days of frustration welled hot until Cleo's cheeks burned with it, and her words spilled forth in an untampered rush. "You know what? I'm tired of being your punching bag. If you want to help your grandmother as much as you claim, maybe stop whining and wringing your hands and *do* something about it instead of blaming everyone else for your failures."

Petra's voice turned as cold as the sleet falling outside. "Even if I did ask your aunt for assistance, do you think she could just wave her magic wand and conjure another ticket? She spent what coin she had already, Miss Jaffray. On you."

Spoiled. Easy. Brat. Tramp.

Petra's low opinion had just reached rock bottom. Cleo lurched to her feet. "I'm sorry for intruding. Enjoy the rest of your evening."

She didn't hear Bayard until he caught up with her outside the club. He'd left his coat behind to chase her down and now he stood rubbing his arms, stamping his feet, his breath coming in quick puffs of steam. "Petra doesn't mean it. She's scared and, honestly, a little jealous."

"You think Petra Kristiansen is the first girl to take against me for no reason? Hardly."

"She's not that bad once you get to know her."

"You could say the same to her about me, and maybe you should." Cleo shoved him back the way he'd come. "Go inside, Lieutenant, before you freeze to death."

His shoulders hitched as if he wanted to say more, but she shooed him on with one mittened hand. "Go. Get back to your date before she accuses me of stealing you away on top of all my other crimes."

"Right. Good night, then, Miss Jaffray."

"Good night, Lieutenant Bayard." Alone, Cleo retraced her steps back to the legation, turning the conversation over in her head. She understood fear in all its forms from the walking on eggshells variety to the blind, blood-draining panic. She'd experienced all of them, sometimes in the same five minutes. She understood Petra's fear as the worst kind: the helpless boulder-in-the-stomach dread for someone you love.

She climbed the stairs back to her attic room, pondered the traveling outfit laid out for tomorrow, the precious ticket propped against her dressing table mirror. *Had* Aunt Daisy called in favors to get Cleo this ticket? If someone found out, could that favoritism be used against her?

Before she could change her mind, Cleo scrawled a quick note, signing her godmother's name at the bottom. Hardly a forgery, but who was to know? Placing it along with the ticket in an envelope, she sealed the flap, addressing it to Frøken Kristiansen c/o Solstrand Guesthouse, Bergen. The chancery office was thirty yards away. Surely there was someone there who could tell her how to get an important letter delivered overnight priority.

She didn't want to go home yet, but she knew someone who did.

Dear Anne,

One would think after a lifetime of social functions and more than two years serving in Norway, I would be immune to the pomp and glamour of an evening at the royal palace. You would be wrong. It's always both thrilling and terrifying in equal measure. I suppose if I were a normal guest—my husband being the official US representative and me his smiling wife—it would make things simpler, but this is so much more interesting. There are times when I have to stifle my amusement at the way in which my very confusing presence causes consternation in courtiers' breasts.

THE PALACE DINING room was ablaze with lights that shone down on men in black tie, some studded with medals, while the women glittered like peacocks on parade as guests worked their way through seven courses and speech after speech. A small string ensemble offered a quiet background to the buzz of grim conversation. King Haakon VII presided over the company, his trim athletic body and direct, uncompromising gaze so typical of the Norwegians Daisy had met in her time here. It was a country comfortable with itself and its traditions. Welcoming of the strangers in its midst, but never gregarious, pandering, or what one would call overly friendly. These qualities only made her love them all the more.

Tonight's reception was more uncomfortable than usual, though perhaps Daisy's perception was skewed seated as she was between the head of the British and German missions, which was somewhat akin to being the buffer between two belligerent schoolboys.

"If you think we're going to believe you were there to survey for a new commercial airline between Norway and Germany, you're mistaken."

"My good friend, you can surmise all you like. The Norwegian authorities understood our aims were benign. I can't help your suspicious nature."

"My suspicious nature . . . it's not my country invading its neighbors."

"Didn't the Norwegians lose two more ships off the northern coast last week? I believe those were British mines they hit, not German."

At one point during the fish course, Daisy's hand curled around her butter knife. She only refrained from stabbing it into an offending thigh when someone stood to offer one more toast.

Just then, Crown Princess Märtha caught her eye. Prince Olav's wife didn't smile, but there was in her expression that of a secret shared. Daisy released her grip on the knife and renewed her efforts to parry the barbs being flung back and forth through the remaining courses and the king's gracious speech.

After dinner, they moved into the great hall, where the string quartet from dinner had expanded to become a chamber orchestra, and music filled the high-ceilinged room. A few took this as an opportunity to dance, and soon Daisy was whirling through a waltz with the minister from Portugal. She felt the stares from a few of the older crowd who believed a woman of nearly seventy should maintain a certain dignity, but she'd long since grown hardened to the itch between her shoulder blades and the thin-lipped frowns as she sailed past in the arms of her dance partner. It was only after a particularly energetic Lambeth Walk that left her breathless with laughter that she slid free of the crowds to find a quiet corner where she might recover.

"I envy you your stamina, Madam Minister. These functions never fail to exhaust me." Crown Princess Märtha had detached herself from her husband and now shared Daisy's corner, shimmering in a gown of pale blue, diamonds winking at her throat.

Daisy had always found the princess charming; intelligence

glowed in her wide eyes and strength honed her finely boned features. Since Queen Maud's death two years prior, the crown princess ruled the ladies of the royal court, and it was obvious King Haakon thought the world of his Swedish-born daughter-in-law. He wasn't the only man to be bowled over by her quiet kindness. Daisy had heard from more than one source how smitten President Roosevelt had been by his royal guest during her recent visit to America.

"I'll probably pay for it in the morning with aching joints, Your Highness, but I love a good knees-up." She sipped at her champagne, wishing instead for a cold glass of water. "Luckily for me, parties are in my job description."

"The late queen loved to dance as well."

"Who do you think taught me to defy convention without a backward glance?"

A noise from across the room drew their attention. The British minister roaring over some disagreement, others smoothing the troubled waters. Her Royal Highness gave a small shake of her head. "You showed admirable restraint this evening. If the gentleman from Berlin had not changed the subject, I wasn't certain you wouldn't have used that knife on him."

"Was it that obvious?"

"To all these men? No," she replied. Her voice was low, barely audible over the music, and she leaned close as if this was a conversation meant for Daisy's ears alone. "But I'm a mother, and I've worn that very same look when my daughters are bickering over a doll they both desire. How much greater the animosity when it's the world in contention."

"So long as the countries involved adhere to the international rules of law that Norway follows so strictly, then all will be well," Daisy said just as quietly, falling back on a familiar theme she'd used to good effect with visiting journalists and anxious businessmen.

Her Royal Highness was not so easily swayed. "And if they do not?"

Daisy could lie. Pretend she hadn't seen the contents of diplomatic pouches that told of growing concern among neighboring mission heads and their army of intelligence officers. But it was obvious the princess would know it was a lie as soon as the words left her lips. "If, God forbid, it comes to war, seek me out, Your Highness, and I'll do what I can."

"You or your country?" the younger woman asked.

It was a rash, unthinking offer, and Daisy had no idea what Washington would say should it come to pass that she had to make good on it. No, that wasn't quite true. She knew what the career diplomats would say, the politicians and bureaucrats who weighed every action like misers with their scales. But she couldn't rescind it now. Not with the princess considering her carefully with features showing both determination and an intuition lost to the rest of her nation. Daisy would worry about her superiors when she had to and not a moment before.

The irony not lost on her, she held out a hand as if sealing a gentleman's contract. "Consider it the offer of one mother to another."

The princess paused for a moment before clasping Daisy's hand, her face seeming to smooth in relief. "Thank you."

She drifted away at that point, her public smile once again in place as she joined a group nearby, the sound of laughter dissipating the solemnity that clung to Daisy. She felt that familiar tickle at the back of her neck, the sense of someone watching her with disapproval. But it was no grand dame with an overinflated sense of self-worth this time. It was the king.

CHAPTER 4

Dear Anne,

It's been a long day, and I'm as weary as I've ever been since stepping off the ship in Bergen's harbor to take up this post. The slow drip of the war is tiring—the daily briefings that bring endless counts of ships, planes, men. The maps with their color-coded dotted lines crossing miles and frontiers. The conversations and arguments. The warnings and justifications. You grow numb to it if you're not careful, so then when events occur that require decisive action and quick thinking, it's like trying to jump-start one of those old Ford ambulances of ours in a heavy January freeze. I'm not sure whether I'm the ambulance or the frustrated, desperate driver. I suppose history will tell . . .

The *Blücher*. The *Lützow*. The *Emden*. The *Kondor, Albatros,* and *Möwe*." Daisy read off the list as she pinched the bridge of her nose in an effort to alleviate a blossoming headache.

"And those are just the cruisers and torpedo boats," Mr. Whitney sniped from his chair across the room, brows beetling as he read from the file.

"I can read," she replied mildly, flipping through the report.

Part of the foreign service boys club, the vice consul had been a thorn in her side since she'd arrived in Norway. More recently, he'd been furious when he was passed over for transfer to another posting, blaming her for submitting a poor service evaluation. In fact, it had been her recognition that, despite his insubordinate attitude, he was too valuable to lose. Looking back, it might have been smarter to praise him to the skies and suggest he might put his superior diplomatic skills to better use somewhere else— Outer Mongolia sprang to mind. None of those thoughts ever made it to her face or crept into her tone. What was the saying? Keep your friends close and your enemies closer? Daisy wouldn't go so far as to label Mr. Whitney an enemy; he remained a valuable part of the chancery staff. But he was someone she managed with a careful hand.

"Bloody Norwegians." Whitney flung down the folder. "How'd they let it come to this?"

"We're privy to the same intelligence as they are," Daisy replied calmly. "How did *we*?"

He clicked his jaw shut, but his face grew red with swallowed words. Daisy sighed. Arguing got them nowhere. He was clearly as frustrated as she was and subsisting on little more than coffee and cigarettes. She pushed aside her irritation and smoothed her face into conciliatory lines. "Opinions aside, what's your professional assessment?"

Mollified, he leaned back, steepling his fingers under his chin in thought. "I'd lay odds they're heading out to meet the British, ma'am. The Jerries won't let their mine laying off Narvik stand."

"Perhaps. But that doesn't explain why they're grouping at the mouth of the Oslofjord, does it?" She consulted her map, scanning the long, jagged waterway that drove straight north to the capital's heart.

"You asked for an assessment," Whitney argued. "If you choose to ignore it, that's up to you." He heaved himself to his feet.

"Good thing the builders finished that new bomb shelter in the basement. I expect you'll be sleeping there tonight; rest those old bones of yours while you have the chance." He smiled to make it seem as if he was joking, but Daisy wasn't fooled.

She answered him back with a smile of her own. "Old is for others, Mr. Whitney. I'm getting younger by the day. Must be the climate. That being said, I'm long past the age where camping is enjoyable. If those ships are aiming for Oslo, they won't be here before tomorrow at the earliest. I'd rather start a war after a good night's sleep in my own bed, wouldn't you?"

After he left, she choked down her lunch in between phone calls to the Foreign Office, the legations in Copenhagen and Berlin, the consulate in Bergen, and her contacts in Trondheim, Narvik, and Stavanger. Was this a German feint to draw the British into battle? Or was it something bigger? Bolder? It was like staring at the scramble of scattered puzzle pieces. Trying to fit them together until the picture emerged. So what piece was she missing? What clue didn't she have?

Rubbing her tired eyes, she snapped on the radio, settling into her favorite chair to gaze on her favorite view: the mountains to the far west, hanging like hazy shadows against the pale sky. She took up her embroidery, sorting and matching threads, another pattern with blank spaces and missing pieces that would take work to bring into focus.

At one point, she spied Cleo passing outside the door. A light step, a sultry whiff of Tabu perfume.

The girl always had been a chameleon. She could slide through a space without notice or draw every eye if that was her intention. She'd certainly not inherited that mercurial quality from either parent. Both Letitia and Paul were as easy to read as a pair of children's primers. But Cleo was quicker to find the angle and turn a moment to her advantage. In a man, it was a trait that would win praise. But women were still raised to be timid approval-seekers, which made Cleo's ingenuity a blot on her copybook. Normally Daisy would have fostered Cleo's clear thinking. Turned against her, she found it as irritating as everyone else did.

Movement flickered at the edge of her vision. "Do you plan to hover all night, Clementine, or is there something you wanted?"

She could practically hear the huff at her use of that detestable name.

Cleo's hair was damp and dark as if she'd just left the bath, those short choppy curls of hers barely touching her ears. They made her look painfully young and far more like her father. Paul's hair had been that same shade of expensive Swiss chocolate. He'd had the same long straight purposeful nose, those green eyes flecked with gold. In fact, there was very little of Letitia in her daughter except perhaps for her boyish slenderness, not at all the fashion these days when luxurious curves were all the rage.

"I only wanted to say how much I appreciated what you did for me in securing that ticket." In and out like the threads of Daisy's embroidery, Cleo's fingers laced and relaxed. The pulse in her throat as rapid as a bird's. "But in the end, I couldn't use it. Not without feeling like I was abandoning Micky. You understand, don't you?"

By the time Daisy had learned of Cleo's deception, it had been too late to call ahead to Bergen and explain the situation. That ship had sailed—literally. Miss Kristiansen's grandmother was on her way to New York. Daisy could rant and fume or she could find the angle and adapt. Perhaps Cleo was more like her than anyone.

"Have you written your mother to explain?" Daisy looked down at her own hands, which lay relaxed upon her lap. An old woman's hands, she realized with a start. Freckled. Knobby. She never felt old, so it was always a surprise to see herself in a mirror and notice the gray hair, the sagging neck, the thickening of her body.

"Not yet." Cleo studied the tops of her shoes. "I will. It's just hard to find the right words."

Daisy's gaze narrowed. "They don't need to be perfect. They just need to be from you." Cleo nodded and started to turn away, but Daisy stopped her. "Do you know what an SS-Junker School is, Cleo? It's used for training by Germany's secret police forces. Gestapo. The SS-D. One of these schools opened in Zakopane shortly after the invasion. Did you know about the school? Or the other Gestapo facilities located in Zakopane as part of the German annexation of that country?"

Cleo's answer was clear in the way she closed her eyes, knuckles white, body rigid.

"How well did you know your trumpeter?" Daisy continued. "Did he ever talk to you about what took him to Poland in the first place?"

"Work, of course. He'd hired on with a jazz band out of Kraków."

"My information says that his father's family was from Kraków. He had relatives there."

"Sure, but nobody Micky had ever met. His grandparents emigrated ages ago."

"Did he ever speak about the invasion of Poland? How he felt about it?"

"He griped about the inconveniences, the new regulations. Nothing that could have been seen as treasonous or worth being arrested over. And it was only to me. He never spoke out where anyone might hear him."

Daisy took up her hoop and needle. "Let's hope so."

CLEO SLIPPED OUT of the residence in the confusion of dinner preparations for the new French ambassador. It didn't take her long to find herself back at the same smoky nightclub with its flickering candles, hothouse flowers, and starry-eyed couples rocking against one another on the tiny dance floor as the band played.

The same maître d' met her at the door, glancing over her shoulder in search of her date.

"Bord til en, vær så snill." Cleo held up a finger. "Table for one."

He sat her near the kitchen, bringing her a bottle of wine and a bowl of creamy fish soup. She sopped it up with a thick hunk of crusty bread and tried not to think about similar nights in similar clubs listening to similar bands. It wasn't until the group bowed their way offstage for a break that she realized they were speaking English—American English.

Homesickness twisted her gut.

Before she could talk herself out of it, she followed the familiar rise and fall of her mother tongue backstage to a cluttered dressing room that doubled as a storage closet. Brooms and mops stood in a corner beside a mirrored vanity ringed with Hollywood lights where the singer checked his thick wavy chestnut hair. The horn section slumped together on a broken sofa heaped with cushions—one reading a battered copy of *War and Peace*, the other juggling a dinner plate on his lap. A third man, bony and tall with a bird's sharp face and skin as dark as mahogany seemed to be sleeping on a pile of old newspapers tied with twine, his arms crossed corpse-like over his chest. Seated on an upturned bucket, another lighter-skinned man in a jaunty green bow tie tapped out a jazz beat on the wall.

"Well, hello there." Spotting her lurking in the doorway, the drummer paused in his tapping, his smile slow and lazy, his gaze roaming over her body even beneath the shapeless coat she wore. If he hoped to surprise a blush out of her, he was doomed to disappointment. She'd been ogled by far more experienced lechers in her twenty-five years.

"Excuse me," she said. "Not to intrude, but I'm looking for someone."

"Aren't we all, sweetheart?" The drummer laughed.

"His name is Micky Kominski. He plays trumpet. Maybe you've heard of him?"

"Depends. What do you want him for? Has he skipped town? Does he owe you money? Are you"—his gaze settled on her stomach—"in the family way?"

She wrenched her coat tightly around her. "He went missing in Poland."

The man reading looked up from his book. "Poland? What the hell was he doing there? Doesn't he know there's a war on?"

The drummer leaned against the wall, sticks still tapping. "Sorry, doll. We've been working here in Oslo since the beginning of the year. Sam over there doesn't like to drive his precious rattletrap van into battle zones."

The man reclining on the newspapers opened one sleepy eye. "Make fun of Athena all you want, but she gets us where we need to go."

"Athena?" Cleo ventured.

"The van," Drummer explained with a roll of his eyes and a flutter of his sticks. "Sorry, doll. Hope you find him, though."

Cleo should have expected it. She'd received the same answer everywhere she went. Common sense told her to give up. Even if Micky hadn't died in the café's bombing, there were a thousand different ways he could have been hurt or killed in the weeks since. But giving up on him—on her search—meant saying goodbye. She couldn't do it. Not yet. Not so long as there was a chance he could still be out there. A chance he needed her.

Not many people did.

After the snug warmth of the club, the wind slapped her awake. Streetlights reflected golden off the snow and bounced back from dark windows of neighboring apartment buildings. Cleo burrowed her hands into her coat pockets and hurried back to the legation, slipping up the drive and hoping to sneak in through the kitchens and up to her room without being seen. A rustle in the bushes and a crunch of a boot heel on the gravel checked her pace. A dark figure stood in the shelter of the portico. "We need to quit meeting like this, Miss Jaffray."

Even with only the glow of his cigarette to illuminate his features, it was easy to see the lines dug into the lieutenant's face, the way he stood tense and angry. Or was it fear that held him taut as a wire? "You look as if you've seen a ghost."

His gaze met hers, his eyes wide and almost lost. "I don't know what I just saw, but it sure as hell wasn't good."

Whatever had him jumpy as a cat, she wasn't going to stand out here and interrogate him. Her feet were already frozen, and the cold was making its way simultaneously up her legs and down her back. "Come on. I have a surefire remedy for chasing away ghosts."

"Brandy?"

"Better."

The kitchen was quiet and dark but for a few lamps left burning in case the minister woke and wanted a glass of milk or a cup of tea in the middle of the night. The smells of bread, sugar, and gravy lingered in the warm air.

Bayard fell into a chair as Cleo moved around the kitchen, searching out milk, cocoa, sugar, a saucepan. Two mugs. "I want to thank you for helping Petra," he said, color slowly returning to his face. "After the way she treated you, I didn't expect it."

"I didn't do it for Petra. I did it for me. It was a selfish act—pure and simple."

"If you say so."

"Here." She pushed a mug across the table at him, hoping to

change the subject. "Mother always says a good cup of cocoa makes bad things go away."

He sipped cautiously before smiling his thanks. His shoulders lost that hunched defensive posture. He rubbed his face with his hands, erasing the tension though shadows continued to cloud the edges of his gaze.

"Care to tell me what's going on, or is this one more thing I'm not supposed to know or can't know or everyone's too busy to tell me?"

"Might as well. If it's what I think it is, we'll be up to our necks in it sooner rather than later."

That was ominous. Cleo sipped at her own cocoa, for the first time wishing she was back in the nursery with Mother tucking her up with a kiss to keep the monsters away.

"I just got back from the German embassy." Bayard stared into his mug, a frown between his arrowed brows. "A friend of mine in the Norwegian foreign office invited me along to watch a peace movie the Germans were showing."

"Sounds dull. What was it? Rosy-cheeked blond children frisking in an Alpine meadow? Hearty hausfraus and their polka-loving husbands eating sausages and clinking frothy tankards at Oktoberfest?"

"I wish." His haunted look was back, and a muscle jumped in his jaw. "It was a documentary film about the bombing of Warsaw. It was horrible. So much devastation and death. You wouldn't believe it."

"Wouldn't I?" She gripped her tea towel like a lifeline. "Though I can't imagine why they'd show such a film."

"They explained it was a way to promote peace, for God's sake. They claimed it was to show what would happen to anyone who resisted the Nazis' attempts to defend it from English aggression. We were all so shocked, no one knew what to say. It was . . . it was . . ."

"Absolutely bonkers?"

That surprised a faint smile. His brown eyes softened. "You could call it that." They finished their cocoa in silence. He set his mug in the sink. "You may regret you gave that ticket away."

"I'm not leaving until I find out what happened to Micky. Is he alive? Is he dead? Has he been detained or imprisoned? Someone out there knows."

"That reminds me." He sat up, fishing in his pocket. "A courier dropped this off for you." He handed her an envelope.

Cleo slid a finger beneath the flap, unfolding the heavy, expensive stationery. The handwriting was bold and black and arrogant. "It's from Herr Brauer's secretary. I'm to meet with him tomorrow morning at the German chancery."

"He has news?"

"I'll find out tomorrow." Her words were cut off by a low moaning wail that skittered up her spine. She locked her knees together to keep from diving under the table.

Bayard's face assumed his earlier stricken look of shock. "Stand to. Here we go."

MIDNIGHT AND THE streetlights still burned.

Cleo stood at her window, fingertips pressed to the cold glass as she strained to catch the drone of aircraft, the whistle of falling bombs. This wasn't the first air raid drill she'd lived through— there had been one while she was staying in a town near the Slovakian border and two more as she passed through Austria along with a stream of fellow refugees. She'd followed instructions and the crowds as they made their orderly way to the designated shelters and waited patiently for the authorities to tell them it was safe to go home. There had been no real sense of alarm or panic. Poland had given the Germans confidence. The West's subsequent inactivity had boosted it.

In Munich, where she had been dozing in a railway station, the sirens had wailed again. By then she'd grown used to them so, with nowhere to go, she'd simply pulled herself deeper into her coat and continued to sleep. In the German city of Kiel, there had been no sirens, but whispers of an attack had sent people into the street to search the night skies along with the antiaircraft batteries.

One a.m. and Oslo was finally plunged into darkness. Cleo could hear the staff scrambling in the blackout, laughing and chatting as if they were enjoying a children's parlor game like sardines or hide-and-seek.

There was a suffocating claustrophobia that came with being unable to see. It stole her breath. An eerie numbness crept into her fingers and feet. Using the faintest overlap of shadows as a guide, she worked her way from the window to the bed, settling back on the duvet, digging her fingers into the fabric as if it might anchor her in place and keep her from simply fading away to vapor. In her fancy, she imagined them coming to wake her in the morning and finding her vanished into thin air—disappeared like Micky.

Would they spend any more time looking for her than they had for him? How much did her name count? Her pedigree? Her Sutton Place relations?

Silly question: if war spared those with the proper connections, her father would have lived to come home rather than ending in a French military cemetery, one name among thousands, among hundreds of thousands.

A phone rang and was quickly answered. Hurried footsteps passed by in the hall outside her door. The earlier laughter died out, replaced by a murmur of conversation. The phone rang again. A car arrived in a crunch of gravel. Doors slammed. Voices rose and fell, though she couldn't make out what they said. At one point, Cleo heard Bayard shouting blackout instructions.

Aunt Daisy's voice—sharp but not frantic—cut through them all.

Silence resumed.

Did you know about the school? Or the other Gestapo facilities located in Zakopane . . . ?

Not at first. The war had come on them so suddenly, waves of infantry and tanks streaming through town in the first wave of invasion, that they'd had no time to be afraid. It wasn't until the flood of refugees from the devastation in Warsaw and Kraków, Grodno and Katowice began to arrive that fear sat in her belly like a rock. Micky let them sleep on the floor of their apartment while she offered up what money she had to help them on their journey. But that had been before the Germans and the Russians cemented their grip and the stream of refugees seeking shelter in Zakopane thinned then stopped altogether.

Whenever she talked about following those making their escape, Micky convinced her it was safer to stay put rather than venture out onto the choked roadways and overcrowded trains. It would be fine, he reassured her. Just don't be smart, don't break any laws, and, last but not least, don't draw attention to yourself.

It had worked.

Zakopane, isolated among the forests and peaks of the Tatra Mountains, grew quiet. The shops and cafés that had closed during the invasion reopened. At the Czarny Kot, the band's jazz set was replaced by military marches and Vienna waltzes and music straight out of the last century, but the German officers on leave lapped it up, paying for endless rounds, each toast to victory sloppier than the last.

Then the crackdowns began.

The arrests started.

And even quiet, out-of-the-way Zakopane grew dangerous.

She closed her eyes, but now the unrelenting black was shot

through with afterimages of broken bodies and fire-blackened beams that, even months later, made her pulse flutter and slithered icy over her skin. Twenty dead, most of them German officers. Was Micky among them? She'd assumed so until a letter had been pushed under her apartment door, sending her out of Zakopane to risk the road at last.

She opened her eyes, hoping to erase the memories that came with the darkness, and pulled a blanket around herself. The cold continued to seep into her bones until she shivered, unable to get warm.

A knock at the door brought a clerk with a flashlight asking if she wanted an escort to the new basement shelter.

Cleo shielded her face against the blinding light. "Has Mrs. Harriman gone down?"

"No, miss," he replied. "She's on the phone."

"Then it must not be too bad. I'll stay here." She refused to hide in a basement while the rest of the city remained unfazed though, once he was gone, she wished she'd asked him to leave his flashlight.

Two a.m., and the lights flickered back on in the residence followed by a slow cascade as switches were thrown and fuses reset all over Oslo.

The phones quieted. Conversations dwindled. The residence settled into sleep.

All except Cleo.

She returned to her window and watched as the city's shadows shrank back into alleys and doorways like the monster receding back under her bed.

CHAPTER 5

Dear Anne,

No doubt future generations will question how we could have been so caught off guard by events. We should have known this was coming, but we were blinded by our own hopes. Hope that we would never get to this point again. Hope that the world had learned its lesson. Hope that we had insulated ourselves with laws and long-standing tradition. But we forgot that war is also a long-standing tradition. Denmark fell within hours. The Germans' sights are set on Norway now . . .

A ringing phone startled Daisy awake. Kim gave a sleepy woof from his bed by the radiator. The glowing dials of her bedside clock read three a.m. Her heart sank. Nothing good ever happened this time of the morning.

She fumbled for her glasses, knocking over the carafe of water beside her bed. The receiver slipped through her shaking fingers. Her heart banged against her chest. But her voice remained rock steady. "Harriman here."

"The ships have entered the fjord, ma'am. The Germans are headed for Oslo."

Cold washed through her, not a draft from the ill-fitting

windows, but an inner chill that no amount of quilts could banish. What the Norwegian government had worked so hard to avoid barreled toward them in a churn of ships' propellers.

What was there to stop them? Not much, if the reports on her desk were accurate.

Daisy refused to panic. That's what they wanted—both the Germans and those few among her staff ready to pounce with whispers of incompetence, inefficiency, and inexperience. She would remain calm and measured, an eye within the storm. No matter how much she felt otherwise. Even as she rose and dressed, she was formulating plans, making lists, reviewing options.

The German attack might have caught her by surprise, but not out of ideas.

The next hours were a blur of restrained confusion as cables were sent, letters were written, and phone calls made. Miss Kristiansen arrived at the legation as if it was just another day at the office. Only careful scrutiny uncovered the tremble in her lips and the shock clouding her blue eyes.

"Were you able to get through to Washington, my dear?"

"No, ma'am. I believe the Germans are in control of the telegram office. They could not guarantee our message would be delivered."

Daisy tried not to twitch. Morale hung by a thread. She was their leader. They took their energy from her.

The chancery offices buzzed with a mix of excitement and fear while the residence filled with anxious questioning staff and their families, essentials gripped in hastily packed suitcases, children kept close with sharp words from tired mothers. News came that King Haakon and his family, along with members of the Norwegian parliament, planned to travel to the town of Hamar by special train as soon as it could be arranged.

"Will they surrender?"

"Will they fight?"

"Where's the Norwegian military?"

"Where's the German navy?"

"What about the British? Will they counterattack?"

"What does Washington say?"

Daisy ignored the barrage of questions. It was easier than replying that she didn't know. Best to look confident. In command. Doubt would race through this crowd like wildfire, and she'd never restore order. Lucky for her, the drone of aircraft overhead and the answering thunder of distant gun batteries cut through the deafening chatter like a knife.

"We'll send the legation's families north to Sjusjøen until we better understand the situation," Daisy advised, her voice holding a bark of command that quelled any argument. "Lieutenant Bayard, see to it."

"Yes, ma'am." His face was as stoic as granite; only a slight tightness around his eyes gave away his frayed nerves. Soon cars were rounded up, a route mapped, luggage stowed as groups were organized and parceled out among the transport they'd scrounged. "And you?"

Washington would require up-to-date reporting of the situation. With direct communications impossible, that would mean routing all cables and phone calls through Stockholm. It would also mean sticking close to the Norwegian cabinet as decisions were made. She couldn't do that here in Oslo. "Mr. Cox will stay behind with the rest of the foreign service staff to take charge of the legation here. I'll follow the Norwegian government by car." She paused on her way up the stairs. "You haven't seen Cleo this morning, have you?"

"Not since last night, ma'am. Should I look for her?"

Another low boom shook the residence, rattling china and fluttering curtains. Black smoke rose over the rooftops to the north. "You have your hands full. I'll see to it."

"If you don't mind me saying so, ma'am," he said with a cheeky smile. "Your hands seem just as full."

In the study, Miss Kristiansen was packing up her typewriter along with extra ribbons, ink and pens, pads of paper. Boxes were open on the floor, half filled with confidential files. Others sat waiting to be carried downstairs.

Crossing to her desk, Daisy opened the bottom drawer, pulling loose a wooden partition to reveal a small cavity at the back. From there, she removed a box containing the State Department's codebook. Nothing to mark it as important or of interest. But at this juncture, its safety rated higher than hers.

Wharton's *Buccaneers* was on her nightstand. She peeled off the blue dust jacket, wrapping the codebook inside. Then, after unsnapping the lid of her overnight case, she settled the disguised book amid her travel essentials, shoving it beneath a girdle and surrounding it with a pair of hose, garters, her toothbrush, an extra face cloth, and her nightgown. Satisfied the book was as safe as she could make it short of shoving it down her brassiere, she snapped the case closed. "We'll keep this case separate from the rest of the luggage, Petra. We can't let it out of our sight."

"Of course, ma'am. I'll take it down with mine." She set the case beside the pile of boxes.

By nine thirty, the residence was quiet. Rooms that only hours earlier had been swarming with people were empty. The families were safely away under the care and protection of the lieutenant. Across the courtyard, the deputy chief of mission scattered what staff he could spare to satellite offices in Bergen, Trondheim, and Narvik.

"You're sure Miss Jaffray left with the others?" Daisy asked.

"Everyone has gone, ma'am," Petra replied, pulling on her gloves.

Daisy moved through each room as if assuring herself she'd not left a light burning or a pot on the boil, adjusting a pillow here, straightening a drapery there. Would she return? There was no way to know, and so she offered a silent farewell to the comfortable rooms where she'd made a home for herself over the last few years. This wasn't the first time she'd uprooted her life, but it was certainly the most dramatic exit.

Kim continued to pad at her heels, the old dog sensing the wrongness of the situation but unable to understand. Daisy had tried all morning not to think about saying goodbye to him. She and the grizzled shepherd had been companions since he was a puppy. A true friend when those she loved were an ocean away.

"And you're sure you saw Cleo go?" Daisy asked one last time.

"Ma'am, please." Even Petra's smooth facade was cracking beneath the growing pressure. "German troops have already taken the Sola airfield, and the naval base at Kristiansand. There's nothing to stop them from adding Oslo to that list. We must go now."

Her heart breaking, Daisy scratched Kim behind his ears, bent on aching knees to kiss his soft nose and stare into his brown eyes. He whined, pushing himself against her until she threw her arms around him for a last farewell. Then, before she could change her mind, she handed him off to a footman and hustled into the back seat of the car, Petra squeezing in alongside her.

"Where's Fröislie?" she asked, surprised to find the unctuous Mr. Whitney behind the wheel.

The vice consul swiveled around in his seat. "Your regular chauffeur chose to report for military duty, ma'am," he explained. "I was a driver in the last war, so when they couldn't find anyone else on short notice, I said I'd step in."

"How fortuitous for me," Daisy responded blandly, showing none of her misgivings. Driver was hardly a task for one in his position, so what did he hope to gain by putting himself forward in such a way? Men like him were sly at manipulation; they slipped it unawares like tasteless poison into the tea. She would need to be careful, an added difficulty in a sea of such.

"Next stop Hamar," Mr. Whitney announced, before throwing the Ford into gear.

Daisy blocked out Kim's plaintive barking by focusing on the next few hours, the next few days, what she would say to her president, to Norway's king. Air raid sirens groaned to life, drowning out her dog's barking, which scraped along her bones like nails. Eyes forward, she clenched her purse in gloved hands and refused to look back.

The story of her life, Anne would undoubtedly tell her.

IN THE GRAY light that comes before dawn, Cleo stood across the street from the German chancery. Bundled in a coat and hat against the early morning chill, her breath frosting the air, she watched as men in uniforms came and went, heads bent together in muttered conference. Sometimes they were accompanied by other men in heavy wool coats over nondescript suits. The uniforms didn't bother her. It was the suited men who sent shivers up her spine. She'd seen men like these before. Bland as milk with quiet, thoughtful voices and cold eyes that drilled straight through you. They had turned up in Zakopane shortly after the German takeover. She and Micky had learned to give them a wide berth. Today, she stepped back into a doorway to stay out of the wind and remain unseen until she decided what to do.

Other than the early morning activity and steady stream of visitors, there was nothing to mark the day out as special. No spidery swastikas on bloodred backgrounds unfurled from every window. No loudspeaker blaring the German national anthem to announce their intentions. No steely-eyed soldiers with guns bristling.

Not yet.

But they were on their way.

Coming downstairs for cocoa in the middle of the night, Cleo had heard Aunt Daisy take the phone call. Heard the taut quality behind her clipped speech. The furious response that followed. The air raid sirens had long since ended and lights burned all over the city. Families throughout Norway slept on, not realizing the war had come to them.

She had dressed quickly in the dark, slipping out of the residence in the mounting confusion. Not trusting the trams would be running this morning, she'd walked the short distance to busy Drammensveien, where early-morning commuters hurried to their jobs as if it was any other day. It might already be too late— Herr Brauer taken up with weightier matters and no time to spare for missing persons of no consequence. But she wouldn't know if she didn't try.

Her father had a grave. He had his name listed in an official register of war dead. He had medals in a box.

Micky had none of that. He'd simply walked out of their apartment one evening and never come back.

If she didn't fight for him, who would?

She was hours early for her appointment, but she was certain the German minister would be dressed and in his office. After all, it wouldn't do to greet his country's invading army in his pajamas. She felt in her pocket for his letter, gripping it tightly as she stepped off the curb, darting in behind a long sedan as it turned in through the gate, crunching over the snow and ice.

She followed the two men who emerged from the car as they headed up the steps and through the doors where a buzz, much like what she'd left behind her in the American residence, met her. The difference lay in the tension, which had a more exultant quality. People moved with brisk efficiency. Faces aglow. Steps assured. Not a trace of fear or worry. No pale cheeks. No darting eyes.

They were *that* confident.

"May I help you?" A battleship of a woman in her midfifties, blond hair threaded with gray, looked up from her typewriter. Her voice was sharp as glass as she gave Cleo a quick, dismissive once-over.

Setting aside her nerves, Cleo curled her lips into a condescending smile of her own, and in her best Swiss-finishing-school German replied, "I have an appointment with Herr Brauer." She fished out the letter, practically slamming it on the desk like a winning hand.

"I'm sorry, Miss Jaffray," the battleship answered without hesitating. "The minister is unavailable."

"But I have an appointment." She sounded like a petulant child, but she was too close to simply walk away without a fight.

"I couldn't help but overhear." Cleo hadn't noticed the man standing in the corner until he was at her shoulder, his expression one of shy curiosity, his English as posh as that of any Etonian schoolboy. "You're Miss Clementine Jaffray?"

"Yes, that's right."

He folded his newspaper, tucking it under his arm. "I'm very sorry you aren't able to speak with the foreign minister directly, but Herr Brauer has explained the situation surrounding Mr. Kominski and asked that I look into it, as I was recently stationed in Zakopane."

She clutched her purse and steadied her breathing. "Is there any news?"

"I've taken the time to write to the administration of the Generalgouvernement für die besetzten polnischen Gebiete— the government of the occupied region in Poland—and district officials in Kraków. They still claim Mr. Kominski died in the café bombing. As you're aware, it was a catastrophic event, and many of the bodies they recovered were not easily identified."

Cleo choked back the thick, sour taste at the back of her throat while the man snapped his fingers at the bouncer of a secretary, who was at his elbow with a tray and two mugs of hot sweet tea within minutes. Cleo felt the warmth seep back under his sympathetic gaze.

"From what evidence they've gathered, they feel confident in their conclusions. We're inclined to believe the correspondence you received afterward was merely the work of an unscrupulous con artist preying on your grief for his own criminal ends. You should count yourself lucky this person didn't show up at the expected rendezvous. There's no telling what might have occurred."

"What on earth do I have that a con artist would want?" she asked helplessly.

"You have connections to many powerful people in your country. Is it so hard to fathom why someone would want to cultivate a relationship with you?"

"Are you implying Micky was an unscrupulous con artist?"

"I'm saying we're looking at all angles in our search." As if to forestall an argument, he barreled through her protest. "I'm sorry. I know none of this is what you wanted to hear, but I can assure you we'll continue to keep our eyes open, and if Mr. Kominski does turn up, we'll let you know as soon as we can. You have my word."

Without quite knowing how, she'd been maneuvered back to the front doors. He shook her hand, apology in his warm gaze as if he was sorry he didn't have better news. Out on the street, a fire engine roared past, its bell clanging. "You should get home, Miss Jaffray. It's not safe out here today."

"No, it's not." She tried not to show her disappointment or her anger. None of this was his fault, but she didn't have Herr Hitler in front of her. Just this man with his soft hands and his Mayfair vowels who had been absolutely useless. She speared him with an Alva Vanderbilt sneer. "Speaking of tragic events and unscrupulous con artists, give my regards to your boss."

A little childish and very dangerous. She blamed her sass on a lack of sleep.

He merely inclined his head with a grim flash of his Aryan blue eyes.

Back on the busy street, snow dusted the cars and buses heading out of the city. Some shops had shuttered while others did a brisk business as nervous customers stocked up on essentials. Smoke rose to the north. There was a chatter of gunfire. Overhead, German bombers were being worried at by a pair of biplanes, the Norwegians diving and swooping ineffectually against the modern and more heavily manned Dorniers.

Cleo picked up her pace, her heart thudding against her ribs. Aunt Daisy would wonder where she'd gone. She'd be worried sick. She rounded the corner onto Nobels Gate and took the remaining streets almost at a run. A few cars sat parked haphazardly in the courtyard. A clerk hurried from one building to the other with his arms full of files. From inside the residence, Aunt Daisy's dog howled, his lonely heartbreaking wail fighting against the deeper groan of the air raid siren.

"Aunt Daisy? I'm back!" Her office was empty. So was the drawing room and her upstairs study. Her bedroom was as neat as a pin, but her dressing table was bare, and her closet had clearly been rummaged through in a hurry.

"Lieutenant Bayard? Petra?" Cleo came downstairs to find Kim pacing the kitchens while two maids and the legation's housekeeper, Mrs. Nilsen, chattered in anxious voices. "Where is everyone?"

"Madam Minister is gone." The housekeeper turned her mug of tea around in her saucer. "They are all gone."

"Gone where?"

"North." She hunched into her blouse, her face pinched. "Haven't you heard? The Germans are coming."

"Look outside," Cleo replied. "They're already here."

CLEO SAT AT the kitchen table, pulling bits of ham from her sandwich to feed to Kim. Since she'd arrived, Aunt Daisy's dog had glued himself to her leg and refused to budge.

"At least he is quiet. All morning with the howling. Enough to set my teeth on edge."

Mrs. Nilsen was one of the few who remained when most had left to be home with family. The housekeeper moved around the kitchen in search of occupation, racing to the window at the sound of every automobile, jumping at every distant rumble that shook the pots on their hooks and the glassware in the cabinets. She had worried her apron into a wrinkled mess, and she'd lost at least three hairpins since Cleo had sat down to eat.

"You really don't need to stay on my account, Mrs. Nilsen."

"You can't stay here alone. What would Mrs. Harriman say?"

"I'm not alone. There are plenty of people working just across the way." She wasn't trapped and on her own this time. She was trapped along with an entire diplomatic staff. That had to count for something.

"It is not safe. Not with German soldiers loose in the city."

"I don't think they'll bother attacking the US chancery. Besides, I have Kim. He'll see off any real villains." The dog was currently snuffling up crumbs, his tail thumping against the table leg, but Cleo was sure he could be ferocious in a crisis. He licked her ankle before laying his head in her lap. Well, at least he *looked* ferocious. Maybe that would be enough.

The radio was on, but neither of them had been paying attention until an announcer introduced Herr Brauer, the German foreign minister.

Mrs. Nilsen turned the sound up, her apron clutched in both hands now, pink splotches high on her pale cheeks.

"Den norske regjeringen bør stoppe å gjøre motstand." His voice rang out clear and proud and determined. *"Vi kommer som venner og allierte av kong Haakon."*

Cleo caught maybe one word in every three, but the drift was obvious. Mrs. Nilsen practically wrenched off the knob in her anger. "Friends and allies, bah! They are not welcome in our country."

"Please," Cleo urged. "Go home to your family while things are calm. Please."

"Very well, but if I should be with family, so should you." With a final glance around the spotless kitchen, she buttoned her coat and took up her purse. "You should go to your aunt. The town of Hamar isn't so far."

With what little money Cleo had left in her purse, it might as well have been the moon.

"I'd probably get there and find out that Aunt Daisy had come back here to Oslo. No, I'll stay put and hold down the fort. It'll be fine. You wait and see."

Mrs. Nilsen was finally convinced and with instructions on how to use the range and where the extra blankets were kept just in case it grew cold again, she departed, relief clear in her ruddy cheeks.

Cleo hunkered down in the living room with Kim draped across her lap as they both listened to the muffled sounds of distant explosions along with sporadic clatter of gunfire.

By noon, the city was calm, though there remained a heavy atmosphere that reminded her of summers on the Hudson—the crackle in the air that presaged a coming squall. Kim padded up and down the stairs, pacing room to room, scratching at doors as if expecting Aunt Daisy to be there with a word and a treat. Cleo sympathized completely. She had that same unsettled impatience that wound tighter with every turn of the hour and chime of the clock.

What was going on out there? Had the Germans succeeded in taking the city? Were the Norwegians fighting back? Where were the British? Was the king safe? The radio was no help, and the one time she tried to visit the chancery, she was pushed aside when she wasn't being ignored completely.

She came back to the residence to find Kim scratching and whining at the kitchen door. "It's time for your afternoon walk, isn't it?" He sat down at her feet, his gaze drilling a hole in her forehead. After ten minutes of being stared at, Cleo flung herself out of her chair to search for her purse and a leash. "Right. A short one just to see what's what then we come straight back. Got it?"

She wasn't the only one tired of hiding indoors. Groups of worried residents conferred in front of shops or clustered on street corners, casting wary glances over their shoulders. Many whispered about a British counterattack. The late queen's countrymen coming to Norway's aid to repel the invaders. Cleo patted the lining of her coat out of habit, her documents safe and sound, just in case.

She headed south, crossing over the wide boulevard of Parkveien before skirting the royal palace grounds on her way toward Karl Johans Gate, where the sounds of a marching band drowned out the murmur of a frightened city. But it wasn't Norwegian soldiers that came marching up the hill. Instead, a long procession of Wehrmacht gray marched past the stunned spectators. The drumming of boot heels falling in unison against the cobblestones accompanied the bass drum rhythm as row after row passed, eyes forward in a show of triumph.

Silence fell. No one jeered or shouted or wept. They were far too stunned.

Not Kim.

The dog strained at the leash, barking furiously. The fur down the ridge of his back bristled in anger. Foam gathered at the corners of his mouth.

"Hush. Down, boy. Down, Kim." But Cleo's commands were ignored as she wrapped the leash around her hand to hold him back. One soldier glared and a few muttered curses, but none broke ranks.

Out of nowhere, a bottle came spinning to smash in front of an officer, the shards leaping to cling to his heavy coat and cut his cheek. A few teens shouted jeering insults as the procession passed the university buildings.

Following the infantry came a unit of soldiers on motorcycles, helmets and goggles turning them into unidentifiable enemies, more frightening by their anonymity. Kim practically yanked Cleo off her feet, his fangs bared in a show of rabid fury. Up ahead, a group of students taunted the parading soldiers, shouting and throwing rocks. The marching band scattered. One of the motorcyclists gunned his engine, peeling out of the phalanx to chase after the protestors. That was all Kim needed. He pulled free, throwing Cleo to her knees, skin scraped, blood welling from scratches across her palms and a pain throbbing in her ankle.

"Kim! Come back!" Cleo shouted. *"Kom tilbake!"* she added in Norwegian to no effect. He was a bad dog in two languages.

Scrambling to her feet, she chased him as quickly as sore knees and a twisted ankle would allow, pushing her way through the crowds who were dispersing at commands barked in German. Telling them to go home. To remain peaceful. To be calm.

She trailed Kim to the end of a narrow alley near St. Olavs Gate where the motorcycle rested on its side, leaking oil, its back wheel rotating slowly. The German soldier straddled it, trousers torn, leg bleeding, his pistol pointed at a boy kneeling in the snow, his hands behind his head. He was no older than sixteen, his brown hair streaked with sun under a greasy cap.

"Stay back!" the soldier shouted, swinging his pistol wildly between the boy and Cleo, who skidded to a stop on the icy pavement, hands in the air to show she was unarmed. She couldn't breathe. Her toes curled into her shoes. Her legs and shoulders went numb with cold and fear.

"Get your damned dog away from me," the soldier shouted. His movements were jerky and nervous as he eyed Kim, whose lips pulled back in a dripping snarl as he crouched to spring.

"It's nothing personal." Cleo inched toward Kim, the dog tantalizingly close and the leash strung out in a dirty wet loop just a foot away. "He's got a taste for wheels. He once chased a milk wagon two whole miles."

The bullet whistled past her head to smash chips of brick and stone from the wall behind her, a bee's sting on her cheek where shards bit into her flesh. She flung herself to her knees, throwing her arms over her head, forehead pressed into the slush. Gravel dug into her knees and snow seeped cold into her stockings. She smelled gasoline fumes and damp wool. She tasted the iron tang of blood in her mouth. "Stop! Are you crazy? Don't shoot!"

After making it out of Poland by the skin of her teeth, was she really going to die because of a damned dog? The unfairness of it all made tears burn in her eyes.

The second gunshot vibrated her bones like a tuning fork. Her blood froze solid in her veins, her brain blank with terror. Spots burst at the edges of her vision. If she could have burrowed into the brick wall, she would have. Kim's barking was almost frantic, high with terror.

The third shot never came.

She squinted open one eye then the other to find the motor-cyclist sprawled in front of her, blood pooling over the cobbles, turning the slushy puddles of snow around him bright red. Kim had disappeared again, but the boy remained, a smoking revolver clutched in his hand, his face waxy gray with shock.

Cleo scrambled to her feet. Her stomach rolled up into her throat. Just before she threw up, the boy grabbed her arm and pulled her toward the mouth of the alley. "*Vi må dra nå,*" he said in Norwegian. "We leave before more soldiers come."

"Is he dead?" she squeaked.

"*Jeg vet ikke. La oss dra.* I do not know. We go. Go now."

Stunned, she did as she was told, following the boy back up the alley. They made it as far as the corner when Cleo bounced off a broad chest. Buttons bit into her shoulder. She was nearly over-come by the odors of musky cologne and hair oil. In those few terrifying face-to-face seconds, she memorized every inch of the German soldier, from his gray infantry uniform down to the blue flecks in his hazel eyes. No doubt he was doing the same to her.

"*Fräulein?* What is wrong?" The boy's hand tugging on her never eased its tight grip. She was wrenched free of the soldier's hold and propelled down the street, his shouts following after. "Stop! Stop, I say!"

Back twitching up into her scalp, Cleo ran.

CHAPTER 6

Dear Anne,

I'm writing this to you from the back seat of my Ford so pardon the chicken scrawl. Every bump, I'm jostled by my secretary, her lap filled with accordion folders. My feet are resting on a typewriter case. Mr. Whitney, my driver, is sharing the front with all the luggage that couldn't fit in the trunk. The roads out of Oslo are choked with traffic as anyone who can is leaving. It's taken us two hours to travel what under normal circumstances would take twenty minutes. Tell poor Letitia that Cleo is safe with the rest of the chancery's families in the north away from the fighting . . .

Ahead and behind them as far as the eye could see was a line of cars and trucks, crowded buses, taxis, delivery vans, even a few horse-drawn wagons, wives and children bundled in coats and hats amid all the possessions they could carry, husbands walking alongside muscled draft horses, their ears twitching in agitation, shod hooves scraping sparks from the roadway. Everyone was stunned, faces stricken white, voices muted as they questioned what had happened, how it had come to this in such a short time. Miss Kristiansen's gaze was long, her face set in stone, as she gripped the boxes of folders.

"Is it safe?" Asked more as a distraction than because Daisy was concerned she'd left the codebook behind.

Petra didn't need to ask what Daisy meant by "it." She nodded. "Yes, ma'am."

"Right." Daisy paused then added, "Good. Very good."

Two hours into their journey, they descended toward the low-lying Nitelva River that bordered the village of Lillestrøm. On the left, train tracks paralleled the roadway while low scrubby hills sprinkled with birch, pine, and small stands of ash rose to the right.

"Stop for a bite to eat, ma'am?" Mr. Whitney asked hopefully.

By now, Daisy's hips ached from the cramped car and hunger pinched at her stomach, but she checked her watch and sighed. "No time. We're already hours late."

Mr. Whitney hunched back over the wheel, taking the next turn with an unnecessary sweep of gravel that tossed them against their piled cases.

The hungry silence was interrupted by the growl of an airplane, its German markings all too identifiable. A bold Norwegian pilot rose to meet the enemy, machine gun fire snapping like pebbles thrown against glass. The snaking line of automobiles ground to a stop. Drivers peered through the morning sun to catch a glimpse of the dogfight.

"They must be targeting Kjeller airfield," Daisy commented as more bombers approached, driving the little plane off.

The attack sent men and women tumbling from cars and trucks. Others streamed from nearby shops and houses.

"We're sitting ducks out here." Sweat shone on Mr. Whitney's face as he gripped the steering wheel.

"The train station here has a tunnel that runs between the platforms," Miss Kristiansen offered. "Maybe there is room for us to shelter there."

"Right," Daisy said. "Gather the essentials. Leave the rest. We make for the station."

Whitney pulled onto the sidewalk, cutting the engine. The three of them grabbed what they could carry.

"Let me help you, ma'am." He tried to take Daisy's elbow.

She brushed him off. "I'm capable of walking on my own, thank you." Pins and needles tingled her legs, but she gripped her handbag and lifted her chin. She'd be damned if she was treated like a doddering grandmother.

In the gloom of the tunnel, a group of uniformed men surrounded a striking woman in a blue feathered hat. The two little princesses, Astrid and Ragnhild, hung close to their mother's skirts while she cradled three-year-old Prince Harald in her arms. Daisy greeted the crown princess with a small bow. "I'm glad to see you safe, Your Royal Highness."

"War has come to us, just as you predicted." She might have been commenting on the weather, but Daisy understood all too well the effort it took to appear unconcerned and the reason for it in the children huddled at her side like chicks.

"I'd hoped to be proven wrong."

"What will you do now?" Her Royal Highness asked.

A stray bomb fell nearby, shrapnel tearing into a building, sending a spray of glass over the street.

"Me or my country?" Daisy responded carefully.

The crown princess noted the response and answered with a cool smile. "Is there a difference?"

"I expect it will depend upon what His Majesty decides to do."

Dust sifted from the ceiling as another bomb exploded. Daisy flinched. Someone cried out. Ragnhild and Astrid stood wide-eyed but unafraid in the company of their mother. Harald buried his face in her shoulder.

"He will not run, if that's what you're asking," Crown Princess

Märtha replied steadily. "The king and Prince Olav will stay and rally our people against this invasion." There was a small tremor in her shoulders, her hold on the little prince tightening until he squirmed. "As will I."

THIS WAS THE second time in twenty-four hours Cleo found herself standing across the street from a chancery watching the comings and goings. Only this time, the man at the gate was one of Aunt Daisy's staff. He was in a heated conversation with a German soldier, a rifle slung over his shoulder. She couldn't hear what they were saying, but she had a sick feeling that crawled cold up her spine until she shivered.

Don't be smart. Don't break any laws. And, last but not least, don't draw attention to yourself.

She'd broken all three of Micky's rules for survival in the space of five minutes.

"Bor du her?" The boy again. He must have followed her. And if he'd followed her, who else might she have attracted in her headlong escape? She glanced around as if expecting to see armies of Wehrmacht spilling from every building. *"Bor du her?"* he repeated, pointing at her then at the gate where the soldier's voice was growing louder. "You live here?"

"I used to."

Was it coincidence there was a German soldier parked between her and the residence? Was he looking for her? Should she brazen her way past and hope for the best? Slink away and come back after dark? What if the soldier came back too? Was she safe as long as she was within the legation grounds or did accessory to murder negate any diplomatic protocols? Aunt Daisy couldn't have left town at a more inconvenient time.

"This is your fault," she hissed. "You killed him."

"Because he would kill *us*," the boy replied logically.

"Try telling him that." She pointed to the soldier.

Movement caught her eye. A brown and brindle body slinking low to the ground, sliding in and out of the shadows along the sidewalk. It crossed the street, shimmying its way toward the men at the gate, tongue lolling in a wide toothy smile.

The German unshouldered his rifle, but the clerk stopped him as he grabbed hold of Kim's collar, dragging the shepherd into the courtyard and closing the gate with a clang. At least Aunt Daisy's beloved dog was safe. If only Cleo could be so lucky.

"Vi kan ikke bli her." The boy grabbed her arm as if to pull her away. *"Soldatene vil finne oss."*

Cleo shrugged her incomprehension. "I don't speak Norwegian. You don't happen to have a dictionary, do you?" She racked her brain. *"Ordbok?"* She pretended to flip pages.

He took a breath, his frustration visible. "We cannot stay here," he replied slowly, pointing to the soldier. "We must go."

"Where?"

He grinned and opened his coat to reveal the revolver shoved into his waistband, making the universal gesture for shooting, ending with a cold-blooded smile. *"Jeg kan ikke bli i Oslo.* I leave the city. Join army."

"Hvor?" She searched her brain for the right word. *"Hvor . . . hæren?"*

"North. We go north." He motioned again. "Come."

She gave one last look at 28 Nobels Gate, kicking herself for a fool. "Right. Let's go."

They joined the growing crowds observing the Germans' arrival. Trucks rolled through the streets interspersed with additional infantry troops, weapons conspicuous as they smiled and chatted and pretended to be invited guests when, in fact, they were prison guards, the Norwegians only now beginning to realize it.

Cleo tugged at the boy's sleeve. "This way. I have an idea."

The nightclub was closed. Shades drawn and a sign posted at the door. Cleo led them down a narrow alley at the side of the building cluttered with trash bins to a scuffed door that was—she turned the knob—unlocked.

"Presto chango," she whispered as she opened the door.

The back passage off the kitchen smelled like cigarettes, stale beer, and old cooking grease. She followed the sound of voices coming from one of the dressing rooms.

". . . *regjeringen har flyktet . . . Nasjonal Samling-bevegelsens rett til å overta myndighetene . . . Vidkun Quisling som hodet . . .*" A deep commanding voice boomed from a scratchy radio. Not Herr Brauer this time, but someone equally vocal.

"What's this clown Quisling saying? And what the hell kinda name is that anyway?"

"I don't know, Dud. Take it up with the fucking Norwegians."

"We should head to Stockholm. It's getting too hot in these parts."

"Can't. We haven't been paid yet. Besides, it's crazy out there. We'd never get through."

"We should try. I don't want to be stuck in the middle of a goddamned war."

"What do you think, Emmitt? Fish or cut bait?"

Cleo glanced over her shoulder to make sure the boy was still behind her and put a finger to her lips.

". . . *motstand er ikke bare ubrukelig, men direkte synonymt med kriminell ødeleggelse av liv . . .*," the man on the radio shouted.

"What did he say?"

"I. Don't. Know," someone repeated more emphatically. "How many times I gotta tell you, Paulie?"

Now that Cleo was here, she began second-guessing her idea, but options were thin to none. It was these guys or walk to Hamar.

Confidence was all in the attitude. Cleo banged through the door as if she belonged there, eyes snapping. She took up position, a hand on her hip, her chin raised as she surveyed the group like a general his troops. "Hi, fellas. Remember me? I need your help."

As if they were under attack, the horn section jumped up from the couch where they'd been lounging, the drummer assumed a swordsman's stance with his sticks, while the singer merely looked annoyed at having the radio broadcast drowned out and shushed her loudly. It was the bass player who finally spoke over their surprise. "Hey. You're that American broad."

"That's right. And this is . . ." She turned back to the boy, who was nervously reaching for his ancient revolver. She placed a reassuring hand on his shoulder while giving him a steely-eyed shake of her head. He dropped his arm back to his side. "This is . . . What's your name?" All this time and she didn't even know her partner in crime's name.

He pointed to his chest. "Einar."

"This is Einar," Cleo repeated. "The two of us need to get out of the city."

"Good luck with that," the singer harumphed. "The Germans have thrown up blockades all over the place. Nobody's going anywhere."

Einar seemed to understand. He stepped forward, chest puffed out. "But I must join army. Fight for Norway."

"More power to ya, kid," Drummer said, sliding his sticks into his jacket pocket. "What has that got to do with us?"

It was obvious the drummer was in charge. Cleo focused all her persuasive talents his direction, offering him a winsome smile, a flirtatious flash of her wide eyes. Betty Boop, the lieutenant called her. If you got it, flaunt it. And pray like hell it worked. "We need your help getting him there. Getting both of us there, actually."

"And how do you figure we're gonna do that?"

"Athena." She pointed to Sam, the bass player, whose mouth thinned to a suspicious line under her scrutiny. "Your van. You can drive us to Hamar in it."

"Hello? Roads? Barricades? Men with guns?" He fought back, but he did it with a shifting, uncertain gaze, as if he knew how easily he could be outvoted.

She pressed her advantage. "The Germans won't stop a bunch of American musicians. You can get through the barricades."

"Then what?"

"Take us to Hamar, and you can name your price."

"What the hell's in Hamar?"

"My godmother, Daisy Harriman, who also happens to be the US minister to Norway."

"Says you!" Sam argued, clearly trying to finagle his way out. "Roosevelt wouldn't put any broad in charge."

"Don't be a sap." Drummer rolled his eyes. "Mrs. Harriman *is* in charge. I've seen her name on some of our work visas."

"Fine. But how do we know she's *her* kin? She could be feeding us a line."

Drummer cocked her a look. "Hate to say it, but he's got a point."

"Maybe, but think about it. The nightclub gig is a dead-end now the Germans are here. You'll be lucky to get the money you're owed much less anything more. My godmother will pay handsomely to see me safe. What have you got to lose?"

She had them. She could feel it.

"What do you say?" She scanned the room, but it was Drummer she focused on. It was his answer that counted. "Trust me. A few hours on the road, and you get whatever the manager here owes you plus"—she paused for only a moment—"twenty percent."

Drummer sighed as if aware he'd been outmaneuvered but was

still unable to resist. He played an up-tempo riff on a tabletop. "Load 'em up, boys. We're taking this show on tour."

CLEO WAS STUFFED in the back of the van, wedged between instruments and luggage to the point she could barely breathe—not that she wanted to among the competing odors of pomade, cologne, cigarette smoke, and dirty socks. The windows steamed with their breath. What she wouldn't give for a good blast of Norwegian winter air right now to clear her lungs and cool the sweat damping her clothes to her back in a clammy funk built of heat and nerves.

"This way." Einar, sitting in the middle of the front seat, directed them in a circuitous route through the city. She held her breath every time the van slowed, her muscles tightening until they grumbled forward again in a painfully slow trek north and then east. At last, Oslo fell behind them as the landscape widened out into empty vistas of pine forests, dirty slushy piles of snow pushed onto the verges. Now and again, they passed red-roofed farmhouses surrounded by snug barns and sheds nestled into the wrinkle of snowy hills. A man on skis stopped to wave. A cart being pulled by a shaggy yellow pony waited at a train crossing. But there were no roadblocks and no soldiers, neither German nor Norwegian.

Drummer cranked down his window, and Cleo gratefully leaned forward over the driver's seat, gulping in fresh air. "Now that we're traveling companions, I should probably know your name, doll."

"It's Cleo."

"Nice to make your acquaintance, Cleo." Drummer alternated between scanning a road map and staring out the windshield as if scouting for tanks or incoming bombs. "Dud back there is on trombone. Paulie beside him is our trumpeter. That handsome devil there is Norman; he's our singer." He pointed each member of the band out with a nod of his head. "And you know our bass player, Sam." He jerked his head toward the whippet-thin driver, who was hunched over the steering wheel, muttering about pot-holes. "I'm Emmitt, drummer extraordinaire. I'd offer you my calling card, but it's in my other tuxedo. Maybe I'll have my but-ler send it to you."

"Is it that obvious?"

"Oh yeah, sweetheart, you reek of old money, which makes me have to ask what a flash girl like you is doing here anyway? Shouldn't you be hanging with the boys at the country club or taking tea with your governess or something?"

"After a year away, I'd have thought it wouldn't show."

"You can't hide class, doll. It wears you like a stink. What's the saying? You can take the girl out of the penthouse, but you can't take the penthouse out of the girl."

"You made that up."

"True, though." Sam slapped the steering wheel and laughed his agreement while Einar swiveled between them as he struggled to keep up with the conversation.

"Care to fill us in on why you had to leave Oslo in such a hurry?" Emmitt pressed. "You and the kid here aren't . . ."

This got Einar's attention. He grinned.

"What? No!" Cleo replied. "Nothing like that. He told you. He wants to join the army."

"And you're helping him out of the kindness of your heart, Park Avenue? Girls like you don't generally put yourself out for anybody unless there's something in it for you."

She should be offended, but he wasn't wrong. Not totally, and not in this instance. "There was a small misunderstanding with a German soldier."

"Sorry I asked. Don't say another word. I don't want to know."

He turned back to his map for a moment before leaning over the seat again. "So if the Germans catch up to us and find you . . ."

She'd spent the past few hours hoping he wouldn't ask and now that he had, she still only had one answer. "It won't come to that." She held up three fingers. "Scout's honor."

"You better hope so." Gone was his good-humored teasing. "And this payday better be something special."

On that, they could agree.

She peered over her shoulder through the steamy rear window at the road behind them, empty of pursuers—for now. But if that soldier had been at the legation because she'd been recognized, would they keep looking now that they knew she'd left Oslo? Was she being hunted, or was one soldier's death amid a war not exactly at the top of the army's to-do list? She rubbed her arms to ease the nervous goose bumps and counted the miles, but dread swirled in the pit of her stomach.

Norman dozed while Paulie and Dud argued over who was a better second baseman—Joe Gordon or Lonny Frey.

"You're crazy," Dud argued. "Gordon was better in almost every category—RBIs, home runs . . ."

"But look at Frey's on-base percentage and his batting average for the year," Paulie shouted his rival down. "Plus the man could lay down a bunt like an angel. I guarantee Cincinnati doesn't make the World Series without Frey."

"How long have you all played together?" Cleo asked Emmitt to distract herself and drown out the stream of competing baseball statistics.

At first he didn't answer, and she wondered if he was going to give her the cold shoulder all the way to Hamar. He'd been awfully interested in that map for the past half hour.

"Too long," he replied finally. "But the way things are heating up over here, we'll be headed back to the States soon. One last booking in Stockholm then we're homeward bound. I expect we'll split up once that happens. Paulie has a gal in San Francisco and Sam's dad wants him to settle down and help him in his hardware store."

"And you?"

"Not sure what I'll do. Europe's been good to me. A far sight better than any juke joint or roadhouse in the States. Besides, you watch. We'll *all* be back over here before too long, trading in our zoot suits for military green."

"You think the US will join the war?"

"We did the last time."

"And fat lot of good that did us," she snapped. "We're right back where we started."

"True." His wide face was grave. "We had to try, though, didn't we?"

CHAPTER 7

Dear Anne,

It took us all day to get to the town of Hamar only to be told there was no room at the inn. My traveling companions proved their mettle throughout the ordeal. Mr. Whitney, despite his unpredictable temper, was more than capable of handling the Ford. I think he almost enjoyed the excitement of being back behind the wheel again, reliving his glory days of wartime service, though he'd never admit it. Poor Miss Kristiansen, on the other hand, discovered she'd left behind the suitcase containing most of her clothes. The typewriter that she remembered is small consolation . . .

The town of Hamar curved against the long narrow banks of the Mjøsa. Normally, Daisy would have been peering out the window, taking in the architecture and landscape, asking about local industries, transportation infrastructure, taking notes to review ahead of meetings with her economic advisers. Today, she barely noticed more than a passing blur of gray water and icy froth, a teeth-achingly bright blue sky, the way her joints ached, and how a horrible crick in her neck made speaking painful. They'd stopped only once to allow her to phone the legation in Oslo. That was hours ago, and her bones were making sure she paid for it.

Mr. Whitney stepped forward to help her from the car, but, once again, she refused his hand, forcing herself to step lively toward the community hall where the Storting, Norway's parliament, was in session.

"Mrs. Harriman!" Sir Cecil Dormer, the British ambassador to Norway, waved her down, his long, thin frame wrapped in a heavy coat and muffler, the tips of his elfin ears pink with cold. "Glad to see you made it unscathed."

"By the skin of our teeth," she said with a brave laugh. "Is anyone else here yet?"

"Who isn't, is the better question." He waved his arm to encompass the communication vans lined up outside a building housing journalists and broadcasters. A frantic-looking man in an overcoat and hat barked orders at a policeman, who in turn barked at the locals. A train whistle blew as passengers streamed out of the station. "I'd say most of Europe is represented in some capacity." He leaned in with a gallows smile. "Everyone except the Germans, and they're on their way, so a reliable source informs me."

Miss Kristiansen caught up with Daisy as they crossed the street. "There are no available hotel rooms, ma'am," she explained. "But the village of Hösbjör is just a few miles farther along. Rumor is that's where the royal family's staying."

"With rumors like that, who needs spies?" Sir Cecil winked and tapped his finger alongside his nose. "Go on, Mrs. Harriman. I imagine this caravan won't be too far behind. Not with Jerry on the march."

Daisy wished she could stay and witness the discussion going on a few feet away in the noisy hall. Roosevelt would need her information and her educated opinion. But her educated opinion in this instance was to carry on to Hösbjör. If the royal family planned to pause there, she'd learn just as much without the crowds.

The hotel they came to stood on a high bluff overlooking a

forested valley, a white building shining against the spring snow-melt. The lobby was quiet. Two Norwegian military officers stood on the drive. Another two stood by the concierge's desk. One disappeared and reappeared behind a pair of doors, his gaze intent as if he was casing the layout in anticipation of a raid.

Daisy adjusted her hat in the mirror above a handsome mahogany sideboard. "See to our rooms, Petra. You look dead on your feet."

"Where will you be, ma'am?"

"Untangling the first thread in this Gordian knot."

"Would it have anything to do with that phone call you placed on the road?"

"You'll find out soon enough." She winked. "Go on. I'll be along as soon as I can."

The doors into the lounge were closed, the murmur of conversation audible in the quiet of the hotel's nearly empty lobby. A young man in military braid answered her knock with a raised brow. "*Ja?*"

"Tell His Majesty that Mrs. Harriman would like a word at his convenience."

He frowned as if to bar the door, but a voice called out from deeper inside, and the young man reluctantly stepped aside.

"I apologize, Madam Minister." The president of the Norwegian parliament stood up from his place at a long table, his blunt features strained, his mouth a fold of displeasure. "Young Captain Bakke didn't recognize you."

"No need to explain, Mr. Hambro. In times like these, it pays to be careful."

"You know Mr. Wedel and Mr. Lie."

"Gentlemen, don't get up," she addressed the weary-looking lord chamberlain and minister of supplies as they heaved themselves to their feet before settling her gaze on the two men sitting at the head of the table. Crown Prince Olav, blond and handsome, his hand curved around a cup of black coffee, and His Majesty King Haakon, his face drawn and pale with eyes sunken from lack of sleep, though they remained razor sharp. "It is always a pleasure, Mrs. Harriman. But I assume you didn't come to pay a social call."

"I'll come right to the point. Herr Brauer and I spoke just a few hours ago."

A ripple of consternation passed over the room before the king settled it with a quiet look. "What does the German minister have to say to you that he has not already said so eloquently to my people?"

Wedel sat up while Lie's hands fisted upon the table in front of him. Prince Olav remained silent, but his eyes moved between his father and Daisy, his finger nervously tapping the rim of his saucer.

"He wants to arrange a meeting, Your Majesty."

"I'm sure he does." Daisy gave His Majesty credit. Not even a flicker of surprise lit his gaze. He might have been having a chat with his tailor. "Meanwhile, Mr. Quisling anoints himself the head of a new government in Norway. He apparently has the Führer's full confidence, if not the Norwegian people's."

"I heard about the announcement," she answered, hoping not to be drawn off her task.

"Did you also hear the capital is in the hands of the Germans, with more of their troops arriving every minute?" His Majesty demanded. "Who was there to stop them? Cadets barely out of short pants. A few royal guards who found themselves outmanned and outgunned." His voice was raspy with unspent anger. His eyes sparked as he surveyed his advisers, who paled but did not shrink under his fiery regard. Then as quickly as it came, the storm passed and he settled stiffly back, fingers clenched white around the chair's arms. "You are a very long way from home, Mrs. Harriman."

"We both are, Your Majesty." She pretended she didn't notice the strain in his voice as he tried to understand how events had spiraled so quickly out of his control. "It wouldn't be the first time I've found myself caught up in the middle of a war."

"No, of course. You were in Austria when the last war broke out, weren't you? Should I be worried your ill luck is contagious?"

She could sense him testing her, not out of malice but out of necessity. A man losing friends needed to trust the ones he had left. She held her ground and his gaze.

Whatever he saw in her, he sighed and turned back to his papers. "I appreciate your desire to assist, Mrs. Harriman, but sometimes what serves us best in peace is not necessarily what serves us best in war. You understand."

Completely. He had accepted her as minister so long as her job was lobbying, glad-handing, and hostessing. Skills she could handle with her eyes closed and standing on one foot. He wasn't yet ready to trust her with more. Could she blame him when there were those among her own staff who remained skeptical? No. That would be a waste of her energy that was better spent changing his mind.

"And Herr Brauer?"

"We will meet him in due course, though I don't suppose he'll like what we have to say." His grimness vanished in a charismatic smile, the man who could charm any reception hall or ballroom. "I would beg one favor, if I might . . ."

She made the obligatory noises, but who denied a king his favor? Certainly not her.

"Under the circumstances, the safest place for Her Royal Highness and the children would be in Sweden. She would have the comfort of her parents and the protection of her uncle the king to see her through this trying time." He lifted a hand to his son at the far end of the table, his youthful features hollowed but still sharp with determination. "And Prince Olav would not have the distraction of family in harm's way."

That long-ago palace dinner. That quiet conversation.

His Majesty knew and was calling in his chits.

"I take it Her Royal Highness isn't on board with this plan."

"I'm sure she would listen to you, woman to woman."

There it was again. As if females were beyond the ken of normal men and only someone of their sex could understand their fickle natures when in fact what it boiled down to was that she was being banished so the men could get on with their work. Already they looked anxious, shifting in their seats. Checking watches. She smiled until her teeth ached. "It's my pleasure, Your Majesty, but I'm sure Crown Princess Märtha is stronger than you think." She paused before adding, "Most women are."

As final words, they lacked pizzazz but were probably better than slamming the door in a huff, which is what had crossed her mind.

Miss Kristiansen met her back in the lobby. "There is a phone call for you, ma'am."

Daisy took up the receiver. "Harriman here."

"Lieutenant Bayard, ma'am." The line crackled as he shouted over miles of telephone wire. "I'm ringing to let you know we've arrived safely in Sjusjøen. I'll see that everyone is organized before joining you in the next day or two."

"I hope Cleo didn't give you any trouble." There was a long silence at the other end. "Lieutenant? Are you there?"

Daisy could hear the blood rushing in her ears, the concierge speaking to the bellboy. The rattle of the elevator door. Her hand clutching the receiver went damp and clammy.

Bayard cleared his throat. "I thought Miss Jaffray was with you."

* * *

SAM PULLED UP at a fork in the road near the village of Minnesund, where a group of Norwegian militia had set up a roadblock. Einar jumped out as soon as the van slowed to a halt. In rapid-fire Norwegian, he chattered away at the older bearded man who looked to be in charge.

The man shook his head.

Einar pulled aside his coat to show his revolver. Even in a foreign language, his frustration was clear.

The man shook his head again.

Einar climbed back into the van as the soldiers let the van pass.

"What did he say?" Cleo asked.

"They do not want me. They tell me to go home." He folded his arms across his chest like a truculent child denied a sweet. "I won't. I will fight. Soldiers in Hamar, they will take me. I will guard the king himself."

Leaving the makeshift checkpoint, they continued on, following a river that flashed in and out of sight through a scrub of pines and leafless, gray-trunked birch.

"You said you were looking for a friend of yours—a trumpeter," Emmitt said with a rustle of his map. "Ever find him?"

Cleo hunched her shoulders deeper into her coat despite the heat. "Not yet."

She thought back to the man she'd met at the German chancery. He'd said he'd served in Zakopane. She didn't recognize him, but that didn't mean much. There had been so many officers and staff passing through town it was impossible to recognize them all. Only the most influential stood out to her: Weissmann and his deputy, whose name she couldn't remember. They'd been regulars at the café. Micky had pointed them both out to her one evening and warned her to steer clear. As if she needed the warning when every day was a minefield and safety was a mirage. A month later the café was a charred ruin and Micky was missing. Was there a connection? Had Micky followed his own rule, or had he slipped up and made enemies?

"Espa," Einar said, indicating a village of low red roofs standing out amid the gray sky and the white snow.

"I'm starving," Dud groused, shutting his book with a thud. "Has this backwater got a restaurant? Better yet, a bar?"

"Dud's right. I need to stretch my legs before I become a permanent pretzel," Norman piped up.

"I have to take a piss like you wouldn't believe." The chorus grew louder. The band was getting restless.

Cleo couldn't blame them. Her left foot was asleep, and she'd had a cymbal sticking into her side for at least twenty miles.

Sam pulled over, and Einar hopped out to speak to a man on a tractor, loping back over the hard ground to deliver his news. "He's heard from friends farther south and west that Germans are close."

"Right," Emmitt snapped. "I don't know about the rest of you, but I don't want to be here with my balls hanging out when the Germans roll in. We don't stop again until Hamar." He glanced sharpish at Cleo. "Then we eat and drink on the US minister's dime."

With much groaning, they clambered back into the van as Sam shoved it into gear. The engine sputtered and stalled. He turned the key, but the engine wouldn't kick over. After a few minutes of high-pitched whirring, a thin stream of white smoke rose from under the hood. "Shit! Dud? Take a look, would you?"

"Athena's your fucking van, as you're always so quick to point out."

"Fine, but I don't know jack about engines. You spent six months working in a garage."

"I washed 'em. I didn't fix 'em." But he did as he was told, pushing the hood up to peer inside.

Einar got out, and he and the man on the tractor exchanged a long conversation that involved a lot of pointing and head shaking before Einar returned with a smile of triumph. "He says he can fix."

"I don't want some local yokel fiddling around with Athena," Sam grumbled. "What if he ruins her?"

"And Dud won't?" Emmitt griped. "Besides, it's that or walk."

"Thank you for helping me. I go now." Pulling up his coat collar, Einar started up the road.

"Where the hell is he going?" Paulie growled.

"I knew this was a bad idea," Sam muttered.

Cleo jogged after Einar, pulling him to a halt. "You can't just leave now. Not like this."

"Germans come," he stated simply, his round cheeks puffed with determination. "I join army and fight."

He continued trudging up the road, his knapsack banging against his hip. His wool hat was pulled low over his head to keep out the damp cold. Cleo watched him go, expecting him to turn back before finally realizing that wasn't going to happen.

"Hold on!" She hurried to catch up again. She heard Emmitt call out, but she ignored him. "We can't just leave them stranded in the middle of nowhere."

"They are safe here," Einar said. "You stay. You will be safe too."

She wished she was as confident of that as he was. "You saw those soldiers asking questions at the legation."

He sized her up before shaking his head. "It is a long way to Hamar on foot. You are a girl."

"What's your point?"

He frowned, not understanding the words, but most definitely understanding her tone and body language if his sheepish blush was any indication.

"I'm tougher than I look," Cleo added, "and if you're going, I'm going with you."

The boy grinned in easy surrender. "Together then. We both find army. We both fight Germans."

Cleo didn't want to fight Germans, but she felt herself grinning in response.

"Hey!" It was Emmitt jogging to catch up to them. "The old man says we're stuck until tomorrow." He eyed Cleo with a narrowed gaze. "You're ditching us, aren't you?"

"I have to get to my godmother. Besides, it's safer for you if I'm not here when the Germans turn up."

"And that payment you promised?"

"If I've left Hamar before you arrive, I'll send it care of your next booking."

"We've got work at a dance hall called Virveln in Stockholm, but I won't be holding my breath." He dug his hands into his coat and stamped his shoes on the packed snow to keep circulation in his toes. His cheeks glowed with cold and cynicism.

She threw her arms around him in a hug. "Be careful. You and all the boys."

"You too, Park Avenue." He shook Einar's hand. "Take care of her, you hear? Or you'll answer to me."

Einar grinned and saluted as he'd seen Cleo do earlier. "As she says it, scout's honor."

Dear Anne,

I'm beginning to understand what poor Letitia's been up against all these years. And here I thought she was exaggerating. But like father, like daughter . . .

THE LIEUTENANT'S VOICE still buzzed at the other end, but Daisy wasn't listening. Her hand trembled, and she stilled it before anyone assumed she was afraid for other reasons. An old woman, confused and anxious. It was the last thing she needed. She'd felt Mr. Whitney's gaze more than once during the trip. She imagined him making notes of every crack and wobble, proof she wasn't up to the task.

She shook off her suspicions. She was running on no sleep and little food while traveling hither and yon with an army nipping at her heels. Was it any wonder she began to look over her shoulder? Now Cleo was missing—again. The girl was worse than a magician's assistant. Now she's here. Now she's gone. Was she still in Oslo? Or had she gone haring off on the ghost of a rumor about that man of hers? Stupid, feckless child.

Daisy sank into a nearby chair, her heart fluttering uncomfortably in her chest.

"Ma'am? What's happened? Is it the lieutenant? Is he safe?"

Returning to Oslo was impossible, and there was no one to send back to look for her. "Petra, get me Mr. Cox on the phone."

A few minutes later, Daisy was speaking to an earnest young clerk whose dread of being the bearer of bad news rang through the wires. "Miss Jaffray's room hasn't been touched, ma'am. All her clothes and shoes are still in the cupboard, but she's not here. No one's seen her since she went for a walk with Kim early this afternoon. The dog came back. Miss Jaffray didn't."

As Daisy set down the receiver, her exhaustion seemed to triple, her limbs heavy, and yet she burned with anger. "I could throttle that blasted girl," she complained to Miss Kristiansen over dinner. "She's not at the legation. She's not with the lieutenant. Where could she be?"

"She had an appointment with Herr Brauer this morning, ma'am." Her secretary's tone never changed, but the inference was clear. "Perhaps someone at the German chancery might have an idea of where she went."

Of all the days to be knocking on the Germans' front door.

Cleo's timing was impeccably horrible. Daisy chose to remain stubbornly positive in the face of disaster. "I don't see Herr Brauer having time to chat with my foolish goddaughter today of all days, do you?"

"No, but, if you'll pardon me saying so, ma'am, she doesn't seem like a young woman who lets a war stand in the way of what she wants."

"A fair reading of her character."

"A family trait, ma'am?" Miss Kristiansen suggested, her features thawing into a glimmer of a smile.

"Normally I'd be encouraged at this display of initiative. Today I just want to box her ears." For the first time since Lieutenant Bayard's explosive revelation, Daisy let herself take a deep breath that wasn't weighted with lead. Until she knew differently, she would assume Cleo was alive and well. It was really all she could do. "It's too late to learn anything more tonight. I'll ring again in the morning. Maybe they'll have news."

She hunched back over her dinner, but her appetite was lost. She pushed her lamb around her plate before choking down a few roasted potatoes, distracted by a quiet conversation at a nearby table.

"Do you think the king will surrender to the Germans' demands?" came the whispered words.

"As far as they're concerned, it would do just as well for him to be dead" was the hushed response. "With him and the prince out of the way, all that's left is a vulnerable widow and three small children. Easily manipulated. Easily used."

A scenario already anticipated by the king, who was obviously under no illusion as to the veracity of German guarantees. What Hitler wanted, Hitler got. And if he wanted Norway under the nominal rule of a child king, he'd do what he could to make it happen.

The diners departed, leaving Daisy to finish her coffee in peace. When the French attaché entered the room, his whole body vibrated with news. "A company of German paratroopers are on the way here now. We can't count on Norwegian defenses holding out for long. The royal family and parliament are being evacuated immediately to the town of Elverum."

As one, the room abandoned their dinners, shouting for luggage to be organized, bills settled, cars to be brought around. No one panicked, but no one lingered either. Outside, Daisy searched for the Ford amid a strobing array of flashlights and handheld electric lanterns.

"Over here, Mrs. Harriman!" Mr. Whitney waved from the far side of the yard before hurrying to assist with her bags. "What do you think?" he said, pointing to the enormous American flag he'd tied to the roof with twine. "Should keep the Germans from taking potshots at us."

"Let's hope. Have you seen Miss Kristiansen?"

"Here I am." Petra moved through a sea of cars, all rattling to life, Daisy's overnight case clutched to her chest.

"Safe?" she asked softly so as not to draw Mr. Whitney's attention.

Petra placed a hand tellingly over the case as if she protected a child and answered in a near-whisper. "I won't let it out of my sight, ma'am."

Daisy knew she was being absurd, but her gaffe over Cleo rankled. If she could misplace her goddaughter, who was to say she wouldn't lose the codebook?

The road to Elverum was narrow and winding. Deep snow filled the ditches to either side and glowed blue under a bomber's moon. A parade of headlights flashed over long stretches of forest broken by farm fields, meadows, and small family farms. Daisy imagined she could hear the sounds of an advancing army, but there was only the hum of tires against the macadam, the squeak of seat springs, and Mr. Whitney's nervous tapping against the steering wheel as he drove. Petra was silent, her face flashing in and out of shadow.

As they rounded a corner, cars ahead of them slowed and braked. "Looks like another roadblock, ma'am. Elverum's just a few miles farther on."

They crept forward, a car at a time. Men were hewing logs, dragging branches across the road. Some in the uniform of the Norwegian Royal Guard. The rest in heavy coats and scarves, their faces muffled by caps and collars against the overnight cold. Now and then, she caught a glint of a rifle barrel, a grim face here and then gone. Daisy counted a few dozen men at most. Not nearly enough to stop a determined German advance.

Daisy rolled down her window. "Everything all right, Colonel?" she asked, drawing the attention of a red-cheeked man directing the placement of a machine gun.

Spying the American flag, he grimaced at her accent but inclined his head in a respectful nod. "You arrived just in time, ma'am. We're closing this road to traffic—friend or foe—once His Majesty is through."

"I wish you luck."

"Not to boast, but one of mine is worth ten of theirs."

"Your men are that skilled?"

"No, ma'am. My men are that angry."

CHAPTER 8

Cleo tugged a thermos from Einar's knapsack and took a swallow of sludgy coffee, compliments of the truck driver who'd picked them up on the road near the village of Tangen. They'd parted ways when he turned off to make deliveries, and they'd found a ride on a farm wagon pulled by a teeth-grindingly slow tractor. Hitching rides proved easy. Traffic was thick, a snaking line of cars and trucks and buses making their ponderous way between valleys as they headed north and east. Everyone they met asked the same questions—had they seen the Germans? Did they know what the government planned? Would the Norwegians fight back?

She wished she had answers.

Einar seemed to be immune to the exhaustion that dogged her with every long mile. He traveled with the eagerness of youth as if they were on a big adventure rather than running ahead of a deadly German army. As if his ancient revolver and enough confidence to sink a battleship could change the tide against trucks and tanks and machine guns. It would have been endearing if she hadn't wanted to strangle him with his own knitted scarf.

Outside the village of Bekkelaget, they faced another road-block. Another group of soldiers. And another rebuff of Einar that left him sullen and quiet, but it had also offered up valuable information that almost made Cleo lose what little self-control she had left. The Norwegian government had left Hamar for the town of Elverum farther east.

As if to prove their claim, planes roared low with a throbbing rumble Cleo could feel in her sternum. For a moment, she was back in Zakopane, shielding her eyes against a late summer sun as wave after wave of bombers flew toward Warsaw and Kraków. Beside her, Micky had muttered under his breath, and when fear drove her to seek out his hand, it was as damp and cold as her own. This time, it was Einar who slid his mittened hand into hers. His scent of wool and spruce filled her nose.

"*Vi er nesten fremme.* Almost there."

Adjusting their direction, they marched on, thumbing rides when they could, trudging through snow and slush along the verge of slippery roads when they couldn't. As darkness fell, and they grew closer to Elverum, lights flickered over fields from nearby farmsteads while traffic increased. A line of cars roared around a bend. A convoy of buses soon followed. A half hour later, an open truck rumbled over a low ridge, carrying armed soldiers in white coats that blended in with the gray dusk and the tree-shadowed snow. A staff car, all chrome and purring engine, sloshed mud against her legs. Cleo kept an eye out for Sam's van, half in hope and half in dread. But no battered van appeared. She sent out a wish they were safe and warm. Then cursed them for being safe and warm.

She knew she wasn't thinking straight. It had been a very long, very confusing day.

By now, Cleo could barely see her hand in front of her face. She followed Einar as much by hearing as by sight—the crunch of his boots, the huff of his breath, the occasional gurgle in his stomach. Dulled to exhaustion, her brain focused on putting one foot in front of the other. She nearly banged into his back when he stopped suddenly in her path, his head up, a hand going to his belt.

"What it is?" She stood ankle deep in the snow, trying to hear whatever sound had spooked Einar, when there was a murmur of voices caught on the air, the creak and snap of branches, the rasp of a saw followed by the chink of heavy chains.

A farm hugged the road. Figures moved over the yard and in and out of the sheds and barns, erecting a makeshift barricade. Logs and barbed wire and abandoned cars waited to be pushed across the road. She sighted along the hill toward a low ridge where the glint off a muzzle revealed more soldiers hunkered in wait behind a stone wall.

"Are they German?" she whispered over the thud of her heart and the roaring in her ears.

Einar grinned like a fiend. "Norwegian."

He pushed on with renewed energy. Cleo followed more slowly, ankles rolling on hidden stones and uneven ground. Down below, a long, low sedan slowed at the roadblock. A soldier leaned into the window, his voice loud against the quiet night. He pointed up the road. Another voice responded, one Cleo recognized.

"That's Aunt Daisy!"

She lost her footing in her rush to catch up to the car, her feet skidding out from under her. She landed hard, the breath wheezing from her lungs. Her back jammed into a root. She called out. "Wait! I'm here!"

The men on the ridge stood up, and she immediately felt the prickle of more than one rifle trained on her.

"Wait!" She held up her hands. "American! I'm American!"

Einar was behind her somewhere in the dark. Nearby a dog barked frantically.

The car slid back into drive and disappeared as a hand gripped her arm. A voice burned in her ears. A gun was trained at her head.

"I'm American," she whimpered.

* * *

SHE'D COME SO close. Twenty measly little miles separated Cleo from Aunt Daisy. Might as well have been two thousand. No matter how she'd argued, she'd been told to stay put and follow orders. If she'd done that in the first place, she'd be nicely tucked up in her bed in Oslo rather than cold, hungry, and reeking of soiled straw and pig shit.

She huddled in a corner of an old barn, counting the young men sporting hunting rifles and determined expressions who came and went as they prepared for battle. A few looked no older than Einar. Schoolboys playing at war. They shifted uneasily, hands trembling and throats tight. No matter how Cleo did the math, she came to the same conclusion—they were woefully outnumbered. As the last of the soldiers departed, Einar and a man in an officer's uniform approached Cleo, alone in her corner.

"What's happening?" she asked, looking between the officer and Einar, whose face glowed like a lit fuse.

"Germans are close," Einar translated for the officer. "We will trap them like fish in a net and then . . ." She noted the word *we* as he slid a finger across his throat.

"What's that got to do with me?"

Einar shoved his revolver into her hand, the butt warm from his coat pocket, and she almost leaped out of her skin. "What's that for?"

He mimed shooting someone before moving off to take up his own position shouldering a borrowed rifle.

She risked a peek through the rough slats of the barn. Below, where the road passed the farm, a group of soldiers had hefted logs across the road until the pile stood nearly a dozen feet high. Others looped and twisted roping metal barbs over and under and through the barricade. Out of the corner of her eye, she caught the flash of moonlight off a rifle muzzle on the far side of the road, a shift of shadows as soldiers hunkered down to lie in wait. Anyone traveling the road to Elverum would be stopped by barbed wire and barricades. Anyone attempting to force their way through would be mowed down by the platoon of waiting Norwegian soldiers.

That was the plan, anyway. Simple but effective.

She heard the Germans before she saw them. A clamor that made no attempt at subterfuge or subtlety. The first in a line of buses stopped at the barrier, the rest idling behind it. Men got out to inspect the barricade. Orders moved up and down the column. Guards with rifles hopped from the backs of trucks, peering into the trees where nothing moved.

Her breath shallowed then caught at the back of her throat with a metallic tang that turned out to be blood from where she'd bitten down on the inside of her mouth.

A shout carried up from the road. There was a moment when everything sharpened in her mind, the air clean with pine and snow, the fast-moving clouds throwing shadows over the land-scape to trick the eye. Then the night exploded.

Muzzle flashes and the high-pitched rattle of a machine gun seemed to come from everywhere. She pressed herself into the floor of the barn, the straw dust catching in her throat as she fought to make herself as small as possible. There was a buzz in her ears, a roar that pumped angry at her temples. Her head seemed to vibrate with the noise.

A muffled shout burst through the underwater ringing in her head. Two soldiers beat at flames that ran ahead of their attempts, slithering up the ancient beams of the barn, catching in the thick dry straw litter, chewing through the loft to drop embers that smoldered in coats and panicked the soldiers who fought to escape. Black smoke seared her throat. Cinders burned her skin and hands. She couldn't see. Couldn't breathe.

A hand caught her own, pulling her blindly. She crawled and stumbled forward until she broke free of the burning barn. Einar, his sooty, grinning face alive with the thrill of battle, helped her to her feet, pointing toward the brow of a nearby hill. "Go that way."

Keeping hold of the revolver, she covered her mouth and nose with the cuff of her coat. Eyes stinging and weepy, she crouched and zigzagged her way to the safety of the tree line. Behind her, flames shot into the air, swirling skyward in a cyclone of embers and smoke. A grenade exploded to her left, shaking the ground, throwing chunks of dirt and shrapnel in every direction.

From the ridge of the hill, she could see the battle being played out like a chess game.

The Norwegians, despite their numbers and inexperience, proved worthy successors to their Viking ancestors. They were ferocious in their attack. The buses offered some protection to the Germans, but with no way to go forward, they were forced to retreat back down the narrow road. The officer had said the attack would be like trapping fish in a net. Cleo would say it was more like shooting fish in a barrel.

A snap of a twig behind her caused her to spin, her hand sliding the revolver free of her coat. A man stood twenty feet away. Even in the uneven shadows from the burning barn, she could tell he was German. Had he come up here to circle around and come at the Norwegians from behind? Had he fled at the first shot, hoping to lose himself in the chaos? Was he hurt? Was he armed? A thousand thoughts tumbled through her brain at once, but even as her heart threatened to jump clean out of her chest, she was steadying her sights on the man.

"Don't move." She spoke in German through the deafening roar of her pounding heart and her heavy breathing. "I'll shoot. I swear I will."

"Will you, little bird?" He stood still, but there was no fear in his stance, only a watchful scrutiny. "Are you sure about that?" His smile gleamed white and toothy in the dark—or maybe she imagined it. His tone was certainly enough to send shivers up her spine.

"I'm very sure." The revolver was old and heavy, her sweaty palms cold on the metal. Her wrists ached from targeting it at his chest—or where she thought his chest was.

"I don't think you have it in you." He took a step toward her. "I think you're going to let me go."

She pulled back the hammer. "I mean it!" she shouted. "I'll blow your damned brains out."

He took another step toward her. She had a brief thought of shouting for help, but who would hear her way up here? She was on her own.

"Give me the revolver, little bird." His voice was slow and persuasive and trickled like cold water down her back as he moved closer.

If he reached her, she was dead. She could see it in his eyes. He was furious and desperate and she was easy and alone.

"I won't tell you again." Cleo hated the squeak in her voice.

"You're right. You won't." He lunged.

She dodged, her boots sliding out from under her, sky and branches and snow swirling above her as she fell. The gun exploded, knocking her back, every tendon in her shoulder screaming in a wrenching pain. As her head hit the ground, there was a crack of gunfire, and someone shouted something in incomprehensible Norwegian.

Then nothing else.

Dear Anne,

I'm far too old for this to-ing and fro-ing over the countryside one step ahead of calamity. My nerves remain steady. My knees less so. And the less said about making decisions after thirty-six hours without sleep, the better. But after a good night's rest and a hearty breakfast served to us by the hostess of our guesthouse, I'm much refreshed and ready for whatever new adventures await.

Postscript:

I spoke much too soon . . .

"She's coming around," Petra said, relief flooding her tired features.

Cleo's unfocused gaze moved from Petra to Daisy to the Norwegian boy who'd turned up in the dead of night babbling nonsense about murdered motorcyclists, a van full of musicians, and an ambush that almost led to Cleo being burned to a crisp, then shot through the middle.

"Am I dead?" Cleo asked, her voice raspy and thick with smoke and confusion.

The weight that Daisy had been carrying since her phone conversation with Lieutenant Bayard lifted, but nothing eased her exasperation, which continued to simmer low in her gut like a pot on the hob. "You damned well should be. What on earth were you thinking, haring across Norway without the sense God gave a goose? This isn't a game, Clementine. You, of all people, should know that."

Cleo winced, her hand gripping the slightly musty wool blanket they'd found in a cedar chest, and Daisy almost—*almost*—felt bad for shouting. "No, ma'am, you're right. It isn't."

Cleo contrite *and* apologetic? Now Daisy did feel bad—and scared. Cleo had always brazened her way through every tight spot and unpleasantness, arrogance carrying her when cleverness failed.

"She will live, yes?" the boy asked, worry clouding his bright blue eyes. His face was streaked with dirt, his hair matted and unkempt under a thick wool cap. He reeked of smoke and sweat and the sour odor of pig.

"It's going to take far more than a knock to that hard head of hers to lay her low."

He might not have understood all the words, but he caught the gist. A grin broke over his face, and Daisy realized he was younger than she'd first thought—no more than sixteen at the most. She couldn't help but recall the last war and the legions of boys just like him, gray-faced and broken after four years in the trenches. Would this be his fate? Forced to grow up far too quickly amid death and bloodshed? Did he have a mother at home worrying? A sweetheart awaiting his return?

"Thank God you're alive, Einar." Color slowly returned to Cleo's face. She tried to sit up, wincing at strained muscles and sore ribs, tentatively touching the sticking plaster on her forehead, the bandage on her neck. "Did we win?"

"Of course." He puffed out his chest, lifted his chin. "I took the bad man out—blam!" He aimed his finger and shot. "Then when they all run away, we bring you here."

Outside, a truck horn sounded, followed by a shout.

Einar glanced out the window. "I go now. You're safe here."

Cleo gave him a kiss that turned him pink as a peach. "Stay out of trouble." When he started to go, she grabbed his wrist and held him back. "Thank you."

He grinned again and gave a final wave as he headed out the door. Petra mumbled a few words about antiseptic and slipped out after him, leaving Daisy alone with Cleo. She lay back on the sofa and started to close her eyes.

"Don't you dare!" Daisy scolded. "Not until I'm finished raking you over the coals for behavior bordering on criminal."

"Einar told you about the soldier on the motorcycle?"

"Einar told me all sorts of things, and if only half of them are true, I'm beyond furious. Did you really leave a German soldier lying dead in an alley?"

"Einar killed him, not me. If it makes any difference, he seemed happy enough to leave *us* dead in an alley."

Daisy breathed in slowly through her nose and out through her mouth. Anything to keep herself from saying more than she ought. A headache—which she attributed solely to her goddaughter's cockamamie antics—banged against her temples.

She paced the parlor like a lion in its cage, relieved that they had the guesthouse to themselves after the British had fled farther afield to stay ahead of the German forces. No need to play the polished diplomat. She could be as tired and cranky and put out as she pleased.

Petra returned, bearing a breakfast tray, which Cleo dug into as if she hadn't eaten in days. Maybe she hadn't. Daisy's guilt washed fresh through her. How could she have left the girl behind? It was an inexcusable lapse. She couldn't afford any more of those. Not with Mr. Whitney watching her like a hawk.

"The Norwegian foreign minister, Dr. Koht, is on the phone for you, ma'am," Petra said. "He wants to fill you in on the current negotiations with the Germans."

"The phone lines are still working?"

"For now. Stockholm left a message as well. Apparently, Herr Brauer would like a word with you too."

So she was to be the middleman between Norway and Germany. Daisy was reminded of her conversation about motherhood with the crown princess. If only she could send both men to their rooms without any supper.

"Right. You stay here, Miss Kristiansen. Make sure my god-daughter doesn't leave this room without an escort. She has a bad habit of vanishing." She pointed at Cleo. "And you—I am in no mood to play child-minder so stay put until I get back."

"Herr Brauer . . ." Cleo looked up from her boiled egg and toast, trouble in her gaze.

"What about him?"

"I went to see him yesterday morning."

"Doesn't take no for an answer, indeed," Daisy muttered through gritted teeth. "And?"

"I didn't get in to see him, but there was another man there who seemed to know who I was. He said he'd help find Micky, but I've been thinking—" Cleo was interrupted by the rattle of windows in their panes, and a growl that vibrated the walls and floor of the tiny guesthouse. Bombers headed toward Elverum. "I've been thinking about the school in Zakopane you talked about." Cleo gripped the blanket. The scrapes and bruising on her face and up into her singed hairline made her look unbearably young and painfully fragile. "Do you think Micky may not want to be found?"

CHAPTER 9

Dear Anne,

Was it my influence that brought about the meeting between King Haakon and Herr Brauer? Or was I merely one of many voices? I can't say for sure, but however it was brought about, the two men are closeted alone together only a few yards away. Oh, to be a fly on that wall . . .

Daisy waited outside the school in Elverum, tucked into a corner of the building to avoid the wind. She didn't try to stay out of sight. Nobody paid much attention to a gray-haired lady of mature years. She was invisible unless she chose not to be. But now, invisibility suited her. She'd come directly from her phone call with Stockholm, leaving Miss Kristiansen in charge of Cleo. Heaven help the poor girl.

Though which girl she referred to varied by the minute.

As soon as she'd heard that His Majesty planned to meet with Herr Brauer, she'd made arrangements to be there—if not in the meeting, which proved impossible, then on hand to hear the outcome. Now two hours into her vigil, she began to think she could just as easily have waited somewhere warmer.

She stamped her numb feet in the snow drifted against the bricks.

The German bombers had come and gone, targeting the artillery school on the edge of town, leaving behind rutted streets and pock-marked windowless buildings. A burned-out truck sat crumpled in the road. Glass littered the sidewalks, sparkling like ice.

The cold seeped up from her toes to her ankles. Sleet prickled her cheeks and speckled her coat. Still she waited. At last, a side door opened as two gentlemen emerged from the school. One pulled on his gloves. Another settled his hat more squarely on his balding head against the worsening weather. She didn't need to see the soldiers coming to attention, the gawking cadets on parade, to recognize him.

"Your Majesty." She crossed the schoolyard, the pain of warmth returning to her limbs making her hobble on pins and needles.

His guardsmen closed ranks against her, but he waved them away with an imperious hand. "Madam Minister, I am glad to see you well after last night's adventures."

"I could say the same, Your Majesty. You took an awful risk coming back here after the attack."

"Herr Brauer took the bigger risk. I have friends close by. He does not."

She'd heard a rumor that the German foreign minister had arrived in Elverum alone and blindfolded to meet the king. Whether that was true or not, there had certainly been a hint of cloak-and-dagger about the situation. The meeting had been one-on-one, no functionaries or clerks allowed, not even Crown Prince Olav by the king's side. Daisy had seen them all waiting as she had been, their faces furrowed and careworn, stubble graying their jawlines. After a bit, they'd drifted off to seek shelter out of the weather. She'd remained steadfast at her post. Her tenacity had paid off in this quick quiet interview with His Majesty before his staff hurried him away.

"Is Herr Brauer demanding that Norway surrender?" she asked.

"I hope you mentioned to him the recent speech made by his Führer in which he stated that a nation bowing to violation without offering resistance does not deserve to live."

King Haakon ran a hand over his face. He'd grown older over the last days. His eyes had sunk within their sockets and his gaze was clouded by dark thoughts, but he remained straight as a poker, his shoulders wide as if he might carry the country on his back. "Are all Americans this pushy?"

"I like to think of us as determined and persistent, but pushy suits."

"It would seem you have prior knowledge of Germany's demands. Listening at keyholes, Mrs. Harriman?" His narrow face was sharp as a blade, his mustache drawn low over a mouth bitten with frustration. Out of the corner of her eye, she saw the approach of men in dark hats and overcoats, others in uniform. Her time alone to make her government's case was limited.

"It's only a guess based on their recent actions in Denmark. Your brother King Christian capitulated to save his throne. I imagine Herr Brauer—and now Mr. Quisling in Oslo—hope that you will do the same."

His Majesty took a moment to answer. Daisy was wise enough not to fill the silence. "He has asked me to return to Oslo," he explained. "My family and my dynasty will be safe from harm so long as I dance to Hitler's tune."

"So long as you surrender," she persisted.

The cadets had long since dispersed, the streets emptying as afternoon dusk descended along with an icy sleet that hissed as it fell. Light escaped from a window here and there, arrows of gold against the blue snow, but a blackout thickened the already dense shadows. The men surrounded the king, jostling to exclude her, to push her from his path. She refused to be sidelined. She planted herself like a tree, unwilling to be ignored. "Have you made a decision as to what course you'll take?"

"If I have, do you think I would share it with you?"

A fair question, but one she'd anticipated. "Sir Cecil Dormer and the British have bolted for the safety of Sweden. Norway's friends are a bit on the lean side currently, but I count myself among them."

Her words obviously struck a chord. Why else had he not already signaled his guards to remove the obstreperous old lady in his way?

"Her Royal Highness admires you, Mrs. Harriman." His face softened at mention of his daughter-in-law. "Märtha finds your candor refreshing and your ambition and energy qualities she would wish her own daughters to emulate. I'm less convinced."

Daisy didn't allow his skepticism to faze her. She'd been underestimated before. "It's my father's fault, Your Majesty. He was a man who should have had sons and reconciled himself to the lack by bringing up three girls in the exact same manner as he might three boys. It led to a certain freedom not always appreciated in this day and age."

"Your president is one that seems to appreciate it."

"Yes, but he's always been ahead of his time. A trait we share. I've sent word to Washington, and I'm currently compiling reports to be passed to the United States through our embassy in Stockholm. If you would just—"

"Do not take offense, Madam Minister, only I am not certain what you or the United States can do about this situation, no matter how many reports you send or how much you have the president's ear." He tipped his cap, the signal that his patience—and their conversation—was at an end. The soldiers took up position to either side of him as he prepared to head to his car.

"You'd be surprised at how much it takes to offend me, Your Majesty." Daisy hustled along beside them, unwilling to let him escape without offering a last word. "But I wouldn't count us Americans out completely. As you say, we're pushy. We might be of some use to you yet."

He settled himself into the back of the car that would take him to the safety of Nybergsund, a dot on the map that, for now, remained safe from attack. Stress dug grooves into his thin face, gray with fatigue. He sat hunched as if in pain, though his expression remained fired with grim determination. He had sought to keep his country at peace, but he was not bowed by the prospect of war.

Daisy watched as his car drove off, unsure whether she'd made her case or not. Twenty yards up, the car came to a stop. The king's window rolled down, and he beckoned her over. "Have you thought any more about my request?" he asked.

"Is the crown princess in Nybergsund?"

"For now, but they are bound for the border and then Stockholm."

"She won't leave you and the crown prince behind without a fight."

"No. She won't. But she *will* leave."

"OUCH! THAT STINGS." Cleo practically leaped off the couch, every sore muscle screaming in protest. "Holy cow! It needs cleaning, not scouring. If I didn't know better, I'd say you're doing that on purpose."

Petra sat back with a barely concealed roll of her blue eyes. "Why would I hurt you on purpose, Miss Jaffray?"

"Oh, I don't know, let's see . . . because you don't like me? Because you think I'm a spoiled brat? Because you think I'm causing Aunt Daisy trouble by being here? Because you think I'm interested in your boyfriend? The reasons are positively endless."

"I'm not hurting you on purpose," Petra said, before adding in a not-so-quiet mutter under her breath, "*dum jente*. Now let me see to this burn before it becomes infected." After cleaning the scrape on Cleo's neck with soap and water, she slathered it in petroleum jelly.

Cleo gritted her teeth against the sting. Her head sloshed with an ache that sizzled down into her shoulders, and her smoke-singed throat hurt. "Beauty, brains, and now nursing skills—anything you can't do?"

"Make you be silent." Petra moved to the scrape on Cleo's shoulder.

"Did you just try to be funny?" Cleo squeaked around the sting of antiseptic. "You actually have a sense of humor? Who knew?"

Petra concentrated on stoppering the bottle, cutting a piece of gauze, searching for the surgical tape. So much for trying to be friendly. Cleo should have known better. The woman had Norwegian snow in her veins.

Outside, the farm where they were staying was alive with a growing number of refugees seeking shelter: families displaced by the bombs; businessmen caught on the road; men, young and old, some with rifles, some carrying only shovels and axes, but all determined to join the fight. She could hear their voices, the sound of engines, the squeak of boots across the spring snow. Was one of them Einar? No. He was away with those soldiers from the roadblock. She said a prayer for his safety, though she didn't really believe anyone was listening. Still, a little otherworldly help couldn't hurt.

". . . can't believe he came back . . . pray it's not a trap . . ." Right outside the window, a man's deep voice, rounded *o*'s and flat *a*'s. American? British? Cleo's head hurt too much to decide.

"Same could be said of Brauer" came the answer, this voice decidedly British.

The competing voices swam into a buzzing drone like a hive of bees then faded farther into the background as sleep stole over her.

She dreamed of the German motorcyclist, his face and that of the soldier at the barricade merging and melting into one unnerving featureless mask. Why hadn't she pulled the trigger when she had the chance? Why hadn't she killed the man? He'd have killed her, and she just stood there, frozen. Unable to move. Was she a coward? Was she the weak little bird he'd accused her of being?

"I never thanked you properly for helping my grandmother get home." Petra's voice shocked Cleo awake, her joints pulled into place as she sat up.

Her eyes flew to the clock on the wall. Barely a few minutes had passed, but it felt like she'd dozed for hours. Her brain was mushy as if she'd drunk too much. "I wasn't using the ticket," she replied thickly. "No sense letting it go to waste."

Petra's lips pursed, digging deep grooves to either side of her mouth. "You do not make it easy to be kind, Miss Jaffray."

"Takes one to know one, Miss Kristiansen."

Petra's blue eyes flashed dangerously. "I do not think life is always a joke, if that is what you mean."

"Isn't it?" Cleo's lethargy clung like a wet blanket, and she was desperately thirsty. "Think about it. A week ago, your greatest worry was whether your boyfriend was flirting with me—he wasn't by the way. Today, we're fighting over our supply of boiled eggs and hoping the Nazis don't drop a bomb on us. If that's not completely absurd, I don't know what is. Believe me when I tell you, there's a fine line between comedy and tragedy."

"And you straddle it, pretending at one and scoffing at the other." Petra cleared away the antiseptics and gauze then boiled a kettle on the gas ring. Cleo would have asked for a cup of tea if she didn't think Petra would fling it at her.

"You never answered my question," Cleo ventured in an attempt to mend fences. "What do you have against me other than that I don't take life seriously?"

Hefting the typewriter case onto the table, Petra set it up along with paper, pens, and a pile of notepads. "Maybe it is because I have responsibilities and people who depend on me, and you are given every advantage, every privilege, and you toss them aside as if they are nothing. Toss your family . . . your fiancé . . . aside as if they are nothing. How can you do that?"

Years of practice. The flip remark hovered on the tip of Cleo's tongue. The tossed-off comment that would direct the conversation into safer channels. But the words tasted sour now. Petra's opinion pricked a tender spot, a part of herself Cleo avoided at all costs. The part that said it was better to be the one doing the leaving than the one being left.

"If it's Georgie Cliveden you're worried about, he married six months after I left him standing at the altar. His bride's father owns a tin plating concern in New Jersey, and she's his sole heir. Believe me, no hearts were broken there. In fact, I probably did him a favor."

Petra violently shuffled her papers. "You laugh and you joke as if it's all a game and yet, as you say, we are in the middle of a war with no idea what will happen next."

"That's the point. Not knowing what happens next. Not caring what happens next." Unconvinced, Petra continued to glare as if she might burn a hole through the table. Frankly, Cleo was feeling less sure about that line of reasoning herself, but she wasn't going to let Petra have the win. "Look, you're an ant and I'm a grasshopper and never the twain shall meet."

Obviously not the response Petra expected. Her face registered annoyance compounded by confusion, as if she was unsure whether Cleo was mocking her or not.

"You know . . . the fable," Cleo continued. "The ant is hard-working and practical while the grasshopper fritters and frolics and enjoys life."

"Isn't that the one where the grasshopper is starving when winter comes and begs the ant for help only to be turned away to die?"

"Well, old Aesop was a tough cookie. I prefer to imagine an alternative where the ant and the grasshopper become friends in the end and enjoy the long, hard winter on the ant's food and the grasshopper's cheer."

"Ridiculous. Why should they be friends? The ant does all the work, and the grasshopper does nothing."

"He brings joy."

Petra sniffed her dismissal of this nonsensical notion. "Where have you brought joy? To your mother? Your jilted fiancé? Your godmother? It seems to me you bring nothing but worry and trouble, Miss Jaffray."

She punctuated her statement by feeding a clean sheet of paper through the typewriter's rollers and settling into her work with a zip and a ding and a rattle of keys.

Conversation over, but not before Cleo felt the punch of Petra's criticisms like a fist to the chest, resentment burning hot behind her breastbone like a bad case of indigestion. And just like indigestion, the burn quickly faded, replaced by a sour, uncomfortable feeling of guilt that squirreled her stomach.

Tuning out the rattle of typewriter keys, Cleo stared out the window, watching the long silver shadows slide over the snowy hills, trying to excuse away her actions and coming up empty. For so long, she'd fought against others' expectations. When had she stopped expecting more of herself?

She pulled herself up on unsteady legs, suddenly desperate to be sick.

"Where do you think you're going?" Petra looked up from her spread of papers. "Mrs. Harriman said you were to stay here until she returned."

"Can't talk. Gotta puke."

Petra scrunched up her nose and turned back to her typing. ". . . grasshopper . . . ant . . . *dum jente* . . ."

Cleo dashed for the toilet, where she was splendidly and furiously sick.

Dear Anne,

I understand His Majesty's continued mistrust of our country's intentions and I sympathize with his plight. You know as well as I do that the current political climate in the United States means there's little hope for direct aid of any kind crossing the Atlantic. The president will need to find other, subtler, ways to assist and abet the war effort. If anyone can do it, it's that wily fox Roosevelt . . .

"WHAT DO YOU think happened at the meeting?" According to Miss Kristiansen, Cleo had slept most of the afternoon, but now she was restless, unable to relax, and pelting Daisy with incessant questions.

Daisy was equally unsettled as she turned over her conversation with the king, thinking of all the things she should have said.

"I'll wager His Majesty told Herr Brauer to piss off," Cleo answered her own question. She paused in her pacing to lean a hip against the table where Miss Kristiansen was typing up the latest coded cable to send on to Stockholm, the codebook in its borrowed dust jacket open for reference. Petra protected her work as best she could while simultaneously slamming each key as if she pulled a trigger. Cleo, oblivious, bent closer and pointed out a spelling error. Petra ripped the page out with a muttered curse and started over. Five minutes later, Cleo was back, this time with a cup of tea and a plate of cookies she left at Petra's elbow. Petra ate half and left the rest, which she pushed back across to Cleo. Daisy would never suggest it, but the two women reminded her of a pair of squabbling sisters. Sparring one minute and making up the next.

"I'm sure the German minister pressed every conceivable argument," Daisy pondered aloud. "I'm sure he spoke of the need to spare the Norwegian citizens any needless bloodshed that a protracted war would bring to the country. And I'm absolutely sure he pointed out the fact that the Germans have already taken a good chunk of the country with ease and will likely do the same with the rest."

"And *then* His Majesty told him to piss off," Cleo said.

Daisy couldn't help the smile.

Mr. Whitney banged into the cottage, declaring, "Ma'am, you have to hear this." He flipped on the radio, dialing it up and down through whistles and the hiss of static until . . .

". . . The Germans have invaded the country with bombing and every other means of destruction. Germany has violated every right of a small nation wishing only to live in peace . . ."

Petra's fingers stilled upon the keys. Cleo sat on the arm of the couch, her hand unconsciously touching the bandage on her forehead.

". . . the people of Norway will strain every nerve in their effort to raise anew the liberty and independence which a foreign power has tried to crush with brute force . . ."

"That's done it," Mr. Whitney declared, snapping off the radio. "King Haakon's told the Jerries exactly where they can stuff their negotiated surrender. There goes the chance for any diplomatic solution."

Daisy felt the vice consul watching her as if to gauge her reaction. So much work over the last twenty years wasted. The world was ripping itself apart despite the tireless efforts of countless diplomats and pacifists. Had it all been for naught?

"We are at war," Petra said softly.

"You've been at war since yesterday morning, my dear," Daisy said. "It's simply official now."

"What's your plan now, ma'am?" Mr. Whitney asked.

What *was* her plan? She ticked through a to-do list in her head before spreading out a map of Norway on the table. Obviously, their next stop would be Nybergsund, where the royal family and their government was hiding. The village was about sixteen miles from the Swedish border. Close enough for the crown princess to make a quick escape if she needed to, but would she? Would Sweden have them, if it came to that? It would be a precarious position for the neutral country, especially with this firsthand experience of how little Germany honored neutrality. And then what? German troops poured into Norway from the south and west. How on earth could His Majesty, with his scattered and outnumbered forces, ever hope to throw off such an organized incursion?

With British help? Perhaps. But Daisy wasn't convinced the British had the manpower or the willpower if circumstances proved difficult, which of course they would. Hitler had rolled over half of Europe without breaking a sweat while Chamberlain dithered and appeased and wrung his hands.

"Should I ready the car, ma'am? We could be in Nybergsund in a few hours if the roads are clear."

"Hear that?" Cleo stood at the window, but there was no vagueness in her gaze now. She was focused, her body taut. "Planes."

"We're safe enough here." The growling vibration knifed up Daisy's spine like nails, but she remained in her chair, judging distance and direction. "They'll be headed for Elverum again."

But the noise grew until the sound of the bombers shuddered

along the floorboards and up into her calves. Outside, there were shouts and calls. Lights in the main house were switched off and curtains drawn. "Cleo, get away from the window. Petra, douse the lamp."

Daisy gritted her teeth and clutched her fountain pen until it snapped under her grip, ink spreading black and cold over her fingers. The ground shook with the concussive punch of exploding bombs. Moonlight was overtaken by an orange glow that turned the far woodland bright as a city. The blasts came closer in a chain of overlapping sound like ocean waves, rattling dishes, knocking prints from the walls. Papers slid to the floor along with an open drawer of pens, paper clips, and staples. Petra gathered them up, tossing them into the closest file box, when the whole house shook with a roar that pushed against Daisy's eardrums and punched her chest like a fist. A window blew out in a glittering spray of glass. She couldn't hear anything but a high ringing in her ears.

"Get out!" she shouted, her feigned indifference no use to her now.

"The codebook!" Petra shouted.

She shoved it in her coat pocket as Cleo dragged her toward the door ahead of Mr. Whitney, who lent Daisy an arm. This time she allowed it, grateful for his strength and angry at herself for being grateful.

The four of them followed the stream of panicked refugees into the woods. The shriek and whistle of bombs stuttered like a string of firecrackers, blowing holes in a nearby shed, taking out a row of parked trucks and a tractor, obliterating a far-off fence.

Behind them, a car swerved into the yard, tires sliding on the ice. A door was flung open, a man nearly toppling from the driver's seat. In the glow of the flames, his face was blade sharp and fierce.

"Well, look what the cat's dragged in," Cleo said, not even bothering to hide the shake in her voice. "Lieutenant Bayard."

CHAPTER 10

Cleo woke to the smell of burnt toast the next morning. Or maybe it was burnt coffee. Or maybe the house was on fire. At this point, nothing would astonish her. She rose slowly, but her soreness was gone and all that was left was a lingering stiffness in her joints and an itch where her skin healed under the thick bandage.

The influx of refugees arriving after last night's attack meant they no longer had the guesthouse to themselves. An insurance adjuster, a man who sold appliance parts, and a grocery delivery driver took up residence in the parlor, a blank-faced family of four whose house had its roof blown off sat in silence around the dining room table, and the queue for the lavatory was at least five deep.

Cleo found her way to the kitchen, where Bayard toasted bread to go with the tin of sardines Petra was forking onto a plate.

"There's our wounded warrior," he proclaimed. "You've had quite an adventure."

Petra pursed her lips in irritation and turned back to her task, her movements quick and angry.

If Cleo thought they'd come to a détente, she'd been mistaken.

She found a chipped mug in a cupboard and reached around Bayard for the pot of coffee on the stove. This close, she could see a spot on his cheek that his razor had missed and smell his scent of aftershave and diesel fuel. She chalked up the heat steaming along her skin to the paraffin stove. That had to be it. She could be accused of a lot of things but stealing another woman's man wasn't one of them.

"Doesn't seem like the adventure's over yet." Leaning against the counter, she cupped the steaming mug, hoping it hid the flush in her cheeks. "Have you seen Aunt Daisy this morning?"

"She's trying to get through to Stockholm. Not sure if she's having much success though. Telephone service is spotty at best."

"What do you expect?" Petra snapped, slamming her plate down. "The Germans are everywhere."

Bayard's shoulders inched higher, his grip on the toasting fork tightening. He kicked out a chair and sat down at the table with his plate of sardines and toast. "Eat up. We need to get on the road as soon as we can."

"What's the rush? If you hadn't noticed, it's a little dangerous out there."

"You should have thought of that before you decided to treat this war like a child's game and nearly got yourself killed." Petra's words hit like a slap, and Cleo felt herself taking a step back as if she'd been physically assaulted. "If you only did what you were told. You're just like—"

"Enough!" Bayard's sharp response was unexpected. He played the diplomat so well that catching a glimpse of the soldier came as a surprise.

Cleo played it off with one of her patented smiles and a toss of her curls. "It's all right. Miss Kristiansen knows how us grass-hoppers like to play." She finished her coffee, setting her mug in the sink. "I'll be waiting at the car whenever the rest of you are ready to go."

As soon as she left the kitchen, she could hear their voices quiet and quick. Hardly the murmur of lovers. This was an argument conducted in whispers.

She'd assumed Petra would be overjoyed to see the lieutenant swoop in out of the shadows. Instead she'd been prickly around him since his arrival as if he was a stranger or as if he was someone she wished was a stranger. It didn't make sense. Mr. Whitney wasn't much better. Rather than being relieved at having another man to share the responsibility of getting the US minister safely through a war zone, he seemed put out by the lieutenant, and as the night wore on, the two of them started to remind Cleo of two cockerels in the same coop.

Only Aunt Daisy had been genuinely happy to see Bayard, though in a rather official way, pulling him aside for a full debriefing that lasted into the small hours of the morning. Cleo had fallen asleep to their quiet voices in a nearby room, weirdly at peace in a way she hadn't been since Oslo.

She wandered outside to where Mr. Whitney readied the Ford. Two cans of gasoline sat by the trunk beside a box of supplies while he secured the American flag to the roof with rope. "I heard the Norwegians watched the Germans marching into Oslo with smiles on their faces."

"Then you heard wrong," Cleo answered, feeling her temper flare at the sneer in his tone. "They were in shock, same as you'd be if you saw foreign soldiers marching up Pennsylvania Avenue. But they weren't smiling. And they sure as hell weren't welcoming them."

"*You* sure didn't." He bent to offer her a cigarette. "You put a bullet in one of them. Right between the eyes. Must have been quite a fight."

She inhaled, feeling the burn down her airways before the nicotine loosened her lungs, which in turn loosened her body.

She leaned against the car, trying not to notice the dents and pockmarks in the paint from last night's attack. "Yeah, that was just what it was."

"I wonder if the minister will be including that little nugget in her official report to Stockholm. I wouldn't think so, would you?"

Cleo looked up, but he had already tossed his cigarette away and was back to loading the car.

THEY DROVE SLOWLY over the bridge and through the town of Elverum—or what was left of it after last night's attack. Barely a building remained except for the hospital. Bricks and lathing lay scattered in grotesque piles. Here a pipe leading nowhere. There a sofa, still smoldering in a street. Flames licked at a burned-out bus. Men and women salvaged what belongings they could from the ruins, packing them into crowded cars or onto the backs of flatbed trucks.

Petra was as white as the handkerchief she gripped in her hand, but her eyes burned hard and bright, and there was a ferocity to her silence that made Cleo cringe. Aunt Daisy, on the other hand, regarded her surroundings with studied concentration as she filed and counted and memorized. Every broken building. Every displaced civilian.

Bayard and Mr. Whitney, crushed into the front seat of the Ford together, were the only two who seemed unmoved by the destruction. Or perhaps it was only that they were already so focused on their own animosity, there was no space left for anything else.

Was it merely a pissing match between two men jockeying for favor with their boss, or was there something more? Something to do with that crack Mr. Whitney had made about Aunt Daisy's reporting to Stockholm?

Once or twice, Cleo caught Whitney watching her in the rear-view mirror, but whenever she tried to catch his eye, his gaze slid back to the road, and she was left with a growing knot in her stomach.

"Shit," Bayard breathed as Mr. Whitney dropped the car into first gear to creep around the bloodied carcass of a dead horse, its flanks riddled with machine gun bullets.

In a nearby field, more dead horses lay where they'd fallen, their blood staining the churned snow. Not plow horses or shaggy-coated cart ponies, these were cavalry mounts from the cadet school. Destroyed as if they were any other piece of military equipment to be put out of commission. Five. Eight. Twelve. Cleo stopped counting.

A lifelong equestrian, Aunt Daisy twisted her face in sorrow. "What a waste."

Leaving Elverum behind, they took the road north, but soon came to a roadblock. Backtracking, they tried a side road that passed beneath a shattered forest of pines but were stopped by the ruins of a bridge. Whether destroyed by Germans or Norwegians, it was impossible to tell.

"Now what, ma'am?" Mr. Whitney asked.

"If we can't go north, we go south and see if there's a detour."

With Bayard manning the map, Whitney turned the Ford around, wheels spinning and sliding in the ice, his driving experience the only thing keeping them out of drifts and ditches. But the roads in every direction were impassible, either by snow or by barricades of wire and felled trees. As the hours passed, the windows fogged with their breath while they shared a package of crackers Bayard found in his kit. A low afternoon sun reflected off the snow and shone in every mud puddle. They'd been driving all day and still hadn't made it farther than a few miles from Elverum.

"I suppose the one consolation is that if we can't get through, neither can the German army," Aunt Daisy offered up as once again they were forced to stop, the bridge ahead lying in concrete chunks ten feet below the roadway.

Whitney backed the car up to take a narrow lane they'd spotted a few miles back. But as he jammed the car into reverse, the rear end fishtailed, sending them into a snowbank. He shoved it into first then into reverse then into first again, hoping to rock the car out, but they were stuck fast, the wheels spinning until gray smoke rose from the muffler to mix with the thickening shadows. Bayard got out to push, but the snow was too deep and the car too heavy.

"Blast," Aunt Daisy muttered. "It's already getting dark."

Petra heard them first, her head lifting like a hound catching the scent. The rest of them fell silent and still at the now-familiar sound of airplane engines. Bayard shaded his eyes as he followed their path. "They're heading for Elverum again."

Aunt Daisy kicked angrily at a tire. "Maybe there's a farm farther along this lane. Someone with a tractor or a plow horse to pull us free."

"I'll go, ma'am." Bayard was already pulling on his overcoat, settling his cap.

"Not you. Whitney can go. He can take Miss Kristiansen with him. She can translate if need be."

"I know Norwegian," Bayard argued.

"Maybe so, but your accent is appalling. We don't need someone mistaking you for a German and blasting a hole through you." She raked Mr. Whitney with a scowl. "Well? What are you waiting for?"

"Yes, ma'am." He pulled on his gloves and wrapped his scarf tighter against the dropping temperature before grabbing a flashlight. As he switched it on, his gaze caught and held Cleo's. This was her chance to get him alone and find out what he intended.

Maybe she could persuade him to forget he heard about what she'd done in Oslo.

"I'll go." She ignored the damp seeping over the cuff of her boots and planted her tam firmly over her ears.

"No, Cleo." Aunt Daisy's voice was hard, the boss not the relative in her tone. "I asked that Miss Kristiansen—"

"We won't be long." Ignoring the order, Cleo stepped out ahead of the flashlight beam, pushing through the snow. "I'm sure I saw lights nearby." She gave a final wave. "Come on, Mr. Whitney. Keep up."

"Clementine Verquin!" Aunt Daisy shouted that wretched horrible humiliating name as if it would make Cleo listen.

She smiled into her pulled-up collar. It never had before.

CLEO SLIPPED AND sloshed up the rutted lane in Mr. Whitney's sullen company, her socks and stockings clinging to her frozen toes, her nose running with the cold. He offered her a hand over a slippery patch of ice—so not a complete jerk. She thought about ignoring his gesture but then her feet nearly slid out from under her, and she grabbed him by the forearm. He chuckled under his breath but didn't let her fall.

Now that she was alone with him, she wasn't sure what she planned to say or do. Plead her case? Defend Aunt Daisy?

Maybe she was wrong. Maybe there had been no hidden threat behind his words. Maybe she was imagining things. Jumping at shadows. Feeling guilty. But there had been something in his tone that worried her. Something that set the hairs at the back of her neck to tingling. She'd had that same feeling the day Micky left their apartment. The sense that something was not quite right. She'd ignored it once. She wouldn't do it again.

"Look, I think we got off on the wrong foot," she said, working up the courage.

Mr. Whitney grunted, swinging his flashlight up, the light falling on the vague shadows of a farmyard, sheds and barns secured against the night, a snug steep-roofed farmhouse with a lamp in the window. It reminded Cleo of Christmas cards or a Currier and Ives scene—minus the bombs and soldiers, of course.

"Keep quiet and do as I say," he growled. "Got it?"

An argument simmered in her chest, but she swallowed it back. Antagonizing was not the way to win him over. She nodded as he banged on the door, setting off a ferocious barking inside. "Hello? Anybody home?"

Not a sound came from inside except for the dog's continued growls and snarls.

"Maybe they think you're a German soldier trying to get one over on them," she offered. "Let me try." Before he could argue, she banged on the door. "Hello? I'm American. A-mer-i-can. I'm friendly. *En venn.*" She peered in through a curtained window. "*En venn!*"

After a long minute, there was a latch thrown and the faint squeak of hinges. A figure peeked through the crack. He held a large knife in his hand. Mr. Whitney backed up. Cleo smiled broadly with her hands raised and palms open to show she was unarmed. "How do you do? I'm Cleo Jaffray. I'm awfully sorry to bother you so late, but our car is stuck, and we hoped you might be able to help us get it out." She racked her brain for the right words. "*En bil* . . . um . . . *en bil.* An automobile." She mimed driving. "Snow. Trapped in the snow." She made screeching sounds and thumped her hands against the doorframe to illustrate being trapped, all while trying to ignore Mr. Whitney's chuckles. "*Nei . . . nei gå.* No go." Where was Einar when she needed him? "We're stuck. Can you help?" She ended her performance with another broad, guileless smile.

It must have worked. The door opened wider, and they were

ushered into a cozy front parlor. Three children sat on the rug by the fire playing a board game while a middle-aged woman with streaks of gray in her brown hair knitted to the sound of the radio. Cleo smiled and offered thanks in every language she could think of while the man of the house pulled on his coat, gloves, and hat; gathered a lamp; and explained the situation to his family.

"What are you people doing on the roads?" he asked in perfect English, shutting the door firmly behind him. "Don't you know there's a war on?"

Mr. Whitney gave a bark of brittle laughter while Cleo jogged to keep up. "We're on our way to Nybergsund actually. You wouldn't happen to know the best way to get there, would you? Only our driver"—she shot a hard look over her shoulder—"can't seem to find a way through the roadblocks."

"Hang on. It's not my fault," Mr. Whitney sputtered.

"Nybergsund?" The farmer shouldered open the heavy barn door and led them inside, where the air smelled sweetly of manure and hay. A sleepy cow eyed them from her byre while chickens rustled and murmured from their roosts. "What do you want there?"

Mr. Whitney stammered an answer as Cleo replied smoothly, "We were hoping to catch up with some friends, but then this horrid business with Germany started, and we're afraid we're going to miss them. We're in a dreadful rush."

Mr. Whitney cleared his throat as if to warn her she might be laying on the posh a smear too thick. What did he know? She'd survived for months on charm, finishing-school polish, and, when necessary, wide-eyed ditziness. If it worked, why change?

The farmer led an enormous, deep-chested draft out of his stall and snapped him into the crossties. The horse shook its shaggy head as the farmer moved quickly to harness him. Cleo scratched the big bay behind one ear and inhaled the sweet, dusty aroma of horse.

"There's a way." The last harness buckle secured, he grabbed a coiled length of heavy rope, which he handed off to Mr. Whitney before unsnapping the horse and leading him outside, where it stamped and puffed in the slush and mud. "Or was. Not sure how things stand these days."

They started back up the lane, but by now night had fallen and there was only Mr. Whitney's flashlight to see by. Above, stars mixed with snowflakes. Cleo's breath came in puffs and a stitch pinched at her sore ribs. "I don't remember it taking this long. Could we have missed a turn?"

Mr. Whitney paused to look around, swinging the light up over the trees. "A plane. Can you hear it?"

It was barely a growl over the wind and the creak of the trees, but the horse shifted in a jingle of buckles, and Mr. Whitney doused his light, plunging them into invisibility. The sound grew louder. The plane passed overhead, fire trailing from its left engine as it struggled to stay aloft.

The farmer spat a few words in Norwegian that were clearly meant as an insult.

When the plane disappeared behind the tree line, the farmer tugged his horse forward as they resumed their trudge through the snow, falling thicker and faster now. They'd gone only a few steps when the ground shook and the sky exploded, silhouetting the trees in flame, lighting Mr. Whitney's face with an eerie glow and reflecting in the horse's wild eyes as it tossed its head and sidestepped in fear. The farmer controlled him with a sharp jerk on the lead while Cleo soothed him with a stream of nonsense that had always worked on her hunter back home.

A car horn sounded. Three quick blasts followed by three long ones then three more quick. Cleo's heart stopped. "SOS! Aunt Daisy's in trouble."

CHAPTER 11

Dear Anne,

Catastrophe! Will write more when I can . . .

Petra only wandered a short way into the woods, but the pilot jettisoned his bombs as he went down over the hill. We found her lying beneath those pines," Daisy shouted over the ringing in her ears.

Trees and sky and road swirled in a kaleidoscope of blowing snow and ash, and she put a hand against the car to steady herself. Flames lit the lieutenant's stunned face and reflected in Mr. Whitney's dark eyes like devilish pinpricks. Only Cleo seemed unaffected by the confusion. She took charge with crisp commands that seemed to cut through the shock like a knife, directing the men in their efforts to load Miss Kristiansen into the Ford.

"Gently into the car. Gently," Daisy added her voice as chorus. "For God's sake, don't jostle her."

Smoke scoured Daisy's throat and made her eyes sting and water. Her calf ached where she'd stumbled, and something wet and salty slid between her tightly pressed lips. Tears? Blood? She slid onto the front seat of the Ford, which had been extricated from its snowbank, the farmer going ahead to warn his family of their arrival with a wounded woman.

"The house is up around this bend, ma'am. The family's name is Peterson." Mr. Whitney's voice echoed down to Daisy from a long tunnel, and there was a low hissing like radio static filling her throbbing head.

"Can you hear me, dear?" She draped herself over the front seat in order to take Petra's hand, trying not to notice how cold it was, trying not to slide her fingers farther up her wrist to check for a pulse. "It's going to be all right, Petra love. You'll see."

The words rang hollow, but they were all Daisy had to keep the panic at bay.

"She's cold as ice." Cleo sat in the back, cradling Petra Kristiansen's head in her lap. Blood soaked the sleeve of her coat, black and sticky under the car's faint dome light. "I think she's in shock."

"Keep her warm. Take my coat if you must," Daisy suggested, but Cleo was already shedding her own coat to tuck around Petra. The girl must be freezing herself; she wore only a thin wool sweater, but she showed no sign of the chill as she murmured quiet nonsense and smoothed the hair back from Petra's forehead.

"What did you say?" Daisy asked.

"I told perfect Petra she couldn't allow some boorish Nazi with bad aim to get the best of her." Cleo's gaze shone bright and angry and scared.

The poor road and the squeak of struts, the iron scents of sickness, gasoline, leather, and blood, the sense of urgency screaming through every vein. Daisy steadied her breath as memories of the last war flooded her like a spring tide. But back then she'd had strapping regiments of capable Red Cross Motor Corps girls by her side, and there had been the anticipation of a good meal and a soft bed at the end of the journey.

Tonight, she was lost in the middle of nowhere, and the injured was not some anonymous soldier, but one of her own. Someone she cared about. Someone who counted on her.

"Watch out, Mr. Whitney," she scolded after a particularly teeth-jarring slam of the axle into a deep hole. "Speed won't help if she's flung about like a rag doll. An ambulance driver needs to match promptness with vigilance. Do I need to take the wheel and show you how it's done?"

She sensed his resentment in the sudden stamping of brakes, but he kept his mouth shut and they swung into the farmyard without incident. The house and outbuildings formed a break against the wind and a lamp burned in the window.

A tall woman, her graying hair scraped back off her forehead beneath a blue kerchief, stood silhouetted in the doorway. "Come. Bring her inside. Quickly. Quickly," she called in Norwegian.

~~Between~~ AMONG the four of them, they bundled Petra into the house, where they were guided toward the kitchen with its enormous corner fireplace, a squat cast-iron baking oven crouched beside it. Pretty lace curtains were drawn tight against the dark, holding in the faint aroma of yeasty bread. "Put her on the settle there. It's warm from the oven, and we will build up a fire."

Through introductions, Daisy forced herself to remain calm despite the nervous energy flooding her system. She drew slow breaths through her nose. Focused on the unusual pattern in the crocheted blanket covering Petra: the skill in the knots, the way the colors blended from blue to yellow to red and back again, the strength and softness of the wool.

Any other time she would have engaged Fru Peterson in a conversation about her handicrafts, pestered her for advice on how to get that beautiful floral design at the edges. She would have admired the woman's skill and shown off the half-finished sweater she was knitting for her youngest grandchild that now sat at the bottom of her trunk.

As Fru Peterson stripped Petra of her coat and shoes, she scattered the children with orders to gather up lamps from the bedrooms and bring them to her while inviting her guests to wait in the parlor. She tried to shove Daisy toward the door, but she planted herself like a tree and refused to budge. "Miss Kristiansen's in my charge. I'll stay."

Fru Peterson nodded even as she moved around the room, gathering supplies, putting a kettle on the hob, ordering the children one by one to set the lamps close so she could see as she knelt beside Petra, examining the girl slowly and thoroughly from the gray cast to her features, the cuts on her arms to the bruises on her ribs and the way her right ankle swelled.

"She needs a doctor," Daisy urged. "Or maybe the Red Cross hospital in Elverum?"

Fru Peterson shook her head as she cleaned each cut with antiseptic. "We've no phone to summon a doctor even if he agreed to come this far, and the roads are dangerous." She settled a blanket over Petra, who by now was waxen and pale, her skin damp with sweat.

Petra jerked and tried to sit up, her eyes shocked open as she took a gasping breath. "The codebook," she declared in a rush of English and Norwegian as she fought to sit up. "Is it safe?"

"Easy, little one." Fru Peterson eased her back onto the cushioned bench. "You've been in a bad accident. You need to rest."

"It must be made safe."

Fru Peterson shot Daisy an aggrieved look. She, in turn, gestured toward Mr. Whitney. "Make sure the luggage is brought in from the car. Take special care of my traveling case."

"Ma'am?"

"Just do it."

She knew she was being high-handed, but right now dancing around Mr. Whitney's sensibilities was beyond her.

A blast of cold air stung Daisy's cheeks as the door opened again on the farmer and the lieutenant, stamping the snow off their boots, dusting the ice from their hair. "There are fires to the south and west. Elverum is burning."

"Dear God, preserve us." Fru Peterson crossed herself while her children watched from doorways and the top of the narrow stairs.

"It's not safe to travel any farther tonight," the lieutenant said, reverting to English, his hair glittering with melted ice and his face shadowed by worry. "Peterson has offered to let us sleep here. We can head out in the morning and hope to catch up with . . . with our friend."

"If he's still alive," Mr. Whitney muttered.

"Of course he is, and that's the last I want to hear of such defeatist talk," Daisy fumed.

Fru Peterson gave her an odd glance, making Daisy wonder how much English she understood. "Tore," their hostess said to the oldest boy, dark of hair and eye like his mother. "Settle our guests. I will stay with the girl for now." She gave an impatient jerk of her chin toward Daisy. "Go with my daughter. Lillie will see to that cut on your cheek."

"I have a cut?" For the first time, Daisy noticed the sting where a splinter had slashed her cheek. She touched her face, fingers coming away red and bright with blood. "It all happened so fast."

Their eyes locked, Daisy seeing the same weary resignation she felt weighing down her own body, aching in places she couldn't blame on the blast.

Fru Peterson nodded. "So it did."

CLEO SHIFTED HER hips to the left, her arm to the right. She pushed a second cushion beneath her head, but there was no getting comfortable on the lumpy couch. Not that it would have helped. Sleep was impossible tonight, even without Mr. Whitney's snoring. Every time she closed her eyes, the flicker of flames danced across her lids and memories of Poland chattered to life like a movie house film reel, playing over and over in her head.

Micky, wrapping her in blankets and tucking a hot water bottle beside her. Teasing her about wearing her necklace to bed under her flannel pajamas. She'd not wanted him to leave, but he'd been insistent. An important meeting, he'd said, giving her a kiss on her feverish forehead. "Mrs. Nowak will check in on you."

If she'd known it was the last thing he'd say to her, she might have pushed him for something more profound.

She'd been ~~woken~~ AWAKENED by the shake of the building and the clang of fire engines passing in the street. Mrs. Nowak had brought the news along with a bowl of soup and crusty bread warm from her bakery ovens. The Black Cat was gone, destroyed in a blast that some blamed on a gas leak and others on sabotage. When Micky wasn't home by midnight, Cleo grew worried. When he didn't turn up at all the next day, she started asking around. Could he be one of the nearly two dozen dead in the explosion? No one could say for certain, but after two days of silence and gallons of tears, she'd finally come to believe it.

Then his letter arrived.

Since then she hadn't known what to believe.

She still didn't.

Could Aunt Daisy be right? Could Micky have done something that brought him to the attention of the SS? He was a musician, not a spy or a soldier. She tried shuffling the pieces, looking at the clues from different angles, but the questions remained the same. The memories rewound. The film started again. No matter how many times the images slid past, she couldn't change what happened and she couldn't come up with an answer that made sense.

She finally gave up trying, opening her eyes on the beamed

ceiling of the farmhouse. Her hands trembled, and there was a knot in her stomach, the same one she'd carried with her since that night. Most of the time she ignored it. Not tonight. Not with Petra lying injured in the next room. Tonight it squirmed like a living thing, threatening to climb its way back up her throat.

Mr. Whitney remained a lump in the corner, but Bayard's chair was empty. Through the parlor's curtains, she saw a figure bundled in coat and scarf by the farmyard pump. She rose quietly, pulling on her coat as she let herself out of the house.

Bayard looked up at her approach. "You should be asleep."

"So should you," she replied, the cold air burning in her lungs, "but if your chair is as uncomfortable as that torture device they call a couch, I can understand why you're not."

"Whitney's snoring doesn't help." He tried to spin it as a joke, but neither of them laughed.

"Speaking of Mr. Whitney, what do you know about him?"

"Not much," Bayard answered. "He's a vice consul. A State Department fossil. Bleeds ink. Guards his little consulate fiefdom like a junkyard dog. Why?"

"No reason." She ignored the question in his gaze by asking one of her own. "This is going to sound crazy, but could you teach me how to shoot?"

"A gun? You're right. It's crazy."

"I'm tired of being powerless. Of being the victim and at the mercy of others."

"That's what Petra's sister said—or as good as." She couldn't see his face, but his tone was as brittle as the ice on a nearby pail.

"Her sister?"

"Sofia Kristiansen. She's a doctor at a clinic near Dombås. She couldn't get through to Petra so she sent word by me that she was leaving her job to join the army. She said she couldn't sit by while her country was being attacked."

"That was why Petra was so upset this morning."

"Her parents are cut off in Narvik. Her brother's somewhere at sea. And now Sofia's running off into who knows what. Petra's worried sick about them. Ironic, isn't it? Here she's the one fighting for her life." He fumbled for a cigarette, lighting it with shaking hands. For the briefest of moments, there was something in his hollow gaze that made her insides sit up and take notice.

She shook it off, but the dirty feeling of betrayal remained. "I'd best get back inside before I catch pneumonia. Good night, Lieutenant."

He grabbed her wrist as she turned to go. She could feel the warmth in his fingertips, the strength in his grip. See the flecks in his eyes like steel splinters and the way his expression shifted ever so slightly. "I'll teach you if that's what you really want."

She stepped away, and his hand dropped to his side. He drew a breath that held nothing but regret before letting her go.

Dear Anne,

My secretary has been wounded. We're taking shelter with a very kind family whose farm lies just off the main road. The Petersons are the epitome of Norwegian hospitality paired with a spirit of practicality, and I have no doubt that poor dear Petra is in the most capable of hands, but I can't help questioning my decision to follow the government rather than staying to nurse her . . .

"THE CAR'S READY, ma'am," Mr. Whitney said, his somber visage made even more morose by the salt-and-pepper stubble graying his square bulldog jaw and the bags under his eyes. Like all of them, he'd slept in his clothes, giving him a raffish air of morning-after dissolution.

"All the luggage stowed safely?"

"Yes, ma'am."

"Has Mr. Peterson found a way through that doesn't involve abandoning the Ford for horse-drawn sledges?" Daisy broke the icicles at the farmyard pump with a bang of her hand before brushing her teeth. She knew her own appearance was less than pristine—it would take an army of maids to get the wrinkles out of her suit—but she would at least greet the day with fresh breath and every hairpin in place.

"He thinks so. But we need to get on the road as soon as possible." He checked his watch. "As in now."

"What about Miss Kristiansen?" Bayard asked when told of the plan. "Do we just leave her behind?"

If Mr. Whitney was somber, the lieutenant was downright dismal. Daisy didn't blame the poor man. She felt equally disconsolate, but she'd spent half the night spinning over possibilities in her head. None of them were winners. Only one made sense.

"I understand your concern, Lieutenant, and I respect you for it. I feel the same. But our mission is clear, and I need you beside me to carry it out. I've left the number for Ambassador Sterling in Stockholm, where they can send word. When she's well enough to travel, we'll arrange her passage over the border into Sweden."

"And if the borders become impassible?"

That had been one of the possibilities that had kept Daisy awake and she'd come up with no solutions. If the Germans were successful in closing the borders, Petra would be trapped. Their only hope was that the Norwegians would overcome their initial disorganization to rally. But that was a thin hope with each fleet of bombers that passed overhead. His Majesty had declined the Germans' offer of a negotiated peace. They had answered by doubling their efforts to subdue Norway by force, pouring troops and machinery into the country.

"I'll stay with her, Aunt Daisy," Cleo offered.

Daisy took a breath and counted to ten before she spoke. "Impossible."

"Why? You need Lieutenant Bayard and Mr. Whitney. I'm just a passenger, one you didn't even expect. I can stay with Petra, and when she's better, we can travel on to Stockholm together."

"And your travel papers? They'll never let you across the border without them."

She patted her coat. "Safe and sound."

"Why am I still not filled with confidence?" Daisy pulled on her gloves. "I promised your mother I'd look after you, Clementine."

Barely a ripple on the surface, but Daisy saw the shadow pass over her features, the dark entering her gaze. "I can do this. Let me do this." After a moment, she added, "What if it was Phyllis? You'd want someone you could trust to stay with her."

Bringing up Daisy's granddaughter was hitting below the belt. Just the sort of sucker punch she'd begun expecting of Cleo, who didn't miss a trick when it came to getting what she wanted. "I think you know the answer to that question very well, which is why you asked it."

"Ma'am?" Mr. Whitney urged. "We need to be on the road now if we're going to make Nybergsund."

A sense of inevitability took over. Daisy's choices taken away one by one. She expected a glimmer of triumph, but Cleo's features were pensive rather than triumphant.

"Right. But as soon as Miss Kristiansen can travel, you need to leave. No dallying. Once there, go immediately to the American legation and ask for Mr. Sterling."

"Where will you be?"

"That remains to be seen." When Cleo frowned, Daisy tried to cheer her up with a confident smile. "Buck up, my dear. I'm an old campaigner. This isn't my first war, remember." Mr. Whitney held the car door for her. "You're sure we have everything?" she asked as she settled herself against the seat.

"Yes, ma'am. Every box, case, file, and report. Even a typewriter, though I don't see any of us using it between here and Nybergsund."

"Maybe in a pinch we can throw it at the enemy."

"Enemy, ma'am? I believe America's official stance remains one of neutrality."

"My secretary is injured, and I've been dodging bombs for the last twenty-four hours—not exactly the actions of friends," she snapped, realizing by the cunning glint in Mr. Whitney's eyes that she'd been goaded into a loss of temper.

Lieutenant Bayard cleared his throat, and she submitted to his subtle command to shut her mouth before she said something she shouldn't.

Strapped into his skis, Mr. Peterson waited at the head of the lane to guide them through the maze of barricades and roadblocks while the rest of his family offered their farewells and best wishes. Daisy tried not to worry over what might happen to them. Her burden was already greater than she wished. She forced herself to keep her eyes on the road and the days ahead. But the thought still intruded: she was too old for this.

Adventure, indeed.

CHAPTER 12

Dear Anne,

I've written pages describing my days and been remiss in never once asking about yours. AM says your health is still up and down. I know how you hate to be dictated to, but please listen to the doctor's advice. Despite all our efforts, this war in Europe will be worse than the last. We'll need as many of the old guard as we can muster to build a new and stronger army of heroines to face what's coming . . .

The road ran alongside the ice-covered Glomma River. Smoke rose from small farms nestled into the hills. A herd of shaggy cows huddled under a stand of birch trees. They met no traffic and, other than the smoke, there was no sign of life. Curtains were drawn. Yards were empty. A tractor stood snow-covered in a barnyard. It was as if the population of this little valley had simply vanished.

"It's damned eerie is what it is," Mr. Whitney muttered under his breath as he gripped the wheel while Bayard scanned the skies for planes. Twice now, they'd stopped the car at the sound of engines, a shadow of black crosses sliding over the snow. Daisy felt them along her bones and in her jaw like a dentist's drill.

If she closed her eyes, she was back in France—dashing along sodden roadways under splintered trees, past scarred and crumbled villages on her way to the French headquarters at Senlis through Château-Thierry and Belleau Wood, Rheims and Compiègne. But she *wasn't* in France. And this *wasn't* the last war. It was a disastrous new one, a scar barely healed over and now ripped open once again.

The Norwegians had set up their blockade at the perfect spot. Ribbons of barbed wire wrapped a stockade of newly cut logs stretching from a steep wooded hillside to the icy banks of the river. The soldiers who waved them to a stop were all painfully young, and all of them eager for any news she could give. They crowded around the car, rifles slung over broad shoulders, faces ruddy and wind-chapped, bright against the white of the uniforms.

Was it true three busloads of German soldiers had been driven over a cliff when their Norwegian drivers chose death over collaboration?

Had the king and Crown Prince Olav really hidden in the woods during a German air attack on their hotel?

Did the government really send military call-up notices through the mail?

Rumor and fact mingled, a painful reminder of the confusion sown by the Germans' rapid advance. Daisy had no answers to give, though she hated admitting it.

"We need to pass," Daisy said after explaining their situation.

An enormous oak tree of a man sporting a thick yellow beard stepped forward. He studied the Ford, the hillside, the river. Daisy could almost see the calculations going on behind his bright turquoise eyes. At last, he nodded. "Do you trust me?"

An odd question, but what choice did she have? "Implicitly."

His teeth gleamed from deep within his frosty facial hair before he turned to shout orders to his men. It took a moment for Daisy to comprehend the enormity of her trust.

The officer—Myre, his name turned out to be—beckoned her to follow, his hands in their gloves as large as dinner plates. "This way."

Together, they descended the hillside one treacherous step at a time. Along the edge of the river, the surface was frozen. Farther out, the current churned with ice floes and a flotsam of rotted logs and splintered branches.

Mr. Whitney and Lieutenant Bayard skirted the riverbank. She shuffled after them, Myre's meaty arm keeping her steady. That was when she heard the familiar roar of planes. She froze, feeling the push of adrenaline through her veins but no panic.

The noise grew louder, the sound drowning out the shouts of the soldiers slowly maneuvering the Ford down the hill.

"Almost there. One step at a time." The words, deeper in tone than even the planes' growl of engines, acted like a balm to her bruised eardrums. She gave a grim smile and allowed Myre to practically carry her around the barricade and back to the road.

The planes passed, one waggling his wings, but none of them made any move to attack. Were they headed to Nybergsund? Had the king's defiance put a bull's-eye on his back? Had the Germans decided it was preferable to kill a king they couldn't coerce?

She held her breath as the team of soldiers eased the Ford along the river's edge, the ice groaning and creaking under its weight.

"You are lucky it has been a cold winter," Myre remarked as the men, with much shouting and gesturing, hoisted and shoved the car back up the hill to the road on the far side of the barricade and began removing the chains from the tires.

An odd sort of luck, but true nonetheless.

The sun glittered over the snow, but the air was icy and carried a promise of a storm to come. A snow that would close roads, ground planes, snap telegraph and telephone wires. Slow the enemy. *Play to the Norwegians' strengths*, she thought as she glanced at the nearby line of skis sticking upright out of a snowbank.

"Be careful," he warned. "Word is that the bridge this side of Nybergsund has been bombed and the town is under attack. We are hoping for a British counterattack to relieve the pressure on our cities, but we have heard nothing."

There was a challenge in his gaze. Daisy felt scoured as if by an arctic wind. But since parting ways with Cecil Dormer and his wife in Elverum, she was as in the dark about British intentions as he was. "Is there anything I can do for you or your men to thank you for your help?" she asked.

"Could you get word to my wife in Oslo? Her name is Anna. If you could let her know I am alive and safe. There wasn't time before, you see."

Daisy started to prevaricate when she caught the desperate hope in his face. "I'll see she gets word of your situation."

He quickly found pencil and paper and scratched her address and phone number down.

Mr. Whitney leaned on the horn, chivying her along like a mother hen with a wayward chick. She frowned at the presumption and turned back to address her furry knight in shining armor, but he and his men had already slipped away, the trails of their skis disappearing into the trees.

THE LITTLE GIRL pointed to a chair.

"*Stol*," Cleo answered.

The girl pointed to an oil portrait of two grim elders hanging on the wall.

"*Bilde*."

A table.

"*Bord*. Come on, something hard."

The girl sighed as she kicked at the legs of her stool. At last, she said, "*Jeg er lei av å lære deg. Jeg skal leke med kattungen min. Ha det.*" Then hopped off the stool and headed for the door without a backward glance.

"Wait a minute," Cleo complained. "I got *goodbye*, but the rest of what you said whizzed right over my head"—the door closed, leaving her talking to herself—"*and* she's off."

There was a muffled groan of pain quickly stifled. "She said she's bored with teaching you and wants to play with her kitten." The words were as raspy as dried leaves, but Cleo had never heard anything so beautiful in her life.

"Petra? You're awake!" She slid off the kitchen table and flung open the door the youngest Peterson had just closed. "Fru Peterson! She's awake," she shouted before turning back to Petra, whose eyes remained bleary and half closed, bruised hollows within a face white as chalk. "Golly, you had us worried. Can I fix your pillow? Are you warm enough? Maybe a glass of water?"

Petra closed her eyes. "You can stop shouting. My head feels like a soft-boiled egg."

Fru Peterson bustled in to fix a deliciously smelling bowl of something from the stove, which she tried offering Petra. "I'm sorry. I am not very hungry."

Fru Peterson reluctantly set the bowl to the side with a frown. "My husband will be here soon with the doctor and have you up on your feet in no time."

Cleo caught a hint of something in the woman's gaze that worried her. "Can you come with me, ma'am? There's something in the parlor I want to show you," she said with a pointed look.

Out of earshot, Cleo practically pinned Fru Peterson against the wall. "Why would you say that about the doctor when we know Elverum's been bombed to smithereens and the hospital, if it's still standing, will be overrun with wounded?"

"Because in her case, hope is the only medicine I can offer."

Fru Peterson's expression frightened Cleo. She slid a hand across a chair back before gripping it tight to stop the downward spin of her fear. If she didn't acknowledge it, it wasn't real. "Tell me the truth—how long until you think Miss Kristiansen will be well enough to travel?"

Fru Peterson glanced over her shoulder to the kitchen. "I don't know."

Cleo tiptoed back in to find Petra lying quietly, her eyes closed. Her hair was fanned out on her pillow and her hands were crossed over her chest. Like a corpse ready for burial. Cleo touched her shoulder, praying she wouldn't be cold. Petra's eyes flew open, her pupils dilated, giving her gaze an oddly haunted look in her gray face.

Cleo exhaled on a muttered curse. "I thought you were dead."

A smile tipped Petra's mouth. "Not yet."

Cleo pulled up a chair. "Come on, then. Eat up. Fru Peterson says this is the best thing for invalids. Puts hair on your chest."

"Are you never serious?"

"You'd be surprised how serious I can get, but humor staves off the panic—usually."

"Is there a reason to panic?"

"Says the woman who was blown up."

Petra consented to a sip of the broth, but her heart clearly wasn't in it. "You know what I would love right now? Cloudberries."

"Sounds like something out of a child's story."

"They grow in the wild. We go out every August and pick them. We have a spot that only our family knows about. My father guards it like a state secret. Mother makes jam with what we don't eat straight off the stem." After a few bites, Petra pushed away the bowl. "I can't eat any more."

"You've barely eaten enough for a bird, but I'll let you sleep."

"No." Petra grabbed Cleo's wrist, her grip frighteningly weak.

"Please stay. I do not want to sleep anymore. Not yet. I can continue your lessons."

"You'll soon be as bored as Katye Peterson."

"I'll risk it."

"Now you're laughing at me."

"As you say, humor staves off the panic." As if she'd said more than she wished, Petra fell silent, fiddling with a loose thread on her quilt. But only for a moment before she composed herself, courage locked into place. "I am surprised you would be interested in learning Norwegian."

"I figure it's good to know more than *yes*, *no*, and *thank you*."

"I have heard you speak—and listen," Petra replied. "You know far more than that."

Cleo leaned close. "Don't tell Katye. She'll realize I'm not a prodigy."

"But you have other languages. I have heard you."

"I've always felt it was good to know what people are saying about you in as many languages as possible."

"I expect that made it easier to search for Mr. Kominski."

"Easier to ask the questions, but the answers didn't come, no matter what language I spoke. They still haven't."

"Do you believe he is still alive?"

In the early days, Cleo would have answered immediately and with certainty. She'd have shoved aside her doubts as useless and unhelpful. But now, how to answer Petra? Once she could have sworn she'd sensed his presence, that she had only to close her eyes and he was there. She had only to follow that feeling like an unspooling thread and he would be there at the end of it. She'd not had that feeling in weeks. When she closed her eyes, there was only the roar of flames and a fading voice on the wind. Did that mean he was dead? Or did that mean the doubts had won, and she was giving up?

"I don't know what to believe anymore" was Cleo's answer. "The more I go over my time with Micky, the less I feel I really knew him. Maybe if I had a photograph to remind me, but all I have left is this necklace he bought me for Christmas." She ran a finger over the cheap pink costume diamond nested within its encircling faux-ruby setting. She smiled when she saw Petra's distaste. "It's hideous, I know. But he was so proud when he gave it to me. All smiles and excitement. How can I get rid of it?"

"It is hard to lose the people we love."

"Bayard told me about your sister."

"Sofia has always been the brave one, the strong one. If she decides she wants it, there's no stopping her." Petra's eyes fluttered closed, her breathing shallow and even, her last words barely more than a whisper. "Like someone else I know."

Dear Anne,

Forty miles has turned into what feels like four hundred as we seek to reach the village of Nybergsund. I'm reminded of the last time I felt as if a vast conspiracy of diplomacy was ranged against me— 1919 Paris as we struggled and fought to birth Wilson's promise of a League of Nations. At least then I was younger, the company was exhilarating, and the dining sublime. Sadly, I can't claim any of those benefits this time around. It's been a packet of crackers, a thermos of weak coffee, and a pair of grumbling men for companions. Their grumbling has not improved despite my attempts to lighten our situation with amusing anecdotes. How can anyone not be cheered by my story of being trapped in a corner table at Henri's and inadvertently eavesdropping on the Prince of Wales's conversation because I was too embarrassed to squeeze past him? You would have laughed, Anne. In fact, I believe you did when I relayed that story to you right after it happened . . .

* * *

DAISY CLOSED HER diary, bookmarking her letter to Anne. She'd no idea when, or indeed if, her letters would get through to her sister-in-law. Would they come to her one at a time in a trickle of overdue mail or all at once in a deluge of airmail envelopes? Either way, the act of writing down her observations and experiences helped to cement them in her own mind. The way Mr. Whitney tapped the steering wheel as he drove, a repetitive Morse code mixture of boredom and frustration. The frequent stops as they were passed from roadblock to roadblock, with little new information to show for it, but a growing list of scribbled names and hasty messages for wives, mothers, and sweethearts.

All is well.

I am safe.

Hope to be home soon.

Every message a pin stuck in a map between Elverum and Nybergsund. But like her letters to Anne, she had no idea when or if they would ever be delivered.

The bearded soldier's warning proved to be inaccurate. The bridge into the village was intact, though the road to either side was churned and cratered, debris filling the icy ditches and scattered over the roadway so that Mr. Whitney had to slow the Ford to avoid damaging the undercarriage. They crept across, every bump causing Daisy to twitch as if the span might collapse under them at any moment, but they made it without mishap and were soon in the village—or what was left of it.

Mr. Whitney flagged down a man sifting through the ruins. Gray dust coated his face and hair, making his age impossible to guess. His coat hung loose, and he wore a pair of slippers as if he'd flung on the first clothes to hand when the bombing started.

Daisy rolled the window down. "Excuse me. We're looking for

someone in charge. I believe members of His Majesty's cabinet arrived in the last day or so."

The man paused, his hand clutching a leather-bound book singed at the edges, the pages glued together in a soggy mess. He eyed the car and the American flag with confusion. "Who are you?"

"This is Mrs. Harriman, the US minister to Norway," Mr. Whitney jumped in before she could answer.

The man combed a hand through his hair before eyeing his fingers as if surprised they were still attached to his hand. "Why should I believe you?"

"Why would we lie?" Mr. Whitney replied, his voice rising as he fought back his irritation. "Who else would be flying the damn Stars and Stripes?"

"Nazis lie. They killed my little girl as she crossed the street here. You could be a Nazi." He turned back to the wreckage of timber and brick. "What danger was she to anybody?"

"Look here . . ."

"Enough, Mr. Whitney." Daisy's tone brooked no argument. She'd not intrude on this father's grief. "We'll find someone else to ask."

They stopped more than once, but no one knew where to find the Norwegian government. No one knew what direction the king and his son had traveled. No one knew who was in charge. Or if they did, they were keeping it close to the vest. Mistrust and skepticism had become the village's watchwords. Best to remain silent. Invisible.

Nybergsund was no more, and its inhabitants, all but ghosts.

Snow had started falling again, and the afternoon light was uncertain. Mr. Whitney started his infernal tapping. "We're not getting anywhere with these people. Maybe we should go west— back the way we came."

"Back to Elverum?" Bayard asked.

"Back to Oslo. We can ask the Germans for safe passage."

"I have a duty to report on the situation," Daisy said. "Washington needs to know what's happening on the ground."

"Fine, but there's nothing to report. And we don't know what's happening." Mr. Whitney's volume rose as his temper frayed. "We can't even get anyone to talk to us."

Daisy could feel Lieutenant Bayard bristling, but Mr. Whitney had a point and a lifetime of serving in diplomatic posts around the world. What were they accomplishing driving in endless circles?

"You know I'm right, Lieutenant." Mr. Whitney pressed his advantage. "Miss Kristiansen's already been hurt. How long do you think an American flag and God's luck will keep us safe?"

"So we just give up and run back to the capital with our tail between our legs?" Bayard fired back.

Daisy intervened before it came to blows. "Enough. Both of you. I can't hear myself think with the bickering."

They mumbled apologies, but it was obvious the argument hadn't ended, merely been put on hold. "We have to face facts, ma'am," Mr. Whitney said, replacing his driver's cap with his vice consul's seniority, wielding the gravitas of a career man who'd studied diplomacy like a science. "The Norwegian government and its royal family have left Nybergsund, and we've no way of following. Our best option is to return to Oslo, where we can regroup and consult with Mr. Cox and the rest of the foreign service officials about our next steps."

Daisy felt herself folding under the logic of his arguments. In Oslo, she might be able to reestablish contact with Washington, Stockholm, and Berlin. She might be able to look upon the situation with more than just rumors to direct her actions. And once she had a grasp of events on the ground, she might have a better view toward her next move.

Might.

She glanced at Lieutenant Bayard, but this was her decision to make.

"It's dangerous out here. We've seen it firsthand," Mr. Whitney added. "Continuing on is risky, with no guarantee of success. No one would blame you for calling it quits and turning back, ma'am."

Wouldn't they? Her insides squirmed just imagining the pitying reactions when she turned up back at the legation. "Thank you for your thorough read of our situation, Mr. Whitney. Now, if you'll just turn the car around, we can get moving."

"Back to Oslo, ma'am?" he asked a little too smugly.

Three roads led out of Nybergsund, any one of which could have been taken by the king and his cabinet. Had he gone north toward Lillehammer and Sjusjøen, where the US legations' families waited in relative safety? East into Sweden? No matter his desperation, His Majesty had made it clear he had no intention of slipping over the border to give the Germans a propaganda win. South? What would be the point? He would be driving straight into the German armies swarming up to press the Norwegian forces against the border.

With no way of knowing where the Norwegian king and cabinet were hiding, she had no way to complete her mission of supplying Washington with information. So, if she couldn't fulfill her duty, perhaps she could fulfill her promise.

"Ma'am?" It was Lieutenant Bayard, his expression concerned as he hunched deeper into his coat.

She smiled, suddenly sure of her decision. "We're going to find the crown princess."

CHAPTER 13

The Petersons' parlor was as hot as an oven, but Petra's features remained blue-tipped, and her teeth chattered as if the cold had seeped into her bones. Cleo fanned herself with an accordioned newspaper dated Monday, April 8—the last normal day in Norway.

How long before this grew to be normal? It hadn't taken them long in Poland. Mere days until one learned to avert one's gaze, ask no questions, and never ever get involved.

That had worked right up until Micky vanished.

"The dog is brown." Despite Fru Peterson's care, Petra's voice was still colored with smoke and pain, as if her lungs had been singed in the blast, and Cleo had to lean close to catch every word.

"*Hunden er brun*," Cleo repeated the phrase in Norwegian.

"Where is the closest train station?"

A little harder. Cleo had to think about it. "*Hvor er . . . hvor er . . . nærmeste . . . togstasjon?*"

Petra's lips curved in a sad Madonna smile. "Your pronunciation is horrible, but you're correct. Now here's a tricky one. *Man skal ikke skue hunden på hårene.*"

Cleo rolled the words back and forth in her brain but came up empty. "Something about dogs, but after that I have no idea."

While everything else about her had grown weaker by the

hour, Petra's gaze remained keen as steel. It zeroed in on Cleo with unerring accuracy until heat warmed her cheeks. "It is an idiom," she explained. "It means, literally, you shouldn't judge the dog by its hairs."

Was this Petra's roundabout way of apologizing? Now Cleo *was* worried. Petra didn't look like someone who second-guessed her decisions very often—if ever. "I'll be sure to remember that one."

Acknowledging Cleo's words with the barest of nods, Petra winced, a flicker of pain passing over her face, eyes squeezed shut.

"We've been at this for over an hour. You should rest."

Petra grew quiet and then silent, her eyes fluttering closed. Her skin shone like pearls, great shadows scraping out the flesh under her eyes, hollowing her throat and shoulders. And there was a finality to her gaze that frightened Cleo.

This fear blossomed into a sudden and overwhelming need to feel cold air on her face and wake up from this growing sense of unreality that made breathing hard and thoughts spin like snow-flakes. She smoothed the quilts over Petra then fled to the farm-yard, ashamed by her cowardice.

The sun reflected off the snow, blinding her as she emerged from the dim, overheated kitchen. She squinted, eyes watering, as she made her way to the shed, where the cows gathered in a jostling, stamping crush at the gate waiting to be fed.

Peterson forked hay over the gate to the herd while one son filled the trough and another dropped fresh straw down from the loft. Both boys were in their teens, square-jawed and earnest like their father, but there was none of the usual banter between sib-lings, no joking or laughter. They went about their work with a sense of resigned inevitability.

She leaned against the gate, rubbing the broad forehead of the closest cow. Raised in the heart of New York City, she'd never been the accomplished equestrian Aunt Daisy was, but Cleo had always enjoyed the peace of the stable, resulting in more than one flustered nursemaid finding her among the animals when her mother's grief and expectations seemed insurmountable. "Is there anything I can do to help?" She rummaged through her recent lessons. "Help you? *Kan jeg hjelpe deg?*"

"I speak English." The older boy handed her the pail. "You can get water for the chickens." He pointed toward the pump just as a thud shook the beams of the loft, followed by the angry crack of a curse. *"Faen i helvete!"*

"Det er nok!" Peterson shouted. "That's enough!" He addressed Cleo with an apologetic shrug of his shoulders. "Forgive my sons for their disrespect. They are desperate to join their friends who have already left to fight. But I need them here, and their mother would be heartbroken."

Her father hadn't been much older than these boys when he exchanged his new marriage for short-lived glory in the skies over France. The junior Petersons, at least, had the excuse that it was their country being overrun. What was her father's reason? Did he care that Mother's heart would break? That his child would never know him as anything other than a portrait on a wall? A name held over her as a threat? A ghost she could never live up to, but could never shake?

Cleo filled the pail with icy water before lugging it across to a pen, where a few hens scraped at the mud while a handsome rooster presided from the door of a coop. One of the younger Peterson children gathered eggs into a basket.

"Frøkken Jaffray! Come! Quickly!" It was Fru Peterson. She flapped her apron like one of her flustered hens.

Cleo dropped her pail and raced for the house.

Petra was sitting up, her face gone from gray to a horrible shade of bruised and dingy purple. She clutched a copy of an Edith

Wharton novel to her chest, her eyes wide and terrified as she fought to catch her breath. Pain was now clear in every brittle movement. "We have to find Madam Minister," she gasped. "This very minute."

Before Cleo could answer or even step farther into the room, Petra gave a strangled sob and collapsed, the book falling to the floor in a spill of pages.

"IT IS MY fault," Petra moaned, her words slurred and thick as if she'd been drinking. "All my fault." She'd been unconscious only for a few minutes, before coming around in a shuddering convulsion of limbs as if fighting to pull back from an invisible brink.

"Easy now." Cleo pressed a cool compress to her forehead. It was all she could think to do, though it seemed completely inadequate to the situation. Like a sticking plaster for a severed limb. "What's all your fault?"

Petra craned her neck from side to side as if checking they were alone, her hands picking at the blankets, her hair, her skin. At last, she pointed to the novel, which sat on the floor at the end of the couch. "It was in my coat pocket."

"What's so important about a copy of *The Buccaneers*?"

"It's not. It's"—she dropped her voice to a whisper—"a State Department codebook. Mrs. Harriman was ordered to guard it with her life, and now it is here—with me." She started shaking again, her jaw clenched so hard, Cleo imagined she could hear teeth cracking under the strain. "It's my fault."

"It'll be all right, Petra. Honest." Cleo hurried to reassure her before Petra's anxiety grew dangerous. Her face was sunken as if being sucked dry by some unseen force, the bones of her skull clear beneath her blue-gray skin. "When we get to Stockholm, we'll turn it in at the legation. No harm done. Just lie back. Take a deep breath. I'll make sure the codebook is returned. Nobody will ever know it was missing. I swear it."

"The word of a grasshopper?" Petra asked with a hint of her old scorn, though the sting was gone.

"We grasshoppers might be flighty, but we're tenacious. Just ask the Egyptians."

Petra smiled. "Not even death stops the jokes."

"Death is the biggest joke of all," Cleo answered simply.

Petra relaxed back into the blankets, eyes closed, and Cleo slipped away to confer with Fru Peterson. She might not be able to make Petra better, but she could make her smile and that would have to be enough.

When Petra woke next, Cleo was waiting with a bowl and spoon. "More soup?"

"Better than soup," Cleo replied. "Taste it."

Petra's face broke into a smile and for a moment a blush of pink colored her gray cheeks. "Cloudberry jam."

"It's store bought, but it's the best I could do in a pinch."

After a few bites, she laid back, her voice drifting. "I guess you bring joy, after all." Cleo thought she'd fallen asleep, but it was only a respite as she regathered her strength. "When I was little, my great-grandmother died." Petra paused, her breathing wet and raspy. "I remember sitting under a table listening as the grown-ups laughed and told stories about her, the sillier the better." Her words came slow and barely audible over the frightened pounding of Cleo's heart. "They all left with smiles on their faces. I didn't understand how they could be happy when *I* was so sad."

"My mother told me stories about my father," Cleo said. "In all of them, he was this amazing hero that everyone admired. I started out sad, wishing I knew him so I could tell stories about him too. Later I realized nobody could be that perfect. And I stopped being sad. And I stopped listening to the stories—and my mother."

"You sound like my sister, Sofia. She never listened either. If someone told her to go left, she'd go right just to spite them."

"Where is she now?"

"I wish I knew. She left the hospital where she worked to become a medic for the military."

Cleo took a bite of the jam left in the bowl. It was tart and tingled on her tongue, but there was a grassiness to the aftertaste, a wild flavor she'd never tasted before.

"Will you tell stories about me when I am gone?" Petra asked.

Fear skittered over Cleo's skin like ice. Dread clamped a fist on her shoulders, lead sat in her belly. She dropped the spoon back in the bowl, the jam turning bitter on her tongue. "I won't need to. You'll be there to tell your own story."

Petra fell silent. Her fidgeting ceased. "I do not think I will leave this place."

"Don't be ridiculous." Cleo's panic rose into her chest, up her throat, itching at her scalp, cold and slick. She wanted to run, but her legs wouldn't hold her. "Peterson said the roads are open. We can get you to the hospital in Elverum."

Petra put her hand over Cleo's, willing her to stop speaking. She turned her head to the pillow, and the coming darkness caught in the folds of the drawn curtains. "I'd rather stay here." Her voice was no louder than a sigh, but it seemed to echo in Cleo's head. "This place feels like home."

An hour later, Fru Peterson came in, laundry basket on her hip. "He's putting petrol in the truck now. We'll have her to the hospital in no time."

Cleo's eyes burned, her cheeks wet with tears. "She won't be needing the hospital."

Dear Anne,

We've crossed the border into Sweden. At last, a real bed and a bath-tub of my very own. I'd love nothing better than to wallow in hot water before collapsing into dreamless slumber, but duty calls, and by now, I'm sure Washington is wondering if I'm still alive . . .

THEY LEFT BEHIND the well-armed Swedish troops gathering at the border, their artillery and armored transports holding a tenuous battle line that until a few days ago seemed safe, a backwater that barely needed guarding much less defending. As they bowled through the dark countryside between walls of deep snow, the engine lulled Daisy into a semi-doze where her dreams were filled with the roar of airplane engines and the sing of falling bombs. She jolted awake, stretching to relieve the tension cramping her muscles, the guilt and fear pinching at her chest.

Petra and Cleo would be safe. Of course they would. Safe and well under the care of the kindhearted Petersons. She must remain optimistic. Dwelling on what she couldn't change would only sap her energy for what she could.

She breathed slowly and evenly, focusing on the conversation from the front seat, where Lieutenant Bayard acted as navigator for Mr. Whitney, the two of them speaking quietly about crossroads, turnings, and the safest route up the mountain to Sälen and the hotel recommended by an officious border agent with a thin mustache and a high reedy voice that had made Daisy's head ache.

It was only when they pulled up in front of the handsome Högfjällshotell resort that the dark fears she'd carried with her since Elverum faded under the bright lights spilling out from the hotel's windows to illuminate the wide treeless slopes. If she hadn't spent the last days dodging German bombs, she might have almost believed she was here on a skiing holiday, her cases filled with thick woolen sweaters and stout walking boots rather than the confusion of papers and files and ledgers stuffed into the trunk and piled along the floor under her feet.

As they pulled into the parking lot, the Ford's headlights picked out a man leaning in a doorway smoking a cigarette. Two others hovered in conversation by an enormous sedan, its engine plinking as it cooled. A third group exchanged information like plotters at a coup. Hounds catching a scent, all of them stood straighter, eyes focused on the car and its ragged American flag as it crunched to a stop on the frozen snow.

"Looks like the press got here ahead of us," Mr. Whitney mumbled before stepping out of the car as a hotel porter hurried over to collect the luggage. "Damn parasites."

Once Daisy might have felt unsure facing a phalanx of eager reporters, afraid of speaking out of turn or stepping on diplomatic toes, but the last few years had supplied her with a steady faith in her abilities. She'd come to enjoy the journalists and broadcasters who'd attended her dinners in Oslo—their clever conversation, their honest unfiltered opinions, their insight into global politics usually as prescient as any State Department official. They were a good source of information and, in many cases, a good source of fun.

"We all have our jobs to do," she said, climbing creakily to her feet before turning on her well-rehearsed minister's persona like a flashlight against the gloom. "The trick is to learn more from them than they learn from us."

The reporters started forward, but before they could get a word out, Bayard stepped in front of Daisy with an arm extended like a Princeton running back. "A few minutes before the inquisition, fellas. It's been a long three days."

They fell back, but Daisy could sense their curiosity and their eagerness. What had she seen? What did she know? What might she let slip that their readers and listeners could gobble up with their cornflakes and coffee? She'd be happy to indulge them, but right now she wanted a bath, a bite to eat, and a bed—in that order.

The hotel was crowded, the usual wealthy guests and Swedish nobility exchanged for displaced diplomats and government officials from half a dozen countries. There were hugs and shouts of greeting and relief every time the doors swung open. Britain's Sir Cecil Dormer and his wife, Lady Mary, were safely ensconced in the lobby bar; Poland's minister to Norway, Mr. Neumann, passed Daisy at the elevator; and the irrepressible French foreign minister's wife, Madame de Dampierre, had commandeered a radio in one of the lounges and was practically leaning an ear to the speaker in her search for the latest news.

"Mrs. Harriman?" Lieutenant Bayard caught her in the upstairs corridor, already fitting her key into the lock. "The switchboard has the legation in Stockholm on the line. The ambassador is anxious to speak with you. There's a secure line in the hotel manager's office."

She shoved the key into her coat pocket, bidding a regretful farewell to any chance of a rest.

On the phone, Freddie Sterling breathed a huge sigh of relief. "We've been worried sick, Daisy. Three days and not a peep out of you."

"I've been rather preoccupied trying not to be blown to smithereens. Speaking of which, any word on His Majesty and the crown prince? Are they safe?"

"Our guess is as good as yours. The Norwegians aren't talking, which makes sense when they can't be sure who else might be listening. But we've heard the crown princess and her family are safe in Sweden—for now."

Safe and staying in the same hotel, according to a harried front desk clerk who imparted the information at the same time he apologized to Daisy for the overtaxed plumbing system and arranged for supper to be sent up to her room. Sterling satisfied for the minute, Daisy started once more for the elevator. This time she was interrupted by a shout and a hand on her sleeve.

"Mrs. Harriman, Arthur Menken of the United Press." He flashed his press card before maneuvering her toward the bar with the prowess of a lion singling out a wounded gazelle. "A word if you don't mind . . ."

Another gentleman, this one thirtyish with knife-edged cheekbones and dripping in cologne, joined them before Menken could move in for the kill. "We've heard rumors of your amazing journey," he flattered in rapid-fire French, "and would love to interview you for *Paris Soir*."

Exhaustion dogged Daisy, but there was also a restlessness after her conversation with the US ambassador to Sweden. A need to be doing something, moving forward, making plans. It took her like that sometimes, this odd eagerness. Her late husband, Bordie, had often witnessed her single-mindedness, and while he might not have always understood it, he didn't stand in her way when the feeling took hold.

"Gentlemen, I'm flattered at the attention and would certainly welcome a drink if you're offering." From the edge of the crowd, Lieutenant Bayard cut toward them, his shoulders squared as his jaw. She held him off with a look as she settled herself between the two reporters, a finger of whiskey materializing like magic in front of her. She raised the glass to her lips with a cool smile. "I'll be happy to answer all your questions, but first I have some questions for *you*."

Daisy allowed them an hour of her time before pushing back her chair. "And there you have it, gentlemen. I expect you have deadlines to make. And I have a bed calling my name. I'm sure I'll see you in the morning."

They rose when she did, seeing her off with murmured ac-
knowledgments, but she knew as soon as her back was turned
they'd be scrambling for the phones, shouting down the miles
in hopes of being the first to scoop the world. Lieutenant Bayard
escorted her to her room like some sort of unofficial bodyguard.
Kind, but hardly necessary. He hovered as she slid the key into
her lock, pushed open the door, and switched on the lamp. There
was a manner to his presence as if he wanted to speak but couldn't
find the words. He didn't need to. She felt the same, but sharing
their worry wouldn't ease it, and she'd not seen a real bed in days.
There would be time for confidences tomorrow.

"Sleep well, Lieutenant." A wish? A command? He nodded as
she closed the door, immediately feeling the slump in her shoulders slide into her waist and down into her ankles.

The duvet was thick as frosting on a cake and there were four
snowy white pillows. The radiator creaked with sauna heat and the
room's carpeting was thick enough to dig her toes into as she peeled
herself out of her clothes and sponged off in the sink while she waited
for the bath to fill. Her cases had been brought up earlier and were
now lined up neatly in a row under the window. It was only as she
rummaged through her overnight case for her cold cream that her
heart slid up into her throat. Where was the codebook?

She sank onto the bed, her belly in knots, trying to recall when
she'd seen it last. Petra had been using it at the guesthouse. Daisy
remembered distinctly seeing it on the table beside her just before
the air attack that sent them running into the yard. Had she seen
it since? She squeezed her eyes shut in hopes of jogging some flash
of memory. She paced the room, retracing each step and each
minute over the last frantic days, but it was useless.

The case was here.

The codebook was not.

CHAPTER 14

Dear Anne,

Our mountaintop hotel has taken on the aspect of a country house party. Friends flung together by circumstance making the best of it as we jolly each other along. Even at my age and with all I've seen in my life, I remain amazed by the resilience of the human spirit and its ability to find the light, even in the midst of tragedy.

After twelve hours of blissful, uninterrupted sleep, Daisy woke with gritty eyes and swollen ankles, but these were nothing compared to the weight pressing her into the mattress like an anchor. She toyed with the idea of staying in bed, playing sick like a child avoiding a test, but it was a thought she abandoned almost as soon as it surfaced. Hiding would get her nowhere, and she hated the idea of anyone thinking she was infirm or needed coddling. Instead she rose and dressed for breakfast, ticking over her options like checking off a bulleted list—item by item, idea by idea.

One: Return to the Petersons? Out of the question. Bayard would wonder why on earth she'd come all this way only to re-trace her steps, and now that she was here, any hasty departure would bring unwanted scrutiny.

Two: Inform Lieutenant Bayard? No. At least, not yet. Not until she'd heard from Petra or Cleo. Hopefully the pair were already on their way to Stockholm. If they were lucky, they might even be there by tonight and that blasted codebook with them. Besides, the lieutenant had enough on his plate. She'd not add to his load until it was necessary.

Three: Admit her failure to Freddie Sterling when she spoke with him next and ask for his advice? He was always so helpful and infinitely patient, but widening the circle of accomplices only shared the trouble. It wasn't his problem to solve.

By the time Bayard knocked on her door to escort her to breakfast, she was no nearer to a solution, but her usual optimism allowed her to greet him with a bland smile of welcome that hid a multitude of sins. Breakfast further restored her confidence, the babble of various languages strangely soothing to her troubled conscience. Downstairs, Madame de Dampierre was back at her radio, King Haakon's voice acting to quiet the crowded room. Even for those who didn't understand Norwegian, the gravity of the words was evident. "Our position is such that today I cannot inform you where in Norway I myself, the crown prince, and the government reside . . . We commemorate those who gave their lives for our fatherland . . . God save Norway."

A chorus of the Norwegian national anthem rose over the clink of cutlery and the bang of waiters' trays. Daisy felt her cheeks ache and a lump clog her throat. Thank heavens for the lively French countess. She abandoned her radio to join Daisy, exclaiming over the deliciously outrageous rumors of a Norwegian plot to sneak their gold reserves out of the country under the very nose of the Germans in a scheme that sounded like something out of a spy novel. Daisy found herself laughing right along with her, never letting on she'd had these rumors confirmed as truth last night along with even more outlandish tales of near-death escapes, courageous acts of valor, and heroic stands against overwhelming odds.

The madame's eyes twinkled with laughter. "I feel almost as if we are in one of these ridiculous Warner Brothers movies with car chases and twirling mustaches." Conversation dipped as the crown princess passed through the dining room. "And imperiled heroines, of course," Madame de Dampierre added under her breath.

Daisy excused herself and followed Her Royal Highness outside, shivering as she closed the terrace doors behind her. The Alpine air was damp. Steel-gray clouds clung to the mountains, obscuring distances and muffling sound, giving them the sensation of having left the outside world and its troubles behind. It took only a glance at the solitary woman striding the shoveled paths to realize not everyone shared her impression.

Misfortune breeds isolation. People don't know what to say, how to behave. Daisy had seen it in the long years of Bordie's protracted illness and then after his death. Friends, awkward and unsure of their footing, used distance to mask discomfort. Bordie's sister Anne was one of the few who'd remained steadfast. This kindness endeared her to Daisy, cementing their friendship in the way only shared hardship can.

Did Her Royal Highness have such a friend?

If she did, she wasn't close to hand.

Daisy was. She would do what she could.

Despite the temperature, the crown princess wore no gloves or scarf, and her coat was thin, fashionable rather than utilitarian. "Your Royal Highness, I hope you don't mind my intrusion, but are you quite warm enough?" A brisk tone, a mother chiding her chick. Normally she'd not have dared, but sometimes it paid to cut through the niceties and get straight to the point. "Perhaps we should return to the hotel for a nice hot cup of coffee."

The crown princess had been staring up at the broad, treeless rise of the mountain, a small frown wrinkling her brow as if she was contemplating whether to strike out for the summit, but by the time Daisy caught up, her face was as smooth as new plaster.

"We were guests here just a few years ago, did you know that?" Daisy knew that enigmatic expression. She'd applied it just this morning. The world would see only what was allowed, nothing more. "During the day, we hiked and skied, and in the evening, we danced and drank and ate. It was glorious." The crown princess worked at a spot on her coat's cuff, back and forth in a small, nervous gesture. "Everything has changed now, all but the mountain. The mountain is exactly the same. As it will be a hundred, a thousand years from now." For the first time, she met Daisy's gaze, her eyes unreadable in the dim morning light. "That's a reassuring thought."

Daisy let her talk. Maybe that's all she needed, someone to offer her an ear to bend as she worked through the last few chaotic days. "You must think I'm mad nattering away about nothing."

"I think you're brave," Daisy replied. "You and the children."

"They are the only reason I agreed to leave Norway. If it had been me alone, I would not have been swayed so easily."

The weapon used against women since the dawn of time. Conditioned from birth to see motherhood as a sacred vocation, any woman who dared put her own desires first was considered unnatural and lacking in proper humanity. Men, on the other hand, valued rugged words like *freedom, independence, individualism*. Daisy had been fortunate in having both a husband who took pride in her ambitions and the wealth and station that allowed her to step into public spaces where most women were excluded. The crown princess's plight reminded her that even women moving in the highest circles could still be tethered by expectation and love.

"The Germans nearly had them at Nybergsund. Did you know?" Her Royal Highness continued. "They escaped and hid in the woods while bombers destroyed the village. They're being hunted, driven north like game before the hunters' guns."

Daisy could see the willpower it took for the princess to stand here quietly in the snow while her husband and father-in-law remained back in Norway. She was a person of action, much like Daisy herself. Sitting and waiting was anathema. She needed to be active, in control.

"They know the country as the Germans can't. And they have their countrymen to protect them."

"That's what my mother says."

"Princess Ingeborg is here?"

"She arrived a few days ago. We will be traveling on with her to Stockholm and staying with them until events allow us to rejoin His Royal Highness the crown prince."

Until, not if.

She turned back to the mountain in obvious dismissal, leaving Daisy to pick her way back over the uneven ground to the hotel's terrace, slowing to nod to the fashionable woman bundled in fur and pearls smoking a cigarette out of the cold when she suddenly recognized her as Princess Ingeborg—sister to King Haakon of Norway and King Christian of Denmark, sister-in-law to King Gustaf of Sweden, and Crown Princess Märtha's mother. Daisy had seen her only a few months earlier, but the current crisis had flattened her fine-boned features like soft wax, loss and grief for her scattered family swimming in her gaze.

"Mrs. Harriman," she said with a gracious acknowledgment of recognition, "do I look a hundred years older than I did before? One brother who has lost his country, the country of my birth. Another hunted like a wild animal. I'm not sure who my daughter is angrier with right now—the Germans or her father-in-law." She stared out at the crown princess, who remained frozen beneath the pines with her unseeing eyes fixed upon the rocky, rising ground.

"It will go better for her once she and the children are settled with you in Stockholm."

Lines pinched at Princess Ingeborg's drawn features. "Let's hope Sweden remains the refuge she's expecting it to be."

Daisy left the woman and returned to the hotel, suddenly anxious to pen a quick reassuring letter to her daughter, Ethel. Lieutenant Bayard intercepted her inside, looking scrubbed and official. "Ma'am . . . a moment?"

Her traitorous stomach clenched in anticipation. Had he discovered her blunder over the missing codebook? Was there news of Petra and Cleo? "Something the matter, Lieutenant?"

"We've had word from the legation wives back in Norway."

Dear Anne,

I've tried to imagine what Mrs. Cox and the other wives are going through. This unsettled lack of information is unbearable for me; how much more so for the families of my legation staff, who don't have my sources to fall back on?

"Captain Hagan tried to get through to Sjusjøen, where our families are staying, but he couldn't make it due to heavy snows." Lieutenant Bayard filled Daisy in over drinks in the hotel's lounge. She stuck with coffee but she understood the lieutenant's indulgence in an early scotch.

"They're safe?"

"For now, ma'am, but events on the ground are changing hourly. There's no telling how long before operations make their escape impossible."

Here was her chance to turn her doubts into practical action.

"The Norwegians are near Lillehammer. We can join them there, and hope the roads north are clear. I'll pack immediately. Inform Mr. Whitney we'll leave within the hour."

She didn't wait for his response. She'd learned early that waiting for permission got one nowhere. Better to behave as if the path was laid, the blessings bestowed. First with her family and then Bordie. Later, as her horizons expanded into government with her appointment to the federal Commission on Industrial Relations, it took boldness to be heard, confidence to be listened to, and a well-developed sense of humor to laugh off the slings and arrows that would inevitably follow.

It was only as the lieutenant departed to make arrangements that she realized she wasn't the only one among the Jaffray family to use this same "ask forgiveness, not permission" approach to life. She'd accused Cleo of following in her father's footsteps by doing the very same thing. In Daisy's case, it had won her power and respect. Paul had died an untimely death. What Cleo would gain from following this philosophy remained to be seen.

She returned to her room to put together a suitcase. As she paused in the middle of rummaging through trunks for a spare hairbrush, she was reminded of the missing codebook. She twitched with guilt over such a ruinous blunder, but it was her desertion of the girls that gnawed at her. She could only pray Petra was back on her feet and that she and Cleo were on the road to Stockholm. If they weren't . . .

A knock on the door startled her out of the downward spiral of her thoughts. "Come."

Bayard eyed her clothes on the bed with the usual expression when dealing with recalcitrant children and stubborn old biddies. "Are you certain this is wise, ma'am? Maybe you'd be better off traveling on to Stockholm with Her Royal Highness and Princess Ingeborg."

"I'm here to gather information, Lieutenant. I can't do that shipwrecked in a hotel in Sälen."

"The Germans are bombing the roadways. You won't hear them until they're right on top of you and by then it'll be too late."

"Did you ever wonder *why* the Germans are massing so many forces along those roadways? *Why* they're bombing places like Elverum and Nybergsund—towns and villages with absolutely no strategic value? If the royal family won't cooperate, it's better they're out of the way altogether."

"All the more reason you should accompany the crown princess to Stockholm."

"She is in the more than capable hands of her mother, who I very much doubt would appreciate any interference from me."

"Do you think that's really who His Majesty is concerned about?" He hurried through her deepening frown. "Of course, she's important, but it's Prince Harald he's desperate to keep safe. He's the heir to the throne if his grandfather and father are killed. And in German hands, he's a convenient puppet to prop on the throne while they do as they like."

"But he's not *in* German hands."

"No." Bayard looked away, but not before she caught the hard straight line of his mouth and the steel in his eyes. The polish of the ministry attaché stripped away to bare soldier's steel. "Not yet."

The hairs lifted at the nape of Daisy's neck, a strange prickling sensation as thoughts settled and just as quickly moved on. She sought to grasp them before they vanished, but the lieutenant ruined it by clearing his throat and breaking her concentration.

"I know you hate delegating these missions to others, but if anything should happen to you—a sitting US minister—think of the untold repercussions in Washington, not to mention how it would hurt your family."

Was he right? Was her safety more important than her work? Was she running away from her worries by running into danger?

She'd been in plenty of dangerous situations: border skirmishes along the Rio Grande, the war-torn French countryside, striking miners' camps in Colorado. Had she been running then? Bordie's death had rocked her, had changed the landscape of her life, leaving her unmoored. Her work and her daughter had been twin anchors during those dark days. No saying which was more essential to her sanity.

Perhaps she *should* stay behind. Bayard's argument wasn't as far-fetched as it sounded, and, while Sweden meant safety from German bullets and bombs, there were plenty of subtler ways Hitler could get what he wanted. Stockholm would be just waking into spring. She could review options with Sterling, consult with Ray Cox and the others in Oslo. Begin rebuilding her network of connections that would enable her to monitor the invasion from afar. No more pulse-pounding air raids or trigger-happy soldiers, no more biscuits washed down with sludgy coffee or hours spent scribbling notes in the back of her trusty Ford. It would be just the respite she needed.

The phone on her desk rang. She answered it, switching into Norwegian to accept the call coming through from Stockholm. Was Ambassador Sterling looking for another update? Passing along messages from Washington?

"I hate to pile on when you're already dealing with so much." Even over the wires, Freddie Sterling's voice was warm with sympathy. "But I have some unhappy news from home."

Was it Ethel? One of the grandchildren? Daisy gripped the receiver in a sweaty hand. "Go on."

"Anne Vanderbilt's been admitted to the hospital. They don't believe she'll survive the next few days. I thought you should know."

The gnawing in Daisy's gut clawed its way into her throat, where it sat like a rock. Bordie's older sister had survived so much tragedy, so much loss. The death of three husbands. Three children—Barbara only last year. But she never faltered, pushing through her grief, using it to propel her forward. She and Daisy were yoked together through marriage but kindred spirits in ambition and strength. They had encouraged one another. Propped each other up. Anne was a remarkable woman and a remarkable friend. Daisy felt old age clutch at her with new strength.

She couldn't remember what she said to Freddie. Whatever it was, it satisfied him, and he rang off. Her skin was cold, but her heart banged against her ribs like a rolling tympany. She stared at the wall, the flocked paper, the fingerprint smudge at the edge of the mirror. The hotel pen beside the hotel stationery.

She flung herself to her feet, unable to stand it a moment longer. If running meant a reprieve from the crowd of emotions settling like weights, she'd run as far and as fast as she could.

She found Lieutenant Bayard and Mr. Whitney waiting for her by the Ford in the hotel's courtyard.

Mr. Whitney caught sight of her first, tossing his cigarette away as he opened the trunk. The lieutenant's scowl darkened his handsome features, his eyes tired and clouded with his own thoughts. "You're not going to change your mind, are you?"

"If I'd allowed the men in my life to dissuade me from risky endeavors, I'd be one of those curtain-twitching grandmothers whose sole purpose is offering unwanted advice and knitting unwanted sweaters."

She couldn't be sure, but she thought she saw Mr. Whitney glance at her as if he wished she might be strangled with her own ball of yarn. Lieutenant Bayard merely nodded his acceptance as he took his place in the front seat.

Forward momentum carried her. If she stopped now, she'd find it impossible to start again. She settled in the back of the car. "I knew you'd see it my way."

FATHER MAGNUS REMINDED Cleo of Santa Claus. He was round with a windburned face, a long white beard, and a voice like warm honey. But instead of gingerbread or cloved oranges, he smelled of a combination of incense and woodsmoke. He didn't seem at all put out by having to speak to her, not in the warmth and comfort of the parlor, but here in the cow byre, where she'd come to escape the Petersons' well-meaning but smothering concern.

"She'll be well taken care of, Frokken Jaffray. You have my word." His English was perfect. Two years of seminary in Minnesota, he explained. "She will lie among her countrymen."

Petra Kristiansen shouldn't be lying anywhere except maybe on a bed in a Stockholm hotel, but Cleo didn't say that. She didn't say anything. She gripped the top bar of the gate, her nails digging into the wood, and fought back tears. She didn't even know why she was crying—for Petra lying cold and still on a slab in the Peterson's woodshed? For Micky missing in the chaos of invasion? Or was it an accumulation of tiny sorrows and shallow cuts that added up to this flood of self-pity and hopelessness?

"Fru Peterson asked that I give this to you," he continued. "She found it in the young woman's pocket when she was preparing the body for burial." It was an envelope addressed to Petra's sister, Sofia. "I trust you'll find a way to deliver it."

Cleo shoved the envelope into her coat pocket. "I'll make sure of it."

"Peterson tells me you need transport into Sweden," he said with a tap of his pipe against the gate. "Gather your things."

A half hour later, she found herself sitting in the front seat of an enormous car that looked as if it would be more at home carrying Hollywood starlets to a movie premiere than hurtling around the hairpin turns of frosty Norway. Her driver was a dour-faced woman, silver hair styled flawlessly and tucked under an expensive feathered hat. Her smart suit and pearls appeared odd after Fru Peterson's flour-dusted aprons and hand-embroidered scarves.

Cleo recognized the type immediately—she'd grown up around them. Wealthy. Entitled. Assuming the laws didn't apply to their kind. Without asking, Cleo knew this woman came from money, probably inherited rather than earned. She owned land, not a small farmstead like the Petersons. Something grand and ancestral, where the work was done by others. Her days were probably spent in leisure. If they had been in America, it would have been on the golf links or the tennis courts, or at the card table. Cleo had no idea what Norwegian society did for fun, but no doubt it was similarly pointless and repetitive. Yet tucked amid the lunches, dinners, and cocktails would be the Lady Bountiful charity work: raising money, making speeches, sitting on committees. Aunt Daisy's career had begun under such circumstances as had those of many of her friends and family: Anne Morgan, Anne Vanderbilt, Roosevelt's first lady, Eleanor.

Perhaps Cleo was sitting beside the Norwegian equivalent. She snuck a look from under her lashes, but her hostess remained focused on the road ahead, her narrow chin thrust forward in a face set in bullish lines, pink feather bobbing with every bump. A more unlikely warrior would be hard to find. For some reason, this reminded Cleo of Petra and the tears started all over again.

The woman took one hand off the wheel long enough to rummage in her pocket for a handkerchief, which she handed over, all without taking her eyes from the road.

"*Takk.*" Cleo wiped her cheeks. After the week she'd had, she must look a positive fright. But the woman had said nothing about the mismatched unlaundered clothes, the ladders in her stockings, the lack of makeup or powder. She'd simply ushered

Cleo into her car, no questions asked, at least not of Cleo. She might have grilled Father Magnus before agreeing, but that had been done behind closed doors. In Norwegian too fast for Cleo to catch.

"How do you know Father Magnus?"

The woman's brows lowered, her gloved hands tightening on the steering wheel, but she kept silent. It had been this way since the journey began. Did she assume the less she knew of her passenger, the better off she'd be? Did she resent this intrusion on her time and her valuable gasoline? Or was she merely focused on potential dangers from German planes to jumpy border guards to icy roads?

"My cousin Randolph has a car like this, only his is gray and he calls it Lulu after a singer he used to date, though I'm not supposed to know about that."

Cleo didn't know why she kept trying to make conversation. It was obvious the desire to chat was not shared. Maybe because she'd never met a challenge she could walk away from. Or maybe—and more likely—because silence meant time to think and Cleo didn't want to think. Not about what she'd left behind. Not about what might be lying ahead.

"Come to mention it, my cousin Chester called his schnauzer Lulu. I wonder if she's named after the same singer."

Cleo was practically catapulted into the windshield by the force of the woman's stomp on the brakes. The car grumbled as it idled, the only car on this stretch of country road. The woman reached across Cleo, turning the door handle. "Go."

"I don't understand. Go where?" The road they were on was barely a road at all. More like a break in the trees. They'd left the comfortable landscape of farmsteads behind them as they drove, the terrain growing wilder and emptier.

The woman pointed to a line of telephone towers that passed

overhead on their march up a low hill to the east. "Follow the wires. The border is on the other side."

"You can't just abandon me alone in the middle of nowhere."

The woman continued to point until Cleo reluctantly did as she was told. She'd barely closed the car door when the woman shoved it into reverse, turning the enormous car with the dexterity of a race car driver before heading back the way they'd come.

Alone, Cleo followed the towers as she'd been instructed, her muscles loosening under a bright afternoon sun. There was no indication she'd crossed the border into Sweden. No fences or gates. No outposts manned by uniformed guards. The trees spread unbroken in every direction and the road looked as if it was a track for wagons hauling timber out of the forest. Could it be this easy? Or would soldiers leap out at her as soon as she rounded the next bend? If so, what to do with the codebook?

Old movies always showed the hero swallowing the incriminating evidence, but she could hardly chew and digest an entire book in the next five minutes, and it was too big to fit into the lining of her coat where she kept her travel papers. She could chuck it away under a bush or bury it in a hole where no German raiders could find it, but that would leave Aunt Daisy at the mercy of those who might accuse her of negligence. Out of options, she secreted the slender book down her blouse before buttoning her coat to her chin to hide the odd bulk and corners. Barring a bear hug, it should be safe enough.

The putter of a motorcycle broke the quiet. Shoulders back and chin high, Cleo stepped into the road as if hailing a cab outside Grand Central Station.

CHAPTER 15

"Thanks for the lift." Cleo waved to her ride as he spun his motorcycle in the crowded hotel parking lot, flinging gravel, mud, and snow in a reckless arc before hitting the gas, scattering everyone in his path.

It would take a hot bath and a stiff drink to relax limbs frozen from hours riding pillion, but she was safe and out of Norway. Ignoring the curious stares, she headed inside, smoothing a hand through her windblown hair while trying to hide her skirt, which had suffered from mud, slush, and a hot engine. The lobby resembled an international conference, with at least five languages vying for dominance between the doors and the hotel's concierge desk. She searched for any sign of Aunt Daisy or Bayard, but other than a pair of reporters shouting into the hotel's house phone—"*C* as in *cat. O* as in *Oscar. T* as in *tiger*"; "Did you get that, Lenny?"—there was no sign of any American contingent.

A harried desk clerk sighed over a stack of telegrams while a woman in a floor-length silver fox coat bellowed at him in French as if he was deaf rather than Swedish. Cleo interjected her request in between the woman's steady stream of demands. "Do you speak English?"

"English, but not gibberish," he replied sharply while continuing to fend off the formidable woman, who had begun waving her arms in a belligerent fashion.

"Actually, it's French she's speaking, not gibberish. Please ring Minister Harriman's room and tell her that her goddaughter has arrived. Better yet, what's her room number? I'll go on up and save you the bother."

"Room 411, but she's not there, miss. She departed for Sjusjøen yesterday."

Bayard and Aunt Daisy had discussed the legation's families, but neither of them had mentioned risking life and limb to go back into Norway after them. "Did she say when she'd be back?"

Cleo had spent the entire noisy, bone-jarring ride from the border holding back tears and wishing for Aunt Daisy's gruff comfort. Someone to hug her and tell her it would get better while at the same time scolding her to stop sniveling and do something more with her anger than wallowing. Someone to ease the guilt that sat like a rock in her stomach, making eating impossible but drinking necessary. The higher the proof, the better.

Not that the desk clerk cared—or even noticed. He shrugged his indifference as he was pulled away by a shout from his manager, who had joined the fray with the Frenchwoman, now tugging at the manager's shirtfront, her face splotchy red.

"*Takk* for nothing," Cleo replied, using his distraction to slide behind the counter, quickly locating and pocketing Aunt Daisy's room key.

"Stop!" he shouted as she hoofed it toward the elevator. Of course, *now* he decided to be observant.

"Madame Aubert is asking for news of her husband and children, by the way," Cleo called back over her shoulder, translating the woman's almost incomprehensible French as the doors slid closed. "She's distraught, not crazy."

Safe for the moment, Cleo slumped against the wall of the elevator, pushing the button for the fourth floor.

"That was most considerate of you."

Cleo straightened self-consciously, only at that moment becoming aware that she wasn't alone on the elevator. A handsome woman in her midthirties, brown hair swept up off her neck, clothes simple but obviously bespoke, held the hands of two little girls in matching pinafores. "Let us hope she is able to obtain news of her family." Her voice was deep and smooth, each English syllable carefully pronounced.

"And that the news she receives is good." Cleo rubbed at the grime embedded in her palms and pretended she didn't smell of grease and sweat and Mr. Peterson's herd of swine—did swine even come in herds? Cleo tried to clear her head, which was growing thicker by the minute.

"Mama, she smells," the younger of the girls whispered in Norwegian.

"I understood that," Cleo replied, putting Petra's language lessons to use.

Was she tired? She couldn't remember catching more than a few hours of sleep over the last few horrible days. But this felt like more than exhaustion. Maybe it was shock. She was jittery and at the edge of tears but also cold—so damned cold. She clamped her teeth in a grimace of a smile to keep them from chattering.

The older girl gave her little sister a hard nudge. "Astrid, don't be rude."

Astrid slid Cleo another sideways glance.

"You must forgive my daughter," the woman apologized.

"She's not wrong," Cleo replied. "I do radiate a rather pungent aroma. I'm beginning to offend myself."

"She may be speaking truth." A small smile tipped the solemn woman's lips. "But she will need to learn when tact will serve her better."

"*Jeg beklager, mamma*," the little girl apologized.

The elevator doors opened, and Cleo stepped out. "A wise woman once told me, *Man skal ikke skue hunden på hårene*, which is a Norwegian way of saying 'don't judge a book by its cover,' no matter how smelly it is."

The two little girls laughed, and for a moment their mother's smile brightened her eyes before the doors closed on them all.

Thank God. She was alone. She could fall apart without a gawking audience. Cleo followed the numbers to the end of a quiet corridor and let herself into her godmother's room. It was obvious the housekeeping staff was as overworked as the front desk clerks. Aunt Daisy's bed was unmade and her clothes lay over a chair, awaiting the laundry. A room service tray lay uncollected on a table. The contents of the Ford sat in a pile of boxes and crates by the desk. Pulling the codebook from inside her coat, Cleo packed it, still in its disguise, among the files. Just as if it had never been mislaid.

Hopefully wherever Petra might be, she breathed a sigh of relief.

Cleo wanted nothing more than to crawl into bed and lose herself to unconsciousness. Instead, she forced herself to strip, bathe, and rinse out her clothes in the sink. By the time she was clean and warm and wrapped in a bathrobe pulled from Aunt Daisy's luggage, her mind had settled from its earlier frantic spin. Outside, a cold sleet hid the distant mountains and caused lights to flicker on in the courtyard. The hotel had the feel of a solitary ship in a storm. Hopefully no icebergs in the vicinity.

Ignoring the lump in her gut, she poured herself a whiskey from the room's bar. Then a second. The third finally thawed her frozen insides. The fourth softened her bones and gave the world a hazy glow, but the words Cleo had rehearsed over the long miles slid through her muzzy brain.

The ache in her belly expanded up into her chest, and the last days caught up with her like a wave crashing over her and pulling her out to sea. Her head ached. She wanted to be sick. Curling up under the duvet, she drew her knees in against her chest in a desperate attempt at warmth or security.

With sleet tapping at the windows, Cleo floated away on the whiskey, but just as she was about to sink into sleep, she felt herself falling. A sense as real as the odor of wool steaming dry on the radiator, the smell of roses caught in the pillows, and a firm hand shaking her shoulder.

"Clementine Verquin, what on earth are you doing here, and in my bed?"

That bloody awful name banged against her skull.

She smiled at the familiar scolding and snuggled deeper into the duvet, finally able to drift to dreamless sleep.

Aunt Daisy was back.

Dear Anne,

I've arrived safely in Stockholm, Venice of the north. You'd love the bustling elegance of the city with its glorious architecture and wide boulevards, though right now it's bursting at the seams with newly arrived refugees from Norway. I've taken rooms at the Grand Hotel, though I'm already on the lookout for a place outside of the city, somewhere quiet where I can regain my bearings. We have lost one of our own, and our hearts ache for Miss Kristiansen's family back in Norway. We held a service for her, the small chapel brilliant with flowers. Poor Cleo has taken the death hardest of all of us. I am reminded of how the British described the death of a soldier in the last war. They would say he has "gone West." I imagine Petra taking ship, perhaps in one of her ancestor's dragon-prowed boats, for lands uncharted. I hope this note finds you in better health . . .

* * *

WHO WAS SHE fooling? Her beloved Anne was not likely to recover. Daisy's old friend had been ill for too long, her body exhausted by the heart condition that had plagued her for years. Yet she'd never allowed her poor health to distract her from the family she adored or the causes she championed.

Daisy could learn a thing or two from Anne.

Instead, she stood in a corner of the Stockholm Palace's ornately gilded Pillar Hall, watching the swirl of guests—not a familiar place or a usual practice. She'd always felt comfortable at the center of the crowd, at the heart of a situation. From her earliest days shepherding her beloved Colony Club from a half-baked wifely complaint to the overwhelming success it was today, she'd taken pride in her ability to chart a course through the roughest waters. Truly her father's daughter, she never felt more alive than when she was shooting blockades, outrunning hurricanes, and bringing her ideas safely to port. It wasn't hubris. Simply a testament to hard work, unremitting energy, and an iron will that didn't allow her to dwell on the worst. That confidence had begun to sour with the news of Anne's stroke and taken a mortal blow with news of Petra Kristiansen's death.

Cleo had reeked of whiskey as she filled Daisy in on the circumstances surrounding her secretary's death. With bloodshot eyes in a face gray as the April weather and a tremor in her usually confident voice, she relayed the details with bullet-like precision. She finished by pointing to the codebook, which had miraculously reappeared at the bottom of a file box.

Daisy took her first deep breath in days, the band pressing against her temples finally easing. "Where did you find it?"

Cleo went still for a moment, her eyes dark with thought. "It was my fault. I was looking for something to read and grabbed it off the table at the guesthouse outside Elverum. I didn't realize what it was until later."

"I recall Petra having it last."

"No. It was me," Cleo answered firmly, her expression allowing no argument, and Daisy let the explanation stand, curiously encouraged by this unfamiliar selflessness, yet sensing a wariness as if Cleo was testing the ice, weighing how far to step.

"Very well. I appreciate your confession and the return of the book. Both mean a lot."

More than Cleo would ever know.

The trip from Sälen to Stockholm had been made in almost complete silence. Lieutenant Bayard spent the time transcribing his notes on the military situation in and around the Gudbrandsdal Valley, though his gaze was bleak in a face etched with misery. Cleo gazed out the window, her stare unfocused, her fingers worrying at her necklace like it was some kind of good luck talisman. Once in a while, she let out a sigh as if she meant to speak but settled back almost immediately once more into lethargy. Only Mr. Whitney remained untouched, or perhaps he was simply too busy to grieve while he took charge of arranging their journey, his pomposity coming in handy as he harangued railroad officials, porters, hotel clerks, bellhops, and waiters, smoothing their path like a steamroller run amok. There was a moment when it seemed he might confront her, his expression pained and oddly uncertain. Daisy almost took pity on his obvious discomfort by inviting him to dine with her, but there were limits to her desire for self-immolation. If he wanted to have it out, he knew where to find her.

Instead, relieved at having his irritating arrogance directed at others for a change, Daisy took the opportunity to catch up on her work, the distraction derailing any temptation to wallow in self-pity or second guesses. As the train grumbled south and east across Sweden, she read over all the correspondence that had piled up in the days she was out of reach: dispatches and telegrams from Mr. Atherton in Denmark, Mr. Kirk in Berlin, and Mr. Moffat in Washington as well as updates from Mr. Cox back in Oslo. Secretary of State Hull's praise of her courage under dangerous conditions raised her flagging spirits, and she tucked his message away to reread whenever she needed a boost. Comparing her notes of the last few days with Lieutenant Bayard's observations, she pulled all the disparate events of the past week into a coherent narrative that she passed along to Washington almost as soon as she settled herself into rooms at the crowded Grand Hotel.

"Mrs. Harriman, I am glad to see you safely back with us after your journey to Sjusjøen." Caught wool-gathering, Daisy smiled at Crown Princess Märtha, who had joined her in the corner, or perhaps she had always been there. Uncertain of her standing in this new place, much like Daisy herself. She wore a floor-length gown in a frosty sea green and an unreadable expression as her gaze passed over the assembled guests. "I heard there was trouble outside Dombås."

"The bombing of a railway tunnel where one of my staff was taking shelter. He's fortunate he wasn't killed."

"Others of your staff were not so fortunate."

"No. They were not." Daisy took a coupe of champagne from a passing waiter, forcing herself not to gulp it down like medicine. "And you?" she asked when she had a moment to recover her aplomb. "It must be a comfort to be back among such familiar surroundings."

"Familiar, yes. But not as comfortable as I imagined." Daisy continued to follow the princess's gaze but could not see who she was watching as she said this. "I hope Miss Jaffray is recovering from her ordeal."

Daisy felt her stomach involuntarily clench, though why she couldn't say. Only that Cleo and Her Royal Highness in conversation seemed like a moment rife with the potential for calamity. "I hadn't realized you'd been introduced to my goddaughter."

"Not formally. We shared a lift at the hotel in Sälen, but it was one of the most entertaining ascents I've ever taken. I hope we can meet again under better circumstances."

"Any encounter with Cleo is bound to be interesting. She has a knack."

Her Royal Highness smiled, a real, honest one this time. It made her face glow, and Daisy was struck again at the woman's vibrance and her strength. "Don't be too hard on her, Madam Minister. She looked as if she'd had a bad time of it. But she was lovely to the girls and quite a champion to one of the French delegation's wives, whose family was trapped in Denmark."

Mr. Hambro, president of Norway's parliament, interrupted their conversation. He was grim-faced, but his body, unlike so many weighed by the current crisis, seemed more robust. A statesman rising to the occasion rather than shrinking from it. Traveling discreetly back and forth over the border, he was a steady source of information, and Daisy made a note to reach out to him before he disappeared once more into Norway.

The crown princess's smile vanished, but she touched Daisy's sleeve before she drifted away. "I know of the promise His Majesty forced on you in Elverum."

"He was concerned for your safety."

The princess cast a wary glance over her shoulder at Hambro waiting patiently for an audience. "I can assure you, he still is."

IT WAS AFTER midnight by the time Aunt Daisy returned to the hotel, but over the past year Cleo had grown used to rising at noon and going to bed as the sun was coming up. More recently, sleeping had become downright dangerous, a minefield that left her the next day with an oppressive sense of dread and a headache that gnawed at the base of her neck. Not sleeping did the same, but without the nightmares. She counted that as a win.

Tonight, Cleo had taken up residence in the lobby, curled in an armchair with a book in her lap, though it remained unopened as she used the busy hotel's comings and goings as a distraction. Phones rang. Bellhops pushed past with loaded luggage carts. There was a constant purr of conversation in a world of languages.

When Aunt Daisy arrived, she surprised Cleo by not immediately taking the elevator up to her room. Instead, she passed through the lobby to one of the hotel's private reading rooms. After a few minutes and a stop at the hotel's café, Cleo followed. Aunt Daisy sat at a corner table by the window, a lamp throwing long shadows into the cherry-paneled corners. She looked as if she'd been in the middle of writing a letter, but now she stared unseeing into the darkness, her tired gaze unfocused and the skin beneath her eyes ashen. She slid a hand over the half-written page but not before Cleo saw the name scrawled at the top of the page.

Dear Anne . . .

"I'm sorry about Mrs. Vanderbilt. I know you two are close."

Aunt Daisy motioned to the seat across from her. Cleo sat, pushing one of the cups of coffee she'd brought with her across the table, keeping the other for herself. "It's not cocoa, but it'll have to do."

Aunt Daisy took a sip while Cleo let the silence spin out without trying to jump in and fill it. At first it felt awkward and uncomfortable, but after a moment, she felt her shoulders relax and her chest loosen. "Is it bad?"

Her godmother tucked the unfinished letter into her handbag. "There's always hope."

It was obvious as she said this that she didn't really believe it. It was an instinctive response built from a lifetime of looking on the bright side.

"She was a charmer like all the Harrimans," Aunt Daisy continued. "But she was kind as well, which I think is a far more admirable trait. From the moment I knew I would marry her brother, she was a generous sister and a loyal friend."

"Mother says she was a heroine for her work in the last war. How she used her own money to assist the French troops, raised funds for hospitals, ambulances, and medical equipment."

"Anne didn't just raise funds. She did the hard work, the dirty work. She nursed. She drove. She ran canteens. She mucked in wherever it was needed and never once complained. But she wasn't the only one. There were an army of heroines all doing the same. Doing what they could because it was the right thing to do."

Cleo bit her lip, following Aunt Daisy's long gaze into the darkness. The weight was back, pressing down on her abdomen, making the coffee stir uneasily. "If it wasn't for her, my father would still be alive."

Aunt Daisy sat up, her eyes going wide before she mastered her response and the diplomat's veil took hold. "Your father's death was the result of bad weather and bad luck. You might as well blame the fates or shake your fist at God. It comes to the same thing in the end."

But now that Cleo had spoken, she needed to follow her accusation to its end. To hear what Aunt Daisy would say to refute the claim. To convince her it wasn't true. "But it was Vanderbilt money that funded those American pilots. It was influence and pressure and the lure of glory over French skies that sent him to war."

Aunt Daisy sighed in agreement. "Anne was hardly the moving force, nor were the Vanderbilts the only wealthy family to lay their money on the line, but I suppose in a small sense you're right. Neither she nor her husband believed America could stay neutral in the face of German aggression. They believed we had a duty to our friends and allies to do what we could with what we had. That standing on the sidelines and watching wasn't an option."

Cleo picked at a spot on the tablecloth, her chest aching as if someone had punched her. But for the first time, she saw her father not as the dashing flyboy of her imagination but like Einar or the young Peterson sons or the soldiers at the checkpoint. Angry. Afraid. Leaving homes and families behind because the alternative was impossible.

"It's hard to imagine it now, but it was a time of doing, Cleo. Of seeing problems and wanting to find solutions. Not just in the face of war, but in the face of any injustice that cried out for a solution. The last war brought out the best in so many." The veil slipped, and Daisy's eyes swept up to pin Cleo like a butterfly to a board. "It remains to be seen if this one will do the same."

CHAPTER 16

Dear Anne,

I have heard it said that if you do not give a dog a job, he will make one for himself. So long as my official orders from Washington are to "stand by," I will throw myself into the work I feel most equipped to tackle, which is assisting my Norwegian friends as best I can. I might be without a chancery to call my own, but I am not without resources or connections . . .

completely understand, Mr. Trainor. And I've sent your information on with a request for additional funds to be used to assist American citizens with evacuation. If you call back in a week, I hope to have a better answer for you."

Mr. Trainor did not want to call back in a week and made sure Daisy knew it along with how he was personal friends with Secretary of State Cordell Hull and she'd be sorry when he made a formal complaint—oh and by the way, this is what happened when women were put in charge instead of staying in the kitchen where they belonged.

Right up until that moment, she'd been sympathetic to poor Mr. Trainor's plight. Mustering every last drop of empathy, she managed to get off the phone without informing him of just what he could do with his misogynistic bullying. Still, she felt as if she'd been flayed alive by the time she slid the receiver back into its cradle, and it was only ten in the morning.

Daisy had thought her days on the road had been long and chaotic. Now she looked back on them with an almost nostalgic feeling of freedom, from ringing phones and clattering typewriters; the constant jostling of reporters for the latest reports; the breaking headlines, and the reams of papers moving across her desk in a blur of cables, telegrams, reports, filings, letters.

There were not enough hours available for the demands of her position, and always there was one more name on a list of those to meet, one more letter from a panicked family member requesting information or assistance, one more luncheon invitation, drinks meeting, evening reception. After a hectic week spent at the Grand Hotel in the heart of Stockholm, she chose to retreat to the resort town of Saltsjöbaden, a short train ride outside the city. At least there she had the comfort of distance to buffer her from the pulls on her attention. Her days and evenings might be crowded, but her nights could be spent in quiet pursuits like knitting or listening to music on the wireless.

Last night had not been one of those nights.

She had been up to all hours in conversations with Sterling and his deputies only to be met by reporters as soon as she returned from the American legation. Stevens from the *Christian Science Monitor* and Callendar from the *New York Times* trailed her through the hotel lobby, asking for her take on the arrival in Oslo of Reichskommissar Terboven and what she thought of the British withdrawal from southern Norway. She hated to shoo them away, very often they gave as much as they gathered, so she spent another hour chatting over drinks at one of the hotel's bars and didn't make it to her bed until nearly dawn. A few hours of sleep and back into the city to do it all again, so she was not at her best by the time the telegram from Alexander Kirk, the American chargé stationed in Berlin, arrived on her desk that evening.

"He's certain?" she asked Mr. Whitney, who, even in silence, had a way of radiating effrontery.

"It came direct from the German administration in Zakopane."

"So he never made it out of Poland."

"Doesn't look like it."

Daisy rubbed at the space between her brows where the tensions of the day gathered and ran over the conversation in her head. How she would offer the news. How Cleo would take it. Once she might have been able to predict with relative accuracy the stubborn shock and frantic disbelief that would follow such an announcement. Now she wasn't as certain.

Cleo had always been a whirlwind, age turning the tantrums of her youth into the brashness of adulthood. That had changed somewhere between Oslo and Stockholm. Perhaps it had been Miss Kristiansen's death that caused this new composure. Perhaps it had happened earlier. There was no way of pinpointing or maybe there was no point in time at all, but a series of moments, one building on another like blocks. It was as if the winds had calmed, allowing a space for questions and for doubt. A space for forgiveness.

Daisy reread the telegram as if she might catch some inner meaning behind this new information. But the words were sparse, and one could make of it as much or as little as necessary. Kominski was dead. Cleo had her answer.

That was an end to it.

Or it should be.

As usual, it was close to midnight before she arrived back at the hotel in Saltsjöbaden. Instead of pausing for a nightcap or a restorative cup of tea, she headed up to their suite. She'd settled on the direct approach as the best way to deliver her news. It's how she preferred it. She assumed Cleo would be the same.

Their suite was spacious with a lovely view of the water. She found Cleo preparing to go out—clipping on a pair of earrings, searching her closet for a serviceable pair of shoes. Her short choppy curls had grown long enough to brush her shoulders.

"A late dinner?" Daisy asked, envious of the young's seemingly unending well of energy.

"I'm going to the Virveln dance palace. There's someone there I owe a visit and payment on a debt."

"Your man with the van?"

"Well, to be perfectly accurate, it wasn't *his* van. Athena belonged to Sam."

"Athena?"

"The van's name was Athena. Not sure why. Something to do with a barmaid in Greece, but Emmitt . . . he plays the drums. He was the one who convinced Sam and the others—"

"Cleo, for heaven's sake, stop talking." Simple. Straightforward. Beating around the bush was for cowards. "I've had an answer to our inquiries from Berlin."

Cleo's body went stiff as a board, her lips a twisted slash of crimson in a face gone gray. "Micky's dead, isn't he?"

"I'm afraid so, my dear." Daisy waited for the shock to expand into disbelief and then suspicion. Instead, Cleo straightened the gaudy pink diamond and its wreath of costume rubies against the hollow of her throat. A touch as if to anchor herself in the present with a reminder of the past.

"I shouldn't be surprised, should I?" She turned back to the mirror, her eyes awash in tears or perhaps it was a trick of the reflection, for when she faced Daisy next, there was nothing but hard angles and stubborn planes. "We're at war."

* * *

A CROWD OF young people milled outside the Virveln dance hall, laughing as they jostled and debated whether to go home or head somewhere else, where the beer was cheaper, the girls prettier, the band hotter.

Cleo pushed her way past them and into the lobby, pausing at the coat check before taking a moment to freshen up in the retiring room. Women chatted as they reapplied lipstick, added an extra dab of perfume, lamented over torn hems, laddered stockings, crushed toes. Cleo let the crowd leave before she stepped to the mirror. She smiled, frowned, tipped her head to the right, tipped her chin up. All as if she might see Micky's death written on her face. A visible mark no amount of Max Factor would hide. But there was only an odd sallow-green cast to her skin that she blamed on the poor lighting.

Mother had told Cleo once that she had known the exact moment of Father's death—that she had felt a pain in her chest and immediately fainted dead away, and when she had come around, she had known his soul had departed. She would not be convinced, no matter how Cleo argued, that it was far more likely that at seven months pregnant and suffering from indigestion, she had simply grown lightheaded and lost her balance. Now here Cleo was looking for signs and portents, unable to believe Micky could die without a clap of thunder or a shift beneath her feet to mark his passing.

Breathing in the ballroom's all too familiar scents of perfume, hair tonic, and sweat, Cleo felt a dizzying sense of déjà vu that had her steadying herself against a wall. If she closed her eyes, she could imagine herself back in the Black Cat, Micky shredding it on the trumpet for an audience that couldn't get enough. The musicians around him had changed over those final months; Ady and Arthur saw the writing on the wall and left for Paris, Szymon fled east ahead of the German advance. Micky had merely bent to the current regime like a reed, playing what he was asked without question, the good American renouncing his degenerate music. What he'd convinced Cleo then was smart business, she began to see as simple cowardice.

It pricked at her grief like a burr. If Micky had been wrong about that, what else might he have been wrong about?

Women sat along the edges of the dance floor, swaying to the music and shooting wistful glances at the men leaning against the walls smoking cigarettes and elbowing each other like schoolboys at recess. Every few minutes there would be the tap on the shoulder that would send another couple out into the scrum on the dance floor.

Cleo wasn't interested in kicking it up with a Lindy hop or a tango. She ignored the looks and the invitations as she slid her way toward the stage, where the band was killing it with a stripped-down version of "Swingin' the Blues" that had the place rocking.

She counted heads. There was Norman trading his crooner's microphone for a hot piano, Sam working his bass like a madman. Sweat beaded on Paulie's forehead as he led the band on his trumpet, Dud right behind him on the trombone, the two of them throwing the melody back and forth between them like a ball. She stood on tiptoe to see over the crowd of dancers for a glimpse at the man behind the high hat, snare, and tom who held them all together with his crazy rhythm. He caught sight of her and grinned, bringing the music to a crescendo before fading out.

All five safe in one piece. She felt a knot in her gut loosen.

An announcer took the stage, sending the dancers scattering to the bar for another drink and leaving Cleo alone at the edge of the stage. The band set down their instruments to towel off and recover, except for Emmitt, who shouted, "Hey, Park Avenue! You're alive! Dud bet me fifty bucks we'd never lay eyes on you again. The bastard owes me."

"You're all well? You made it out without any problems?"

"All present and accounted for, though we had to put poor Athena out of her misery outside of Torsby. Paulie played taps and Sam wept like a baby." He searched the ballroom. "That kid with you?"

She shook her head. She'd tried not to think about Einar when Aunt Daisy's conversations turned toward updates from battlefields around Rombaksfjord in the north to the town of Åndalsnes in the south. She convinced herself he was safe when soldiers trickled over the border into the camps, wounded or ill and recounting tales of firefights and nonstop air attacks and artillery the Norwegians had no hope of countering. But it was as much a story as all the others she'd told herself: That Micky was alive and safe. That Petra would recover. That the world wasn't on fire.

Emmitt seemed to recognize her thoughts. "I'm sure he's aces," he said with a brotherly squeeze of her shoulder. "He looked like he could take care of himself."

She reached into her handbag. "I came to bring you what I promised." She handed him an envelope. "Well, maybe not quite what I promised. Aunt Daisy wasn't as pleased to see me as I let on."

He shoved the envelope into the breast pocket of his jacket. "Since most of them were expecting you to skip out completely, this is pure gravy."

One of the stagehands gave a shout. "I'd best get back." Emmitt seemed to realize this was a final farewell. His face dropped into somber lines, mouth pulled against the stubble of his face. "Take care, Park Avenue." He looked around at the crowds already jumping with anticipation of the next number, at the bright faces of the young men and women. "For some reason the say-ing 'fiddling while Rome burns' keeps running through my head these days."

IT HAD BEEN a week since Cleo said goodbye to Emmitt and the others. A week since Aunt Daisy had shattered her hope with the news of Micky's death. She'd barely made it out of bed the first few days, and when she finally did, she stayed hidden away in her tiny cubby of a hotel bedroom, playing endless games of solitaire.

She expected Aunt Daisy to drag her out by her ears at any moment, but that wasn't her godmother's way. She had the an-noying habit of sitting back and making one come to their own conclusions. It meant that Cleo could grieve undisturbed, but it also meant days of uninterrupted introspection. A sifting through of memories and choices and what-ifs that left confusion in their wake.

This afternoon, Cleo shuffled the playing cards before placing them one up, six down; two up, five down; three up, four down. Through to seven before she laid the deck at her elbow on the table, taking up the first card. A five of hearts. She scanned the cards in front of her, searching for a spot to set it down.

Voices carried from the parlor, where Aunt Daisy was enter-taining guests. She'd invited Cleo to attend, but she'd demurred under the pretext of a headache.

Not entirely a lie.

Just not entirely the truth either.

Still, it was almost impossible to hide oneself completely away. The suite her godmother had taken, while larger than most, re-mained cramped. Only the sea view from Cleo's window gave the illusion of space. Otherwise, it was like living in a shoebox.

No move. Cleo flipped the next in her pile. Ace of spades.

"'Heart of oak are our ships, heart of oak are our men . . . We'll fight and we'll conquer again and again.'" Aunt Daisy had a way of speaking as if she was addressing an unruly crowd of suffragettes in front of New York City Hall.

The response to this recitation was lost in the laughter that followed.

Cleo's hand hovered over the spread of cards, but her mind couldn't take in the specifics of suits and numbers. Aunt Daisy had broken her concentration, her thoughts flying in a million directions like shrapnel. Cleo blinked, her vision a wash of blurry tears. She hated women who cried. Moping was even worse. Yet here she was wallowing in woe-is-me tears, which made her angry *and* pathetic.

Petra was dead.

Micky was dead.

Losing them had broken Cleo's increasingly fragile notion that war happened to other people. That she was a mere bystander, grieving on cue for the bad things that happened, but never truly touched by them. Seeing it all through the lens of someone who could always just turn away.

She couldn't turn away now.

If someone killed a person you loved, that made them your enemy. That's how it worked. A little voice reminded her that her father's death had also come at the hands of Germans, and it had never bothered her before. She silenced the voice by telling herself that she'd never loved her father. His death didn't count.

Cleo flipped the next card. Seven of diamonds. And the card after that. Five of diamonds. And the card after that. By now, she wasn't even trying to make a play. Her brain was stuck, habit carrying her forward.

"I've been invited to speak about my experience in Norway with the American Women's Club next week." Aunt Daisy's voice carried up the stairs.

"Of course you were" came the reply. "You're all anyone can talk about these days." Cleo didn't recognize this woman's voice, though the round breathiness to her vowels seemed vaguely familiar. "Your name's on every editor's lips from San Francisco to Bar Harbor. You've put the plight of the country on the front page."

Cleo set down the rest of her deck, following the sounds of luncheon being finished off with coffee and cake. Not because she was hungry—she wasn't. But because this woman's voice reminded her of someone. She stopped short of barging into the parlor, but she stood on the threshold and listened.

"As it should be, Mrs. Thorson," Aunt Daisy replied. "Refugees are pouring across Sweden's borders, hundreds every day. They'll need help with housing, food, clothing, medical care, and that's just in the first few days."

"We had a cable out of Chicago from a new group calling themselves Norwegian Relief. They're already organizing committees across America to help with fundraising efforts. Donations will be used to assist with the very basics at first, but they have grand plans for future needs that might arise. Minister Bulls has already begun preparations."

A third voice, but not nearly with the back of the theater volume of the other two. "The amount of work is staggering. One looks at the enormity of the situation and simply despairs. How can we possibly do it?"

"How do you eat an entire elephant? A bite at a time, Inge." There was a scrape of a fork on a plate as if to demonstrate. "A bite at a time."

Cleo felt her heart flutter in her chest. Of course. That's where she'd heard that voice before—or one so similar as to make her chest hurt. Petra had spoken with the same swoop and swing of Norwegian combined with the flat sharpness of English.

"Won't you come and join us, Cleo?" Aunt Daisy called out. A command couched as a question. Trapped, Cleo pushed wide the door and stepped into the parlor.

Aunt Daisy was lunching in company with two older women, broad-beamed and businesslike in traveling suits dusted with crumbs. But these were no minor-league paper pushers if the pearls and the unmistakable scent of Joy perfume was any clue.

Aunt Daisy introduced them with a sweep of her arm. "Mrs. Sillen and Mrs. Thorson are part of a group working with the Norwegian Refugee Office."

"You poor dear," Mrs. Sillen tutted, her round, dimpled face and pink rosebud mouth scrunched in concern. "Your aunt told us of your loss. Such a tragedy."

"Tragedy is an act of God, Inge. This was an act of war." Mrs. Thorson's accented voice held none of Mrs. Sillen's pillowed sympathy. "What will you do now, Miss Jaffray?"

What *would* she do? Go home like everyone assumed—and probably hoped—she would? Shut away her unanswered questions along with her anger and her grief and her guilt? Go back to living in the big house on Fifty-Seventh Street, the seasons delineated by the events on her mother's social calendar, her father staring down on the two of them, censure in his unblinking gaze?

If you were only more like me, he always seemed to say.

Some of her indecision and her pain must have been visible because Mrs. Thorson reached into her handbag and pulled out a business card. "No time to dillydally. Come see me when you decide you want to fight back."

CHAPTER 17

Dear Anne,

These letters have become habit. Somehow it's easier to collect my thoughts when I imagine you at the other end, unfolding the heavy paper, rummaging for your reading glasses, and talking back as if I was in the chair across from you rather than half a world away. I had a curious conversation with Clementine—Cleo, as she calls herself these days. I've always thought Letitia was wrong to hide the truth about Paul. I understood her reasoning when her daughter was little, but it serves nothing but her foolish pride now. I wish you could make her see sense. You were the only one who ever could . . .

Daisy set aside the letter to finish later. She was due to a luncheon this afternoon. Spring had come to Sweden, and with it an almost lighthearted atmosphere. She wouldn't quite call it ostrichlike, but there were moments when that was how she felt.

Today's luncheon at Hasselbacken was an informal affair, outdoors under a sky like cream with the sweet scent of spring flowers underpinned by the more savory odors coming from the restaurant's kitchens. Her mouth watered with anticipation. Waiters moved like dancers through the crowd, and there was an air of pleasure that felt out of place under the current circumstances.

Not that war wasn't on everyone's mind. Despite the champagne and canapés, the talk was businesslike. Diplomats and business executives felt each other out over contracts and supply shortages; staff officers and military exchanged news from the fronts around Narvik and Namsos. Pastel dresses and new spring hats rubbed up against bespoke suits and military braid.

"I'd never been so happy to see a real bed and have a real wash as when we reached the hotel in Sälen." Daisy had repeated her story so many times that the details felt as if they'd been lived by someone else.

Once upon a time there was an American minister . . .

The absurdity made her smile.

She drifted from conversation to conversation like a bird gleaning seeds—a name here, an opinion there. She pocketed these disparate bits of information away to be unpacked in privacy later, where she could look for patterns and try to uncover the picture they made. At one point, she caught sight of Lieutenant Bayard in conversation with Herr Kilcher, a gentleman Daisy recognized from the German press office. Since Petra's death, the lieutenant had thrown himself into his work. She wished she could talk to him about his loss, but she was his boss, not his mother. He'd not appreciate her interference, and she'd not risk angering a comrade and a friend.

The afternoon shadows circled, and clouds spread thicker over the sky, leaving a damp chill that smelled like rain. The guests moved indoors in twos and threes, taking their talk with them. Daisy followed more slowly, enjoying the last of the light falling over the hedges and beds thick with daffodils and purple pansies. It reminded her of the house in Mount Kisco she'd shared with Bordie early in their marriage. Not in any concrete way she could put into words. It was only a feeling that slipped away just as you reached for it, a sweetness of memory that faded too quickly to catch hold of.

"Are you coming, Daisy? I'm holding a seat for you at our table." Estelle Bernadotte called from the French doors thrown open to the gardens. The dark-haired American-born countess was one of those who worried over Sweden's growing relationship with Germany. Her husband shared this unease and pushed to train his beloved scouts to assist in the country's defense should the need arise.

"Be right there." She lingered a few more moments, but the light had faded, and the memory was gone. As she climbed the steps to go in, she caught sight of Herr Kilcher again at the far edge of the terrace sharing a smoke with another man. As she watched, he tossed away his cigarette and made his farewells, joining Daisy as they headed inside.

"Is your friend joining us for lunch?"

"I'm afraid not, Madam Minister. Kriminalinspektor Heimmel just arrived in the capital and has much to do."

A pricking between her shoulder blades made Daisy turn back for one final glance at the stranger on the terrace, who met her gaze and returned it. Caught, she offered him a casual smile. His response was polite rather than friendly, a warming in his deep-set eyes that traveled no farther. She continued into lunch on Herr Kilcher's arm, laughing at his stories and all the time wondering what a Gestapo officer was doing in Stockholm.

IT TOOK THREE days for Cleo to take Mrs. Thorson up on her offer. Three days for her anger to grow like a tumor until no amount of cocoa could settle the ache in her gut. Aunt Daisy watched her leave for the train station, her features arranged in their usual deadpan expression but for a moment's pleased wrinkling at the edges of her eyes.

The walk from Central Station to 37 Banérgatan was long enough to allow Cleo to enjoy the spring sun before she was plunged into the windowless office deep within the imposing five-story building that housed the Norwegian legation. Mrs. Thorson barely raised an eyebrow when Cleo turned up. She merely smashed out her cigarette in an overflowing ashtray, poured herself a new cup of coffee from the hot plate on the cabinet behind her, and handed Cleo a stack of files with a minimum of instruction. "You'll find it tedious, but it's necessary," she explained.

She was right. It *was* tedious. The Swedish authorities weren't particularly interested in assisting the Norwegians in their struggle. Not when they had the Germans watching for any hint they might not be as neutral as they claimed. The Refugee Office was barely unpacked before it had been overwhelmed by the arrival of refugees spilling over the long, unguarded border between the two countries.

A typical morning saw Cleo crisscrossing the city in search of temporary housing for the newcomers: schools, church halls, hotels. Afternoons, she knocked on doors and made endless phone calls soliciting donations of food, bedding, clothes, and medicine. Some days she traveled from hospital to hospital to check on the injured and ill. Other days, she answered phones, wrote letters, took messages, and chased down officials.

But work was exactly what Cleo needed. Slowly, the rock in her gut shifted as she put her anger to use. She couldn't help Petra or Micky. They were gone. But she could help others. She could tackle her corner of the war one bite at a time.

Aunt Daisy had her own war to fight, the two of them ships passing in the night as Cleo's work took her into the city before dawn and her godmother was usually out when Cleo returned home with just enough energy for room service and a bath before she fell into bed, too tired for dreams.

One evening as Cleo fell asleep over her soup, she felt a hand upon her shoulder and breathed in a familiar rose and vanilla perfume. "Mother?" she murmured, confused about where she was.

"Hush, child. You're no good to anyone like this."

She was helped to her feet and into bed. "I wanted to tell you about George, Mother. I really did. But you were so proud."

"Still am, child." A duvet was drawn up to her shoulders and the light put out.

Not her mother. Her world shifted into focus, her brain coming awake long enough to realize where she was and who the shadowy figure in her doorway was. "Aunt Daisy?"

"I didn't want you drowning in your fish soup. Hardly a dignified way to go."

"No one would be surprised, though, would they? I haven't led a very dignified life until now."

"I won't disagree." Cleo smiled into the dark at the dry retort that was so typically her godmother. "But Georgie Cliveden, Clementine? Really? What were you thinking? Not since the old man made his fortune in railroads a century ago has there been a single member of that family who could think their way out of a paper bag."

"Why didn't you say something?"

"Would you have listened?"

"Probably not."

Light from the parlor threw Aunt Daisy into silhouette, but now and then Cleo caught the outline of her features—the long, straight nose, the high cheekbones, the strength in her shoulders—rimmed in silver. Aunt Daisy folded her arms across her chest. "You should have trusted your mother. You should have told her how you were feeling. She'd have thrown a fit—that woman could have gone on the stage in one of Bessie Marbury's productions—but in the end, she'd have understood. Maybe more than you realize."

Cleo tried and failed to imagine that conversation. "It felt easier to run."

"It wasn't, though, was it?"

She closed her eyes. "I'm not running anymore, Aunt Daisy."

"No, child. And how do you feel now?"

"Exhausted."

A soft chuckle was her answer. "Means you're doing it right, then."

Would Mother have understood? Or would it have been another chance for her to throw her chronic disappointment in Cleo's face? It was only when all was quiet and the last light snapped off that she rose from bed in search of stationery and a pen.

It had been weeks since Aunt Daisy had told Cleo to write her mother, and she'd meant to—really she had. But she couldn't ever seem to find the right words and tomorrow always seemed like the better option. Not anymore. Tonight, the words crowded her mind, sentences writing and rewriting themselves until the only way to quiet the ache in her head was to put them down on paper, her handwriting messy and crisscrossed as she fought to squeeze everything she wanted to say onto the flimsy airmail paper.

In the morning, she propped her letter against the desk lamp. With any luck, Aunt Daisy could include it in the next diplomatic pouch home. With more luck, she'd find out if her godmother was right or merely being kind.

THE PATIENT WARD at the Sophiahemmet hospital was crowded but clean. The nursing sisters in their starched black-and-white pleated caps were efficient as they moved from bed to bed. Mr. Bjornson was recovering from appendicitis and anxious to be discharged. But where he was to go upon his release was the reason Cleo had been sent here today. Leaving behind a thriving business and a comfortable home, he had arrived in Sweden on skis with nothing to his name but a rucksack containing a change of clothes.

He wasn't the only one.

There were hundreds just like Mr. Bjornson scattered throughout Stockholm and more arriving all the time. Mrs. Thorson and the others at the Norwegian Refugee Office had desks piled high with cases, which meant Cleo was never idle. A new feeling, and one she rather liked.

"Will you be able to help him?" the gray-haired hospital matron asked—in English, thank heavens. Cleo's Norwegian was much better than it had been when she arrived at the Oslo ferry terminal in March, but she'd no handle yet on Swedish.

"We'll do all we can," Cleo replied, an incredibly useful line that worked in an amazing amount of situations, though not, it seemed, on the matron, who offered her a firm handshake at the hospital's entrance and bid her goodbye with "We will all be called upon to do what we can, Miss Jaffray. What we need to do now is the impossible."

She was reminded of Aunt Daisy's comment about an army of heroines. Was she a new recruit? It made her feel both insignificant and necessary, a tiny cog in a great machine.

"Miss Jaffray, this is a surprise." She looked up at the familiar drawl to find Lieutenant Bayard pulling on his coat. She'd not seen him since their arrival in Stockholm. He was thinner, grimmer, paler. Maybe she was too. But even a changed Bayard was a welcome sight.

"So formal. And here I thought being nearly blown up together meant something." As soon as she said it, she cringed. How could she be so stupid? "I'm sorry. That didn't come out right."

"The phrasing could have been better, but I knew what you meant." Even his smile seemed to lack vibrancy, as if part of him had been washed out or drained away. "I heard about Mr. Kominski. I'm sorry."

Cleo's throat closed around a lump, but she breathed through it and soon enough it faded back to a manageable pain. She spent her days thinking about people like Mr. Bjornson so she didn't have to think about Micky. It hadn't been as difficult as she thought it would be. His face, once haunting her every dream, had grown fuzzy and indistinct like a photograph out of focus. She couldn't remember how he sounded or his laugh or whether his favorite song was Glenn Miller's "Solo Hop" or "Blue Moon" by Benny Goodman. Only his scent lingered, a strange mix of cologne and breath mints.

She clung to that, as if letting that final piece of him go would mean she'd not loved him as much as she thought she had, that all that searching had been for nothing. That she could have given up and gone home months ago, putting away this new version of Cleo to make room for the return of Clementine.

A shudder rippled through her that had nothing to do with the salty wind off the water. She anchored herself with a brief touch of the necklace, the pink glass diamond warm and smooth but so heavy as if Micky's gift—his memory—began to weigh her down. She thought about trying to explain to Bayard some of what she was feeling, but it felt cruel in the face of his own loss. Or maybe he would understand better than anyone. She didn't know and was frightened to ask and risk scaring him off. "Are you here to visit someone?"

"An old reporter friend from my time in Berlin. He barely made it out of the country before the Nazi authorities arrested him."

"For what?"

"Do they have to have a reason these days?" Without thinking, they fell into step together, leaving the hospital to make their way down Engelbrektsgatan toward the park. She hadn't asked for his company, but she was glad of it just the same. He was a familiar face in a foreign city. Someone who recognized the strain around her eyes and the nervous tic in her jaw and didn't question it.

"Aunt Daisy says you've been too busy for social calls," she ventured, shy around him in a way she'd never been before. "Barely an hour to yourself."

He gave a grunt that could mean anything or nothing. After another moment, he added, "I could be wrong, but I think she's doing it on purpose."

"Oh, you're definitely not wrong. Aunt Daisy thinks the cure for all ills is constant motion. If you can't beat the blues, outrun them."

"It's kind of her to worry, but I'm doing okay." He cracked a lopsided smile that had a hint of the old Bayard behind it. "And if I had two seconds to call my own, I'd tell her so." He paused on the street corner and took her hand. "I hate to run, but I'm due to meet Mr. Whitney at the American legation"—he checked his watch—"ten minutes ago."

She couldn't help the grimace that passed over her face. Had the vice consul ever acted on his threat to expose Cleo, and thus Aunt Daisy, with tales of her unorthodox exit from Oslo? Or had all that followed pushed it from his mind? She doubted she could be so lucky. Men like Whitney hoarded any scrap of advantage for the moment it would benefit them the most. It was just a matter of when that bomb would blow up in her face. "I wish Aunt Daisy had shown him the door as soon as we got here."

"He's not that bad," Bayard said, albeit grudgingly. "Kind of a jerk, but he can drive like the devil. Saw us through when it counted. You gotta give him that."

"Maybe, but I still don't trust him."

"You think he's a spy for the Germans?" he teased.

She instinctively stepped closer as if one of those passing might be listening in on their conversation. "Maybe not for the Germans."

CHAPTER 18

Dear Anne,

Perhaps it's because I'm a woman, anxious that there should be peace in the world and eager to understand both sides of a human quarrel, but I really do try to maintain relationships even with those who might otherwise drive me to drink. Vice Consul Whitney is one of those men who doesn't believe women should be in public life and treats me like a specimen in the zoo. It reminds me of something Mrs. Blair from the DNC said to me about women entering politics "one room at a time." Maybe one man at a time . . .

According to our latest intel, His Majesty King Haakon, Crown Prince Olav, and the Norwegian cabinet have fled via destroyer to Tromsø. They're out of harm's way for now, but conditions on the ground are changing daily. The area around the city of Narvik is under intense bombardment from both Allied and German forces, making it inadvisable for the minister to travel into the country."

Daisy steepled her fingers under her chin, listening to Lieutenant Bayard's report, checking it against her own reports. "Right. I've spoken to Count Douglas with the Swedish legation—"

"Have you seen this?" Mr. Whitney banged into the office

without knocking, his brows scrunched, his face splotchy with outrage. Daisy should have been angry, or at least mildly irritated. Instead, she welcomed his intrusion as if it had been expected. There was something oddly comforting about his labored breathing, heavy sighs, and raspy grunts, and the tap of his rapid footsteps. So long as he was upset with her, it meant there wasn't anything more disastrous for him to focus his ire toward.

"Join us, Mr. Whitney," Daisy said, keeping her voice light. Maybe she'd be accused of softness, rolling over and showing her belly whenever he barked. He should be put in his place firmly. But that had never been her way.

He shook a sheaf of papers at her. "Have you seen this ridiculousness?"

"You'll have to be more specific. Most of what I see is absurd to the extreme these days."

"This damned news article in the *Der Bund* paper."

"Oh that." She laughed. "Did you see the date on the paper? It was published six months ago."

"I can tell you now if I'd seen it then, I'd have done something about it. As it is, you're content to let such a tissue of lies stand?" He read from the page. "'Mrs. Harriman plays selections from Chopin, Liszt, and Mozart on the piano for Foreign Minister Koht and throws in here and there a few short political remarks.'" He shot sparks at the two of them, seemingly surprised at their lack of shared fury. "Is that what they think? That you're a wealthy amateur pianist who plinks a few pretty notes in between diplomatic crises?"

"Did they really say that?" Bayard asked, his lips twitching with amusement.

"More or less," she replied, then addressed Mr. Whitney, who remained clearly agitated. "I'm sure the poor reporter did his best." She took up her reading glasses. "Where did you get it anyway?"

"A batch of newspapers and magazines just arrived at the legation. This was in there along with a selection of other materials."

"Lovely. Maybe there's mail from home as well. I haven't heard
from Ethel in ages," Daisy said, anticipating a wonderful long
newsy letter from her daughter to read over dinner.

"'Doll . . . delicate lady . . . white-haired . . . no fuss . . .'" Mr.
Whitney was like a dog with a bone. "It makes America a laugh-
ingstock, as if we're sending committee ladies to do the important
work of diplomacy and statecraft."

"You'd be surprised at how much work of real importance originates with committee ladies," Daisy said, a ring of steel in her
voice that caused Lieutenant Bayard and Mr. Whitney to blink
in surprise.

The vice consul seemed to come back to himself, almost as if
he was surprised by his own outrage. He rattled his pages, his face
losing some of its color, and cleared his throat. "Right. Well, so
long as we know where we stand, ma'am." He slammed his way
back out of the office to answer a ringing telephone.

"What was that about?" the lieutenant finally asked.

"I'd say Mr. Whitney's patriotism has, at least for the moment,
trumped his chronic discontent."

"As in 'he can say it, but he'll be damned if anyone else does'?"

"Something like that." Daisy laughed. "Utter nonsense, but
what in life isn't?"

The lieutenant's good humor faded, and there was a worried
look in his eye. "Miss Jaffray thinks Whitney's plotting against
you."

Daisy finally gave up trying to keep her place in the memo
they'd been reviewing. Dog-earing it for later, she focused all her
attention on Lieutenant Bayard, who looked as if he wanted the
floor to swallow him. "Does she? I don't know if I'd go as far as
that."

"You can't say he hasn't tried to undermine your authority. And he's got a chip on his shoulder. I wouldn't put it past him to even an imagined score."

Daisy felt herself settle deeper into her chair, or maybe this added weight was all in her head. Either way, it was a conversation she'd not expected to have and so she was caught off guard. Bayard continued to look equally nonplussed. It gave her a moment to think before she responded.

"When I was appointed minister to Norway, I received a congratulatory letter that said while, on the whole, they were pleased for me, they rather thought women in general should stay out of the male sphere of public life—and this came from a friend."

Lieutenant Bayard had the good sense to see it for the funny story that it was rather than attempt to fill the space with apologies on behalf of mankind. She appreciated that. It *was* a funny story. She had a million of them.

"Mr. Whitney is a man who sees the world he knows disappearing," she continued on to her point. "He can't stop it any more than he could stop the tide coming in. It scares him as it scares me."

"But *you're* what he's scared of."

"Not me. I'm very much of his world and his age. Oh, I might have broken a few rules along the way, but I was always the rarity, the speck in the oil. Annoying but acceptable. That's changing with your generation and the war will only hasten that change. My only regret is that it takes such a cataclysm, but then isn't that just how nature works."

THE ANCIENT KUNGSHOLM Church was full as Norwegians flocked to celebrate their country's Independence Day. Rolling her shoulders, Cleo shifted on the uncomfortable pew, trying to find a spot that didn't hit her in the back or numb her rear. Aunt

Daisy surreptitiously passed her a mint and a scolding parental glance, and Cleo was reminded of her mother, who used to do the same every Sunday.

Cleo's gaze wandered from the altar and its elaborate painting of Jesus ascending into heaven, passing over the rector, Dr. Krook, gesticulating as his voice reached the arched ceilings and shook the tall windows with words like *country*, *king*, *courage*, and *love*. Every face was turned toward him like plants toward the sun. Somber, shaped by pain or grief or shock, white as chalk or blotchy with emotion. A few burned with tears.

News had come only days earlier that Belgium, Luxembourg, and the Netherlands had fallen to the Germans, and France was reeling. Rumors swirled that the British were scaling back their military plans for Norway, their troops being pulled to the larger battles going on across the North Sea. Aunt Daisy, who was already in constant conversation with Mr. Sterling, spent even longer hours rushing among the Americans, the Norwegians, and the Swedes or locked away on the telephone with every contact she'd made over the course of their stay in Stockholm. Cleo's own work with Mrs. Thorson had increased as new refugees arrived hourly and more housing needed to be found, food distributed, and supplies scrounged.

As her attention wandered, Cleo couldn't help but seek out the crown princess and her children among the assembled congregation. What did she think of the unfolding calamities afflicting the Allies? Had she been able to speak to her husband since their separation at the border? Did she toss and turn at night worrying for his safety, wondering what would become of her and her children? If she'd ever see their home again? If so, she kept it well hidden.

Her porcelain features were nearly translucent under the glare of the chandeliers, made more so by her sober outfit of gray tweed and the demure black hat perched upon her dark head, but there was no defeat in her steady gaze. Nothing despondent in the way she gripped her hymnal or bent to whisper to her daughters with that same look Aunt Daisy had flashed Cleo only moments earlier. She was every inch icy royal defiance, her strength drawn from and mirrored by the crowd.

The doors to the church opened with a bang that had everyone sitting up and peering round. There was a draft, warm and sweet-scented, bringing a smile where there had only been tears. And then the singing began. A few voices raised then more until the church vibrated with sound. It bounced off the vaulted ceilings, carrying them along, lifting them up. Aunt Daisy stood proud and erect as if encased in iron, her expression as stern as that of any of the Norwegians she loved, her voice merging with theirs as an enormous Norwegian flag was carried up the altar, students gripping the edges as they made a slow procession to the altar.

An older woman reached out to touch a corner. A grandmother dabbed her eyes. A man dropped his head into his hands, weeping. Cleo felt their anger and their defiance and their love. It seemed to pulse the air as the singing and the crying continued. Her vision watered with unshed tears. Her fingers brushed an edge of the flag as it passed, the rough fabric sliding cool under her touch. So much love and courage bound up in a symbol. Out of nowhere, she was reminded of a small cemetery near the French village of Verquin and a row of cement crosses, each one bearing only a bronze plaque and a French roundel.

A young woman followed the procession before sliding into a pew just across from her. There was something about her that caught Cleo's eye: her thick honey-brown hair yanked back off her forehead and pinned with ferocity, her jawline jumping as she gripped her handbag, her stance as square as a sailor's on a deck in a storm as she sang in a high alto. After a moment, Cleo found herself humming along, the words unknown but her voice rising and falling as she followed the rousing chorus. At one point, the woman glanced over at her, a speculative gleam in her blue eyes. But Daisy nudged Cleo with an elbow, and when she snuck a look later from beneath her lashes, the woman was gone from her seat. A side door swung closed with a quick snick.

After the service ended, the congregation milled in the aisles and on the grounds outside the church as if reluctant to leave each other's company. As she waited for Aunt Daisy, Cleo wandered to a seat near the fence, where she could enjoy a cigarette and maybe slide her feet out of shoes a size too small. Her godmother and the Norwegian president, Mr. Hambro, stood in conversation. As he worked to make his point, Aunt Daisy wore her ambassador's face, grave yet inscrutable.

How many men over the years had been fooled by that steel-trap mind hidden behind a socialite's smile? All but one. Cleo had never known Bordie Harriman—he'd died the year before she was born—but she'd heard enough stories over the years about Aunt Daisy's husband to feel confident he'd never once been taken in by that patina of maternal softness.

At one point in the discussion, Aunt Daisy's gaze zeroed in on a pair of men watching the crowd from just outside the fence.

Suits.

Like the men in Zakopane.

Cleo's insides shriveled. What were they doing here?

"You're that lady from the elevator, aren't you?" Cleo jumped at the tug on her sleeve from a little girl in a robin's-egg blue coat, her blond curls coming untucked from beneath a small red cap.

"That's right. You're Princess Astrid, aren't you? Where's your mother?"

"With Ragnhild and Harald." The little girl pointed toward the church's main doors, where Crown Princess Märtha chatted with

Reverend Schubeler, who'd led the sermon. Her son and Prince Olav's heir gripped his mother's hand while her older daughter, Ragnhild, stood quietly at her side—a perfect little princess in training.

This one had a sparkle in her eye that Cleo recognized.

"You smell better than you did before," Princess Astrid declared.

"And you're just as rude as ever," Cleo teased, her laughter making the little princess giggle.

"Mama says I'm *uforbederlig*." The word was one Cleo hadn't learned, but there was an impish twist to the girl's mouth and the flash of a dimple as she said it that was easily understood. "She says I should be more like my sister. That Papa expects me to behave as a princess of Norway." Her voice dropped at the same time as her smile. "That I should make him proud."

Cleo felt the knife turn in her chest.

Your father would never . . .

Your father always . . .

If your father was here . . .

"I'm sure you make His Royal Highness proud, no matter what."

Astrid's smile bloomed once more, but this time there was no mischief behind it. Instead, there was almost relief.

"Astrid, where are you?" Crown Princess Märtha's voice carried a hint of command touched with fear.

Her daughter wasn't the only one to look up at her mother's voice. The men on the street did too, though had they ever truly focused anywhere else?

"Go on," Cleo urged Princess Astrid. "Quick now."

The little girl dashed back to the group, where she was gathered in with a whisper in her ear that quickly sobered her. She glanced back at Cleo with what looked like a question in her gaze.

"No matter what!" Cleo heard herself calling out to the girl. "Don't you forget!"

Aunt Daisy joined Cleo under the trees, an odd expression on her face. "We should go."

Their departure was interrupted by the young woman from the church. Her bright blue eyes burned as she held out a hand. "Are you Mrs. Harriman?"

Aunt Daisy experienced the same odd feeling of recognition—Cleo could see it in the way her gaze widened, her stance one of wary curiosity. "That's right."

The woman stepped forward as if to confront her, and Cleo's body went cold. Was this a German assassin? Did she mean to shoot the US minister here in front of all these people? But out of her jacket pocket, she removed only a piece of paper, dog-eared and damp, which she offered to Aunt Daisy. "My name is Sofia Kristiansen. I'm Petra's sister."

THE THREE OF them sat at a table on the Grand Hotel's veranda, overlooking the harbor. Now that Cleo had the chance to study the elder Miss Kristiansen more closely, the resemblance to Petra was obvious. The sisters shared the same elegant bone structure with cheekbones like scythes and a gaze like tempered steel. They both had the same Nordic features and both spoke English fluently with the odd quirk of an American idiom thrown in. But where Petra had been all icy pragmatic intensity, her older sister was gruff and aggressive, her voice husky with stress and cigarettes. The idea that she was a doctor was both surprising and made perfect sense. She burned with coolheaded confidence.

"We tried to locate you when we reached Stockholm," Aunt Daisy explained. "We sent word to the clinic in Dombås."

"I left Dombås in April." Sofia ground out her cigarette before taking a moment to finger the lumpy envelope Daisy had handed her at the start of their meal. There was a smudge at one corner and a small tear along the flap. It had been folded and refolded, the creases black with dirt. "I felt I could be more use tending to our troops. I've not really had a permanent address since."

If Cleo closed her eyes, she could see Petra propped up on the pillows of the Petersons' sofa. She could smell the warm scents of vanilla, yeast, and hay that permeated the Petersons' farmhouse. She looked up to see Sofia's gaze upon her—not the cool brilliance of her sister's, but warmer, a golden-flecked aquamarine. The Mediterranean rather than the North Sea.

Cleo looked down to her plate, pushing the peas into small piles, forking the grilled fish to give the illusion of eating. Behind her, someone was talking rapidly in German, too low to make out the words but too loud for her to completely ignore. Was it the same men from the church? It was impossible to know without turning around. The hotel was awash in foreigners of all stripes, friends and enemies. They were seated at adjacent tables in the restaurants and bars, sharing elevators, waiting in line together at the telegraph office. Aunt Daisy claimed she found the constant swirl of people and conversation exhilarating and was preparing to move back from the relative isolation of their hotel in Saltsjöbaden. Cleo found it unnerving and caught herself watching her back in ways she never had before.

Sofia tapped a new cigarette from her pack, leaning in to light it off the candle in the middle of the table. Her fingers were long but wiry with strength and stained with tobacco. "I have joined with a medical team headed north to be closer to the border. We'll be ready if we're needed."

"Ready for what?"

Sofia didn't answer, and Aunt Daisy didn't push, as if she already knew. As if she too was aware of the men behind them.

"Petra was furious with you for joining up," Cleo offered. "She didn't think you should risk yourself at the front."

Sofia ran a finger over the envelope's seal, her short nails bitten to the quick. Another difference between the sisters. Now that Cleo looked for them, they were easy to spot. "Petra was always the peacemaker. As a child, she would act as a buffer between me and our parents whenever we fought. She was the good daughter. She did what was expected. She never looked beyond the safe little life she'd built for herself."

"It didn't end up so safe, though, did it?" Cleo felt her anger rising on Petra's behalf.

"That is war." Sofia spread her hands palms up as if her sister's death had been an unavoidable sacrifice.

Cleo's face burned, and she fisted her fork in her hand. "Where were you when your grandmother was stranded in Bergen with no way to get home? Where were you when your parents were trapped in Narvik? Where were you when Petra was dying? It's all well and good to answer your country's call, but what about your family's? What about those you profess to love? If you're not fighting for them, who are you fighting for?"

Aunt Daisy put down her knife and fork, an embarrassed frown wrinkling her brow. Sofia didn't go so far as to blush, but she did look at Cleo with a considering expression, as if her words had pushed past Sofia's indifference to hit some part of her soft underbelly—if Sofia Kristiansen even had one. Cleo wasn't so sure.

"I'm sorry," Cleo said in a mortified rush, wishing she could take back her words. "You really must excuse me. I have a meeting I need to attend." It was the first excuse that came to her mind as she tossed down her napkin, leaving behind her uneaten dinner and a glass of wine she could really have used right now.

She heard Aunt Daisy making her apologies, Sofia brushing it off. Passing the table behind her, she glanced at the group of men she'd overheard earlier. Nothing about them stood out, but all of them gave her the creeps.

With no particular place to go, she wandered the streets around the hotel, crossing the Skeppsholmsbron, pausing halfway over the bridge to stare out across the water to the royal palace standing squat and square without a single fairytale turret or wedding cake adornment. Instead, it projected strength and permanence, a boulder in a stream, the current forever parting around it while it remained untouched.

It was late by the time she returned to the hotel, but Sofia Kristiansen was still there, leaning against a column at the bottom of the stairs smoking a cigarette. She ground it out under her boot heel and approached. Cleo unconsciously braced for a punch.

"I'm sorry for running out like that," she apologized again and almost meant it.

"There's nothing to forgive. You weren't wrong." Sofia motioned for Cleo to join her out of the rush of the lobby's traffic. The alcove she found was quiet, cushioned chairs circling an elegant cherry table. In her belted twill trousers and collared men's shirt, Sofia looked like one of the hotel staff on a smoke break. "I was wrong—for saying those things about Petra. It's as you said, I wasn't there when my family needed me." She shook her cigarette pack, but it was empty. She crumpled the light blue wrapper with its bulldog logo into a ball, only the *p* in Petterøe's still readable. Then, left without a crutch, she dropped her large bony hands between her trousered knees. "I decided my country needed me more."

CHAPTER 19

Dear Anne,

I've been kicking my heels in Stockholm for weeks. Not that there's been a dull moment among the steady stream of long alfresco lunches and leisurely cocktail receptions, but I would feel better if I knew what my future held—and if I could be certain who I could trust. Do you recall the muddy flats around Centerport Beach on Long Island? It's a bit like that. No way to gauge where the safe spots are or if I'm about to be sucked under. You would argue this is a position I should long be familiar with, but it's different this time. Maybe because I have my promise always at the back of my mind . . .

Daisy skimmed the report she'd received from Mr. Cox in Oslo on the appointment of a new German civil authority to oversee the Norwegian administration, but by the third paragraph gave it up as impossible. Too many other thoughts crowded out the facts and figures so painstakingly collected and passed on to her by the Norwegian legation. Tossing it down, she stood to stretch muscles stiff from hours behind a desk. A new pain in her lower back drowned out the old pain in her knees. She ignored them both as she paced the perimeter of her office.

For weeks, she'd been waiting to hear when she would be

traveling to rejoin King Haakon. She'd filled those weeks easily enough. She'd used the connections she'd made over the last three years within the Norwegian community to gather every scrap of information she could glean, passing it on to Freddie at the Swedish office as well as to Washington. President Hambro had been a great help, bringing news of the Norwegian government on his flying visits between Tromsø and Stockholm. But with each day that passed without instruction, Daisy's unease grew. Was she being shouldered aside? Pushed to the fringes? If she had an ounce of gumption, she'd phone Secretary Hull at the State Department and ask straight out rather than satisfying herself with memos over the potential for rationing and requisitioning of Norwegian foodstuffs.

"Mrs. Harriman . . . Madam Minister . . ." Mr. Whitney stood in the doorway with his queer combination of bullying obsequiousness. "Mr. Seaton just arrived from Washington and came immediately to see you."

The State Department's emissary was young, probably no older than Daisy's daughter, Ethel. Early forties, his wiry hair showing only a few touches of gray, the skin around his eyes just now creased with the tiniest of lines, but his expression kind. No, not kind. It was dismay she saw in his gaze, which didn't bode well. Despite the flicker of warning that curled up her spine, she greeted her guest with a warm smile. "I hope you're here to finally tell me when I might start traveling north to meet up with the Norwegian government."

Her question asked, the knot very slowly loosened as experience took hold.

"I've warned Madam Minister it's not safe," Mr. Whitney interrupted. "Not while the Germans control so much of the country."

Daisy chose not to respond to Mr. Whitney's long-standing

concerns. He was technically correct. If only he didn't take such condescending pleasure in it.

"I can't say for certain what Washington plans, ma'am. I'm sure once the situation around the city of Narvik stabilizes . . ." was Seaton's evasive nonanswer. "Though your work since your arrival here in Stockholm has been invaluable, as is your continuing relationship with the crown princess."

The flicker of warning settled into a knot at the base of her skull. "I'm not sure I'd go as far as to call it a relationship. We've hardly seen her here in the city. She's staying with her parents in the country at Villa Fridhem."

Seaton waved away her modesty and any further conversation about the princess with a clearing of his throat and a deft turn of the conversation. "You gave an interview recently, Madam Minister."

"If this is about that issue with the United Press, I've already been warned." She returned to her desk, where, with methodical, precise movements, she gathered the pages of her abandoned report and slid them into their file before adjusting the blotter and the three fountain pens. Her thoughts quieted. Her breathing slowed. He'd never realize the tension banding her shoulders or the nerves buzzing her skin. She'd not always worn the mask so well; her early days on the job had been marred by gaffes and missteps. Insignificant and easily brushed aside as the growing pains of a new diplomat. They would not be so forgiving now or under these circumstances. "I'd no idea they'd billed it as an exclusive. I certainly hadn't anticipated that when I agreed to speak to them."

"We understand the pressure you've been under; the strain of the last few weeks has been tremendous." Seaton leaned farther forward, the light bouncing off the lenses in his glasses making his expression unreadable, but now that she understood it for what it was, his impatience and his unhappiness were obvious. "No one would blame you for feeling the weight of it."

So she was right. This sojourn in Stockholm was the first step to being pushed aside. She thought she'd be hurt or insulted. Instead, she was angry. "Is it my age or my gender that gives me the free pass?"

"I'm sorry?"

"Let's cut to the chase, Mr. Seaton. Tomorrow I have a meeting with a prominent Norwegian businessman who's been clever enough to convince the Germans to let him cross the border freely as he works to bring needed supplies to the farmers in the northern districts. That will be followed by a discussion with the Germans over their decision to ration food, fuel, and grain reserves. Then there are phone calls to make, telegrams to send, and correspondence to review. Neither my schedule nor my temperament allows for beating around the bush."

"Right." Her loss of temper seemed to lift her in his estimation. His gaze focused on her with a new clarity, his nervous leg quieted under the table. "You've been receiving quite the press coverage in the German papers."

She glanced at Mr. Whitney, who was suddenly very interested in the tops of his shoes. "If you're referring to that ridiculous article in *Der Bund* . . . ," she began.

His expression shifted to something not quite a smile. "That one was a real corker. If only they were all so imaginative. Unfortunately . . ." He pulled out a pile of newspaper clippings. Some she recognized. Some were new. "This one here accuses you of being a British agent. This one a Norwegian agent." He showed her another. "Here they talk about your close connections with the new British prime minister, Churchill, a close friend of his mother's, I believe."

"Honestly, how old do they think I am?" she groused. "And

here I thought the article extolling my skills as a pianist was the most egregious."

"I assure you they get more *interesting*." His use of the word wasn't at all reassuring. He cleared his throat and resettled his glasses. "This one suggests you and Norwegian President Hambro are conspiring to bring America into the war."

"That's preposterous."

"It accuses you of begging the president to gift American ships to Norway to use against the German fleet."

That pulled her up short. She *had* sent a letter to Roosevelt last December suggesting America consider donating a few rusting destroyers lying unused in Philadelphia's shipyards. The Norwegians were a seafaring race, but in their fight to patrol their coastline, they were sadly lacking in equipment. The president had kindly, but firmly, turned her down.

"I don't need to tell you, Mrs. Harriman, that agents of Hitler's government here in Stockholm are listening, watching. Every scrap they can gather is going directly to Berlin."

He *didn't* need to tell her. These weren't the only rumors swirling around the Grand Hotel's parlors and smoking rooms. Stories persisted that the Germans were interested in laying their hands on Crown Princess Märtha and her children, most particularly Prince Harald. She'd seen for herself the men at the edges of the crowd outside Kungsholm Church, sent there to monitor and report back. She'd recognized one of them—the Gestapo officer she'd first noticed at the luncheon at Hasselbacken. So far, Sweden had kept the princess safe. But Sweden's king, the princess's uncle, walked a fine line in his dance with neutrality and enjoyed a friendly relationship with the Germans that stood a closer watch.

"I'll continue to guard my words, but there's not much I can do when the German press invents them from whole cloth." She sensed there was more to be said, but that he preferred to do it without an audience. "Mr. Whitney, weren't you in the middle of finishing that report on the growth in output of Norway's Sokndal and Knaben mines?"

"Of course, ma'am." His face twisted into something that could have been resentment or could have been consent. So hard to tell. It might make him good at his job—an enigmatic face that gave nothing away—but it made working with him damned difficult.

"Right. We're alone, Mr. Seaton. Suppose you tell me what's going on."

"It concerns your goddaughter, Miss Jaffray." He straightened his tortoiseshell glasses, his Adam's apple bobbing. Then he leaned forward to pull out a photograph, not from his zippered case but from his jacket pocket. "I think you need to see this."

CLEO SAT AT the hotel bar, her third gin of the evening in front of her. Ever since meeting Sofia Kristiansen, her nightmares had returned worse than ever. She woke with her heart racing and every muscle flexed in panic, overcome by a sense of foreboding that never quite left her. Moving back into the Grand Hotel hadn't made it easier. Aunt Daisy brightened at the center of tugging influences, drawing energy from the whirl around her, while the constant fun house dissonance of competing languages and allegiances made Cleo dizzy and claustrophobic.

Tonight she had accompanied Mrs. Thorson to a dinner at the America-Sweden Women's Friendship Institute, a group of mostly diplomatic wives, though the local business and expat community were well represented. While the conversation had been one of concern and apprehension, there was a disconnect Cleo couldn't overcome. A feeling that the fight wasn't theirs and all precautions should be taken to keep it that way.

By the time she'd taken her leave, she felt her mood sliding toward the old familiar darkness. For weeks, she'd been able to push it to the edges of her mind, but it had never disappeared completely. Tonight's indifference had fractured her grip. Gin wouldn't rid her of the terrors that plagued her, but it would dull the edges until sleep wasn't the enemy.

She waved the bartender over for a refill.

"If you're looking to lose yourself in a bottle, I'd go somewhere a little more anonymous, especially if you're worried about Whitney and your aunt's reputation."

She looked up into Bayard's concerned face. "Mine being irredeemable, you mean?"

"Nice try, but I'm on to you, Cleo Jaffray. You're not the spoiled little rich girl you want everyone to think you are." His gaze narrowed in on her face, her shoulders, her posture, as if he saw beneath her bluster to a part of her even she didn't understand yet. It took all her willpower not to shrink under his stare. "Come on. There's a place I think you need to go."

It was easier to be led than dragged, and despite her protest, she was glad of his intrusion. It broke her free from what would have been a dismal evening of maudlin self-pity.

Bayard didn't let go when they reached the sidewalk. Instead, he quick-stepped her around the harbor and over the bridge that took them into the city's Old Town. Past the fortresslike royal palace, where Cleo glanced up at the lighted windows as if she might spy the blond curls and cheeky smile of Princess Astrid. Into a warren of crooked, narrow alleyways lined with shops and cafés, clubs and dance halls, where soon enough she was completely lost with no idea how to get back to her hotel barstool. At last, he slowed in front of a narrow nondescript stuccoed building of arched windows beneath a sagging awning.

The door was propped open, letting the sounds of a smooth clarinet underpinned by the brush of the snare spill out into the street. A singer stepped up to the microphone, her emerald dress shimmering under the stage lights. Candles and shaded wall sconces created an intimacy of shadows, flickering over the drinkers at the bar, the couples glued to one another on the dance floor, the men and women packing the tables. A waitress guided them to a seat and furnished them with two martinis. Somehow being given permission made the idea less appealing. Still, Cleo downed her drink, letting it fill the cracks where the memories tried to reach her.

"Come here often?" She said it as a joke, but Bayard didn't even crack a smile.

"You're not the only one feeling sorry for yourself."

The first round of martinis disappeared, as did the second. Her body relaxed as warmth extended along every limb like honey. The replay of unbroken moments began to slow then dissolve. She could focus on the music and the people around her, which is when she first sensed the smoldering tension like a backbeat to the band. It pulsed between tables, made itself felt in a pounded fist, a shouted word, heads grouped close in conspiracy.

"What is this place?" she asked.

"Officially it's called Oväder, but a lot of people have started calling it 'lille Norge.'"

Cleo studied her surroundings with new eyes, seeing the drawn faces of the waitresses, the anger in the barman's eye. The table beside them was in a loud argument over the British takeover of Norway's merchant shipping fleet. The couples on the dance floor clung together like survivors in a lifeboat. The singer wept as she broke into a traditional folk song that ended with raised glasses and shouted toasts from nearly every table. "Long live Norway!"

"Is this supposed to make me feel better?"

"It's supposed to make you realize you're not the only one feeling powerless." Cleo tried not to notice how quickly Bayard's own drinks disappeared or the tension draining his features. She wasn't the only one aching under the weight of useless regrets. That sense of painful solidarity made her bold.

"You don't have to pretend around me, you know," she ventured as Bayard waved over the waitress for another round. "I was there."

He didn't feign ignorance at her meaning. If anything, he seemed to relax a little.

"Petra died. But her death is not your fault any more than it's mine."

His shoulders sank, and he looked away at the growing crowd. "I know that. I do. But I promised her she'd be fine. That morning at the guesthouse in Elverum when I told her about Sofia, I fed Petra this big song and dance about how we'd be safe and not to worry."

Fine. Safe. Don't worry. Micky had said all that and more whenever Cleo brought up the idea of leaving Poland. Comforting lies. Empty and meaningless when the world was coming apart at the seams. "Petra wasn't a child, Bayard, and that wasn't a promise you had the power to keep."

Her words were sharper than she intended, but they had the desired effect. He came back to himself with a nod and an apology. "It's not just guilt over her death that keeps me up at night."

"It's not?"

He met her gaze, the caramel brown of his irises practically melting into the black of his pupils. His brows curved low as if he struggled with a particularly complicated equation. "No."

So much feeling bound up in that word. It slid into her stomach like the heat from her martini and teased along her skin like a touch.

The band swung into a soulful rendition of "Stardust." Bayard stood up from the table and offered his hand. "Would you care to dance?"

This was probably a really bad idea, but Cleo was beyond caring. She laid her hand in his with a smile. "I'd love to."

She'd never noticed how tall he was until she was clasped in his arms. She'd never smelled his woodsy cologne or known that he was a horrible dancer. It was endearing when he wasn't crushing her toes.

"Sorry," he muttered in between keeping time under his breath. "Two left feet."

"Don't they teach ballroom dance at West Point?"

"I'm ROTC so I wouldn't know." His smile took the sting from his words. "But I can see you being all the rage among a ballroom full of generals in the making."

Maybe it was the martinis on top of a stomach already full of gin. Maybe it was the defiant atmosphere that called to her own chronic anger. Or maybe it was the security of being embraced by a man she trusted as she'd not let herself trust since Micky walked out. "Generals are highly overrated."

She laid her head against his chest, felt the scratch of his uniform against her cheek, the steady beat of his heart under her ear, and let herself imagine she was a young deb at a dance with a handsome ROTC recruit.

A cool breeze disturbed the heavy odors of alcohol, sawdust, and hot bodies as the outer door opened and the inner curtains were drawn aside to admit a woman dressed, not for an evening out, but in trousers and a collared shirt under a soldier's jacket. Bayard stepped free of Cleo's arms, and the moment was gone in a drift of cigarette smoke and the fade of the trumpet.

"It's Sofia," Cleo said, slightly dizzy from the dance and her own disturbing thoughts.

"I know." Bayard flushed as if they'd been caught in flagrante delicto. "I invited her."

* * *

"WE CAN STILL win against the Germans." Sofia Kristiansen slammed her fist onto the scarred table. "We can still take back what is ours." She practically grabbed Bayard by the lapels to demand he agree with her. "If only they would listen to General Fleischer, an experienced leader who knows the terrain and knows how to fight."

"Who's they?" Cleo asked, welcoming her buzz as a way to numb herself against the onslaught of grievances and rage.

Sofia hadn't mentioned Petra since she'd arrived—not once. If she mourned her sister, it wasn't evident in the deadly flash of her gaze or the way she clenched her glass of beer. Or perhaps this was sorrow. This desperate need to fight back, to hurt others as she'd been hurt.

That Cleo could understand.

"The Allies, of course," she argued. "The English and the French. They have the men, but they behave as if they have already lost . . . as if they have already given up. They dragged us into this with their provocations, and now they retreat like frightened rabbits."

"They're beginning to look to their own borders."

Bayard had explained that he'd invited Sofia here to discuss what she knew of the state of the Norwegian military on the northern border. But the conversation had quickly escalated into a drink-fueled rant with Bayard barely able to get a word in edgewise while Cleo, stunned at how easily she'd fallen into the lieutenant's arms, had ordered round after round on Bayard's tab.

"So where does that leave us?" Sofia demanded before answering her own question. "With our asses dangling in the wind for the Germans to shoot off, that's where."

Bayard had no answer, or rather the answer was so obvious, it didn't need to be stated out loud. That wasn't good enough for Sofia. "Your government sits by as Europe is devoured country by country. I hear your politicians' excuses. It is not your fight. You have an ocean to protect you. Why should American boys die for countries on the other side of the world? We don't ask for you to fight for us. We ask only that you offer us the assistance we need to fight for ourselves."

Maybe it was the desolation in Sofia's gaze. Or the guilt Cleo felt hearing her old attitudes parroted back at her. Maybe it was Bayard—two Bayards, actually—both of them sitting across from Cleo with their stupid Joseph Cotton straightforward looks while Sofia railed about American cowardice and isolationism. But Cleo heard herself fighting back. At least she thought it was her. It sounded like her voice, though never had a thought even close to this one come out of her mouth.

"Not every American thinks we should stay out of it," she argued, her tongue thick, her mouth dry. A steady pounding that wasn't all the band's bass drum in her head. "My father fought and died in the last war. He didn't wait for his country to send him. He died wearing a French pilot's uniform because he believed we needed to stand together against dictators. There are plenty of Americans who feel the same way now. I guarantee it."

Sofia sat back, more considering now and less contemptuous. But her regard wasn't the one that sent prickles along Cleo's skin or fizzed her stomach despite the gallons of alcohol. Bayard watched her too before pushing his chair back and holding out a hand for her to take. "It's late. We should probably get you home, Miss Jaffray."

She noted his use of her surname and was more hurt than she'd expected. "Should we?" She levered herself to her feet with his assistance, the floor pitching and rolling beneath her. "Yes, I expect we should. I suddenly don't feel so well."

Outside, she drew in a deep damp breath of smoke and salty air that swam in her stomach and made her head spin. Streetlights reflected in every puddle and washed the buildings in gold. Despite the late hour, people still milled in front of shop windows or strolled the cobblestoned alleys enjoying the fine weather. There was laughter and conversation and romance. Normal life in a city oddly untouched by the violence of war that washed menacingly against its borders.

"I never knew that about your father," Bayard remarked as they retraced their steps. At least she thought they did. Surely that was the bridge they'd crossed earlier and that building up ahead looked familiar . . . or maybe it was that building over there.

"I've had that story shoved down my throat since birth. I have no idea if it's even true, but tragic war hero sounds better than heartless bastard." They wound their way down to the waterfront along the Skeppsbrokajen, where sailboats and pleasure craft rubbed up against steamers and workboats. "I wouldn't care so much what lies my mother tells herself, but she expects me to worship the fantasy too."

"Maybe it wasn't about lying. Maybe it was about giving you a father you could be proud of."

"Now who's dispensing the sage advice?" Cleo teased, looping her arm through Bayard's. Unaccountably happy when he didn't pull away.

Shivering from more than the cool night air, she focused on the lights of the Grand Hotel that dazzled on the far side of the water, a million reflections shimmering on the waves like coins in a fountain. She never noticed the broken paving stone until it tripped her. She grabbed at his shoulders. He clasped her around the waist. The two of them clung swaying at the water's edge, the sky whirling overhead like a Van Gogh painting.

Before she could think better of it, she kissed him. Maybe it was more accurate to say she stumbled herself at him. But he didn't let go. His lips were as warm as she imagined, and he was careful as if afraid to frighten her off, or perhaps he was the one who was frightened. With the passing seconds, his kiss deepened. His body against hers was as hard as steel, his breathing ragged. She felt her body responding and clung tighter, her fingers gliding up under his uniform jacket to the smooth heat of his skin beneath. She hadn't felt this way since— No. She wouldn't think of him. Or her. Or any of the reasons why being here and doing this was a very bad idea. Only now that she was thinking, she couldn't stop. And kissing and thinking never went well together.

A bark of laughter from a nearby group of men jolted them both back to reality. Bayard cleared his throat as if preparing to apologize or explain, or worst of all, tell her it was an accident that meant nothing.

Instead, his stammering words were a jumble of noise in her ears as her unfocused gaze spotted a familiar figure standing in a nearby doorway.

The swirl of Van Gogh became a nauseating smear of light and color and her own heavy breathing. She tried to fling herself out of Bayard's embrace, once again nearly plunging them both into the harbor, but he was stronger and held her upright, his considering expression becoming a frown that shadowed the edges of his eyes.

"I saw him," she gasped. "I saw Micky."

CHAPTER 20

Dear Anne,

If only you were here with your perfect combination of eminent good sense and bracing encouragement. I'm sure you would have a few choice words for me on the nature of duty, responsibility, and the burden of leadership and then you would tell me to forget them all where family is concerned. If only it was so easy. If only we were back in those halcyon days of our youth when the world was fresh and the path seemed so easy . . .

Daisy set aside the letter. There was no rush these days. No one waiting to read it. It made it harder to write, but easier to say what needed to be said. All the thoughts in her head that had no outlet could be put down, made real with pen and ink. Sometimes just the task of writing brought her relief and an answer to her question. A new perspective that suddenly sprang into focus like the brilliant flash of a light bulb.

And even when it didn't, the act of writing to Anne kept her alive. She'd had no updates on her sister-in-law's condition nor had Daisy sought them out. It was unlike her to take the coward's way, but so long as she didn't know for certain, she could hope. And hope was a priceless commodity in times like these.

Rubbing the aching spot between her brows, Daisy pulled the accordion folder front and center, spreading out the clippings and notes, with that damned article and its photograph on the top of the pile.

A FAMILY OF SPIES the headline screamed in German, revealing the closely guarded secret that a cousin of the current American minister served as her intelligence agent in Poland and the pair had been instrumental in a bombing that killed over twenty German military along with an unspecified number of Polish nationals. Lies, all of it. Imagined by a so-called journalist and published in a newspaper filled with similar conspiracies, intrigues, and evil gossip. But it was the photograph accompanying the article that Daisy studied inch by grainy, badly lit inch.

It was obviously Cleo. Daisy recognized that big smile and that gaudy costume diamond necklace, even with the photograph out of focus and Cleo standing in the shadows behind a table circled by German officers. One reached back toward her, his face lit with laughter. But it was the man at the edge of the photograph that drew Daisy's eye, the man beside Cleo watching the scene, a cigarette held loosely between his fingers. She could see why her goddaughter had been smitten. Micky Kominski was far too good-looking: deep-set eyes, thick dark hair, and a pair of full lips above a dimpled chin. The caption beneath the photograph read: *Czarny Kot a week before its destruction by a foreign agent.*

Cleo could no more have bombed the café than flown to the moon, but Kominski? Maybe Daisy's earliest suspicions had been correct. Maybe Kominski's death had been more than bad luck. Seaton had reminded Daisy that while no one took stories like this seriously, tensions with Germany remained high, and any whiff of scandal could be enough to derail ongoing talks with Hitler's government. She waited for him to mention Cleo's murderous exit from Oslo as a case in point, but it never came. Perhaps she'd been wrong about Whitney's intentions.

The scrape of a key in the door alerted Daisy to Cleo's return. She watched as Cleo let herself into the hotel suite—palming her key, sliding out of her shoes, glancing around like a hunted animal.

"You're late," Daisy said.

Cleo dropped her key and her shoes to the floor with a clatter. "You scared me, Aunt Daisy. I thought you'd be asleep long ago."

Her words came slow and thick, and her face was as gray as her coat. Daisy would have chalked it up to drink, but there was more to it in the shadows that clouded her eyes and the nervous hitch in her breathing. "I'll phone down for a pot of coffee."

Cleo looked as if she would like nothing less, but she nodded and slumped into an armchair while Daisy rang for room service. It took only a few minutes to push a mug into Cleo's hands. "Here. I changed my mind and ordered cocoa instead."

Suspicion bloomed like spots on Cleo's cheeks. "Mother only ever made cocoa when she was trying to soften bad news."

In an almost repeat of Seaton's movements of a few hours ago, Daisy pushed the article and the photograph across the table. "I think you need to read this. It's a sloppy attempt to discredit me by attacking you, but I thought you should be warned in case someone mentions it."

Cleo winced at the burn on her tongue as she hunched over the clipping, her gaze shifting as she seemed to read it, study the photo, and read it again. "Is this a joke? I never spied, and I certainly never murdered anyone." Her gaze remained fixed on the photograph, confusion creasing the corners of her eyes, digging at her chin. "Do people believe this? That I planted a bomb? That I killed all those people? That I killed Micky?"

"No one believes it." As far as she knew. Though Seaton was decidedly somber as he relayed the information and Mr. Whitney, when he was filled in, questioned whether Cleo might not restrict her activities with the Norwegian Refugee Office to less public roles in the future, though he did it without his usual snide contempt, which Daisy appreciated.

She folded the clipping away while Cleo focused on the froth on her cocoa. Silence spun out as if her thoughts drifted. Daisy might have blamed it on a bumpy return to sobriety if not for the tapping of Cleo's fingers against her mug, an assessing expression on her pale features.

"Did something happen this evening, Clementine?"

"I went out for a drink with Lieutenant Bayard and Sofia Kristiansen."

More than one, by the smell of her. "Dr. Kristiansen is a force to be reckoned with. Despite their differences, she reminds me of her sister in so many ways."

Cleo's face shut down, and Daisy cursed herself for stepping wrong. Petra's death had been a blow whose repercussions still radiated outward like a stone in a pond. She waited, letting the air clear, the memories dissipate. It worked. Cleo shifted in her seat and blew on her cocoa, before settling back, a tightness in her jaw.

"It's funny this article coming now," she said quietly. "Tonight, I mean."

"Funny? In what way?" Daisy ached to pry her open like an oyster, but nudging would get her nowhere. Instead, she let the silence grow until it practically buzzed in her ears.

"I thought . . . I mean it was dark so I couldn't be sure . . ."

"Couldn't be sure about what?"

Whatever Cleo might have been about to say was lost when she covered her mouth, her face going a ghastly green as she shoved back from the table, the mug sloshing cocoa all over the table and into her lap as she raced for the door. "Oh God. I'm going to be sick."

Daisy waited, her own cocoa growing a skin as it cooled, but Cleo didn't return. When Daisy went to look, she found her sprawled asleep across her bed, still in her clothes, tendrils of dark hair stuck to her damp forehead, and the clipping with the photo of Micky Kominski crushed in one hand.

THE HANDSOME WATERSIDE boulevard of Strandvägen and the streets surrounding it were a hub of embassies and legations, government offices, and diplomatic agencies. Americans rubbed shoulders with Germans, whose windows looked out over Norwegians who had coffee with the British while the Swedes monitored everyone. Cleo could walk fifty yards in any direction and hear come-ons and catcalls in ten different languages.

She ignored them all, waiting on a bench by the water and only occasionally checking her watch until Bayard emerged from the American legation at number 7, saw her across the street, and waved.

Her heart did a little flip, which she squashed like a bug. That kiss had been a mistake even if she had relived it a hundred times over the last few days. She needed to pull herself together. She gripped her handbag and told herself she'd imagined what she saw. It wouldn't be the first time she'd conjured Micky out of thin air. That's all this was.

And yet . . .

"You sounded weird on the phone. Everything okay?"

A loaded question and one she ignored. She had bigger fish to fry this afternoon. "That journalist friend of yours—is he still in Stockholm?"

Bayard didn't seem put off by her bluntness. If anything, he relaxed, his hands and jaw unclenching. Whatever he thought she'd planned on saying, that wasn't it. Maybe he regretted that kiss as much as she did. "For now, he's rooming with a friend just outside of the city. Housing is impossible without the right documents."

"What's his address? Better yet, can you take me? He's more likely to open up to someone he knows."

"Do I get to know what you want him to open up about?"

"I'll fill you in on the way."

"Oh, so this is like a *now* kind of thing?" he asked. She waited until he gave a small sigh of assent and an indulgent shrug. "Sure. Fine. What else do I have to do with my afternoon?"

The train took them just north of the city, where it was a quick walk to a long block of uninspiring flats in a working class neighborhood. Bayard led the way up the outside stairs to the top floor, continuing their conversation from the train. "You've said your aunt doesn't believe you were involved in the bombing."

"But how did they even know I was there? And the photograph they used? It doesn't make sense unless someone in Zakopane informed them." She showed him the photo. "See that guy in the back? He was at the German legation in Oslo. He's the one who said he'd help me find Micky."

"Who is he?"

"I don't know. That's why we're here. I'm hoping your friend can tell me more."

A bolt slid back and a round-faced man with sunken eyes answered the door. His smile was tired but friendly. "Lieutenant Bayard? This is an unexpected surprise. To what do I owe the pleasure?"

"Sorry to drop in unannounced, Donald, but—"

Bayard hadn't even finished his sentence when the man noticed Cleo, his gaze sharpening in recognition. "Clementine Jaffray." He opened the door wider. "The spy who took out twenty

German officers in a bombing. Come in, and welcome to my humble home."

She turned her gritted teeth into a smile. "Glad my fame precedes me. Saves time."

The flat was small and utilitarian: a couch and chair tucked into a corner across from a kitchenette. Bath and bedroom down a short hall. A window that overlooked a courtyard filled with trash cans and flapping laundry. Donald moved a tidy pile of pillows to the end of the couch to make room. That was when Cleo noticed the stiff, awkward way he moved, as if he'd been broken and put back together again. But his eyes remained bright as agates and there was a terrier inquisitiveness to his features. "I'm going to assume this isn't a social call."

"Bayard says you were stationed in Berlin. I'm hoping you'll be able to identify the people in this photo." She handed him the clipping.

Donald hobbled to the desk, where he switched on a lamp, studying the photo carefully from corner to corner. Out of a drawer, he took a magnifying glass, which he used to retrace his steps. Cleo felt herself holding her breath.

He stood up, stretching and wincing. "Well, there's you . . ."

"Anyone else?"

"The man in the middle with the cigar is Oberscharführer Kruger and the chap holding the mug looks like a man called Taubert, but I can't be one hundred percent sure." He shook his head. "A shame you didn't get them when you got the rest. Nasty pieces of work."

"And him at the back?" She pointed to Micky.

Donald took a moment before shaking his head. "Nope. Never seen him before. Somebody you know?"

"You could say that."

"You want to tell me what this is about? I'm going to assume that you're not in fact the minister to Norway's private assassin in Poland?"

"If I was, I'd like to think I'd be smarter than to have my photo taken at the scene of the crime." She chewed her lip, trying to decide how much to reveal. "How about this guy? The one in the corner who looks like he's trying not to be seen. Do you recognize him?"

He took up his magnifying glass and stared for a long time, his terrier features seeming to triangle in on the scent. "Oh yeah, I know him. You want nasty? He's your man."

"What's his name?"

"Kriminalinspektor Victor Heimmel. He's Gestapo." He looked at the photo again, his jaw locking. "He sure seems interested in you, Miss Jaffray."

That's what she'd thought too until she looked again. His head was tilted slightly as he tried to avoid the camera so that it looked like his attention was on Cleo, but, in fact, just beyond her and returning Heimmel's gaze was Micky.

If she didn't know better, she'd think they knew one another.

THERE WAS NO time over the following days to do anything with this information but chew on it in the few moments she could spare from Mrs. Thorson's constant demands. Work at the Refugee Office increased as Norway's prospects faltered, and Cleo found herself working later and later to try to keep up. Tonight, she'd stayed long past quitting time, if there even was such a thing anymore.

She emerged from the Norwegian legation to a cool summer rain that washed down the pavement and rattled in the gutters of Banérgatan. It was too late for the bus, and there were no taxis to be had on such a soggy evening. Surrendering to the inevitable slog, she hunched deeper into her raincoat, and did her best to ignore the cold water sliding under her collar and chilling her back. It wasn't dark; it didn't get dark this close to the solstice, but the light was gray and flat and a low fog hung between the buildings, thickening shadows and throwing sound into queer, swirling echoes.

She headed south, splashing through puddles, passing equally dismal people in equally drenched raincoats. A car passed, wipers frantic, its headlights barely cutting the gloom. She was crossing Linnégatan and passing the turn for the history museum when she heard someone behind her. Not footsteps exactly. The rain was too heavy for that. But there was a scrape of stone. A presence felt more than heard or seen.

Her heart jumped into a higher gear, and the cold rain wasn't the only thing making her shiver. She picked up the pace and turned onto Strandvägen, a busy thoroughfare even this late at night. A few people ducked past her, newspapers held over their heads to protect them. A couple raced by sharing an umbrella. Uniforms and mumbled voices in warring accents and of warring nations.

It wasn't the first time Cleo sensed she was being followed. Ever since her visit to Donald's flat in Solna, she'd felt uneasy. Her first thought had been that it was Micky. But when the days passed without a note or a phone call, her certainty faded. If it was Micky, why hadn't he tried to contact her? Maybe it wasn't Micky she'd spotted that night on the quayside. Maybe she'd been seeing ghosts again.

In this instance, ghosts might be the lesser of evils because if it wasn't Micky out there, maybe it was someone looking for him. Someone who suspected that not only was he still alive, but that she might know where he was hiding.

There it was again, a noise barely audible. One that followed her, pausing when she paused, hiding behind the sound of her own footsteps along the cobblestones. She dug into her purse, her hand fisting around her fountain pen, the closest item she had to a weapon. With the other hand, she gripped her necklace as if it was a talisman against evil, her fingers crushing the stone until it cut into the soft skin of her palm.

She kept to the same pace, neither looking left nor right nor glancing behind her, though she felt a tickle at the back of her neck that wasn't the slither of rain down and across her shoulder blades. A hundred yards on, she would have the park on one side, the water on the other. There would be no cover. Her pursuer would be forced to reveal themselves or give up the chase. Of course, she'd be exposed as well, but there was nothing she could do. This was the fastest way to the hotel, and the rain was coming down harder now.

She hurried past the landing stage for one of the tour boats when a body enveloped in a raincoat and hat brushed past her, nearly knocking her down. The voice was low and gravely, uttering what might have been a threat or an apology. No way to tell over the roaring in her ears. She leaned against a building to catch her breath and the figure disappeared into the fog. So too did her stalker. She no longer heard them behind her. She was alone again.

She squelched her way through the hotel's double doors and up the short flight of steps to the lobby then dripped her way into the bar, where she knew Bayard would be, where he almost always was this time of night. She smiled, catching sight of him at his usual spot, a whiskey on the counter before him. "Lieutenant Bayard?"

He looked up, his eyes widening both at her use of his full formal title and the state of her wardrobe, his jaw going loose as if he fought the urge to gape outright.

"It's time for that shooting lesson."

CHAPTER 21

Dear Anne,

Norway is lost. As yet, few have heard the disastrous news, but it won't take long. The boy with his bag of papers standing outside your door in New York City will be hawking the headline by the end of the week at the latest.

The messenger from Freddie Sterling arrived just as Daisy was finishing up her meeting with Mr. Whitney and Lieutenant Bayard.

Daisy took a moment and read the dispatch again just to be sure. She felt her heart flutter in her chest and cold wash across her shoulders. "The Allies have withdrawn their assistance, forcing the Norwegian military to concede to the Germans."

No one moved. No one spoke. The only sound was the ticking of the clock on the shelf and the horn of an approaching ferry outside. Then Mr. Whitney snapped his pencil in half with a muttered "shit" and Bayard flung himself from his chair to pace the room in choppy, angry strides. "Damn it! We should have seen this coming. We've had reports of heavy bombardments by German aircraft on troop positions in the south and maintaining a free north would have required far more men and aircraft than the Allies have at their disposal. I guess with France lost and the British forces trapped there between the German advance and the sea, it's each to his own."

"It makes sense from a military standpoint, but I guarantee our Norwegian friends won't see it like that." Mr. Whitney scratched a knuckle over his chin.

"No," Daisy agreed. "They'll see the western democracies, who they trusted, as abandoning them. I worry this bitterness could send them into the arms of the Germans."

"Have you received any updates on His Majesty and the crown prince?" Mr. Whitney asked.

Daisy shuffled, then straightened her papers. "They've been evacuated by the British and are on their way to London to set up a government in exile."

"Leaving the crown princess behind."

"Yes. Unfortunately. I've heard through President Hambro and others in the country that there are those in Norway pressing for the king's abdication in favor of a regency for Crown Princess Märtha. I imagine this originates among those most unhappy with the Allies as well as those most fearful of angering Reichskommissar Terboven and his boss back in Berlin."

"The Germans would love that. What a propaganda coup to have Prince Harald on the throne and under the thumb of the Nazis," Mr. Whitney commented.

"She'd never agree to it," Bayard shot back. "Not after all she undertook to get out of Norway in the first place."

"We hope that's the case, but the pressure on her is extreme and growing by the day," Daisy replied.

"You think her uncle is one of those pressuring her to return?"

"I think he would do whatever he could to secure the safety of his country. And so does Prince Olav, if the latest reports from

London are accurate. He's convinced Hitler is actively plotting to get hold of Harald."

Bayard tossed the cigarette away. "So we get her out of Sweden. Out of Europe."

"Just like that?" Mr. Whitney looked up. "Snap our fingers and magic her away?"

"Why not?" Bayard answered. "President Roosevelt took a huge shine to Crown Prince Olav and his wife when they visited Hyde Park last year. I'll bet he'd offer his assistance if he was convinced it was the only way to keep the family out of the hands of the Germans."

"I'll bring it up with Sterling, and we'll put a plan together." Daisy turned the page to their next order of business. "Lieutenant Bayard, you're scheduled to leave for Namsos next week?"

"I should be on the road tomorrow, ma'am. But are you sure I wouldn't be more help to you here?"

"I think we can manage for a short while, and with these new developments it's more important than ever we have eyes on the ground. We'll see you as soon as you get back." Daisy closed her file. "In one piece, Lieutenant. That's an order."

"I'll do my best."

"Forgive me. I didn't mean to interrupt." Cleo pulled up short in the doorway, her gaze circling the room. She'd traded her dress for a sweater and a pair of men's dungarees cinched at the waist with a leather belt and her hair was tied back in a pretty pink scarf that heightened the blush in her cheeks when she caught sight of the lieutenant. "I was looking for the lieutenant." She grinned. "We have a date."

Daisy sought out Bayard, who looked like he'd just swallowed a fly. "Go on." She waved the two of them off. "We're done here."

Lieutenant Bayard cleared his throat as he pushed back his

chair. His normally open features slammed closed, not a thought escaping except maybe embarrassment as he and Cleo departed.

Mr. Whitney frowned until the pair were well away. "You suppose there's something going on between those two?" His usual pinched look eased for a moment into something more like sympathy, and he scrubbed a hand through his hair. "It doesn't seem right."

Daisy bent back over her correspondence, trying to keep the cold in her bones at bay. "No. And I'm sure they realize that more than anyone."

"MAKE SURE IT'S in line with the forearm. Firm grip on the stock. That's it. Slight upward angle. You can use two hands if it's easier."

Bayard stood just behind Cleo, reaching around to place her hands in the correct position on the pistol. She shivered at his breath tickling her ear, the heat of him against her back. She glanced over her shoulder with a grin. "Did you see Mr. Whitney's face? I thought he might swallow his tongue."

He shook his head, placing his hand over her hand, moving it a quarter inch to the left, refolding her fingers with a squeeze she felt all the way to her toes. Maybe this wasn't the best idea she'd ever had. Or maybe it was genius. "You like tossing a cat among the pigeons, don't you?"

Telling herself this was important and she needed to pay attention to his words and not the way she fit into the curve of his body or the tingling of her skin when they touched, she made herself focus on the pistol and the target twenty-five yards away at the far end of the field. "If the pigeon is Mr. Whitney, then yes. He's just too easy."

"I can't argue with that. But . . ."

"But what?"

His body tensed as if he was preparing to say something important. Their eyes locked, his almost pained. Would this be the moment? She held her breath, both wanting and dreading what he might say next.

"Nothing," he mumbled finally, returning to his lesson.

Bayard had brought her to an enormous park at the edge of the city with enough space to accommodate a small firing range run by the Frivilliga Skyttevāsendet, a volunteer shooting club with groups all over the country.

Bayard's was such a good-natured face it was hard to see him as the soldier he was. But when he pulled his service pistol from its holster, she could see him settling into his uniform. His center of gravity lowered into his legs as his shoulders widened, and there was a shuttering to his open gaze like a mask falling over his familiar features. It was both reassuring and frightening, like having a favorite dog suddenly show its teeth.

"Arm straight. Not that way. More like this. Steady your wrist and elbow. Use your shoulder. That's it. Eyes level. Even breaths. Don't think too hard."

He had Cleo go over every step until she could load, reload, and fire the .45 without flinching or closing her eyes when she pulled the trigger.

"You've been keeping an eye on Whitney like I asked?" A topic safe of minefields.

"I've kept both eyes on him and come to the conclusion that he's cynical, pompous, and a bit close-minded, but we knew that already," Bayard answered, back on easy footing after their brief awkwardness.

By the end of the lesson, Cleo's aim was still atrocious and her ears rang as if someone had struck a gong right behind her eyes, but she could shoot a paper target from up to fifty yards away. How she would do if the paper target decided to shoot back was a problem for another day.

"You're no Annie Oakley, but you'll do."

"I don't need to be. I just need to do what I need to do if I need to do it. No hesitation. No fear."

"Fear is your body's way of keeping you alive."

"*This* is my way."

"I know you think there's some sort of clue to Micky's disappearance in that photograph, but it's hardly proof of anything other than that Heimmel was in Zakopane when you were, and he admitted to that."

"True, but it doesn't add up. The coincidence of him being in that café? The way the two of them are watching each other? Now someone's following me? It all ties together. I just don't know how yet."

"I wish you'd tell your aunt. Or let me tell her."

"Tell her what? That I think I'm being followed but I'm not sure because I've never seen anyone and they've never done anything to me? I'll tell her when there's something to tell."

They stayed until the light grew uncertain. "We should get back," Bayard suggested. "I leave early tomorrow."

"What do you mean leave?" The hairs on the back of Cleo's neck stood up. "Where are you going?"

"I'm headed back into Norway. Communications between Stockholm and Oslo are still unreliable—no guarantee of who might be listening. Best to get our information firsthand."

"Why you?" she asked weakly.

"Why not?" was his eminently reasonable answer. She wanted to smash him over the head for it.

Somewhere along the way, she'd come to rely on Bayard being there, like a piece of the furniture. Not flashy or stylish, but comfortable and broken in. It wasn't a feeling she wanted to investigate too closely. Not while guilt and attraction were such a tangle. "Be careful. I can't lose anyone else."

"I'll be back before you know it. Promise."

Micky had said much the same and the war had taken him. One more parting. One more goodbye. Her life felt like a series of fractures, none of them fatal, but each one causing a little more damage. At what point would she break?

"You'll be fine, Cleo. You're not on your own anymore. Whatever is going on, you have people you can count on."

He assumed she was worried for herself, which was sweet and so Bayard-like. Or maybe he knew her too well—the old her. The ride back into the city was quiet, both of them caught up in their own thoughts. She didn't want to go back to the hotel. Her room was too quiet, left too much space to think. And mostly what she was thinking was that she didn't want this day to end. To watch Bayard walk away with no guarantee he'd come back.

The words swam through her head, a disjointed babble, more emotion than coherent thought. She stared out the window, seeing the city close in around them, streets narrowing, buildings rising up to either side. Pressure grew at the back of her throat and gripped her ribcage. She only sat up when Bayard passed the hotel on his way onto Stallgatan and up around the Ladugårdslandsviken waterfront. "Where are we going?"

"Trust me," he said with a secretive glance.

"You said that the last time and we ended up in a bar full of angry Norwegians." But she settled back into her seat, the pressure blooming into a warm glow under her skin.

Twenty minutes later, they pushed through the turnstiles at the city's amusement park at Gröna Lund. Above the tight cluster of buildings towered the rolling track of a coaster, the click of ascending cars loud over the organ music and the bang and clank of carnival games.

"Really? I'm dressed like a stevedore and you bring me for a night out?"

He paused, his smile falling into uncertainty. "Should I take you home?"

She grinned and pulled him forward. "Not on your life."

Gröna Lund Tivoli hugged the Djurgården waterfront. Rides, stages, and carnival amusements tucked into a corner of land the size of a postage stamp. Families clustered around the carousel while gangs of rowdy young men with slick hair and dungarees and shiny-faced giggling couples followed the sounds of a jazz band at the waterfront. Bayard and Cleo wandered among the stalls. He dragged her into the fun house. She pulled him onto the coaster. By the time they shared a boat through the Tunnel of Love, her initial surprise broadened like a bubble inflating into happiness.

"There used to be a carnival that would come through town every summer when I was a kid." Bayard handed her a paper bag of popcorn and bought one for himself. "The usual games and sideshows, the fat lady and the sword swallower. You could pay a penny to have your fortune told. My dad would take me every night. He was like a little kid. Couldn't get enough of it."

"Where was your mom?"

"She died when I was twelve—pneumonia. Poor dad was stuck with five kids to raise on his own."

"You have siblings?"

"Two sisters and two brothers. I'm the oldest."

She shook her head. "Why does that not surprise me?"

He gave her a slightly embarrassed smile. "I've been told I'm a bit of a stick-in-the-mud."

"That's harsh. I'd call it an overdeveloped sense of responsibility bordering on mother hen, but it definitely makes sense now."

"Dad did his best, but it was a struggle. He wasn't well when he came back from the war. It was like he was still fighting it in his head. Some days he'd be angry. Some days he couldn't get out of bed." Bayard didn't want her pity. It was obvious in the clipped matter-of-fact way he told his story. It was just the way it was, and he'd made his peace with it long ago. But Cleo took his hand anyway. "Still, every year when that carnival set up, he'd be there with all of us in tow, and it was like a light switched on inside him. For that one week, he was a different person. Then the carnival would pack up and move on and take the magic with it. Dad was back to being Dad."

"Do you suppose my father would have been the same if he'd come home?"

His voice was a shrug. "I don't know."

"Another question I'll never know the answer to. Another experience I never got to have." They had wandered closer to the water. Cleo heard the sweet, high sound of a trumpet and the pounding excitement of a piano. The singer's voice was as thick as honey as he took up the melody. The music made Cleo smile, made her heart beat faster, made the feel of Bayard's hand in hers spark. This time she was the one who tugged him through the milling crowds. "Come on. I want to dance."

His palm pressed against the small of her back and his fingers linked with hers as she led him into the steps. It reminded Cleo of their lesson at the shooting range. He frowned at one point as if he'd lost count in his head. She met his gaze. "Eyes level. Even breaths. Don't think too hard."

His arm slid around her waist, pulling her closer. She could feel the wired tension in his muscles, sense the anticipation like lightning between them. His breath was warm against her cheek. She could smell his shaving soap and the clean, woodsy smell of his cologne. She felt her feet moving, her hips swaying. There was a buzz in her head and a lightness to her body she'd not felt in weeks. Their circle contracted, their movements slowing to a standstill as the dancers parted and joined in an orbit around them. Neither of them heard Goodman give way to Prima until the drummer started his solo, a snazzy Gene Krupa lick of cymbals and snare that made the crowd jump.

It couldn't be.

"That's Emmitt!" Cleo shouted, breaking away to stand on tiptoe to see over the dancers crowding the floor.

It was Bayard's turn to be caught off guard. "Who's Emmitt?"

Cleo pushed through to the edge of the stage to wave him down. His face registered surprise and then delight, and when the set ended he joined her in the wings with a rib-crushing bear hug. "Wow! Never thought to see you again, Park Avenue."

"I thought you and the boys would be heating things up in some club in Chicago by now."

Emmitt rubbed a hand across the back of his head. "I reckon the boys are by now. I decided to stick around here. Save myself a trip back."

"You really think America will enter the war?"

He shared a look with Bayard, the two men seeming to pass some secret message between them. "Maybe not now or even a year from now. But I don't think they can let this fight pass, do you? Us Yanks never have liked a bully." One of the stagehands gave a shout. "I'd best get back, Park Avenue." He started for the stage when he suddenly turned back. "Hold on. I almost forgot. I ran into that guy you were looking for—Kominski."

"Are you sure?" Cleo's mind ticked back over that split-second glimpse on the quayside. So it *had* been Micky she'd seen that night. She hadn't been imagining things. Still, her mind rebelled. It couldn't be. "He's dead. They told me he was dead."

"Well then they told you wrong."

CHAPTER 22

Dear Anne,

I made a promise and, while it has taken me months to fulfill it, I am finally in a position to do so. Word has come from Washington, and I've been tasked with approaching the crown princess with Roosevelt's proposal. All well and good, but if I hear the term "woman to woman" one more time, I'm likely to do a violence . . .

I t took Daisy a week to arrange a meeting with the crown princess. Her Royal Highness had been staying at her family's country house at Villa Fridhem for most of the spring and summer, kept out of public view as if Sweden hoped the world would forget they were harboring the remnants of Norway's royal family. And by the world she meant Germany. But living quietly and keeping every finger crossed wouldn't be enough if Berlin pushed. That was where Daisy came in.

She was advised to appeal to the crown princess's maternal instinct as if they might trade casserole recipes and child-rearing techniques. Discounted were Daisy's years of public service and the princess's canny understanding of politics. And yet, Daisy had conceded to this tack by bringing Cleo along to this picnic at the villa outside Stockholm. Had her entertain the children with tag and hide-and-seek and put on a show of what their life might be in America if Crown Princess Märtha agreed to President Roosevelt's invitation. It wasn't exactly casseroles and laundry, but it would have to do.

The two women sat across from each other in the villa's garden, a wrought iron table bearing the remnants of lunch between them. The princess dusted crumbs from her lap, smoothing her napkin nervously along its edge once then twice more. In the silence, there was only the squeak of hedge clippers coming from the front lawn and the putter of a distant tractor. A blackbird's call from the trees was answered by another in the hedge. Daisy felt the weight of every sound in the princess's silence. She counted the seconds in her head until the princess sat up, her features composed, a new stillness in her limbs as if she'd come to a decision. "We have eaten the cake and drunk the tea. You have complimented my dress, and I have remarked on the weather. Now, I think, we can get down to the real reason you've come today."

Daisy should have known Crown Princess Märtha would see the clumsy gambit for what it was. She was both relieved she no longer had to hide behind a critique of last season's fashions and annoyed with herself for being so obvious. She set her cup in its saucer and turned to business with a fresh energy. "The President of the United States is planning to send a transport for the evacuation of American citizens and others stranded in Scandinavia due to the fighting. He's extended that invitation to you, Your Highness. And your children."

Crown Princess Märtha didn't respond immediately. Instead, she selected an iced petit four from the tray with great deliberation. The only indication she'd heard Daisy was the rapid rise and fall of her chest and the new pink to her cheeks. She chewed over her words with the same care she used to nibble the edge of her cake before speaking. "That is a most generous invitation. You must send President Roosevelt my thanks."

"I'd rather send him your acceptance."

Crown Princess Märtha didn't respond right away, which Daisy took as a small success. She had almost certainly been informed of the German Reichskommissar's demands to depose the King and His Royal Highness and begin proceedings to replace the current Norwegian parliament with one more amenable to Berlin. What was less clear was whether she'd been told of the Norwegians' continued resistance to such a move against their royal family. Or the growing pressures put on the Swedish government and her uncle's increasing concessions to Hitler and his bullies. She put an end to that speculation over a fresh cup of tea.

"I might be hidden away out here, Madam Minister, but I'm neither deaf nor stupid. Though people talk around me as if they believe I am one or the other or both. I realize Hitler is determined to set up a pretender government in Oslo that gives the appearance of being supported by the people."

"Yes. It's the lengths to which they might go that's concerning. If the Norwegian people refuse to give up their royal family, Hitler would be smart to give them what they want but wrap it in a package that suits him best."

"You mean my son." She cast another look toward the children, who were giggling as Cleo settled a daisy chain onto Astrid's head like a crown and Ragnhild begged for one of her own. The young prince nibbled the edge of a shortbread biscuit, his round babyish cheeks puffed out as he giggled and ate. "Your goddaughter is good with the children, isn't she? She makes them laugh. She lets them forget for a little while."

Cleo laid back in the grass, pointing out shapes in the clouds to the delighted children.

"A sailing ship!" one of them shouted.

"A horse!" called another.

"I see a face!"

Her Royal Highness's eyes drifted skyward as if she might join the game. Shadows flickered over her cheekbones and along her pale blue dress. "Would my husband be joining us in America?"

"That's a discussion for others. My only task is to see to *your* safety as best I can. It's what His Royal Highness Prince Olav has asked of me. And it's what I want to do if I can."

"He is worried about us."

"He is right to be." Daisy thought back to those men in the churchyard. They might only have numbered three, but she was certain there were others less obvious in their interest and more determined in their plans.

The crown princess's smile was weary, the expression of one who was born into power and had long since learned the tangled ways of politics. "I will consider your invitation, Mrs. Harriman."

"If I could give a piece of advice woman to woman," Daisy responded dryly, "don't wait too long."

"Promise me, Cleo. You won't do anything rash while I'm gone. Got it?"

"This is Micky we're talking about. He wouldn't hurt me."

"Maybe not." Bayard clearly remained skeptical. "But wait for me anyway. Please?"

For some reason, those words twisted tight around her heart, and she reluctantly agreed.

But the questions banged away at her brain with answers that made sense one moment and were punched full of holes the next. It *had* been Micky she'd glimpsed that night outside the hotel. She hadn't been mistaken. He *was* alive. He was here in Stockholm. She'd been right not to give up. Right to push for answers even when everyone told her she was crazy. So why did she feel as if she wasn't going to like those answers? Or that the answers he'd offer might complicate her already complicated feelings?

Mrs. Thorson, who believed work cured all ills, chose Cleo to accompany her on a trip to the village of Öreryd with a group from the Refugee Office to discuss the creation of a possible transit center. She was still unpacking from that when Aunt Daisy popped her head around the door and told her to grab her hat and coat for an afternoon in the country, which turned out to be a visit to Norway's crown princess. Even Mr. Whitney seemed to understand Cleo's need to keep busy and asked her to review all the foreign papers that arrived at the hotel and flag any news articles that mentioned the US minister to Norway.

Monday slid into the following Monday, and Cleo's nerves frayed like old rope. Aunt Daisy assumed it was worry over Bayard, and Cleo let her go on thinking that. It was easier than trying to explain, though Mr. Whitney almost surprised the truth out of her when he patted her shoulder in a kindly uncle sort of way and reassured her that most of the heavy fighting was over now that Norway had surrendered. Somehow the old blowhard's comfort was worse than his bark, and only made her nerves twist tighter.

What if she waited too long and Micky was gone before she could track him down? Promise or no promise, she couldn't wait any longer.

The bus dropped her off across from a small park a few streets over from Brännkyrkagatan. This neighborhood was more industrial. Blocks of apartments interspersed with office buildings and mom-and-pop shops. Storage yards and warehouses hid behind high metal fences. She headed down a narrow alley of locked gates and steep stairs to where a bulb buzzed in its socket over a cellar doorway, which a man with arms like hams guarded with bulldog ferocity. Another hired heavy propped up the wall just inside the club, where a woman stood spotlighted on a tiny stage barely bigger than an orange crate. She had a voice like an angel, but her face was sallow and lined with too many years and too much booze, and she sang with all the emotion of someone reading their grocery list. The musicians backing her up weren't much better, though what they lacked in finesse, they made up for in volume. Cleo scanned their bored faces, but Micky wasn't among them.

Maybe Emmitt had got it wrong. She couldn't imagine Micky playing in a dive like this, no matter how hard up he might be. The space smelled of stale beer, cheap cigarettes, hair oil, and sweat. Workmen and hustlers mingled with dull-eyed girls in heavy makeup and skimpy dresses. A man at a corner table set off warning bells in Cleo's brain, maybe because he was the only one without a drink in front of him and, in the minute she stood there, he glanced at his watch twice as if he was waiting for someone.

"You take a wrong turn, love?" A weedy bartender in a stained red silk vest and an accent straight out of East London pulled drafts into a pair of mugs.

"I'm looking for Michal Kominski. I heard I might find him here."

Suspicion creased the edges of his eyes and bit into the sides of his mouth. "Never heard of him."

Cleo carried on watching him for a moment, but he refused to meet her gaze, his eyes firmly set on the rag in his hand and an ancient water stain on the counter. "He plays the trumpet," she clarified.

The brute propping up the wall sidled up behind her, his hot sour breath against her ear. "You heard Ted. Nobody by that name's been around here. Best move along."

"And if I don't?" Her voice came high and reedy from a throat that was suddenly hard to breathe through.

She never found out the answer. The door slammed open, letting in a damp draft along with two men who shoved their way to the bar. "Roughing up the customers again, Elia?"

That voice. Cleo's heart thrashed against her ribs. She drew a sick, shuddering breath as she turned to face her rescuer. "Fancy meeting you here, Micky."

THE ROOM MICKY showed her to had been kitted out as a small office with the requisite desk, swivel chair, and file cabinet. An old-fashioned safe squatted at the back, a hot plate on the top beside two stained coffee mugs and a small cardboard box labeled *für Nagant-revolver*, which didn't take a linguist to translate. Every inch of floor space not taken up by furniture held more boxes and crates, these stacked carefully and protected with dust sheets. A gold-edged frame peeked from beneath one of them. An intricately carved mahogany chest from another. Wherever these treasures had begun their journey, they'd all ended in the same squalid place.

"Cleo?" His voice startled her back to the present and this seedy club that stank of desperation and gin. He took her hand. His fingers slid into hers like a key into a lock, only something wasn't right. There was an awkwardness in the way they fit together, like tumblers that don't quite mesh.

"Nice digs," she commented, trying to keep her voice light, untouched by the dread turning her stomach.

"Teddy's an old friend." He gave a sheepish smile and spread his hands. "We're safe here."

"Is there a reason we need to be?" Cleo wasn't ready to give an inch. Not yet. But she couldn't stop staring at him as if he'd materialized in a swirl of paranormal ectoplasm in front of her. Then he gave one of those little boy smiles usually guaranteed to make her heart flip, and for some reason she felt herself slide free of his grip. Felt herself take a reluctant step back.

He folded his arms over his chest, staring at her as if drinking her in. "Wow. I can't believe you're here standing in front of me. You look . . ." He lifted a hand to touch her hair but paused before dropping his arm back to his side. "You look different, Cleo. Good. But different."

She held on to her resentment as if it would protect her, but protect her from what? She'd loved him once. She still did. But now that love was clouded by questions. She hated feeling uncertain, foolish. The naive little rich girl who falls for the first handsome stranger who shows her affection.

His eyes widened then narrowed. Maybe in surprise. Maybe in something else. "You're still wearing the necklace I gave you."

She resisted the unconscious urge to touch the stone at her throat, but she couldn't completely hide the shiver that raced up her spine. "Don't change the subject. I want answers, Micky. I deserve answers. I waited for you in Kassa like you asked. You never showed."

He had the grace to look sheepish. "I meant to. I really did. But I was being followed. It wasn't safe."

"What wasn't safe? When you didn't come home that night, I thought you died in the bombing. That's what they said."

"Who said?"

"The Germans. Then that letter came, and I didn't know what to think. I still don't know."

"Yes, well the bombing was a complete coincidence. I couldn't believe my luck."

"Funny way to describe the deaths of over twenty people, some of them people we knew, our friends."

"Twenty people or two hundred—what's the difference? It's a

drop in the bucket in the middle of a much greater atrocity, Cleo. Besides, most of them were Germans. They didn't belong there to begin with. Serves them right."

There was a coldhearted logic in that statement. Maybe Aunt Daisy's speculation was closer to the mark than Cleo imagined. Maybe that was why Heimmel was watching Micky. Because he suspected Micky of being more than a musician.

"So if you weren't at the café, where were you?"

"I was sneaking over the border into Slovakia."

She found herself using Daisy's trick of silence. Letting it spin out until he squirmed.

"I know it was a coward's way, but it was run or die. Simple as that." He paused. "You knew about the things that went on in the basement of the Palace Hotel after the Germans took it over?"

"I'd heard whispers. I didn't . . . I couldn't believe it. Not then."

"And now?"

She swallowed back her disgust and pushed the nightmares to the edges of her mind. "What does that have to do with you?"

He blinked, pressing his lips together as if he hesitated to speak, but something in her eyes must have warned him she wasn't going to be put off. "I was stupid and got involved in some things I shouldn't have. When the bombing happened, I figured it was the perfect time to get out. The Germans knew I played in the band there. If I went missing, they'd assume I was killed."

"As would I."

"Yeah, well that wasn't the best part of the plan, but I wrote you. I told you to meet me." His voice broke. Sincere or a cunning fake job?

"And then didn't turn up."

"I thought they were onto me. I couldn't risk it. I figured when I didn't show up, you'd find your way home to New York."

God, she hated this suspicion. She wanted to throw herself in his arms, and here she was questioning him as if he was a criminal. "So what are you doing here in Stockholm?"

"Trying to scrape enough money together to make it the rest of the way home." He rose from his chair, taking her in his arms, pulling her close. He was thinner than he used to be, his muscles like rope. She could feel the strength just beneath the surface of his skin. "I missed you, baby."

It felt good to lean into his chest, smell his scent of peppermint, cigarettes, and cologne, letting the worry that had propelled her for so long seep out of her like poison from a wound. She could breathe easy again without the sting of his absence.

"I'm glad you're with your aunt. She can protect you."

"How did you know I was here with my aunt?" She slid free of his arms, smiling in hopes of easing the question in his gaze. "And why do I need protecting?"

Micky tossed off one his patented smiles, but this time she saw the mask slip, the fear in his eyes. "Hadn't you noticed? It's a dangerous world out there."

Something in his words felt familiar. Someone else had said that very thing or close to it.

It wasn't until she was in bed that night that the answer popped into her head—Heimmel of the Gestapo.

CHAPTER 23

Dear Anne,

I just received word from Mr. Cox, who remained behind at the legation in Oslo, that all members of the American diplomatic staff must leave the city by order of the German authorities. He's assured me that all my personal effects have been boxed for ship-ment back to the United States, though when I shall see them is anyone's guess. You'd laugh at an old woman's sentimentality, but I was more concerned about Kim's well-being and was crushed to hear of his passing. It was gentle and hardly a surprise. He'd lived to the fine old age of eleven, but it hurts to think of living at Uplands without him. Wherever there is a dog's heaven, there he surely is . . .

Did it mean anything that their meeting took place in the for-mal confines of the royal palace rather than the relaxed atmo-sphere of Prince Carl's country house? Daisy chose to dismiss her qualms as unnecessary. She'd never been intimidated by pomp. She took people as they came, prince or pauper, and she'd frater-nized with enough of both over the course of her varied career to know which she preferred.

She had arrived directly from the American legation, where

Freddie Sterling had been pressing her for news of the princess's intentions. News she couldn't give him. It had been nearly two weeks since she'd presented the invitation from Roosevelt. Two weeks in which battle lines had shifted like the inrush of a tide; Russian armies washing over Lithuania, Latvia, Estonia, Romania; fleets of German bombers softening the British defenses for what everyone assumed would be certain invasion. Two weeks in which the grip on Norway had tightened to a fist; armies disbanded, equipment destroyed, dwindling hope lying in the pockets of a scattered resistance; deadly burrs to goad and harry the German forces until such time as their king might return.

Two weeks in which Daisy had waited for an answer.

Sources had informed her that King Gustav was advocating for his niece to reject the invitation and had gone so far as suggesting that Prince Olav persuade the princess to remain in Sweden. Daisy wouldn't speculate on his reasoning for such a proposal, but she had her ideas. None of them painted the Swedish king in a favorable light.

Upon arrival at the palace, Daisy had been shown to a small antechamber off one of the larger reception rooms, the air there chilly and stale despite the summer heat outside. Dust glittered in the sunlight from the tall windows overlooking the inner courtyard. Crown Princess Märtha was dressed soberly today: gray silk, a set of simple pearls. Her face shone pale in the light, arched brows over a long slender nose and high cheekbones. A jaw deceptively firm.

Her escort had departed almost immediately, though Daisy imagined he was close by. Listening at the keyhole perhaps.

Daisy cleared her throat, casting a glance at the closed door. Her Royal Highness didn't reply, but there was understanding in her eyes. They might be alone, but whatever was said in this room wouldn't stay a secret for long. "I hear Mr. Schoenfeld at the British embassy has been tasked as the US chargé d'affaires for the Norwegian government in London," Her Royal Highness said.

As an opening gambit, it was good. Proof that despite being hidden away, she was very much paying attention. And not a single reference to a hat.

Daisy ignored the ache in the small of her back and settled down to business. "It makes sense. He's there and we . . . that is, I . . . am here."

"Yes," the crown princess replied, tension in her crossed arms and the height of her shoulders. "But it doesn't make it any easier to accept being left behind, does it?"

Her stare was direct, a challenge even, and Daisy sensed they were speaking on two tracks. She accepted the challenge and stared right back as she answered both the spoken and the unspoken question. "No, it doesn't, Your Royal Highness. But it doesn't mean it's the wrong decision."

Crown Princess Märtha seemed to accept the answer, but rather than seating herself in one of the high-backed chairs or on the striped silk couch across from Daisy, she paced like a lion in a cage, or, more fancifully, like a princess in a tower. Did that make Daisy a fairy godmother? She rather liked the sound of that.

"I received a phone call last evening from Minister Morgenstierne in Washington," Her Royal Highness continued.

This was news to Daisy. She would speak to Mr. Whitney as soon as she got back to the hotel. If conversations were being had, she needed to be kept abreast of them. Otherwise, she risked being made to look a fool. To cover her ignorance, she simply said, "Yes, of course." A noncommittal answer that sounded as if she'd known all along.

"He rang to inform me that I should be ready to leave Stockholm in four days." The princess paused at one of the windows, glancing down at the courtyard below, where voices could be heard, the rhythmic shout of palace guards on the turn. "As I've not yet agreed to travel to America, this was news to me."

"Everyone is anxious to have your safety secured."

Crown Princess Märtha looked up at that declaration, a flicker of doubt passing over her features. Once again, Daisy had the feeling she was being quizzed, but whether she passed the test was anyone's guess.

"I informed the minister that I wanted no fuss upon my arrival in New York—no reporters or receptions. I'd rather as few people as possible know of our arrival at all."

"Of course." Though already Daisy could see the problems with that and wondered at Morgenstierne's response. "So you have—"

"Decided to accept your president's very kind offer—yes."

"Wonderful. I'm sure Morgenstierne will make the necessary arrangements and a proper escort will be put in place."

"Apparently those wheels have already been set in motion." Her Royal Highness paused, one long-fingered hand upon a chair back. "I was told you're to be our proper escort."

The stale air settled at the back of Daisy's throat like lead, but she didn't flicker an eyelash. "It will be an honor, Your Royal Highness."

"Will it?" was her quiet question, with no right answer.

Back at the hotel after a hasty meeting with Ambassador Sterling in which all Daisy's fears were confirmed, she tossed her bag and her coat onto a couch as she roared into the office. Forward momentum was all that was holding her together after being made to look a fool. "Mr. Whitney! Where are you?"

The vice consul ducked out of an adjoining room, his hair rumpled, his jacket hanging off one shoulder as if he was just going out or just coming in. "Ma'am? How did the meeting go?"

"They've tapped me to organize and shepherd the refugees from Stockholm to the northern Finnish port of Petsamo, where a ship will take us to New York. Crown Princess Märtha and her children will be among the passengers."

"Us?" If he'd known ahead of time, he was a very good actor. There was nothing but surprise in his round face. "You won't be returning to Norway, ma'am?"

"That would be giving the Germans what they want: a tacit admission that Oslo is the seat of the Norwegian government rather than London, where His Majesty and his ministers have set up their cabinet in exile." A point that Sterling had brought up in their conversation as if she hadn't come to that conclusion on her own.

"I'm sure the crown princess is relieved to hear that you'll be with her on this trip, ma'am. You and she have always got on."

"So I keep hearing." She kept her gaze on Mr. Whitney, watching for a tic, a tell, a giveaway that would reveal his glee at her downfall, but the man was good. The mask remained impenetrable. As did hers.

He'd never know how deeply this last thrust cut.

THE HOTEL'S VERANDA was nearly empty, which was a rarity these days, but Cleo was glad for the quiet. She'd ordered a pot of coffee, leaving breakfast decisions for Aunt Daisy when she turned up. While she waited, Cleo pulled out the photograph taken at the Czarny Kot, smoothing it out on the table. It was curled at the corners from her constant studying, but the image remained frozen in the flick of the camera's shutter, a moment she wished she could call back from a time she wished she could forget.

Placing a saltcellar on one side and a pepper shaker on the other, she stared at the photo as if she could see past the edges for some clue she'd missed. Read the faces of the men in the picture for a hint of what they might have been thinking in that split second. Was Micky involved in the resistance like Daisy had once suggested? Is that what sent him running? Or had there been something darker behind his flight? She tried shaking off her suspicions, but they clung like burrs, tugging her awake in the middle of the night, posing questions she couldn't answer.

Micky's new friends were obvious black marketeers, but how new were they? And how friendly? And where did Heimmel fit into this story? Was he tracking down a member of the Polish resistance, or was their connection more personal?

She pointedly passed over her own face, unable to look at the smiling girl, her head tilted in pleasant conversation. Oblivious to what was really happening. No. That was the real crime. She'd been aware of Hitler's heavy boot, but so long as it hadn't been her neck beneath it, she'd been willing to turn a blind eye. She couldn't do that now.

"A US official's cousin playing footsie with the SS. You're lucky you have friends in high places. That could have been a public relations disaster." Mr. Whitney stood over her shoulder, looking at the photograph.

"It wasn't like that."

"No? Then what was it like?"

She looked back down at the photograph, the smiling stupid girl, the smug men confident in their success. Even Micky wore a pleased-with-himself expression that made her muscles twitch. She couldn't defend herself so she stayed silent.

"In my opinion, any American that stuck around in Poland after Hitler's tanks rolled through was either there to fight, to spy, or to steal."

"Or maybe they were just foolish."

He threw her a look. "Those are the most dangerous."

He took a seat across from her, barely glancing at the menu. They'd resided at the hotel long enough that they knew the dishes by heart. "The first thing I'm going to do when we hit New York City is go to Katz's Delicatessen and get the biggest pastrami sandwich you've ever seen."

"We?"

"Haven't you heard?" He had the air of someone excited to share a secret. "We've been given our traveling orders—we're headed home. Mrs. Harriman is escorting a group of Americans and others back to the States."

"What about her work here? Can't they get someone else to play scout leader?"

"Probably, but what a crown princess wants a crown princess gets."

"She's going too?"

"I've said too much already." Mr. Whitney bit into his toast. "Who knows? You might still be in bed with the Germans."

"That's not funny."

"It wasn't meant to be."

Fighter. Spy. Thief. Fool.

She knew which she had been. But where did Micky fit?

"The minister and I haven't always seen eye to eye, but she's proved herself over the last months. Even I'll admit that, so I'd hate to see all the good she's accomplished erased because of the actions of a spoiled little rich girl who got in over her head. Maybe it's best all the way around that that Micky chap is dead. He can't cause any more trouble."

Cleo used the return of the waitress as a distraction and hoped Whitney didn't notice the flush of heat in her face.

"Good morning." Aunt Daisy took a seat, glancing at the photograph, which Cleo began to fold away. "Hold on. Let me see that again."

Cleo reluctantly handed it over, shame turning the coffee to sludge in her stomach. But Aunt Daisy didn't seem to be looking at her, she was studying the corner of the picture where Heimmel stood nearly in shadow. "I've seen him before."

"He was the man that spoke to me in Oslo."

"Is he?" Daisy handed her back the photograph. "Well, he's here in Stockholm now."

FROM HER HOTEL window, Cleo watched the goings-on at the market across the street in front of the national theater. Stalls overflowed with crates of vegetables, fresh eggs, and baskets of cut flowers brought in from farms and allotments just outside the city. There was fish fresh off the boats that docked at the waterfront across the street to unload their catch onto trays of ice. A man sold ice cream. Another played a violin, his case open in front of him.

It had become a part of her routine like three cups of morning coffee, her walk to the Refugee Office on Banérgatan and back, her evening Manhattan cocktail, her bedtime cold cream. All the small pieces of her day that kept the worst of the waiting at bay. Then she snapped the light off, and her stomach cramped and her chest pounded and she felt her heart ticking off the seconds and the minutes and the hours and the days.

Cleo felt like her entire life had been spent waiting. Watching at windows. Listening for the footstep on the stair or the hand upon the knob. Counting minutes that never passed fast enough. She'd been doing it for so long that the weight in her stomach and the ache in her chest had become normal.

Don't wish your life away.

Her mother used to tell her that. She didn't understand Cleo wasn't wishing to be older. She was wishing for a day in the future that never came.

Bayard had been gone a month, his silence all too familiar in this life of chronic expectation. At least this time, she wasn't alone in her waiting. She could look to Aunt Daisy for reassurance that all was well. He would come back. Cleo's waiting would end. What to tell him when that happened was the question.

More to the point, what should she tell Aunt Daisy?

She had to say something. Micky was alive. He was here in Stockholm. And she didn't know if that was a good thing or not.

Her godmother was preparing to go out to a reception the French legation was holding. Checking her reflection in a mirror, turning this way and that.

"You look perfect," Cleo offered as a way of breaking the ice.

Aunt Daisy harumphed. "This color reminds me of the blue the British convalescent soldiers wore in the last go-round. All I can see when I look at myself are those poor limbless, wounded boys in their pajamas."

Cleo searched through the closet. "What does green remind you of?"

"Don't be cheeky. There's no time to change." Their eyes met in the mirror, and Aunt Daisy stopped primping. "I haven't heard anything if that's what you're here to ask. I'm sure the lieutenant's fine, my dear."

"That's not it." Cleo sank onto an armchair, hands clasped loosely in her lap. "Or not all of it."

Aunt Daisy stopped in the middle of fastening her pearls to sit across from Cleo, a worry line forming between her brows. "Is it the idea of going home? Facing up to your mother after everything that happened? It won't be as bad as you imagine. It's water under the bridge. Besides, she misses you desperately."

"I doubt that. She was usually telling me what a disappointment I was. How unhappy Father would be if he knew the scrapes I was getting into. How she wished I could be more like him."

"But you *are* like him. Far more than is comfortable most of the time," Aunt Daisy replied. "The scrapes he would get into.

Did you ever hear the story about the time your father stole a goat and turned it loose on the Vanderbilts' tennis court wearing Willie K's straw boater with two holes for its ears?"

"The perfect Paul Jaffray?"

Aunt Daisy chuckled. "Or the time he ran away from boarding school to spend four weeks working crew on a pilot boat in the Hudson?"

"You made that up."

Aunt Daisy shook her head, trying to catch her breath from laughing. "And then there was the time he knifed all four of Grayson Prescott's tires in order to keep him from taking the beautiful and very eligible Letitia Lanier to a ball. In a panic, the Prescott boy borrowed someone else's automobile without asking and got arrested for car theft on his way to pick her up. Paul won the girl, and the rest is history. Good thing or you wouldn't exist."

By the time Aunt Daisy finished, she was mopping tears from her eyes, and Cleo was in stitches. It was a few minutes before either of them could collect themselves.

"Why didn't Mother ever tell me any of this?"

"Your mother spent twenty-five years balancing your father on a pedestal. I'm sure she thought she was doing right. Giving you a father to be proud of. She never realized she was putting him beyond your reach, turning him into someone you could never live up to, no matter how you tried. Maybe if you knew the truth about him . . . about his military service . . ."

Cleo sat up, that waiting feeling poised like a pendulum held.

"We were all in Paris when war was declared and trapped, frantic to get out. Letitia and I spent the days getting passports in order. Paul was sent to the bank to withdraw money. We were to meet at the Gare du Nord and take the train for Bologne. When he finally turned up hours late, it was to tell us that he'd run into an old school chum and the two of them had enlisted in the French Foreign Legion, of all things."

"Were they drunk?"

"Maybe. Or maybe they were simply caught up in the war fever that was sweeping the country. Everyone wanted a piece of the glory before it was all over."

"So much for gallantry and honor and fighting for what he believed in."

"I tried to talk him out of it, we all did, but he insisted on honoring his commitment. He thought it was just another adventure—a few months of playing soldier, and then he'd be home. We all thought that. We all hoped that."

"But it wasn't."

"No," Aunt Daisy said, gripping her handkerchief. "A year in the trenches, and then he transferred into the French flying corps. You know the rest. Your father might have joined up for the wrong reasons, but he stayed and did his best for the right ones. He was no saint, Clementine. Far from it. In fact, you remind me of him in all the worst ways. You're stubborn, impetuous, and disobedient." She stood up. "But you don't back down from a fight even when the odds are stacked against you. For good or bad, you are your father all over again."

Cleo's chest expanded. Her limbs felt prickly with sensation. She could hear the traffic outside the window. The squeak of a maid's trolley in the passage outside the door. A muted babble of conversation as people passed on the way to the elevator. But she wasn't hearing it. She was hearing the slow winding down of a clock as the waiting finally ended.

"I wish Mother had trusted me enough to tell me about Father herself."

"I know, child. Your mother held on so tight to the parts of Paul that made her proud, she forgot about all the other parts that made her love him in the first place." Aunt Daisy turned back to the mirror to repair the damage done by their laughter before making a circling sweep of her skirt. "There. Will I do?"

"You're beautiful," Cleo said and absolutely meant it.

"Flattery will take you far, my dear, but you didn't come here to give me fashion advice. What's on your mind? Speak quickly. My car's waiting."

The words were there, but Cleo couldn't bring herself to say them. Not now. She told herself it was because she needed time to examine this new version of her father, to square the scapegrace of a young man who rattled from one adventure to another with the grim, steel-eyed officer staring down on her in eternal censure. The far less noble reason was sheer cowardice. If Aunt Daisy knew about Micky, would she still be proud of Cleo? Or would she see this as just another mess that she'd have to clean up? One more way in which Cleo had let her down?

"It's nothing," Cleo said at last.

CHAPTER 24

Dear Anne,

We received a batch of newspapers today, months old, of course. There was mention of you in the SF Chronicle *dated last May. For some reason, reading it drove your death home to me all over again and I had to let memory have its way with me. Those chaotic days at the start of the last war, the push and shove to get out of France. Paul's ridiculous tilt at a windmill. Over by Christmas. Isn't that what they said? What they always say? Is it hubris or hope that causes them to say it and us to believe them?*

Daisy folded the page and placed it with the rest of them. "You have a lot to answer for, Paul Jaffray, and if I had you before me now, I'd have half a mind to take you over my knee for your foolishness. And, directly afterward, your wife for hers."

She continued to browse the feast of news from home, chuckling over her newfound fame. THE HEDY LAMAR OF GRANDMOTHERS was her favorite headline, though there were a half dozen articles from papers all over the country, extolling her political acumen, her courage, and her intelligence. If only they'd stopped there instead of going on to praise her trim figure, her Paris fashions, and her well-coifed hair. She wasn't surprised, but she was disappointed.

She couldn't recall a single instance of Freddie Sterling's suits being described or his waistline being evaluated.

She poured herself a drink from the sideboard, snapped on the radio, and took up her knitting. She was halfway through a sweater for Phyllis, and if she worked quickly, she might be able to have it finished by the time the ship docked in New York Harbor. But her mind continued to churn, unable to settle into the soothing rhythm that usually cleared her head and relaxed the tension banding her shoulders and settling into her creaky joints.

Had there been a reason behind her recall to the States? She saw the cold logic of it, but it didn't make it sting any less, especially when she'd been held up as a heroine for her work thus far. Hedy Lamar, indeed!

She thought back over the last few months: those chaotic days around the invasion, the headlong flight cross-country in the royal family's wake, the months of information gathering, picking away at every scrap of news and rumor for the crumbs that could be turned into useful intelligence. Had it been a case of something she'd done? Something she'd not done? Her first thought when she'd heard the news had been that they'd discovered she mislaid the codebook. A thought quickly dismissed. Far more likely was that her conversation with His Majesty had been transformed through diplomatic channels into a State Department command. She much preferred that scenario to the alternative, which was that she'd run her course, and this was her reward for her efforts—being put out to pasture with a pat on the nose and a sugar lump.

She needed to look at it as a reward and not as a punishment. She was going home. Back to Uplands and her comfortable house with the wilds of Rock Creek Park just beyond her back garden. She would have Ethel in for a good, long visit and the grandchildren. She would take the train to New York and see her old friend Anne Morgan and they could mourn lost friends and feast on tales of past glories.

Perhaps she would start her dinner parties up again, gathering the great minds among the press and the politicians around her dining table, reconnecting with those whose passions matched her own. Then perhaps she'd dig in to the real work of the war, for this new horror would be much like the last. There would be suffering and heartbreak and hunger and desperation. And people who would step up and do what they could to help.

She wanted to count herself among those people.

Yes, these were all things she could do.

"Mrs. Harriman, we've just received word." Mr. Whitney didn't even bother knocking. "The *American Legion* is due to arrive at the Finnish port of Petsamo."

"Has the final passenger list been typed up?"

"Not yet. We've had over a thousand names come in from the embassies and legations, but the ship's captain has suggested we should cap the number at nine hundred."

She was reminded of the childhood game of musical chairs. No matter how she chose, someone would be disappointed, left behind. She rubbed the space between her brows, where a headache began to form. "Is he sure we can't squeeze in any extra?"

"He's being overgenerous now, in my opinion. He's imagining nine hundred soldiers used to putting up with deprivation and hardship. Not a rabble of civilians—women and children and the like. They'll be expecting *Queen Mary* luxury. God help us when they see what's lying at anchor in Petsamo."

"A bridge we'll cross when we get there. Any reports on activity along the border we should be made aware of?"

"Now that the Swedish government has agreed to let Her

Royal Highness and the children leave, Terboven and the Germans don't seem concerned."

"Let's hope it stays that way."

AFTER TOSSING AND turning most of the night, Cleo finally fell asleep just as the sun was coming up. She was roused from the sludge of troubling dreams almost immediately by the shrill ring from her telephone and a far too chirpy desk clerk informing her this was her requested wake-up call.

The second time she awakened it was to a bellhop with a pot of life-giving coffee.

The third time was to a knock on her door and Micky, who stood sheepishly in the corridor looking charmingly woebegone.

Panicked, she shot a quick glance up and down the hall. "This is a surprise."

"A nice one, I hope." His smile was the same as ever, as was the slouchy, seductive way he had of leaning against the doorframe. Even his scent reminded Cleo of long, sleepy mornings in hotel rooms similar to this one, a bed covered in the morning papers, the floor covered with their cast-off clothes. So where was the dizzying loop the loop in her stomach or the flutter of attraction in her chest? Her rising heart rate stemmed more from the fear someone would spot him and report his presence to Aunt Daisy than from any lingering attraction.

"Of course. I mean . . ." She opened the door wider, dragging him inside before anyone spotted him. "Of course, but what are you doing here?"

"I was hoping we could get breakfast. I know a wonderful bakery just on the other side of the park." His gaze flicked to her unmade bed. "Unless maybe you'd rather we ring room service."

Cleo cinched her dressing gown sash tighter across her midsection like a warrior donning a buckler before battle. "I have an appointment, and I'm already running late."

She didn't have time to wonder why she felt the need to armor herself against a man she'd spent the past six months desperately searching for, and she definitely didn't have time to shoo him away while she puzzled out this odd sensation. Not if the bedside clock was right. She had a car due to arrive any moment to drive her to a school in Upsala that was being used as a clearinghouse for supplies meant for Norway. Not human, this time. Instead, they were collecting and organizing seed, livestock feed, and farm tools and equipment ahead of a shipment due to go out next week—if the right permits could be obtained and transportation arranged.

"Can't you cancel it for a reunion with an old friend?"

Friend? Was that all he thought they were? It made her ache with regret and anger. "I can't just drop everything. People are depending on me. If you'd warned me you were coming, I might have made arrangements."

"Warned you?" His smile faded. "I thought you'd be thrilled to see me."

"I am. That's not what I meant."

"You used to like surprises."

"Is that what you thought when you surprised me by disappearing?"

"I explained all that. I didn't have a choice." He took a deep breath, his smile turned back on like a light bulb. "We're squabbling like an old married couple. You go wash up and get dressed. I'll wait, and we can at least grab a quick coffee before you have to run off."

He'd always had the ability to turn aside a tense moment, never take anything too seriously. She'd loved that about him. Turned on *her*, however, it was much less appealing.

"Micky, this really . . . I don't think this is a good idea . . ."

Watching him settle in, she gave up. An argument would only slow her down further, but a tiny flicker of annoyance burned through her earlier nostalgia.

After a quick bath, she emerged pink and scrubbed to find Micky seated in front of her dressing table. He'd a plate of buttered toast set on top of her favorite silk scarf and a cup of coffee teetering dangerously on the edge of her open jewelry case.

"Micky!" She rescued both with a magician's skill. "What have you done?"

"I thought this would save you time, and we could still have our breakfast together." He pulled the pink costume diamond out of the box with a flash of the old Micky. "Still can't believe you've got this old necklace I gave you. Figured you'd have tossed it away when I didn't turn up. Good riddance to bad rubbish and all that."

"I was never angry with you, Micky. I was afraid for you."

She dressed in haste, irritation and frustration making her movements sharp. When she laddered one of her stockings, she muttered an oath under her breath.

"Are you okay?"

"No, I'm not okay. I'm running late, and you're behaving as if the past six months never happened and we can just pick up where we left off. We can't do that. I can't do that."

"You've changed, Cleo. You look the same, but . . ." He shook his head.

"Of course I've changed. We all have. It's this damned war." Why was she so quick to argue? This wasn't how it had been. Even at their worst, they'd shrugged off their fights or, more often, made up in their own way. But the thought didn't appeal. She needed him out. "How about if we meet for dinner?"

"Can't tonight. I'm seeing a guy who says for the right amount of cash he can get me the proper paperwork to secure a place on a train headed north into Russia."

"You mean forgeries."

Annoyance passed like a shadow over his face. "Not all of us have wealthy, well-connected relatives with deep pockets."

"That's not fair."

"Neither is playing Miss Prim all of a sudden."

When had desire and loss and desperation turned sour? When had her love begun to fade? Had it happened so gradually she'd not noticed the tiny fault lines, the pin pricks that came with every new question? Or was it now? This moment? This peeling back of disguises to show what lay underneath?

"You act as if you're sorry I turned up, but just remember, *you* came looking for *me*."

That hit like a slap. "What's that supposed to mean?"

A knock at the door interrupted their argument before he could answer. Her heart shot into her throat. Was it Aunt Daisy? Mr. Whitney?

"Cleo? It's Lieutenant Bayard."

There was the missing slow stomach flip and the buzz along her skin and the smile she couldn't stop. He was home. He was safe. A weight lifted from her shoulders.

She cracked open the door to find Bayard looking as if he'd come straight from dropping off his luggage to her door. His uniform was rumpled, his coat smelled of gasoline and leather and cigarettes, and there was a tightness at the corners of his eyes as if he'd not slept much since leaving Stockholm a month ago.

"Am I catching you at a bad time?" He spied Micky. "Oh. Didn't know you had company."

Was it her imagination or did his words sound like an accusation?

"Don't mind me." As if they'd not just been fighting thirty seconds earlier, Micky grinned and slid his arm around her waist as if staking a claim. "Cleo and I were just catching up."

She shook Micky off but not before Bayard's cool gaze shriveled her insides. "Micky was just leaving," she explained.

"Not *the* Micky," Bayard said in a dangerous soldier's tone of voice. "And here we thought you were dead, Mr. Kominski. Cleo must have been overjoyed to discover it was all a misunderstanding."

"Between you and me, she was a bit peeved—you know how women get." Micky's smile was more like a leer. "But I explained the mix-up and made it up to her."

"I'm sure you did." Anyone else seeing the clench of Bayard's jaw and the tension in his pose would have chalked it up to a typical military bearing, but Cleo knew him well enough by now to know he was holding himself together by the thinnest of threads.

"Right. I'll shove off. See you later, doll?" Micky leaned in for a kiss, which she dodged.

On the way out the door, he swung back, giving her a long lazy once-over. "Gorgeous as ever."

It was only after he was gone that Cleo realized he was looking at the necklace when he'd said it, not her.

"Care to tell me what all that was about?" Bayard asked, only now sounding like himself rather than someone at the edge of violence.

"I will, but first I need to see a jeweler about a diamond."

THE JEWELRY STORE was off Odengatan, a main thoroughfare bustling with traffic, but inside the shop, the thick carpets and handsome furniture deadened the sound to a whispery quiet. A young couple eyed engagement rings with wistful longing while an old woman haggled with the jeweler over an heirloom, her eyes watery as she explained its provenance, hoping to squeeze a few more kronor out of the man.

She departed with her money at the same time as the couple,

who had obviously found the prices in this particular shop too dear. Cleo was alone.

She'd done this before. She knew the drill. The jeweler was equally experienced if his suspicious gaze and aloof manner were anything to go by. No smiles or offers to help the madam with something. He simply nodded then waited for her to make the next move.

"What are we doing here?" Bayard asked.

"Fishing" was her enigmatic answer as she approached the counter, where she hailed the jeweler with a summons that would have done her Jaffray forebears proud. "I'd like to have a piece appraised."

"I'm sorry, miss. We don't purchase from private citizens."

"No? So that money you gave that woman just now was merely the act of a charitable philanthropist?"

When the man started to grumble, she reached to undo the clasp at the back of her neck. The necklace slid down her throat before she dropped it into his outstretched hand. "I don't need you to buy it off me, just give me a price."

His gaze sharpened with new avarice, and he pulled out a piece of velvet, laying the necklace out flat before taking up a loupe to study each stone in the gold setting, his gaze widening as it settled on the pink diamond. Occasionally he would write something down on a pad of paper or make a noncommittal noise at the back of his throat. Cleo's heart sped up, her skin growing icy as her nerves stretched. It shouldn't take this long. Not unless her hunch was correct and, oh, how she wanted her hunch not to be correct.

"It is difficult to say, miss . . . there are many factors . . ."

"How much?" By now she could barely stand still, and her throat had gone dry, her tongue sticking to the roof of her mouth. She'd kill for a piece of chewing gum or a mint.

The jeweler looked equally nervy. His complexion had turned waxy, eyebrows lifted into his thinning hairline as he read over his notes once more as if convincing himself of his own observations. "The pink diamond is of amazing quality and rose cut. The setting containing the six smaller rubies is quite unique."

Her suspicions confirmed, Cleo swallowed back the bile souring the back of her throat and tightened her belly against the butterflies. If she collapsed would Bayard catch her before she hit the floor? After Micky's shenanigans this morning, probably not. "How much?" she repeated.

He cleared his throat and fiddled with the edge of the velvet. "If you choose to sell the stones separately, you could maybe get five thousand American dollars for the diamond in the center, but I've seen them go for more. The rubies—one hundred and fifty each, give or take. The piece as a whole? Impossible to say. It is obviously quite old and would bring what a determined collector would offer." She wanted to be sick. She inhaled through her nose and exhaled through her mouth to stave off the nausea. "Where did you say you got this, madam?"

"I didn't. Thank you." Cleo's hands shook as she took up the necklace and clasped it back around her neck. "Ready to go, Lieutenant?"

Her voice sounded queer, almost panicky, but maybe no one else noticed.

"That necklace—you didn't know it was worth that much, did you?" Bayard asked when they were back in the car.

Of course Bayard noticed. He noticed far too much.

And she, far too little.

How could she have missed the clues, laid out as they were like crumbs for Hercule Poirot? The doorman's pugnacious questions. Micky's delight when she turned up like the world's easiest mark. His excitement at seeing she still wore the necklace he'd given her.

His flight out of Poland hadn't been an escape so much as a getaway.

CHAPTER 25

Bayard ignored her plea to take her on to Upsala and Cleo was too numb to protest. Instead, he drove them farther out of the city, where he pulled the car up onto a verge by the shores of a steel-gray lake reflecting back the cloudy sky. "Isn't this where we had our shooting lesson?"

"It is. Feel like firing off a few rounds?"

"You have *no* idea."

He flashed her a smile. "Maybe a hint."

That sparked a laugh out of her, and slowly the lump shifted. "Not much of a proper welcome back, was it?"

"Let's say I've become accustomed to your own charming brand of swirling chaos."

"You're not going to tell me I should have waited for you? That I brought this on myself? That I'm a spoiled little rich girl?"

"You'd just been told the man you love is alive. What else could you have done?"

The man she loved. That's right. She loved Micky. She did. She really did. So why was it Bayard's hand she wanted to hold right now? His gaze that sent goose bumps up her back? She wished she could tell him so, but there remained a reserve between them, a line neither of them could bring themselves to cross.

"What else indeed," she murmured, staring out on the wide park, hedged in shrubs. People wandered the paths while others sunbathed on the grass. "You didn't really bring me here to shoot guns, did you?"

"Actually, I thought you could use some fresh country air to clear your head before it was taken up with fertilizer tonnage and seed yields."

"I grew up in Manhattan. Fresh air makes me break out in hives."

"There's the sarcasm I've come to love."

He realized his words at the same moment she did, and an already awkward moment lengthened to the breaking point. When he leaned over, she thought he was actually going to kiss her and she tensed with a mix of anticipation, excitement, and fear. But he only reached across her for the glove box, where he'd stowed a pack of cigarettes and a lighter. "Only one left. Flip you for it?"

She shook her head, dazed that beneath the sick lump was something tingly and warm, though perhaps equally dangerous. He must feel it too, but his guilt and his grief lingered, and she hesitated to enter into competition with a ghost.

He lit the cigarette, taking a drag before handing it over. She inhaled the sweet burn of smoke, letting the taste fill her lungs, swirl down into the cold, achy spot in her chest.

"Better?"

"A bit."

"Enough to fill me in on what's going on with Kominski and whatever that little escapade was at the jeweler's?"

Her heart sank back into her shoes. What was that old tale of wishes that came true but with a twist of the knife you never saw coming? That was Micky. She'd wished him alive, and now here he was, and instead of rejoicing, she was afraid—for him, for her, and for Aunt Daisy, who would be dragged into Cleo's mess if she didn't keep it all under wraps.

She took another deep drag on the cigarette to steady her rattled nerves. She felt Bayard waiting—the scratch of his uniform sleeve, the shift of his shoulders against the seat, his breath fogging the windows. She handed the cigarette over as a signal she was ready to speak then wished she had something to do with her hands. She shoved them into her lap, clenched into fists. "He told me it was to make up for the jewelry I'd pawned after my mother cut me off. He said it was only paste and wire and colored glass bought off a peddler, but that someday he'd shower me in real diamonds. Show the bigwigs on Fifth Avenue what a scrawny Polish boy from Brooklyn could do."

"But it's not paste and wire."

She dug her nails into the heels of her palms, leaving white crescents against her pale skin. "And no peddler sells diamonds and rubies off the back of a barrow."

"So where do you suppose he got it?"

She stared out at the lake, but she was seeing the snow falling over the rooftops of Zakopane, the wind that blew under her scarf and down her back. The quiet streets guarded by German patrols who watched everything, took note of who gathered and for how long, barked commands at those who lingered, roughed up anyone who looked suspicious, arrested anyone who argued. Empty houses. Vacant shops. The town's inhabitants had become wraiths, moving silently through gray days without end. She'd been one of them.

Micky's gift had been a light within the winter dark, a gift too precious to question until now. She'd truly been the care-for-nothing grasshopper. His sin becoming hers out of purposeful ignorance.

She didn't answer Bayard, and he didn't press. Maybe because he already had a pretty good idea. "Did he explain where he's been all this time, Cleo? He must have realized you'd be upset, that you'd imagine the worst."

"He assumed I'd go home."

"But you didn't." Bayard got there a moment before she did. "And now here you are sporting a necklace that could set him up for life. Lucky break for him."

"Whatever you do, you can't say anything to Aunt Daisy about this. Promise me."

"You want me to lie?"

"I want you to keep quiet, that's all." She gave him her best waif look even though he'd never been susceptible to it before. It wasn't hard. Her heart ached as if someone had scooped it out, and tears burned in her throat. If only she knew whether she was grieving over Micky, Bayard, or her own stupid gullibility.

"Fine," Bayard said. "On one condition—you lock that damned necklace up and stay as far away from Kominski as you can."

"I can't just not see him."

"I'm sorry to be the one to tell you and I know you don't want to hear it, but he's bad news, Cleo. If he's in over his head, you don't want him pulling you under along with him."

Mr. Whitney had warned her about the same thing.

She was beginning to think it might be too late.

IT WAS MIDNIGHT before Cleo returned to the hotel, but no messages waited for her at the front desk. If Micky had come looking for her, he'd left without a trace. A lot like last time. The lobby still buzzed with activity and the bars and restaurants were crowded with diners. She ducked past and scurried into an elevator, hoping not to be spotted. Upstairs, the passages were quieter. A few people about, but it was easy enough to avoid those she knew with a few well-timed dodges into side hallways and, in one instance, a broom closet.

Cleo slowed as she passed Aunt Daisy's suite. Perhaps she was wrong. Perhaps she should come clean about Micky and the damn necklace. She lifted a hand to knock when movement caught the corner of her eye. A flash of gray. A squeak of a hinge. Or maybe just a stir in the air that wasn't the elevator ascending or a late-night guest coming home from the bar, but the feel of someone trying to be silent—and failing.

She followed the prickling sensation down the passage and around the corner to her room. A faint glimmer of light showed beneath the door. She pressed an ear to the panel. A thud and a hissed "fuck" didn't take overly sensitive ears.

Anger bunched in her stomach. She pushed the door open and stepped inside, flipping on a table lamp. The room flooded with light, illuminating Micky hunched over her dressing table, shining a flashlight on drawers pulled open and dumped. Her jewelry case upside down and emptied.

"If you're looking for the necklace, it's not there."

"What necklace? I don't know what you're talking about. The room was like this when I got here."

"I'm not stupid, Micky. That diamond necklace you gave me is worth a fortune. But you knew that already, didn't you? Since you're the one who stole it."

His features smoothed in defeat. "How did you figure it out?"

Cleo's accusation had been a stab in the dark. One she assumed would cause an angry denial, words she could cling to as a way to salvage even a whisper of the love they'd shared. His response kicked the last support out from under her. She was left twisting, unable to grasp the truth even as she saw it all unspooling like a bad film.

"I'm not a fool. Or maybe I should say I'm not a fool anymore."

"It was one time, Cleo. One lousy time, but Heimmel caught me red-handed. After that, I was trapped. It was do what he said or else. I didn't have a choice."

"Gestapo officer Heimmel?" She was right. The two men *did*

know one another. No wonder he'd been so interested in helping her find Micky. He was looking for him too.

"The bastard's cold as ice. When the Black Cat went up in flames, I saw my way out and I took it."

"Along with the jewelry you stole."

"It was a few pieces. That's all. You can't fault me for that. Their owner was dead. Would you rather the Nazis steal it all?"

She didn't answer, too stunned and sickened by what he'd done. Her hand unconsciously reached for her diamond before she realized what she was doing. The stone was dirty. Bought with someone's blood.

"It doesn't matter anyway." Micky's voice was grudging. "The jewelry's all gone. Moving in the shadows is expensive. People can smell when you're desperate. They cleaned me out. I'm flat broke. Barely a cent to my name."

"Which is why you need the necklace."

"Damn it, Cleo. Just hand it over, and I'm out of here. You never have to see me again. I'll pawn it for enough money for a one-way ticket home. You and your soldier boy can live happily ever after, and you'll never hear from me again."

She was furious and horrified and disgusted—with him and with herself for believing she loved him. And still, his words hurt. That he could walk away so easily. That he could forget their months together without experiencing any of the pain she'd suffered. Had he ever loved her? Or had she been a fool—twice over? Her breathing came quick and fast as if breathing deeply might cause the pain to grow and spread.

"Lieutenant Bayard isn't mine. He never was."

"Then you've lost your touch." His voice softened, and his gaze warmed with emotion. "It wasn't so long ago you could get any man to fall in love with you."

She wanted to believe she saw regret in his eyes or maybe a

shred of her grief, which had moved into her throat and made it hard to swallow. But it was clear to her now that he was far better at hiding his real feelings than she ever imagined. This wasn't the Micky she thought she knew. This was a stranger.

"The necklace, Cleo," he insisted. "That's all I want."

She choked back her pain. "And if I don't?"

His chest rose and fell as if he was fighting with himself, his face suffused, his shoulders bunched, arms like cords. Would he hit her? He never had before, but there was a first time for everything. Instead, he studied her from top to toe. She could see the wheels turning. He wasn't beaten. She'd witnessed this trait over their time together, this ability to adapt on the fly, make changes as the situation arose. She'd always seen his quick-thinking cleverness as a strength. Now she saw it for what it was, what he was. A chancer. Always looking for the advantage, uncaring whether he bent the rules so long as he came out on top.

"I hate to do it, Cleo, but you leave me no choice." His features hardened, any lingering persuasive warmth gone. "The necklace or that hoity-toity aunt of yours hears how you helped me loot from the murdered citizens of Zakopane. I'm sure that would go over well. Or maybe . . ." His eyes took on a glitter she didn't like. "Or maybe I'll bypass your aunt and go straight to the press with my story."

Cold washed over her skin. She almost wished he'd used his fists. She could handle a few bruises. They would fade. A story like this would turn the scandal of last summer into a footnote. She'd be tarred and feathered. Worse than that, Aunt Daisy risked being entangled in her disgrace.

"No one would believe you." She hated that her voice came out high and thin.

"No? You're the one with the priceless pink diamond, not me. Clementine Jaffray, the runaway bride suspected of blowing up a café full of Nazis and now stealing from murdered Polish citizens. Think how that'll read splashed across the front page of the *New York Times*. By the time anyone decides to check, the damage will be done."

She stood her ground, her knees wobbly. "You wouldn't dare. You'd implicate yourself."

"Yes, but I have nothing left to lose. You do." He brushed past her, his hand on the knob. "Guess I'll see you in the funny papers."

"Wait." It was her turn to scramble for an advantage, an opportunity he couldn't pass up. "If all you want is to go home, I can get you there."

She could feel him weighing the odds of her words. She held her breath, wondering if he'd call her bluff. All he had to do was walk four doors down and knock.

He took his hand off the door handle. "I'm listening."

HER DEVIL'S BARGAIN struck, Cleo escorted Micky out of the hotel to make sure he didn't take any detours along the way. She stood back out of the wind and watched him jog across the street until he turned a distant corner. Then she waited another ten minutes to assure herself he wasn't coming back.

She gripped her hands together and willed herself to stay calm. She could handle this. Just another twist in a dangerous road. Her plan was simple. Aunt Daisy was preparing the final passenger list for the *American Legion*. What was one more name slipped in among nearly a thousand?

"Have you spoken to Berlin?" Two men approached the hotel speaking quietly in German. Hardly unusual in Stockholm. Aside from the main legation on Hovslagargatan, there were secondary agencies and offices sprinkled all over the city, not to mention the bankers and businessmen residing here, hoping to cash in on the flow of Swedish iron to German foundries.

"If the operation is a success, we'll be promoted."

Cleo held her breath. She knew that voice. She pressed deeper into the shelter of the building, hoping to catch a glimpse of them as they passed her. Hoping not to be seen herself.

"And if it's a failure?" They passed into the shine from the hotel's lights. The first man was in his midforties: thinning hair, thickening waistline, bland face. He was one of the suits. Cleo's nails dug into her palms. Her heart banged in her ears.

"We're rogue officers acting on our own." It was Heimmel. The same narrow delicate features that missed handsome by inches. The same upper-crust voice as smooth as good whiskey and twice as warm. What was he doing here? Coincidence? Bad luck?

The two men pushed through the doors into the hotel. Cleo followed at a distance, watching them jog up the steps to the lobby. They caught sight of a third man, this one wearing Wehrmacht gray. All three moved off toward one of the reading rooms. She slid up the steps behind them, keeping to the edges of the lobby as she followed.

"Miss Jaffray, is that you?" Mr. Whitney wiped his spectacles and settled them back on his nose. His stare through the lenses was oddly perceptive—or maybe she was just feeling guilty. "Care to join me for a drink?"

"Isn't it a bit late?" she asked.

"I always took you for the last one to leave the party."

"Habits change."

"Do they?" He tapped his nose with a cold smile before heading into the bar.

What did that barnacle know? Or think he knew? A worry for later. But it was too late. She'd lost her quarry. She reached the end of the corridor, but there was no way to tell whether they'd continued on or doubled back to the bank of elevators. It was probably just as well. What would she say to explain her presence?

She returned to her room, locking the door behind her. Though if Micky had managed to break in, how secure was she really? She shoved a tipped chair under the handle like she saw done in the movies. Her toiletries case sat open but untouched. Micky had taken one look during his search and moved on, just as Cleo had planned. Aunt Daisy gave her the idea, but Cleo had improved upon it. Beneath an extra pair of underclothes, a bra, slip, and two sets of stockings was a brown paper package containing her sanitary belt, menstrual pads—and the necklace.

She smiled and tucked the necklace back into its hiding spot before climbing into bed. She wished she had Bayard's pistol to keep her company. What was the good of learning to shoot if she had no weapon? In the dark, thoughts crowded her. Micky's scent lingered in the air, his words punching at her most vulnerable spots.

She closed her eyes, inhaling and exhaling in a slow steady rhythm, hoping to empty her mind with each expelled breath. Her body grew heavy. Noises faded. There was a still point with sleep just beyond. She rolled over, and her mind instantly sprang back to life.

Micky hadn't really loved her, but was she any better? Surely if she'd loved him, she wouldn't have allowed her feelings for Bayard to get the better of her. Maybe it was time to admit that her search for the truth had become more about finding an answer than finding her lover.

CHAPTER 26

Dear Anne,

The last of the travel arrangements have been made, the last of the goodbyes have been said, and we're due to leave Stockholm any moment. My trusty Ford is being loaded onto the train for the trip to Haparanda, where we shall meet up with the rest of our company to begin the long drive north. One thousand men, women, and children counting on me to lead them one thousand miles into the Arctic. It's July, so weather shouldn't be a factor. Whether the war will follow us is my greater fear . . .

Stockholm Central Station buzzed like a hive despite the late hour, the soaring arched ceiling of the waiting hall directing the sound back down on travelers' heads until Daisy was dizzy with the noise. The kiosks and cafés did brisk business, with passengers standing in line for last-minute coffees or purchasing newspapers to read on the journey. Farther down the hall, a small knot of smartly dressed men loitered near the royal family's private waiting area. Daisy had checked in with the crown princess earlier. Prince Harald and Princess Ragnhild sat quietly on either side of their mother. Only Princess Astrid showed any curiosity in the coming adventure, kicking her heels against her chair as she squirmed and peppered her nurse with questions.

Daisy followed Mr. Whitney to the platform where their train stood waiting. Porters loaded luggage while clerks checked final lists. "We leave in ten minutes, ma'am."

"Have you seen Cleo? She should have been here a half hour ago." The situation felt very familiar. And very disappointing.

"No one's seen her, ma'am, and if I might have a quiet word?" The vice consul seemed to balance on the balls of his feet, his face aglow with suppressed information.

"You're positively vibrating, Mr. Whitney. Spit it out before you have a stroke."

"I didn't want to say anything, and I had hoped it was a mis-understanding, but"—he drew her aside, pitching his voice low as he leaned close—"it's Mr. Kominski, ma'am. He's not as dead as everyone thought."

She went perfectly still despite the sudden pounding in her temples. "You've seen him?"

"A few nights ago. I saw him and Miss Jaffray together. They seemed quite chummy, if you get my meaning."

And they accused women of being gossips.

She was desperate to interrogate him further, but the two of them had come to a détente of sorts. Any tipping of that precari-ous balance would only make a bad situation worse. "Is that all? You had me worried, Mr. Whitney. Yes, I knew of Mr. Komin-ski's arrival," Daisy lied, effectively quashing his delight. "I'm sorry I neglected to mention it when it happened but it was quite unexpected. Good news for a change."

His agreement was tepid at best. "Did he explain where he'd been, ma'am?"

"In Paris, I believe." It was easy once begun. The lies just spooled off her tongue like thread. "He'd no idea Cleo had been searching for him. A muddle all the way around, wouldn't you say?"

"Yes, ma'am. Very confusing." He paused for a moment as if to prepare for a final thrust. "So you authorized his addition to the *American Legion* passenger list?"

She let the mask settle over her face as the weight of Cleo's lies settled into the pit of her stomach. "Yes," she replied quietly. "I did."

His mischief blunted, he soon left to harangue the porters loading the last of the luggage, but she knew it wouldn't be the end of it. Giving a coveted spot on the ship to her goddaughter's boyfriend was too much of an *I told you so* for every man who ever disapproved of women in government.

She clutched her handbag and made herself smile and offer pleasantries to the passengers as they boarded, all the while feeling herself growing harder, burning hotter. Her thoughts were flooded with friends and comrades from her youth. Brave, intrepid women like her beloved Anne who refused to let the world burn without doing their best to put it out—her army of heroines. She had seen Cleo in that role. Had she miscalculated?

These last few months had wrought changes in her goddaughter that went beyond a harder edge to her features and fearsome shadows clinging to her gaze. Daisy had watched her grow into herself—the willful, entitled girl giving way to a determined and capable woman. Or so she'd thought. Maybe it had been wishful thinking. Maybe she'd wanted to see herself in a new generation, that same drive to step into the world and make a difference. Maybe she'd wanted to see what just wasn't there.

The train gave a whistle. Guards began closing and securing doors. The last porter nodded on his way past, trailing an empty cart. The train would leave. Daisy would be on it. She turned away when she heard a shout coming from the stairs at the far end of the platform. "Wait! Please wait!"

It was Cleo, her traveling case banging against her hip. Hair escaped her pins, flying in a wispy dark cloud around her face, and if you looked closely, she wore one navy and one black pump.

"I'm so sorry, Aunt Daisy. I had some last-minute work I had to finish."

"Would that work happen to include Mr. Kominski?" Daisy hoped even now that Mr. Whitney had been wrong. That he'd jumped to conclusions. But the stunned widening of Cleo's eyes gave the game away. Daisy found her chest tightening with unexpected anger. No, not anger. It was betrayal that burned in her throat like acid. Betrayal, not just of Daisy, but of everything she believed. Of the life she'd chosen to live, the values she cherished. It was as if Cleo had tossed them all aside. As if she'd tossed Daisy aside.

She was tired of being discarded. Tired of being treated like an old fool, the grandmother with the nice hats. She'd earned her place here. She'd scratched and clawed and worked like the devil to make it this far. She'd be damned if Cleo was the reason it all fell apart.

"I had to hear about his return, not from you, but from Whitney, who was quite happy to be the bearer of such titillating news."

"I'll bet he was," Cleo muttered.

"Is there a reason you didn't tell me he was not only alive, but in Stockholm? Or that you'd finagled him onto our passenger list?" Daisy didn't wait for an answer. "I was right. You're very much like your father. Selfish, immature, and a bloody great fool." The words leaped from her throat, cruel and cutting, designed to hurt.

Cleo's chin jerked back as if she'd been slapped, her face flushed. "If you'll let me explain—"

"That's all you've done since you arrived on my doorstep, Clementine. Offered up excuses that I've grown weary of hearing." Daisy swallowed the rest of her words, angry with herself for allowing her emotions to carry her away. Angry with Clementine for distracting her when she needed her wits about her for the coming days. Angry with Mr. Whitney for sowing his suspicions until she questioned everything.

Cleo's eyes glittered with a wash of tears, color splashed high across her cheekbones. "I'm sorry I let you down, Aunt Daisy."

"So am I, my dear. You don't know how much."

CLEO HAD NEVER seen Aunt Daisy lose her temper. She'd always been the one in control—calm, sensible. No bluster or flying off the handle. Not like her mother, who lived at the whim of her emotions. Cleo had learned early on to tune out half the nonsense her mother said, the crushing effusions of love as well as the biting disapproval. If only it was as easy to ignore Aunt Daisy. Instead her words banged against Cleo's throbbing temples.

To combat her misery, she tried reimagining the scene where her reaction didn't give the game away, where her lies tripped off the tongue more easily. She imagined herself telling Aunt Daisy the truth and handing over the necklace, relieved at relinquishing a weight that grew heavier with every breath. But that fantasy hadn't lasted more than a moment. This was her problem. Micky was her mistake. She'd let Aunt Daisy think the worst. If it meant keeping her clear of Cleo's problems, she could live with that.

The bump and rattle of the train worked to ease the stretch of cramped muscles. They passed over a crossing. A convoy of trucks waited for them to pass, headlights spearing the dark. Were they headed west into Norway? Did they carry supplies? Weapons? Soldiers? The village fell behind them, and the train was once more cutting its way north through heavy pine forests and stands of white-trunked birch that shone like pale ghosts in the flickering lights. She tried closing her eyes, but her chest ached and there was an emptied-out feeling in her stomach.

"Coffee?"

She sat up, surprised and blinking at the gray light filtering through the window. How long had she slept? "What time is it?"

"A little after nine in the morning," Bayard answered. "We just pulled out of the town of Umeå. Another six hours or so should see us to Haparanda."

Cleo's back ached from sitting, and grit clung to her eyelashes, but the gnawing emptiness of last night had receded to be replaced by the pinch of hunger. The coffee was black and sludgy, but sweet with a hint of . . .

She looked up to catch him tucking a flask back into his breast pocket. "A little brandy to ease the morning afters." He pulled a paper bag from his coat pocket. "And half a sandwich if you want it. I grabbed it in the station café before we left."

"Are you sure you want to be seen with me?" she asked as she accepted the sandwich and his company. "I'm not exactly woman of the hour these days."

"I heard about that." He sipped at his coffee, hair mussed from his own uncomfortable sleep and stubble shadowing his chin. "She's a reasonable woman. I'm sure she'll come around now that it's over." He continued to stare. "It *is* over, isn't it?" When she didn't reply immediately, he frowned and his shoulders sagged. "It's not over." He looked like he could down the rest of that brandy in one swallow. "What have you done now, Cleo?"

"Micky was going to go to the press about the necklace. He was going to tell them I was in on his scheme. I couldn't let him do that so I made him an offer, which he accepted in lieu of the necklace."

"He's on the train?"

"Don't be daft." She smiled. "He's on a bus."

"Are you crazy?"

"I didn't care about me, but I couldn't let him hurt Aunt Daisy. She deserves better."

"Why didn't you tell her that?" He sighed, already knowing

Cleo's answer and already knowing he'd never get her to change her mind.

"She didn't give me the chance. She was too busy telling me what a bonehead I was." She put on a brave face she didn't feel. "It's just a few more weeks. Just until we reach New York."

"Swirling chaos," he muttered, scrubbing at his face. "You're a hard one to make out, you know that?" There was a tightness around his eyes, but there was also laughter tugging at the edges of his mouth, which gave Cleo comfort that she hadn't burned all her bridges.

"I thought you had my kind all figured out," she teased.

"I did too."

"It's easy to box people in, isn't it? To see only what you want to see and pretend the rest doesn't exist. It's simpler that way. You don't have to work at putting all the pieces together to make a picture that might not be perfect."

"Is that what I did?"

"We all do it."

Aunt Daisy was right. Cleo *had* been spoiled and thoughtless and foolish. But now she knew her father, a man held up to her as the heroic ideal, had been just as spoiled and just as thoughtless. Yet when it was necessary, he'd done the right thing.

She could do that too.

IT WAS LATE afternoon by the time they arrived in the town of Haparanda, where their ship's company would gather for the next leg of the journey. As the train pulled into the junction, it passed a field of enormous canvas tents erected alongside flimsy prebuilt huts. Ambulances and open-bed trucks came and went out of a gate guarded by two armed guards. Cleo followed the line of passengers out of the station and down the street toward their hotel, which, even from a distance, had a decrepit and dingy air.

A woman ignored the guard's shout as she passed out of the encampment. Her arms were wide in welcome, her sharp-boned sun-tanned face making her blue eyes shine brighter. "Cleo Jaffray! Welcome to Haparanda!"

Sofia was dressed like a soldier in a faded jacket and dungarees, her braided hair wound over her head like a crown. The only sign of her medical profession was the red cross on her shoulder bag. She enveloped Cleo in a spine-straightening hug, nearly lifting her off the ground.

"What are you doing here?" Cleo gasped.

"I am preparing to head back into Norway to help as best I can."

"By yourself?" Sofia Kristiansen had the ancestry of a Viking and the tongue of a wasp. Cleo could easily see her taking on a battalion single-handed.

"As part of the American-Scandinavian Field Hospital." Sofia motioned toward the camp behind them. "I am assisting Dr. Fishwick, our chief surgeon. We have enough staff and trucks to outfit a hundred-bed facility, but we are waiting for a shipment of medicine and surgical equipment that is being held up while everyone squabbles over their share of the payment."

"Have you heard anything more from your family? Are they okay?"

Bitterness soured Sofia's mouth, her chin thrust forward, jaw lifted. "I have heard my brother has made it to England, but nothing about my parents for the past month. I am hoping I can find them. Bring them back into Sweden, where they will be safe. Then I can make these bastard Nazis pay in blood for every inch of land they occupy. For Petra and everyone they have killed in their desire for power."

Cleo eyed the medical bag. "Rather bloodthirsty words for a doctor, don't you think?"

"It just means I have a better understanding of how easy it is to kill a man." Sofia smiled when she spoke, but Cleo had a feeling she was all too serious. She reminded herself to stay very much on Sofia's good side. "Come," Sofia said. "Let's find something to eat. You look starved."

She bought both of them a dinner of *pyttipanne*, which turned out to be a lot like ham hash but better. Carrying their food down to a park by the river, they found a bench as the setting sun turned the wide sky rose and gold and orange, reflected in the water lapping almost at their toes. Sofia pulled out her usual pack of Petterøe's and lit one, her gaze focused on the dark line of trees on the far bank. Finnish trees sheltering the Finnish border city of Tornio, which hugged the opposite side of the river from the Swedish border city of Haparanda.

A whistle sounded as a train inched out of the junction on its way back south to Stockholm and civilization. Cleo wished she was on it. She was a city girl. She didn't like the wide vistas of cloud-streaked sky and endless forests of scrubby pine. The remote homesteads and narrow logging tracks broken only by the occasional crossroads town. It was too wild. Too empty. Too exposed. Or maybe it was the company. Sofia, like her sister before her, had a way of seeing deeper than Cleo wished, noticing parts of her she preferred to keep hidden.

Sofia tossed her cigarette away and pulled something from her coat pocket. "This is for you."

Cleo marveled at the enameled brooch: a delicate gold butterfly, its lacy scalloped wings decorated in blue and green. "This was Petra's."

"She wrote in her letter that she wanted you to have it." Sofia pinned it to Cleo's coat. "She said to tell you that you are not a grasshopper. You are a butterfly."

Guilt rushed over Cleo like a wave. "I can't accept it."

"You'd turn down a gift?"

"I don't deserve it. I double-crossed her. I took advantage of . . . of the situation to . . . and with the lieutenant . . . I didn't mean to. Really. It just happened. But Petra . . ."

"Is dead." Sofia's face took on an uncharacteristic softness. The golden glints in her blue eyes shimmered. "Do you care for this lieutenant?"

"More than I should."

"And does he care for you?"

"I don't know. I think so."

"If you are asking for my sister's blessing, you will be waiting forever. She is past being betrayed or being in love. And with the world in flames, she would wish you both to find happiness." Sofia grinned like a devil. "Or maybe she will haunt you for the rest of your lives. Who is to say with Petra? She was full of surprises."

It might not have been a blessing, but Sofia's complete disregard for Cleo's distress was cathartic. As if Petra spoke through her sister. Cleo felt her shoulders drop, the ache at the base of her skull ease, and the sick weight in her stomach dissolve. She touched the butterfly as once she touched her diamond. "Thank you."

Sofia shook another cigarette from the pack and placed it between her lips, pausing with the lighter in her hand, as if a thought had struck. "You head north tomorrow. Into Finland."

"That's right." Cleo ran a finger over the edge of the butterfly's wing.

"I have something else for you. What every good woman should be wearing these days." Cleo jumped when Sofia pushed an unholstered revolver into her lap, but just as quickly she relaxed under the weight of the weapon. "It's a long road through rough country. The Germans hide in plain sight. Dressed as Red Cross workers. Finnish veterans. Even the old man living in a burned-out hovel could be an enemy soldier in disguise."

"Why would they care about a convoy of Americans?"

Sofia's eyes hardened to ice, fury etched into every line bitten into the once soft curve of her cheek, the angle of her cheekbones.

"Of course." The answer was like a fist to Cleo's jaw. "They want Prince Harald." She shuddered now with nerves and cold, a shiver that raced over her skin like an ice cube. "Does my aunt know?"

"There is nothing to know. Only whispers and rumors. Sometimes they are false. And sometimes they are truth, which is why it is best to be prepared."

"If I take your gun, what will you use?"

Sofia's smile was practically feral, her warrior ancestry burning in her gaze. "That will not be a problem." As if her duty was done, she seemed anxious to return to camp. She stood, stamping her feet to bring feeling back into her toes. "I should go, but I will hope to see you again when we have won this war."

When. Not if. It didn't sound so far-fetched when Cleo imagined an army of Sofias marching into battle. But such an army needed supplies and equipment and money to purchase them.

"Wait." Cleo dug into her purse until she felt the wrinkled crunch of brown paper. "A gift deserves a gift." She slid her fingers along the fold until they touched the curve of cold metal, the warmth of a stone the size of a hummingbird's egg. She placed it in Sofia's outspread palm, the enormous diamond a vibrant watermelon pink in the arctic sunset, the rubies red as blood. "This should buy enough to outfit a dozen medical units and then some."

Sofia considered it for a moment before pulling Cleo into another hug that had her gasping for breath. "Petra saw something in you that gave her hope. Now I see it too."

CHAPTER 27

Dear Anne,

I have arrived in the Finnish village of Ivalo . . .

Daisy paused as she sought to grapple her thoughts into some sort of arrangement, before crumpling the page, the pretense no longer possible to maintain.

Anne Vanderbilt was dead.

She knew it. She understood it. And yet it was impossible to stop thinking of her as being just a letter away.

One didn't notice the ground upon which one built a life until a piece of it crumbled, leaving only emptiness. A hole filled with nothing but memories. The two of them had grown old together, intertwined through marriage and friendship and tragedy and work. It was a dizzying feeling, this break. As if a tether had been cut and she was falling free with no net. Anne had been a steadfast presence, a sounding board. Someone who understood Daisy's ambitions because she shared them. That need to be more than what society expected. To use the advantages bestowed by birth for a greater purpose, to work for something bigger than oneself or one's family name.

Had it been the age they grew up in that created this sense of duty? An era of great excess alongside an era of great responsibility? Had those values passed her by when she wasn't looking? Or were there still men and women willing to struggle and fight for a larger cause?

Her thoughts turned to Cleo, the reason for Daisy's discarded letter to her sister-in-law and perhaps her melancholy as well. No, not melancholy. That wasn't a strong enough word for what burned under her ribcage. Pessimism? Discouragement? Defeat? No. She refused to admit defeat. That went against her nature. Always had. As had these dismal broodings. She was built of sterner—and more optimistic—stuff.

They arrived in the Finnish village in the small hours of the morning though the sky had never really darkened much beyond a twilight blue. It was a loud chaotic reunion of arriving buses, travel-weary passengers seeking luggage as they shouted greetings to one another, behaving as if they hadn't seen each other in years rather than hours.

Captain Waddell, one of their escorts, roared to make himself heard over the din while Lieutenant Bayard moved from group to group, answering questions, soothing nerves, calming tempers, and assisting as he could.

Once or twice, Daisy caught sight of Cleo, but only from a distance before Mr. Whitney appeared at her elbow, directing her to the hotel, offering updates on their progress as they climbed the steps into the lobby. The scents of paint and fresh lumber hung in the air from recent reconstruction after the Russo-Finnish War the past winter, but the food was hot and the rooms welcoming after the long trip.

"We're stuck here until the last of the buses arrive," Mr. Whitney grumbled. Always punctilious, he'd grown practically autocratic over the course of the last few days. He hadn't brought up Cleo or Micky Kominski since that morning in the train station, and for that Daisy was grateful. She wasn't sure she'd be as successful fobbing him off a second time. "This doesn't leave us a lot of time to make our rendezvous at the port in Petsamo. I've warned Lieutenant Bayard to make sure all is prepared so we can get back on the road as soon as we can."

"And Her Royal Highness?"

"She's been given rooms in a guesthouse on the premises. She's there now, resting ahead of the next leg of the journey, ma'am."

Rest. It was exactly what Daisy should do, but her mind spun and, with no outlet, she found herself unable to settle. The promised dawn came within a few hours, the sky brightening to a high milky blue streaked with mare's tails. If she couldn't sleep, she'd enjoy a last taste of adventure.

Changing into a country suit of sturdy corduroy and lacing on her boots, she left the hotel unseen by anyone who might stop her. This early, no one would notice her missing. Most still slept, and those who were up and about barely recognized her under her outdoor gear.

"Sneaking away, Mrs. Harriman?"

Daisy froze, slowly turning to see Her Royal Highness leaning against the porch railing, a cigarette in her hand. She wore a handsome dress of forest green to match the dark woods surrounding the hotel, her features smooth though there were shadows in her gaze if one cared to notice.

"You've caught me fair and square, Your Royal Highness. I thought I'd take advantage of our respite to revisit an old haunt. Who knows if I'll have the chance again?"

"Indeed" was the crown princess's caustic response before she tossed her cigarette away. "Best say your farewells while you can. I only wish I could join you."

The Ford sat at the edge of the woods, keys in the ignition. Daisy smiled to herself as she started the car. Driving was like riding a horse. Once you learned, you never forgot, and she'd learned under the direst of circumstances—her lessons etched in the charcoal grays of war as she steered her ambulance over the cratered tracks and muddy lanes of France. This drive wasn't nearly as dangerous, though rumors of German infiltrators had followed them north into Finland.

She rumbled over a wooden bridge, the river below curling with foam over a rocky bed, the water so clear one could see every stone and stick and darting fish. Some thought Lapland disorienting, too lonely, devoid of the color one saw in more temperate zones. Daisy disagreed. In the summer, the sunrise burst like fireworks while the winter nights conjured the shimmering dance of northern lights overhead. The air was clear and sweet with a tang of fir.

Pulling up outside the rustic fishing lodge at Inari, she breathed her first deep breath. But here too, signs of the war with Russia were visible in the discarded crates of old medical supplies and the stripped trees and beaten oil-soaked earth where idling trucks had discharged the wounded.

"Hello!" she called, the lodge oddly quiet for this time of year. Normally, the guests would be gathering as the local guides organized gear and plotted the best stretch of river for a day's fishing.

An older man with a weather-beaten face maneuvered through a side door, confusion and agitation uppermost in his stark, pain-bitten features as he angled his crutches on the steps. "We're not taking fishing parties out today . . . or indeed any day."

"Is something wrong?" She assisted him as he lost his balance on the uneven ground.

He glanced nervously at the road leading away to the east. "Wrong? Haven't you heard? The Russians are on the way . . . or maybe it's the Germans. Either way, every man hereabouts has been called back into service. You should leave, ma'am. Leave before it's too late."

* * *

THE HOTEL IN Ivalo was situated near a small stretch of green that ran alongside the river. Some of the guests had spread blankets on the ground. Children skipped stones or chased each other along the riverbank. Cleo found a patch of grass where picnic tables had been set up under the trees.

"Astrid? *Hvor er du?* Where have you run off to, you naughty girl?" A rather harried middle-aged woman ran from group to group in search of her missing charge.

"Can I help?" Cleo asked.

The woman, recognizing her as the U.S. minister's goddaughter, smiled with relief. "Please. She was playing by the water a minute ago. I turned my back and, poof, she's gone."

"You check up by the hotel. I'll walk along the riverbank. She might have followed the other children downstream."

They separated, each calling out for Princess Astrid. Cleo picked her way over the uneven ground. An enormous stand of firs marched down to the riverbank. Briars and undergrowth tangled their way around trunks, and the air smelled sharply of pine resin.

"Astrid? It's Cleo! Are you here?"

Out of the corner of her eye, Cleo caught a glimpse of blond hair and blue ribbons among the thick shadows and leafy scrub.

"Astrid? Is that you?"

The little princess knelt beside the river, dipping a cup into the water, inspecting the contents, and then pouring them out.

"What on earth are you doing?"

Astrid spun, catching a hair ribbon on an overhanging branch. "Oh. I thought you were the funny man. He was here a minute ago."

"Who's the funny man?" Cleo asked, untangling the runaway while surreptitiously checking her for visible signs of damage.

Princess Astrid held out her cup. "Is that gold? I can't tell."

Cleo wrinkled her nose. "It looks more like mud."

"The funny man said this river is famous for its gold. That I might find some if I tried. He gave me the cup to use."

"That was kind of him."

"He said my grandfather has lots of gold, and that I should be clever and find some for myself."

Was this a homesick child's imaginary friend? Or something more sinister? Cleo glanced around her, but there was no one nearby. "Let's go find Nurse, and you can tell me all about this funny man."

Astrid took her hand and the two of them retraced their steps. "What did your funny man look like?"

"I don't know. Just ordinary."

"Why do you call him a funny man?"

"Because he made me laugh. He told me riddles and he pretended to be a dog. He said he had a kitten for me. That I could take it with me to America if my mother let me. He was going to show it to me, but then you came." Cleo's hand tightened around Astrid's until she squirmed and pulled free. "You're squeezing too hard."

Cleo let go but glued herself to the little princess's side, assuming a guard-dog stance. If she could have bared her teeth, she would have.

The royal family was settled in a rustic log guesthouse set a short distance away from the main hotel. Cleo had seen the small military detail set to guard them, though to her untrained eye they seemed more decorative than capable, and she wondered how much use they'd be if the Germans really did attack. Right now, one was standing in the shade of a pine tree enjoying a cigarette. Another was patrolling the car park, though his gaze kept sliding enviously toward the waterside. She had no idea where the other two were, but they had seemed equally unconcerned about possible ambushes. Maybe she was being paranoid, but Sofia's warnings kept Cleo on her guard, watching her surroundings as she searched for any hint of trouble. She'd seen nothing to worry her—until now.

Maybe Astrid's funny man had merely sought to be friendly. Perhaps he was missing his own little girl or had come upon Astrid playing at the water's edge and sought to keep her safe. But then why did he slip away upon Cleo's approach? Why did he not introduce himself to Astrid or do as Cleo was doing and escort the little girl back to her nurse?

The guard with the cigarette saw Cleo approaching with the princess and nodded her on toward the door. She knocked, but there was no response. Turning the latch, she poked her head inside. "Hello? Anyone home?"

The log house's interior was dark and dominated by an enormous stone fireplace. Doors opened off a cozy central room, and a wooden ladder led up to a sleeping loft. Hardly palatial or even grand. She wondered what the crown princess thought of her temporary accommodations.

"No one is here," Astrid pointed out. "Can we go back to the river?"

Cleo ducked her head into a bath, a small study, and a tidy bedroom that must belong to the crown princess. There was a heady floral citrus scent of expensive perfume and closet sachets though another odor crept along the floorboards and gathered near the closet. She inhaled, trying to figure out what it was. Damp wood? Mildew? Perhaps a small animal had made a home here. A weasel, perhaps.

"Astrid! There you are." The children's nurse hurtled through the door, flushed and wild-eyed. "Naughty girl! I thought you had fallen in the water and drowned."

Astrid didn't look the least bit contrite as she confronted her nurse. "I'm not drowned. And Miss Jaffray is Mama's friend, so it's all right."

"Your mother is cross and asked that I bring you straight to her." She shepherded the little girl out the door and down the front steps, frog-marching her across the car park toward the hotel.

Cleo dawdled until they were out of sight before reentering the cottage, hands on hips. "I know you're here, Micky. I can smell that horrible cologne you insist on wearing. Come out now or I'll holler up one of those guards out there to shoot you."

The soft snick of a lifting latch was her answer.

She was right. It *was* a weasel.

"Do you know what they would have done to you if they found you there? Then what they would have done to me? How would Aunt Daisy have explained the situation to Her Royal Highness? Or to her superiors in Washington?" Cleo choked down her fury until her throat hurt.

"I saw him, Cleo." Micky sat across from her in the hotel dining room, rattling his coffee cup in his saucer, knocking a fork to the floor in his agitation. "Heimmel's here in Ivalo."

"And you thought what? You'd throw some of the crown princess's jewelry at him to keep him happy?"

"It was stupid, but I panicked. I didn't know what else to do."

She carefully set down her knife and fork. Run or fight? Keep quiet or come clean? She was running out of options. "Are you sure it's *you* he's after?"

He considered. "You think he's after a bigger prize?"

"I think this has gone way beyond a ticket home." She pushed back her chair. "I have to go find the lieutenant."

"You'll give me up?"

"I'll do what I should have done in the first place."

"What about me? What the hell am I supposed to do while that madman's wandering around free?"

"Lock yourself in your room. Try not to get into any more trouble."

"Everything would have been fine if you hadn't grown a damned conscience." Micky shoved back from the table, knocking his water glass over, the spill spreading along the table, dripping onto the floor. He paused for a moment as if debating whether to stay and help mop up before hunching his shoulders deeper into his jacket and storming off, scattering diners like pigeons in the park.

Not the first time he'd left Cleo to clean up his mess.

She righted the water glass and mopped at the spill with her napkin. Maybe he was right. Maybe she shouldn't have given the necklace to Sofia. The diamond, though it had hung round her neck for almost a year, had never been hers to keep or give away. Perhaps it would have been best to try to find its rightful owner and return it, though how she would have accomplished that, she had no idea. All she *did* know was that handing it over to Micky was definitely not the right decision.

She put her hand to her throat as she'd done a million times, but this time instead of a gaudy pink diamond in an even gaudier ruby setting, she felt the delicate scalloped edge of a butterfly's wing. Her doubts faded. She might have been a fool in a million different ways and crashed from one crisis to another, but in this instance, she knew she'd done the right thing. Sofia would find a way to turn Micky's crime into a gift of hope.

And right now, hope was all Norway had.

She was sure the owners of the necklace would understand and applaud.

She left the dining room in search of Bayard, who had conscripted the hotel manager's office and was shouting on the telephone. ". . . call me back at this number if you hear anything at all." He hung up, ran a hand through his hair in agitation, then lit up a cigarette. "If it's not good news, I don't want to hear it."

"What's wrong?"

"We've started hearing troubling reports coming in of Russian saber-rattling. We might need to get back on the road sooner than we'd scheduled."

"What does Aunt Daisy think?"

"Your guess is as good as mine." He leaned back, his gaze growing thoughtful. "You're looking a little peaky. Is it the fish from breakfast or maybe the fish from lunch? Hopefully not the fish from dinner last night."

Cleo tried to smile but her face wouldn't seem to relax. She would have killed for a smoke right now, but she'd left her cigarettes back at the table. She shoved a hand into her cardigan pocket, fiddling with a bit of fluff at the bottom.

"Cleo?" Bayard asked again, his smile fading in the face of her obvious worry.

"We might have a problem."

"That seems to be *all* we have right now."

Outside, a car horn blared. Once then twice more. Cleo ran to the window in time to see Aunt Daisy's Ford pulling to a stop. She emerged dressed in rough country corduroy, her boots muddy, her cheeks pink with sun.

"Here she is now," Bayard said. "Come on."

"I can't." Cleo started to back up. "Aunt Daisy's already furious with me—and rightly so. This will only make it ten times worse."

Bayard took Cleo's hand. "Whatever it is, we can beard the lion together."

Aunt Daisy was beaming as she retrieved a line of fish from the trunk. "What do you think, Lieutenant? Dinner tonight?"

Bayard caught Cleo's eye and winked.

Aunt Daisy's gaze flicked from one to the other, dropping to their linked hands and back up to their somber faces. Her own smile vanished. "I don't imagine you're here to greet me because you missed me."

"No, ma'am," Bayard said. "Patrols along the border are hearing rumors. It might mean stepping up our timeline."

"Right. Fun's over." She handed Cleo the fish. "Take these to the kitchen."

Cleo wrinkled her nose as she accepted the line, but she didn't budge. "There's something I need to tell you."

"Can it wait?" Aunt Daisy tried to brush Cleo off as she headed for the hotel, her earlier good humor replaced by a forbidding politeness.

It was only what Cleo expected. It was only what she deserved, but it stung just the same. She felt herself start to step back, to give way under her godmother's cold formality. To let herself be frozen out, the disgraced, unwanted relation she'd been when she arrived bedraggled and bereft back in March on the doorstep at 28 Nobels Gate. But she wasn't that woman. Not anymore. And she wouldn't let her godmother treat her as if she was.

"No, Aunt Daisy." She straightened her shoulders and took a breath. "I'm afraid it can't."

Dear Anne,

I've come a long way from the stage fright that plagued me as I stood on the podium to accept the presidency of the Colony Club. Finding the right words for any situation has become second nature over the last thirty years. And yet Cleo has stunned me to silence . . .

BY THE END of Cleo's confession, Daisy didn't trust herself to speak without shouting. Her chest was on fire. Her ears buzzed.

The scent of fish and the arctic air swirled in her flared nostrils. Just a few short hours ago, she'd been up to her shins in an icy river, nothing weightier on her mind than finding the best lie and perfecting her backcast. Now she was on the brink of catastrophe. No. Not catastrophe. She refused to concede to failure. There had to be a solution. There always was if one worked at it long enough.

"Where's Mr. Kominski now?" Daisy's voice was rough with the effort of not screaming.

"I told him to stay in his hotel room." Cleo stared at the carpet, her fall of dark hair hiding her face. Her fists pressed under her ribs, shoulders hunched, as if she was about to be sick.

"I suppose he can't get into too much trouble there," Daisy replied grudgingly.

"Don't bet on it," Bayard muttered. "A shame we can't lock him in and throw away the key."

Daisy threw a hard look toward the lieutenant, but it was clear that while he might have known parts of Cleo's story, she hadn't been completely truthful with him either. "First things first. Bayard, I want you to gather Mr. Whitney and the others. We'll meet in the hotel manager's office in an hour."

"Yes, ma'am." He and Cleo exchanged a private look on his way out, which Daisy filed away for deciphering at a quieter moment.

"What are you going to tell them?" Cleo asked.

Daisy found her gaze straying to her goddaughter's bare throat, where the stolen necklace had once rested. Who would have thought such a garish, vulgar trinket would be worth so much or cause this amount of trouble? "Only what I need to and not a jot more."

She had an hour. Time to wash off the smell of fish and change into something more suitable. Sackcloth and ashes, perhaps. Cleo followed doggishly along in Daisy's wake as she headed for her hotel suite, taking up position like a sentry, her features slowly returning to life now the worst was behind her.

Her worst. Daisy's was still to come.

Despite the inevitable uproar that was sure to happen when she explained the situation, Daisy felt a calm descend as she thought through this new tangle. A dangerous one, for certain, but hardly the first time she'd been caught between a rock and a hard place. The last months had solidified her immunity to bouts of panic. As long as she remained clearheaded, there was a chance she could battle her way through this latest complication. It all came down to untangling the competing threads. Finding the right one to pull.

"Is there something else? Some additional disaster you haven't disclosed?" Daisy asked, bending over to unlace her boots, then stripping out of her canvas jacket and thick wool sweater. "Because I learned long ago to make do without a lady's maid."

Cleo was no longer gray with panic. Her eyes glinted, and there was an alertness to her pose that usually meant trouble. "I was thinking maybe we could just send word to Stockholm about Heimmel. If he's anticipating an unarmed convoy of women and children, I'd bet a show of force would be enough to scare him off."

"There's no time. We have a schedule to keep. Especially if the reports of movement along the border are true." Her own brain sifting through options, Daisy folded her outerwear back into her suitcase and headed into the bath, a towel over her arm.

"What if we took another route?" Through the closed door, Cleo continued to shout ideas over the sound of running water. "One the Germans won't be expecting?"

Ignoring Cleo as best she could, Daisy washed, rinsed, and toweled off. Free of the smell of fish, she dressed quickly and with care, making sure every seam was straight, her string of pearls in place. For now, she remained the US minister to Norway. She'd damn well look like it. She checked her wristwatch. Bayard and the others would be waiting for her, speculating on why they'd been called together, exchanging guesses and forming opinions. She had to hurry before the chatter got out of hand.

By now, Cleo was firing on all cylinders. She circled the room, a finger tapping against her lip as she tossed out idea after idea, each one more outlandish than the last. "I've got it. We put Her Royal Highness and the children on one of the buses. With all the other families, who's to notice a few extra?" She shook her head and increased her pace. "No, that won't work. Moving the royal family onto a bus would require moving someone else off and there would be questions." As Daisy headed for the lobby, Cleo followed a deferential step behind and to the left like a general's aide-de-camp. "Or *we* travel in the royal car and let the crown princess take the Ford. Better still, *I* take her place in the royal car. No need for us all to swap. I could wear a big hat and a veil. No one would know. What do you think? It would work. I just know it."

Daisy rounded on her with a sharp look and firm hand. "Do you embroider, Cleo?"

"What?" Her eyes widened in confusion at the abrupt change of subject. "I can hem a little. Sew on a button. Nothing fancy."

"A piece of advice, then, from someone with far greater experience; it's always tempting when one is first starting out to go straight for the most complicated stitches. But ofttimes it's the simplest ones that work the best."

CHAPTER 28

Dear Anne,

My father has been much in my thoughts lately. Not the man I knew, but the gallant sea captain of his thrilling nursery tales. The blockade runner piloting his beloved Banshee *through storm-tossed waves, barely escaping the guns of a Union squadron with a dangerous running of the bar. I fear I am infected by this same presence of mind in the face of danger for, like an old warhorse smelling powder, I find myself oddly undisturbed by the growing threats. In this company, I am the captain, and it's my turn to outsmart my enemies . . .*

Daisy joined her most trusted advisers in the hotel manager's office, which Lieutenant Bayard had conscripted with a high-handed bark of an order, practically shutting the door in the man's face as he huffed and argued about delays and inconvenience. Ten minutes later, he was still pacing and grumbling in the outer office, requiring Daisy to raise her voice to be heard.

". . . and that's where we stand, gentlemen." She folded her arms on the desk to signal she was finished. "Thoughts?"

Daisy gave the men time to digest the information. She wasn't surprised by their stunned silence. Even keeping most of Cleo's confession under wraps, what she'd outlined was as far-fetched as a bad Dashiell Hammett novel. As she waited for them to react, she noticed when the hotel manager gave up and went away with one last grouse about inconsiderate Americans. And was very aware of the creak of a floorboard and a sudden draft of cool air that followed a few minutes later when someone new entered the outer office.

Cleo? No. The tread was too heavy. The pungent aroma of bay rum cologne too . . . masculine. This was someone else. Someone far more predictable.

Mr. Whitney spoke up first. Not surprising. The vice consul had grown increasingly red-faced as Daisy explained the issues. "How are we only now hearing about this connection between Mr. Kominski and the Gestapo?"

"Better late than never is how I'm looking at it." Daisy threaded her hands together into a tight knot on the desk, her rings cutting into the soft skin around her knuckles. Only Bayard, watching her out of the corner of his eye, might suspect the tight rein she was keeping on her emotions.

"Of course it is," Mr. Whitney argued. "Miss Jaffray's your goddaughter. It's only through your personal involvement that she's been allowed such liberties. This mess can be traced directly back to her." *And you* was left unspoken but definitely implied.

"Now's not the time to be pointing fingers." The lieutenant jumped to her defense—or maybe he was defending Cleo. At this point, it was one and the same thing.

"Oh please," Whitney snapped back. "We all know you're head over heels for the girl."

Daisy wasn't sure whether the vice consul was brave or stupid. Bayard was twenty years younger and four inches taller.

"And we all know you've had it in for the minister since Oslo," Bayard returned, his voice strained.

"If you mean I've offered her the wisdom of my many years in public service, then, yes, I have."

"You know damn well what I mean, you pretentious ass."

The pressure, pent up over months, burst in a torrent of recrimination and accusation. The two men traded barbs and insults with increasing volume. Daisy started to intercede before closing her mouth and stepping back, letting the storm rage.

"Are they always like this?" Captain Waddell leaned close to murmur in her ear, his bracing gaze bemused rather than shocked.

"It's been a long few months," Daisy replied. "Best let them get it out of their system now. We'll need them at the top of their game if we're going to get through the next few days."

She gave the two men a moment to let tempers cool and hoped Captain Waddell wasn't one to carry gossip back to Freddie Sterling at the Swedish legation. It would be difficult to explain her messy little family—Whitney's hair-trigger temper, Lieutenant Bayard's overdeveloped chivalry, the fact that the only thing predictable about Cleo was her unpredictability.

Like a ship's captain, Daisy saw them as in her charge and under her protection. Her trusted crew who might battle each other bloody but wouldn't hesitate to stand together when faced with a threat. A romantic notion perhaps, but she'd walked enough battlefields and known enough soldiers to see the truth behind the romance. When it came down to it, one didn't fight for one's country. One fought for one's friends.

After it seemed like the worst was over, she stepped in with a lift of her hand. "Gentlemen, I'd rather we direct our hostility toward the *actual* enemy. Miss Jaffray's actions have been extremely rash, but I think we can agree that they've also been crucial in identifying and thus countering any possible attack."

"How do you figure that?" Mr. Whitney grumbled, not quite ready to concede.

"Simple." Daisy steepled her fingers under her chin and smiled pleasantly. "If she hadn't added Mr. Kominski to our manifest, he'd not be here identifying a potential German agent, and we'd be left quite in the dark."

Mr. Whitney huffed his grudging agreement while Bayard grinned at the way she'd deftly parried the attack, and just like that, peace was restored.

Out of the corner of her eye, Daisy caught a glimpse of a shadow moving in the outer office. Could it be this easy? The odious man was either that confident or that stupid. She had a notion which it might be.

"We need to proceed with caution." Captain Waddell leaned against the far wall, seemingly untroubled by this new information, as if preventing an abduction was just another day on the job. "If word gets out, there could be panic among the passengers."

"Agreed. This conversation doesn't leave this room." Daisy skewered Mr. Whitney as she said this.

His face folded into a deeper frown, but he kept silent.

"As I see it, if Heimmel is here for the crown princess and her children, he'll want to keep it as quiet as possible," Bayard offered. "It won't be a full-on, guns-blazing assault that would force the Finnish government to react or cause the Swedes to reconsider their concessions to the Germans."

"So how do you think it will be carried out?" Daisy asked. Now that the first hurdle had been crossed successfully, she sat back in her chair.

"It'll need to be done so that no one's the wiser—at least until they're over the border into Norway, where Terboven and his crew can put out whatever official explanation they want. That it was voluntary. That the crown princess chose to return to Norway and act as regent for her son. That the Germans were merely assisting her in that return."

"In the same way that they weren't really invading the country, merely defending it against British aggression," Whitney muttered.

"I want extra protections for the royal family until we've boarded the ship. Nothing obvious, but eyes should be on her and the children at all times."

"I'll see to it, ma'am," Captain Waddell replied.

Daisy glanced once more at the door, noting the way the latch didn't shut properly, leaving a sliver of light to spear the scarred wooden floor. Cleo had been on to something with her mad plan of swapping cars. Crude and obvious, perhaps, but it made sense under the circumstances. Daisy only hoped everyone else agreed.

She leaned over the desk with urgency, pitching her voice clear and carrying to all corners so no one would mistake her intentions. "I propose an additional precaution in case the attempted abduction is planned for the road between here and Petsamo—the royal family and I will exchange automobiles for the last leg of the trip."

Bayard stood up straight, face grim, playing his part in the drama. "That puts you in the line of fire, ma'am."

"This operation is all about subtlety. It's doubtful, if such an attack is actually carried out, that I'd be in any danger once they realized the mix-up. The ambush of a US minister shepherding women and children to safety—let the Nazis try to turn that to their advantage in the newspapers if they can. No, I'll be safe as houses. And the distraction might be just enough to get the royal family away safely."

"If you're sure, ma'am?"

"I am, Mr. Whitney."

He seemed to chew on his words rather than spit them out as he might once have done. She counted that as progress.

"That's settled then," she said. "Now as for the rumors of a Russian incursion . . ."

The meeting broke up soon after, and the group dispersed to put their plan into motion. Daisy glanced down the corridor, seeing a shrouded figure turning a corner on his way back to the guest rooms.

"Bait taken," she murmured with a quirk of her lips. "A better day's fishing than I expected."

CLEO LAY IN bed, watching the curtains drift in the breeze. Outside, she could hear the sound of the river purring its way downstream, where it would end in the wide, arctic Lake Inari. A few shouts as drivers prepared their buses ahead of tomorrow morning's dawn departure. The slam of a door and laughter in the passage outside her room.

The hotel was quiet tonight. Some of the group had already left, urged on their way after closed-door meetings that had Mr. Whitney scuttling from the lounge to the office telephone and back again with increasing agitation. His brows wobbled like furry caterpillars and his face shone with perspiration.

Was Heimmel out there waiting? The idea made sleep impossible. Buzzing with nerves, she rummaged through her suitcase for her novel. Pushing aside her sweaters, her hand passed over cold metal—Sofia's revolver. Cleo had packed it away after Haparanda, hoping she'd never have to use it. Now, she pulled it out, curving her fingers around the grip, letting its weight settle into her forearm. Thumbing the stirrup catch, she saw the chamber held four bullets. Not enough to stop an army, but more than adequate for one cold-blooded Nazi.

A soft tap at the door startled her. She quickly slid the revolver into her coat hanging over a chair, just in case. "Who's there?"

"Cleo? Are you awake?"

She wouldn't look too closely at why it was disappointment she felt when she saw Micky, stubbled and unkempt, standing there.

Twitching, he glanced over his shoulder before diving through the doorway, closing the door and throwing the chain as soon as he was inside.

"Why don't you come on in?" Her sarcasm was lost on him. He was too busy checking every corner of the room, including under the bed and behind the wardrobe doors. "You think Heimmel's hiding among my blouses?"

"You try having a bull's-eye on your back and see how it feels." He sank onto her bed, head in hands.

"You're not the only one in the crosshairs, you know. Aunt Daisy's not likely to ever speak to me again after this." His blank face convinced her he'd never once considered where she fit into his problems other than as the one who could sort them. Her disappointment gave way to shame. Hadn't she leaned on Aunt Daisy in the same way? No wonder Cleo had found Micky so attractive all those months ago. They were both happy to glide through life uncaring of who they hurt along the way—selfish grasshoppers.

"What are you doing here, Micky? It's the middle of the night."

"I couldn't sleep." His clothes seemed to hang looser. His face was ashen, his cocky grin gone, his snappy gaze dulled. This wasn't the Micky who could bring an audience to its feet or send a dance floor into a jitterbugging frenzy. This was a man who had dug himself a hole that he had no idea how to escape. "Look. I'm sorry I dragged you into this, Cleo. I really am." The most un-apologetic apology in history, but it was clear she shouldn't expect more. This was all he could give. It wasn't much to hang her life on, not anymore.

"I'd say this isn't your fault, Micky, but it totally is. All of it. From the moment we were warned to leave Poland last summer to this second—right here, right now—is down to you."

Anger pressed his features into a stranger's hard, ugly angles.

"Easy for you to look down your nose when you've had everything handed to you on a silver platter. Some of us have had to scrape and claw and fight for every advantage. When you're born on the wrong side of the tracks, you can't eat high ideals or pay the rent with principles."

"Maybe you're right. Maybe I never had to fight. Maybe it made me soft. And maybe that's changing."

He scrubbed his hands over his face, exhaustion slumping his shoulders as the fight drained away, leaving him empty and gray. A shifty-eyed, nail-biting shell of himself. She pitied him as one might pity a stray dog. "If anything happens," he stammered. "I mean if things go south tomorrow and . . . Well, I'm sorry. That's all."

"You stay here. Get some sleep."

"What about you?" he asked. "Where will you go?"

"Don't worry about me. I'll find a cozy little corner somewhere. You'd be surprised at the places I've been able to catch forty winks over the last few months."

"That soldier of yours?" The sneer in his voice was unmistakable.

Just a few hours ago, she'd have been furious, but Micky no longer had that power over her. Her feelings for him had faded. The ache in her heart dulled. Still, she couldn't help but touch the sore spot, testing it for strength, even when she knew it would hurt.

"Was our love a lie from the beginning?" she asked. "Did you mean any of it, or was it all part of your fighting and clawing to convince the silly rich girl that you loved her?"

His silence answered her question.

"Thanks for finally being honest." She started to leave, her hand on the door. "As for that soldier, he's far too good for the likes of me. Just like I'm far too good for the likes of you."

She left him, bent elbows resting on his knees, head lowered. He might even have fallen asleep sitting up. He might not have heard any of it.

She didn't care.

The dining room was quiet and set for breakfast. Long shadows shifted and shimmered where a thin moon rose above the water. A figure watched from a long, built-in bench, his silhouette silvered by the light. If this was Hollywood, he'd be the boy-next-door or the best friend. Loyal. Kind. Unremarkable. The one the heroine looked straight past on her way to her happily ever after.

She was no heroine, and she sure as hell didn't think she'd get anything near to a fairy-tale ending. But she didn't need to look any farther to see him for what he was.

He felt her regard and turned. His expression fell into darkness, but she could see the strong slope of his shoulder, his patience in overlapping shades of gray and silver. "Cleo?"

"Do you hate me too?"

"Not even close." She sensed his smile as he spoke, and the weight pressing on her chest lifted away.

She hesitated for only a moment before she joined him.

"It's not the Ritz, but you should be comfortable enough. I'll bunk out in the lounge."

"You needn't go on my account. I mean . . . there's room for both of us." Cleo lied. The lieutenant's hotel room was far smaller than hers, barely space for a narrow cot and a side table with a lamp. There were no windows, meaning it was like being shut in a closet. In fact, Cleo was beginning to think it might *be* a closet, a storeroom pressed into service at the last minute. "You can stay." After a moment, she added, "I want you to stay."

Bayard hesitated.

"Only if that's what you want," she rushed into the awkwardness.

He took her hand in his own, linked their fingers, palm to palm, regarding their joined hands with nervous surprise. "You know I do."

"Then what's stopping you?" Cleo knew the answer, but for some reason she needed to hear him say it. As if that would make it easier for her to argue her case.

He gave not quite a sigh, but he didn't drop her hand. "You know that too."

It reminded Cleo of the night at the Petersons' farm: the thick, enveloping shadows that made confidences easier, the way both of them danced around each other like new skaters on ice, the way her body buzzed having him close enough that she could hear the steady in and out of his breath, smell his scent of tobacco and shaving soap and sweat, feel the drum of her heart in her chest.

Petra had been mere yards away that night. She felt just as close now. But there was another feeling accompanying her presence, one that made Cleo lighter, happier, oddly settled in a way she hadn't been since Petra's death. A memory surprised a smile out of her. "Remember the club in Oslo? I still can't believe you invited me to join you on your date. Petra was positively livid."

Her change in tone seemed to startle him. He didn't answer right away, as if he was wrestling with his own ghosts. For a moment Cleo thought she'd stepped a foot wrong, the familiar guilt pulling them apart as it had for months. Instead, he drew her closer, his hand cupping the soft skin along her ribcage, his head bowed to hers, nearly cheek to cheek. "She wasn't angry at you. Not that time." She could hear the smile in his voice. "It was me she was furious with. She'd thought I was taking her to hear a string quartet performing Bartók. But I went to buy the concert tickets, and they were sold out. Who knew Bartók was that big a draw? Not me."

Cleo imagined poor Petra expecting an elegant evening of

canapés and concertos and getting Emmitt and his crew in a downtrodden nightclub. "So you figured drag me in and she'd be so busy being angry at me she wouldn't have time to be angry at you? Very clever, Lieutenant. I'd no idea you could be so underhanded."

"Not sure if *clever* is the word. *Desperate* might be more accurate. I nearly bankrupted myself trying to make it up to her. Flowers. Chocolates. I took her to that expensive restaurant on Bygdøy allé. You know what finally did it?"

Cleo smiled. "Let me guess—cloudberries."

His eyes widened in surprise. "How did you know? I had a hell of a time finding any. People around here hoard them like gold." He laughed, but the sting was gone. His body relaxed. "Honestly, I don't know what she ever saw in me. We were complete opposites."

"Maybe that's what she liked." Tears burned the corners of Cleo's eyes and washed her vision in silver. "Or maybe she saw something in you that you didn't even know was there." She felt the question catch in her throat, but knew it had to be asked. "Did you love her?"

Bayard paused as if seeking the right words, and Cleo found it hard to breathe as she awaited his answer.

"Love?" he said finally. "Maybe it would have happened in time, but that ran out for us, didn't it? I admired her and, yeah, maybe I was infatuated at having someone so glamorous choose me when she could have had any man in Oslo. But it wasn't love. I know how that feels, and what I had with Petra wasn't it." His stare made Cleo's insides quiver. He let go of her hand, but only to cup her face. His kiss, when it came, pushed through any last hesitations. Neither timid nor unsure, he backed her against the edge of the cot. She gripped his shoulders to steady herself and then because she didn't want to let him go.

Her hands dropped to his waist then slid beneath his shirt to run along the length of his ribs and around his back, where his muscles bunched as he dragged duvet and pillow down onto the floor.

They fell in a tangle of body parts, laughter turning to something more serious and then silence when there was no room left for words. They took their time. Wanting to make the night last. Finding joy and then comfort. Afterward, she lay cradled in his arms, the slippery uncertainty ripened into something stronger, far more solid. Pieces shifting and rearranging to make something new.

"What will you do when you get back to America?" Bayard asked, shaking a cigarette from his pack, lighting it, and passing it to Cleo.

"First, I need to mend fences with my mother. That won't be easy."

"After all this, she still won't forgive you?" He accepted the lit cigarette back from her, their fingers touching, their heads close together. It was easy, comfortable. Ghosts laid to rest at last.

"I don't need her to forgive me. I just want her to understand me. That might be easier now that I'm starting to understand myself."

"And after that?"

Cleo tried to imagine New York—the house on East Fifty-Seventh, the whispers, the glances, the endless round of a life that went nowhere. Where did she fit in that world? Did she want to fit or had the last year reshaped her in ways that wouldn't allow her to resume her old life? Maybe she'd find a job and an apartment of her own.

"I don't know. What about you?"

"That's easy. A transfer back to active duty."

"You don't like your work?"

"I can be of more use elsewhere. And as things stand right now . . . well . . ."

Cleo thought of Emmitt's premonition of the US entry—maybe late, but, in the end, inevitable. Like the last war when Aunt Daisy, her sister Elise, her daughter Ethel, Anne Vanderbilt, Anne Morgan, and hundreds more women just like them had stepped up to fight. They'd seen the horrors and, instead of running back to their privileged lives, they'd chosen to roll up their sleeves.

Cleo had seen her own horrors. Would she run or would she roll up her sleeves?

CHAPTER 29

Dear Anne,

I am reminded of a conversation I had with Lady Harcourt in London in 1917 after a day spent at one of the hospitals there. "All of my generation of men are dead and now their sons are going too." Perhaps it's because I'm at the killing edge of a new war, but these words feel more prescient than ever. A new generation of men—and women—will be asked to bear the brunt for our failings at negotiating a lasting peace when we had the chance . . .

Disguised beneath the brim of a large, veiled hat suitable for a princess, Daisy surveyed the crowded car park. The weather had cooperated with a cold drizzle. Perfect for camouflaging identities under wide umbrellas and shapeless raincoats as tired passengers were herded aboard the buses for the final leg of the journey.

They had used the excuse of the rain to park both cars at the back of the building, where they could draw right up to the hotel's kitchen entrance. When the crown princess and her children emerged, they were guided quickly into their usual car along with Captain Waddell as an added escort. When he shot Daisy a questioning look, she merely smiled. Perhaps he was used to dealing with the vagaries of superior officers, as that seemed to be enough for him. Daisy's own Ford was standing by, her driver already behind the wheel.

Mr. Whitney had been distracted with last-minute details before joining the rest on the lead bus. By the time he realized Daisy's subterfuge, it would be too late for him to give the game away. Lieutenant Bayard was more difficult to mislead. She drew him aside as he issued final instructions to the last of the buses. "Change in plans. You ride in the Ford."

Like Waddell, he was ever the good soldier and didn't question, merely nodded.

Other than checking the time, Daisy was detached from the chaos swirling around her along with the early morning fog. Her bout of nerves had struck in the small hours as she second-guessed her plan, reviewing possible pitfalls and potential advantages, telling herself this crude shell game was a fool's idea, that it would never work. It was only upon seeing the mad shouting crush of people outside the hotel that she'd hardened her shaky resolve. It was all about the magician's sleight of hand—the skillful distraction that drew the eye one way while the switch was made somewhere else.

Daisy tugged on her gloves like a boxer about to enter the ring and prepared to take up her position at the rear of the convoy in the Ford. Her composure was shattered by the unexpected sound of Cleo in loud conversation with the lieutenant as she blew out of the hotel in a rush. "I can't find him anywhere."

She was supposed to be aboard a bus. The one Daisy was watching grumble into first gear on its way out of the lot. And yet here she was—exactly where she shouldn't be. At this point, Daisy should have expected nothing less.

She dragged the pair into the shelter of the building and out of sight. "Care to explain?" she asked.

"It's Mr. Kominski, ma'am," Lieutenant Bayard replied. "No one's seen him since last night."

The squared-off grip of the lieutenant's .45 dragged against his right hip. Daisy hadn't seen him wearing his pistol during all their months in Stockholm. But now, he kept it close. Somehow, it cemented the reality of the situation in a way her middle of the night nerves hadn't. The weapon wasn't the only change in the lieutenant. Despite being out of the weather, there was a new protectiveness in the way he shielded Cleo, turning his broad back to the rain. The two didn't touch. They didn't have to. Daisy could practically see the lightning that danced between them.

There was something different about Cleo today too, something more than the bruised circles under her eyes or the wary downturn to her mouth. It was in the way she held her shoulders—not boldly but with a certain determination. Daisy couldn't put her finger on where she'd seen it before until she noticed the lieutenant beside her. Of course. It was a soldier's stance. An indefinable way of marking one's space and making others take note.

Cleo stepped in front of the lieutenant in her own show of protection. "Micky came to my room. He was sure Heimmel was looking for him. I let him stay there to keep him safe."

Daisy noticed the turn of phrase. "In your room, but not with you?"

"I was elsewhere."

It didn't take a mind reader to know where Cleo had stayed or that she expected to be raked over the coals for it. Daisy left her response to a mere lifting of an eyebrow. She had larger problems to sort out than her goddaughter's long-lost virtue.

"Someone said they saw him later in the lobby, but that can't be right." Worry roughened Cleo's voice. "Micky wouldn't just leave without telling me."

He abandoned you—again was Daisy's thought, but she kept it to herself. "We can discuss it on the way. Get in. You'll have to ride with us."

Kominski's potential for betrayal had been a hunch. The man was a desperate chancer. Daisy had simply given him something to bargain ~~with~~. It had been his decision whether to risk offering it up. She only wished she could have spared Cleo a fresh pain, one final cut from a man who had caused her so much grief already.

Guilt tried to settle itself around her shoulders, but Daisy shook it off as unhelpful. She'd known she was playing a dangerous game. That there could be victims. So long as none of them were the crown princess or her children, she could say she'd fulfilled her promise.

She'd not anticipated Cleo's presence. She was a piece that wasn't meant to be on the board.

Cleo tried to scan the road for any hint of suspicious activity, but her mind barely registered the blur of arctic pine beyond the Ford's window or the murmur of conversation between Bayard and Aunt Daisy. Micky was gone, and this time she was certain he wouldn't turn up, sheepish and apologetic and begging for another chance.

She curled deeper into her coat, poking at her feelings like pressing an old bruise to test if it still hurt. She'd given more to Micky than she'd thought she was capable of giving. Her love. Her time. Nearly her life. And he'd cheerfully taken them all as his due without offering her anything in return. She should hate him, and yet a part of her still hoped he was all right. If it hadn't been for him, she would have taken the first ship for home last summer. She would have remained the woman she'd been, looking inward and scarred rather than strengthened by her experiences. She sent a prayer out to speed him along on whatever path he'd chosen and smiled seeing her own path unfurling like the gray ribbon of highway they traveled.

"The poor Finns are still struggling to recover from the Russian war. The manager at the hotel said it had only just finished repairing the east guest rooms and the dining room had been destroyed by artillery." Aunt Daisy's stern profile was like granite, but with a touch of humor in her eyes. "I don't know about you, but my room reeked of floor lacquer and paint. The odor was worse than Mr. Whitney's aftershave."

Cleo appreciated her godmother's attempts to lighten the mood. Perhaps there was something to be salvaged after all. Perhaps she hadn't burned every bridge.

Up ahead, the bus's brake lights flashed red. Cleo's nerves stretched tight until she saw it was only a herd of deer crossing the roadway.

"This reminds me of my trip to the North Cape back in the summer of thirty-eight," Aunt Daisy commented. "No snow-capped glaciers, but with the same awe-inspiring majesty, the colors and the way the light moves, and everywhere you look, you see a sight more perfect than the last until you're dizzy with it."

"You're going to miss it." Cleo had been so wrapped up in her own problems, she'd not seen Aunt Daisy's loss.

"Of course, my dear, but over the last days, the call of my home at Uplands is beginning to sound louder in my ear than the siren song of Norway."

The deer having fled into the scrub on the far side of the road, the convoy moved out once more. They drove through acres of forest flattened but for the stumps of splintered trees, and now and then they came across a stretch of military encampment the Russians had used during the war. A group of rough-dressed men picked through the ruins, rifles slung over their shoulders. Cleo found herself searching for any sign they might be poised to attack, but they barely looked up as the convoy passed.

"Veterans of the Finnish war, I expect," Aunt Daisy surmised.

They had left the soldiers behind when the quiet was shattered by a crack, and the windshield spidered out from side to side. A second shot quickly followed, and the car tugged to the right. The driver gave a shout and wrenched the wheel to keep them from going into one of the deep ditches edging the road. Cleo tumbled hard against the door handle, while Aunt Daisy smashed her forehead against the seatback in front of her. The Ford sputtered then died.

"Everyone present and accounted for?" Bayard asked, his tone strained, sweat damping his hairline as he scanned their surroundings.

"A bit rumpled, but in one piece, which is more than I can say for our driver," Aunt Daisy replied. "He's been knocked out cold."

Cleo's elbow was all pins and needles. She flexed and curled her fingers, trying to get feeling back, then shoved her hand into her coat pocket, gripping Sofia's revolver until the metal grew hot under her fingers.

"Look!" Bayard pointed through the windshield to where a black sedan pulled out of a lay-by and swept into place at the end of the convoy just as if nothing had happened. Anyone watching from the buses would never notice Aunt Daisy's Ford was missing—singled out from the protection of the herd like one of the deer they'd just seen.

The convoy disappeared around a bend, leaving them alone in the middle of nowhere. It was eerily quiet—not a breath of wind or call of an animal to break the stillness.

Aunt Daisy straightened her hat and adjusted the lapels of her coat. "I suppose I should give myself marks for success, but it does feel like a hollow victory at the moment."

"You meant for this to happen?" Cleo heard the rise in her voice and took a deep breath to steady herself.

"You were the one who suggested we trade cars with Her Royal Highness."

"A suggestion you clearly ignored."

"Yes, but the Germans didn't know that, did they?" Aunt Daisy was far too pleased with herself. She glanced out at the empty road with an odd eagerness. "One would think the Gestapo would be less gullible, but I suppose desperate times . . ."

"So now what?" Cleo's heart banged against her ribs when Bayard unsnapped his holster and slid his pistol free. "We just sit here and wait?"

"Exactly." Aunt Daisy scanned the empty landscape. "It's his move."

TEN MINUTES PASSED in which Cleo's panic settled back into a manageable sick turning of her stomach and a heart that roared in her ears. If Aunt Daisy and Bayard were equally terrified, they didn't show it.

Aunt Daisy calmly poured cold water from a thermos onto a handkerchief from her purse. "Here. Press this on that knot of his." She handed Bayard the wet compress after he settled the stunned driver more comfortably.

Ten more minutes passed in which Bayard and Aunt Daisy conferred through a series of meaningful looks while Cleo chewed her fingernails to nubs.

"Right. This is getting us nowhere." Bayard reached under the dashboard for a lever to open the trunk. "Hope for a spare or we're walking to Petsamo."

"You can't go out there. What if Heimmel's waiting?" Cleo despised the waver in her voice.

"Here." He reached back, holding out the pistol grip first. "Take this and cover me while I change the tire."

"Are you crazy? I can't."

"It's you or nobody."

"Fine, but I don't need—"

He didn't wait for her to explain or protest. Shoving the pistol into her hand, he let himself out of the car, circling back to the trunk.

Cleo followed, trying to make herself as small a target as possible. The clouds flattened the light. The world was washed in overlapping shades of gray, the pines lining the road still tangled in the lifting fog, making it impossible to see more than a few yards in any direction.

With a mechanic's skill, Bayard went immediately for the trunk and the spare, jacking the car up off the ground and beginning the process of changing out the wheel. Cleo stood guard, the pistol up and aimed, her finger hovering cautiously near the trigger, as she scanned the forest that marched unbroken to the road, the ground rusty with dry needles.

Off to her left, the snap of a twig. She spun, squeezing off a shot, the force jerking at her shoulder.

Bayard poked his head around the corner of the fender. "Don't waste my ammunition on rabbits."

"Why doesn't he show himself?" Cleo gritted her teeth. "What's he waiting for?"

"Between you and me, I'm just as happy if he turns around and heads back—" Bayard's words ended on a pained grunt and the heavy thud of a body hitting the ground.

Cleo sucked in a breath. Sweat swam on clammy skin. Her

blouse felt damp with it. Dread made her want to throw up. "You okay?"

Heimmel stepped out from behind the car. "Throw the gun over there please, Miss Jaffray," he instructed in his impeccable British accent. When she hesitated, his words came harsher and more dangerous. "Or do you want to end up like your lover"—she strangled on a breath—"Mr. Kominski?"

Horror mingled with relief then guilt. Her knees wobbled as she fought to keep them from buckling. "Where's Micky?"

Heimmel's mouth twisted in mock sorrow. "In a lonely country ravaged by war, what's one more body?"

Her vision shimmered with tears, her heart blasted open. Poor, stupid Micky. He'd warned her to avoid the bland men in their nondescript suits. If only he'd taken his own advice.

"Miss Jaffray? Your gun? I won't ask again." Cleo felt the snick of Heimmel's cocked Luger like a thud to her breastbone.

She tossed Bayard's .45 away, her hands slick, a buzzing in her ears.

"Good morning, Herr Heimmel. We haven't been introduced but my name's Florence Harriman. I'm the US minister to Norway." Cleo hadn't heard the car door open, but there was Aunt Daisy staring down her long nose with a look that could freeze blood as she shouted to make herself heard. "If it's the royal family you're looking for, I hate to be the bearer of bad news, but you've been thoroughly scuppered."

Heimmel's confidence faltered as he glanced at Aunt Daisy's enormous hat then into the back seat of the car. "What the hell game are you playing?"

"Three-card monte—choose the cup with the pea under it and you win a prize. You chose incorrectly, I'm afraid."

His posh facade melted away. The manufactured sympathy,

the easy smile, the gentle honey gaze. His eyes narrowed, his jaw working in increasing agitation.

"You trusted where you shouldn't have, and now you're stuck with *us*. Hardly the game you were hunting."

Cleo admired Aunt Daisy's courage, but maybe a little less flippancy while the man had a gun trained on them.

"Why shouldn't I just shoot you now? All of you?" he growled.

"I expect you already know the answer to that question, which is why we're still talking." Aunt Daisy remained unruffled while Cleo could practically hear her bones rattling.

"You feckless old cow. You don't know what you've done."

Aunt Daisy didn't smile, but her face softened into humor. "Nor will anyone else. You go back to Berlin. I carry on to America. It remains our little secret."

That idea didn't sit well with Heimmel, who lifted his weapon. Cleo felt herself freeze with that familiar sense of helplessness. She couldn't move. She couldn't run. She could only watch in horror, a roar in her ears, her heart banging its way out of her chest.

Eyes level. Even breaths. Don't think too hard.

She could hear Bayard in her head, steadying her, setting her on the right course. She found a still point within the panic like the quiet eye within a hurricane. She didn't hesitate. She didn't think. She simply slid her hand into her coat pocket, her fingers curving around the revolver's grip. The still point grew, and time slowed with her breathing. No hesitation. No fear. She pulled the gun free, cocked the hammer, and squeezed off a shot. The bullet struck the tree above Heimmel, sending a rain shower of splintered twigs down around him.

He cursed. Her second shot sent him stumbling backward, clutching his shoulder.

"*Hei!*" A voice from behind them.

"Mitä on tekeillä?" Another voice, this one deeper, rougher. Carrying a hint of violence.

"Is problem?" Rifles now at the ready, the Finnish veterans they'd seen earlier approached from between the trees just as a truck horn sounded. An engine gunned loud from the north as a hauler carrying lumber passed, bending the trees in its wake, tossing gravel like pepper. Another truck approached from the south with a trailer bed of rail supplies.

Cleo ducked off the road to avoid the traffic, and when she looked again, Heimmel was gone.

CHAPTER 30

Dear Anne,

We've arrived at Petsamo. Hurry up and wait is the order of the day while officials cross every t and dot every i before they allow us to leave. Our ship, the SS American Legion, *sits offshore, bristling with gantries, its hull painted garishly in red, white, and blue. Some consider this scant protection in these dangerous waters, but I'm reminded of my own trusty Ford with the Stars and Stripes flying bravely from the roof and take heart this ship will see us home . . .*

Daisy found the simple mechanics of changing a tire soothing after the turmoil of Heimmel's appearance. She'd not been afraid of dying herself—the man was too smart to create an incident that might prove awkward back in Berlin. But there had been a moment when she feared the Gestapo officer might take his frustration out on Cleo and the lieutenant. Their deaths would have caused far less fuss—at least to either government. Daisy would have carried the guilt to her grave.

With Cleo tending to Bayard in the back seat, Daisy took over for the injured driver. As far as he knew, he'd been knocked out cold in the accident resulting from a blown tire. If he harbored suspicions there was more to it, he was wise enough to keep them to himself. By the time she caught up to the convoy, the other sedan had disappeared, perhaps called off by Heimmel when his plan went south. Daisy pulled into line as if nothing untoward had occurred and followed the line of buses the last few uneventful miles to Petsamo.

She only drew up the car when they reached the final turning that would send them down to the busy harbor, where a faded hotel sat above a huddle of wharves, shops, and sheds. Until the outbreak of war, this was a place where summer tourists gathered, though looking down on it now as clouds hung low and stormy, one could hardly credit the claim.

"Why are we stopping?" Cleo asked.

"It seems fitting to take a moment to mark this journey's end."

Cleo gazed out at the gray chop of waves. "You're not on board *yet.*"

Daisy tried not to notice that Cleo didn't use the word *we.* A slip of the tongue? Or was more going on behind her blank stare and nervous hands than the events of the last few dangerous hours? "You did well back there."

"I didn't kill him."

"You saved us. Far more important, if you ask me."

Outside the hotel, Daisy had barely parked the car and straightened the veil on her ridiculous hat before Mr. Whitney swooped in to claim her. "Where have you been? She wants to speak with you."

He didn't have to announce which *she* he referred to; it was obvious by his state of agitation and the way he practically herded Daisy toward the harbor master's office as if she might bolt like an untried colt if he let her out of his sight. "I wish you'd warned me about this plan of yours."

"What would you have done if I had?"

"Stopped you, of course."

"Exactly why I didn't warn you."

"And how would I have explained it to the president if it hadn't worked as you expected? Tell me that."

"With relish, I should say. And a great many *I told her so*'s."

He turned away, muttering something about her contrary nature, which had Daisy smiling all the way to the room where Crown Princess Märtha waited. In her dark blue traveling suit with only a simple set of pearls to adorn her somber, white features trembling on the edge of emotion, Her Royal Highness seemed diminished, as fragile as glass. But her gaze remained clear and depthless as the waters of the fjord, her voice strong. "We are here, and we are safe, Madam Minister," she said, holding out a gloved hand. "You have fulfilled your promise to His Majesty."

Daisy risked a reassuring motherly squeeze of the younger woman's fingers. "Oh no, my dear. Didn't you realize? The promise was made to *you*. It was always to you."

Later, she climbed the hill to their borrowed lodgings, enjoying the loosening of taut muscles, the worry that had dragged her down for so long she'd no longer noticed the weight until it was lifted. The evening air was sweet and clean, the jeweled sky so close Daisy might reach up a hand and touch the streaky clouds that blew east, unimpeded by checkpoints and guard towers, into Russia.

Cleo was sitting on a wooden bench in the fenced yard behind their house. As Daisy watched, she cocked a shoulder, tilted her head, dipped into a pocket for a cigarette. When did she start smoking Petterøe's? Was it the same time she'd started speaking Norwegian like a native? Did it have anything to do with her strange friendship with Sofia Kristiansen? That woman had all the subtlety of a sledgehammer and wore a chip on her shoulder like a badge of honor, but she refused to admit defeat, finding a way when the world told her there was none, keeping faith when the fight seemed over. Daisy admired that tenacity. A nation of such and Norway might be the knife at Hitler's back. Too late to save their own country, but perhaps the hesitation that would keep England free long enough for a defense to be made. It was the best Daisy could hope for these days.

She caught herself focusing on the flick of Cleo's wrist and the shift of her hips and was reminded of a long ago August night like this one and a conversation with someone who had dipped into a pocket for a cigarette with that same smooth slide of spine and shoulder.

Did Letitia see the similarities as well? Were they a cause for comfort or pain?

"You'd never make a good spy, auntie."

"No. I'm far too vociferous for keyhole listening." Daisy's memories melted under the thin moon and the briny scent of the bay. "If you're watching for the northern lights, they're rarely visible in the summer. Not dark enough."

"Maybe I'll have to stick around, then." Her cigarette held loosely between her lips, Cleo flicked her wrist as she struck the match against the bench, cupping a hand over the flame, the cap of her hair curved against her jaw. Daisy felt her breath catch in her throat, an old pain flaring along with the burning tip of Cleo's Petterøe's. If only that long-ago conversation on that long-ago night had ended differently, how changed their lives would be, especially that of this young woman, whose unspent love had nearly broken her.

Light shifted and flickered over Cleo's face, gleamed in her eyes. She seemed older. Harder. Wiser. "Does Her Royal Highness know what you did?"

"What *we* did?" Daisy answered. "No. That's best left between us, don't you think?"

"So it's just as if none of it happened." Cleo almost sounded disappointed.

"That depends. Every moment shapes us. It's how we use those moments, how we build on them to create a life of purpose, one we can look back on with pride." Even to Daisy's own ears, it sounded trite, like something a carnival fortune teller might offer for the price of a penny. Hardly inspiring words. More likely Cleo would ignore them as the ramblings of a dotty old woman. If this was Daisy's second chance, she was letting it slip away.

She waited for Cleo to dismiss her with a laugh. Instead, she exhaled a thin stream of smoke, her expression indecipherable in the deepening blue and shifting shadows of twilight.

"Good night, Aunt Daisy."

Her words weren't a dismissal. Instead, they seemed like a decision, and Daisy found her way to bed in a lighter mood than was appropriate after the day she'd had. She might have flubbed the execution, but the sentiment remained. Their lives were built on moments—choices big and small. Cleo's choices had led her here. Where would they take her next?

Like father, like daughter.

Daisy smiled, imagining her late cousin's surprise—and his pride.

It might even be as great as her own.

CLEO WATCHED FROM the window of her bedroom as the crown princess and her children, along with their small retinue, boarded ahead of the rest of the ship's company. The launch motored through the choppy gray waters toward the American troop ship. Sailors crowded the docks and landing stages to watch the spectacle, caps doffed in respect.

"*Yes, we love this country as it rises forth, rugged, weathered, over the water.*"

The singing grew and strengthened as more voices joined, the sound rolling across the water like deep rumbles of thunder. Her

Royal Highness sat ramrod straight as her countrymen saluted her with the national anthem, her gaze set firmly on what lay ahead, the children equally somber.

"Talk about a rousing send-off." Bayard's voice was thick and raspy with sleep. "That's one for the books."

Cleo turned to where he lay in bed, arms behind his head, the soft light shifting watery over the ceiling and across his chest. His brown eyes crinkled at the corners as he studied her, standing in nothing but a quilt she'd dragged from the bed to wrap around her shoulders.

"Even women stood up and fought as if they were men. Others could only cry but that soon would end."

The song swelled in her chest. She recalled Aunt Daisy's story of the peasant women she'd seen during the troubles on the Mexican border. How they left their cooking pots and laundry to take the place of their fallen sweethearts, unafraid, holding the line, doing what needed to be done.

Were they any different from the women of Aunt Daisy's generation who had brought their talents and money, energy and determination to the battlefields of France during the last war? Then turned around and fought for peace with equal enthusiasm?

An army of heroines, Aunt Daisy had called them.

They would need such an army this time around. Women like Sofia with the strength to take up arms, as well as those like Mrs. Thorson to do the work of piecing broken lives back together.

"You're going to freeze," Bayard said. "Come back to bed."

He took her by the hand, leading her to the cocoon of quilts and duvets piled high and soft like whipped cream. She curled her body into his and closed her eyes, allowing herself to imagine a future of similar mornings, but other images crowded out the dream. Other moments crashed across the backs of her eyelids like fireworks. Every slight. Every sorrow. Every unfairness. Every terror. Her teeth chattered and she felt nervous and sick. What was happening to her? Who was this person? She felt brittle and broken, cracks splitting apart the girl she'd been from the woman she was becoming.

"See? I told you. You're shivering."

His hand slid down her ribs, over her hip, along her thigh. Desire danced along her skin like electricity. It would be so tempting. No one would question it. She had history and form. The kind of girl that played with fire and never learned from her mistakes. But the last year had burned her badly.

"Cleo?" There was a new tautness at the edges of Bayard's gaze. "What's going on?"

"I'm staying."

"I'm really hoping you mean here in bed with me." His smile held more regret than pleasure. "But it's not, is it?"

Cleo didn't answer. Instead, she burrowed deeper into his shoulder as if she could imprint everything about him on her memory: the way he smelled, the smooth feel of his skin, the sound of his breathing. She needed to be able to recall those things in the months ahead when he would be so very far away.

"Does Mrs. Harriman know?" he asked.

"Suspects, I think. Not much gets by her."

"She must be proud."

Cleo smiled. "It's a nice change."

"Where will you go?" She was surprised and relieved he didn't start by trying to talk her out of it. Explaining to her how it was a bad idea. That she was woefully unsuited to such an undertaking. How she must be crazy to even contemplate remaining behind in Sweden. It made her love him all the more.

"Back to Haparanda to start," she replied. "Then maybe on to Stockholm. Mrs. Thorson kept my place at the Refugee Office open for me."

"You've known this whole time you weren't going to take the ship for home?"

"No, but Mrs. Thorson hoped I would reconsider." She laid her head on his chest, smiling at the slow beat of his heart.

"And if I asked you to go home? With me?"

Was this how her father had felt when he'd enlisted? Had it been a drunken spur-of-the-moment action? Had he tried to explain himself to his wife? To make her see what was in his heart? Had she tried to listen? Or was she too caught up in her own loss to understand his feelings?

"Please don't ask. I'd have to turn you down and that would break my heart." She looked him in the eye. "Please."

He hugged her close. "How about if I say that we'll meet again when all this is over."

She closed her eyes. "Save a dance for me."

THEY STOOD ON the wooden dock, water slapping at the pilings, spray speckling their faces. The clouds were low, turning the hills around the harbor to granite. A ship's horn cut through the thickening fog. The launch waited for them; a sailor stood at the bottom of the wooden ladder to help them into the boat.

They would be the last to board. Already, a path was being charted through the mine-infested waters off Petsamo harbor. Passengers were settling into their crowded berths; families and elderly were allotted cabins while the rest jammed themselves belowdecks on hammocks slung side by side.

Cleo tried not to think about the stories of ships exploding off the coast of Norway, a choice between a fiery death or a watery grave. She took her cue from Aunt Daisy, who remained stoic as ever, staring down her long eagle nose at Cleo with a look she couldn't read.

Mr. Whitney scuffed at the warped decking, his hands shoved

into his pockets. There was a new look in his face and his mouth had lost its bracketed sourness. He held out a grudging hand and dropped a set of keys into her palm.

"The Ford? Really?" Cleo closed her hands around the cold metal, squeezing until the jagged teeth cut into her flesh. A pain to take her mind from the dull ache under her ribs.

"How else do you suppose you'll get back to civilization? Reindeer sledge? It's a good car, and I ought to know." He cleared his throat as if his tie were strangling him. "She'll see you safe wherever you're headed."

"You don't think I'm tilting at windmills?"

His eyes widened before his furry brows curled low, his jaw clenched as if to say the words was painful. "I think you're an idealistic fool who's going to make a hash out of things, but who listens to me? I'm just a pompous windbag."

"I'd never call you a windbag, Mr. Whitney." She laughed at his deepening scowl. On impulse, she leaned in for a kiss on his bristly cheek. "Take care of Aunt Daisy for me? You know what she's like. She'll be going a mile a minute until you reach New York Harbor unless she's forced to stand down."

"I've never managed it before. Not sure what makes you think this time will be any better." He shot Aunt Daisy a grim shake of his head before busying himself with passing on the last bags to the sailor waiting in the boat.

Aunt Daisy's embrace was warm and scented with perfume. She held Cleo as tight as a mother might farewell a child. "Are you sure this is what you want?"

"You know boats and I have never got on."

"Not since that ridiculous Van Speakman boy's ketch. I remember that summer." Aunt Daisy sniffed, her eyes watery. "Right. Stay safe and out of trouble. Think you can manage that much?"

Cleo's throat closed around a lump. "Is that what you told my father when he stayed behind?"

"Something similar and equally useless. He did what he wanted . . . and so will you." Her eyes swam with tears, but the corners crinkled with delight. "I notice the lieutenant has made himself scarce."

"We said our goodbyes earlier."

Aunt Daisy eyed Cleo with one of those schoolmarm looks that made a person feel two inches tall. "He's a good one, Clementine. Don't leave it too long."

"Just as long as I'm needed and not a minute longer."

"You'll find soon enough that the need never ends. But I'm sure you'll both be counting those minutes." She gazed around her as if taking one last look at a country she'd grown to love and admire. "Ethel was right. It was one hell of an adventure."

Helped into the boat, she sat at the bow, her coat folded around her, her gaze long as if she was already looking ahead to the next challenge. "What will I tell your mother?"

"Tell her I'm my father's daughter. Just as she always wanted."

Cleo stood and watched as the lines were released and the boat moved away from the dock. She struggled to keep warm against the wind and the cold of second thoughts.

The space between them widened, the chop hitting the pilings. The boat circled. Aunt Daisy waved then cupped her hands around her mouth.

"What did you say?" Cleo shouted. "I can't hear you!"

"I said welcome to the army, Clementine Verquin!"

AUTHOR'S NOTE

Who knew that sitting down on a Sunday evening to watch the latest PBS offering would lead to a book, but that was the case in the summer of 2021 when I first spotted the unidentified gray-haired woman warning Norway's Crown Princess Märtha of the coming confrontation with Germany. Who was this smart, savvy diplomat? It turned out to be Florence Harriman, known to her family and friends as Daisy.

She was born into the Gilded Age New York splendor of Astors and Morgans, Vanderbilts and Whitneys. Later, as the wife of J. Borden Harriman, she attached herself to one of the wealthiest and most prominent families in the nation. Like many women during this new progressive era, she cut her teeth on the pressing social issues of the day such as prison reform, the labor movement, and women's suffrage. In 1912, she moved from New York to Washington, DC, as part of President Woodrow Wilson's Commission on Industrial Relations, where she found her footing amid the political whirl. From her home at Uplands, she hosted reporters, diplomats, politicians, judges, cabinet members, and foreign and domestic glitterati at dinners that became famous among Washington's elite.

During World War I, Daisy's activism increased, first as part of the American Red Cross Motor Corps operating ambulances in France, and then, following the armistice in 1918, as an observer to the peace talks in Paris and a staunch campaigner for Wilson's League of Nations as a member of the Inter-Allied Women's Conference. This life of public service made her eventual tagging by President Franklin Delano Roosevelt in 1937 as the US minister to Norway an easy choice.

There is a danger to telling the story of someone who took the time to tell their own story. Florence "Daisy" Harriman was a prolific writer, completing two memoirs: *From Pinafores to Politics* and *Mission to the North*. These books were crucial reading material, both in establishing the history behind this amazing woman's growing significance in American politics, and also in offering me a window into her incredible adventure in Norway that culminated in her acting as escort to Crown Princess Märtha and her children. Where I could, I have incorporated Daisy's own words into my story, but for anyone wanting to learn more about the facts behind my fiction, I recommend both books as highly entertaining and informative glimpses into the experiences of an influential and witty woman who wrung every last drop out of a long and active life.

As much as Daisy offered up an almost daily record of her journey, my book is historical fiction, which, by its nature, is a reshaping of the facts into an entertaining narrative. In doing so, an author may have to stray off the path on occasion. While Daisy's exploits from Oslo to Stockholm then Finland on her way home are all based on the historical record, there were parts of the story that I altered, condensed, or emphasized for the sake of clarity, pacing, characterization, or plot.

The most central of these is my Cleo story line, which is pure fiction from start to finish, including the thwarting of a German plot to kidnap the royal family. But while Cleo was born of my imagination, many events in her story are grounded in real-life incidents, including her experiences as an American during the takeover of the Polish resort town of Zakopane, descriptions of

the Germans' arrival in Oslo, the battle at the farm in Midstagar-
ten, and finally the important work of the Norwegian Refugee
Office in Stockholm, which assisted with food, housing, and essentials for the flood of incoming refugees.

While I invented Lieutenant Bayard, he is based—very
loosely—on US Air Force Captain Robert Losey, and Bayard's
argument with Daisy over whether she should accompany him
back into Norway to rescue the legation's families is taken from
actual conversations between Losey and Daisy. Neither the real
man nor his fictional counterpart was successful. Sadly, Captain
Losey was killed in the Norwegian city of Dombås and is considered the first official American casualty of World War II.

Vice Consul Whitney is an amalgamation of many of the men
Daisy dealt with during her time in public life. Journalists frequently
referred to her as a granny. Fellow diplomats questioned her work
ethic, despite the fact that her gender meant she had to play the
dual role of diplomat and diplomat's wife. Colleagues' concerns over
Daisy's extensive travel as well as the friend who wrote her a disap-
proving letter upon her appointment as ambassador are both based
on fact, as is the article describing Daisy's piano-playing diplomacy,
which Vice Consul Whitney finds so offensive. As he should.

More than once in her memoir *Mission to the North*, Daisy
referred to the State Department codebooks and her interest in
keeping them safe, including her idea of shoving them down her
blouse in case she was stopped by the Germans. I chose to play
with this idea in the story by having them lost and then found,
though it's Cleo who ends up using her blouse as a hiding place.

During her flight from Norway, Daisy spent time with
Dr. D. B. Fishwick of Bellevue Hospital and the American-
Scandinavian Field Hospital, which worked to bring medical
assistance to the Norwegian battlefront, though whether their
trained staff of doctors, nurses, technicians, and ambulance

drivers included an angry Norwegian doctor with a chip on her shoulder is anyone's guess.

As far as I know, Daisy did not keep up the steady correspondence with her sister-in-law Anne Vanderbilt that I indicate in the book. But the two were close throughout their lives, and both women used their wealth and positions to promote progressive social causes. Anne's death in April 1940 from pneumonia while Daisy was on the run in Norway was a punishing blow.

Last but certainly not least, the German Shepherd Kim's hatred of wheels, which launches Cleo's frantic escape from Oslo in the book, is true. However, it was one of Daisy's other dogs who actually chased the Nazi motorcyclist on the day of the invasion. No deaths resulted, though. Kim died peacefully of old age shortly before the events of 1940 took place.

My story covers only a few short months in Daisy's long life, but her influence on the American political landscape can't be overstated. She had the gift of being equally at home among royalty and business tycoons as she was among farmers in Texas and coal miners in Colorado. She was a force of nature who continued working after her return from Norway, lobbying for electoral votes for the District of Columbia and hosting more than twenty guests every Sunday night for dinner at her Foxhall Road home in Georgetown. In 1963, President John F. Kennedy awarded her the Citation of Merit for Distinguished Service.

Over the course of writing this novel, I've had to repeatedly explain who Daisy was, which saddens me when I realize how quickly she's been forgotten. Florence "Daisy" Harriman was a soldier in my army of heroines with a lifetime of experiences and accomplishments that truly put her in "a box seat at the America of her times." I'm honored to offer readers a glimpse of this amazing woman and hope that by doing so we bring her back to the world's attention for one more bow.

ACKNOWLEDGMENTS

There's something magical about opening that box from the publisher and holding my book for the first time. But it's a magic born of the efforts of so many people, beginning with my amazing and talented agent, Kevan Lyon, who saw the potential for this story when it was little more than a vague idea in a late-night email. Her advice throughout my career has been invaluable, and I'm forever grateful for her support and her friendship.

This will be my fourth book with my wonderful editor, Tessa Woodward, who shepherded Daisy's amazing story from first draft through to bookstore shelves with skill, kindness, and an unerring eye for how to make my words better.

I have to send a huge thank-you to the entire team at William Morrow, starting with Madelyn Blaney, who chases down answers to all my questions and keeps me pointed in the right direction, not always an easy task. Thank you to art director Elsie Lyons, who was amazing—and amazingly patient—as we worked toward the fabulous final cover, and designer Diahann Sturge-Campbell, who pulled the whole look (inside and out) together. Copyeditor Justine Gardner made sure what I wanted to say ended up how I wanted to say it and Robin Barletta guided production with a careful hand. Last but not least, Amelia Wood, Ellie Anderson, and their entire marketing and publicity staff worked hard to get the book into the hands of all you wonderful readers.

As always, I have to give a shout-out to Shelley Kay at Web Crafters for maintaining my fabulous website, AlixRickloff.com, and Tom Martin and Tess Jones at my local bookstore, the Bookplate, a magical shop of hidden aisles, crowded shelves—and a library cat to oversee it all. An enormous, extra special thank-you goes to Henning Jakhelln Kjøita and his crucial English–Norwegian translation help. Any errors are mine alone.

I am forever grateful to my writer friends whose support over the years makes this solitary endeavor far less lonely, especially Laura Kamoie, whose book-titling prowess is unequaled; Maggie Scheck, who boldly read my rough pages; and Aimie K. Runyan, who gave the manuscript that all-important final look before submission.

Last but never least, I send my gratitude and my love to my lifelong cheerleader and a woman who inspires me every day with her strength, her intelligence, and her never-ending optimism, Rebecca Goode. I have a feeling she and Daisy would have been fast friends.

ABOUT THE AUTHOR

ALIX RICKLOFF is a critically acclaimed author of historical fiction. She lives in Maryland in a house that's seen its own share of history, so when she's not writing, she can usually be found trying to keep it from falling down.

READ MORE BY
ALIX RICKLOFF

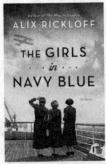

A gripping and compelling dual-timeline novel about three women who joined the Navy during World War I to become yeomanettes and the impact their choices have on one of their descendants in 1968.

"A wonderful blend of smart writing, memorable characters, and World War II imagery all centered on the hunger each one of us has to give love and receive it. A great read for not only devotees of period fiction, but anyone who craves a well-told story."
—Susan Meissner, author of *A Bridge Across the Ocean*

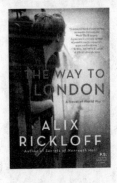

This incredible debut historical novel—in the tradition of Beatriz Williams and Jennifer Robson—tells the fascinating story of a young mother who flees her home on the rocky cliffs of Cornwall and the daughter who finds her way back, seeking answers.